Something About

Jourdyn Kelly

Other books by Jourdyn Kelly:

Destined to Kill

Flawed Perfection (Something About Eve #2) - Coming Soon

~ Table of Contents ~

~ Dedication ~

This is for Mama who is the source of my strength.
For Penny, my best friend, whom without I couldn't have
finished this book. And, to everyone else who has
helped me find the strength to follow my dreams.

~ One ~

Sumptor, Inc. wasn't the most glamorous place to work, Lainey thought as she walked in the old building, but at least it got her out of what was becoming an unendurable existence at home with her husband's constant complaining and criticism. She could have put up with Jack if it had been only her to consider, but she had her sons to think about. Kevin and Darren deserved a home life that wasn't fraught with resentment and discontent. Maybe going back to work would help solve the problem. And if it didn't...Well, she couldn't afford to worry about that now.

In fact, this wasn't the job she had her eye on. It was Sumptor Gallery she was interested in, but knew she would have to work her way up to that. She had deliberately kept her interest in art a secret when she had applied for the accounting job, fearing that if they knew she had been an art history major, it would ruin her chances. She had heard rumors about Sumptor being very picky about the people he hired.

Noises and creaks came from behind the elevator door, and had Lainey leery of the old, rickety piece of machinery, so, she opted for the stairs. She was early and it was only two floors up, anyway. It was the first time Lainey had worked since Kevin was born, and although she was more nervous than she cared to admit, she was grateful for Mr. E. Sumptor, for giving her this chance and meant to thank him as soon as they met – if they ever did. As Lainey stepped out of the stairwell, she nearly ran into the manager of the accounting firm, Meredith Lansky.

"Oh! Hello," Lainey said cheerfully.

"Good morning, Mrs. Stanton. I'm sorry. I didn't mean to startle you," Meredith replied.

Meredith Lansky was a very tall woman in her forties with a regal presence that demanded attention. Her brown hair was tied back in an unrelenting knot and she almost always wore a severe look on a face devoid of any cosmetics. She had to be stern, Meredith thought. After all, she was the manager, and with that title came the responsibility to maintain a sense of authority and discipline.

"You are very prompt," she said now. "I like that. Sumptor will appreciate that quality in you, too."

Before Lainey could answer, Meredith turned away. At five six, Lainey was having trouble keeping up with the taller woman's long strides, and found herself practically jogging to stay in step.

"This is where you'll be working," Meredith said with a grand sweep of the hand as they reached the end of the hall.

The office was tiny, and could have once been a closet for all Lainey knew. An old desk all but filled the room. The computer looked as decrepit as the desk, and the chair...Lainey wondered if the thing would even hold her or if it would topple before she was fully seated.

"It's not much," she heard Meredith saying contritely, "but it will have to do for now."

"It's perfect," Lainey replied with a smile, missing the incredulous glance Meredith gave her as she studied the poor excuse for an office.

"Yes, well, let me introduce you to your co-workers," Meredith said. Lainey Stanton was a peculiar one, she thought, and there was just something about her that didn't sit right with Meredith. Shrugging to herself, she led Lainey to a small group of women gathered at the door of her own, much larger office. "Ladies, this is Lainey Stanton. She'll be taking Margaret's place as supervising accountant."

Everyone gave Lainey the once over, at the same time trying to be discreet. What they saw was a pretty woman in her thirties with dark blonde hair to her shoulders and a delicate face accented by beautiful green eyes. When Lainey smiled, it was warm and inviting. Friendly they would call it. Her gray suit was cut conservatively, but there was still a hint of long slender legs and soft, womanly curves. Unexpectedly, her voice, like aged whiskey, carried a hint of sexuality.

They all welcomed her, all except one, Katherine Bushnell. Lainey knew that Katherine had been up for the job as well, that it had been management's, or rather Sumptor's decision to go with someone from the outside. However, Lainey refused to let Katherine's icy stare bother her. She had been waiting for this chance for nine years now, and nothing was going to ruin it for her. They would both just have to be adults about this.

"This isn't permanent," she heard someone say.

She turned towards the small blonde woman who was standing beside her. "Excuse me?"

"This." The woman gestured widely. "It's not permanent. Sumptor has another building that's being renovated. We all just have to put up with this a little bit longer."

"I see," Lainey responded. "I'm sorry, I missed your name."

"I'm Jackie," the woman replied, smiling. "I work in accounting, too. I guess that makes you my boss."

"It's nice to meet you, Jackie. So, the closet is only temporary."

Lainey was relieved when the women surrounding her laughed. Just as Lainey was beginning to relax, a young girl, wearing far too much makeup, rushed up.

"Sumptor is coming!" She whispered in urgency.

Instantly, everyone stopped laughing. Turning, Lainey saw a middle aged man with horned rimmed glasses and a receding hairline. Next to him was a woman. Although Lainey couldn't see the face of the woman who was talking intently with him, she appeared to be very young and dressed in what looked to be a very expensive, tailored suit. His secretary, no doubt, she thought. How typical that a man facing a mid-life crisis should hire the youngest secretary he could find. The idea made Lainey want to chuckle, but she cleared her throat instead. No need to be so judgmental. After all, he was the owner of the gallery she wanted to work in. Just then the woman lifted her head and smiled at him.

Lainey watched as he blushed, actually blushed, and hurried off down the narrow corridor.

"Good morning, Meredith. Ladies." The young woman nodded her head in greeting, locking eyes with each employee and smiling.

Her voice was soft. Sensual was the first word that came to Lainey's mind. Her blonde hair was pulled back, though not as severely as Meredith's, with strands falling at the sides, framing a face that could bring a man to his knees, with its striking gray eyes, a small, perfect nose and full lips. She wore a black skirt that stopped at mid-thigh, showing those beautiful, shapely legs and a white button down shirt undone enough to show the swells of perfect breasts. Lainey had never seen anyone quite so beautiful.

"Good morning, Ms. Sumptor," Meredith replied. "This is our new employee, Lainey Stanton."

Eve turned her head and looked at Lainey, holding her gaze with smiling eyes. "Lainey. It's nice to meet you. I'm Eve Sumptor."

As they shook hands, Eve raised one perfect eyebrow.

"You weren't expecting a woman," she said knowingly giving Lainey's hand a friendly squeeze before releasing it.

"Ms. Sumptor," Meredith said over Lainey's stunned silence. "I need to speak with you for a moment."

"Yes, Meredith. Excuse me, Lainey. I apologize for the poor working conditions," she said pausing at the door. "It won't be for long, I promise."

Winking at Lainey, she turned to walk into Meredith's office, leaving all of the women staring after her enviously.

"Amazing, isn't she," Jackie whispered as everyone separated to return to work. "I've never seen anyone quite like her."

"Yes, she's beautiful," Lainey agreed. "I was expecting a man. I never imagined that E. Sumptor was a woman, let alone so young. I must've looked like a fool, just staring at her."

"She's used to it, I'm sure," Jackie said, giggling. "I think we all had the same reaction when we first met her. It's almost impossible not to stare. She's so – captivating." Both women turned to watch Eve through the window to Meredith's office.

Inside, Eve was enduring yet another meeting with Meredith about the hiring of Lainey Stanton.

"I understand how you feel, Meredith," she said patiently. "But as I've told you before, Katherine just isn't the right person for the job."

"But she has seniority, Ms. Sumptor. She should've been next in line."

"Seniority doesn't necessarily mean that she's next in line." Eve sighed softly. "I know that you and Katherine are friends, Meredith, but I have to do what I feel is right for the company. Katherine simply doesn't have enough experience."

"Nor does Lainey, she hasn't worked in over nine years..."

"Enough," Eve interrupted. "I've made my decision. We'll try this with Lainey, and if I feel as though it is not working, then we'll try with Katherine. In the meantime, I expect you and Katherine to be kind to Lainey. Is that understood? I think Lainey will do great." Eve turned to look out the window just then, and made eye contact with Lainey once again. Holding the contact for a moment, Eve gave her a small smile. Turning back to Meredith, she said, "I'm a good judge of character, Meredith – as you know."

It sounded like a warning.

"Now, if there's nothing else, I'll get back to work. Have a good day, Meredith."

Since a minute earlier Lainey was looking in the window, Eve sauntered over to her.

"Come to my office in about ten minutes, please," she said pleasantly. "I would like to speak with you."

"Yes, ma'am."

Eve smiled at her, a bold and devastating smile. "Don't call me ma'am. It makes me feel old." Then with another wink, she turned and walked away.

Eve sat at her desk, surrounded by paper work. She tried concentrating on the report in front of her, but her mind was on other things besides work. There was something about Lainey Stanton that had intrigued Eve from the first moment she set eyes on her, although she wasn't sure what it was. Lainey had a classic beauty, the sharp, yet delicate features with soulful green eyes, and a wonderful mouth that bowed down slightly at the edges. Eve shook herself and tried focusing back on her work. It must be the painter in me, Eve thought. She could notice the inner beauty of a person as well as the outer, and Eve noticed Lainey. She drummed her fingers on the desk as she thought about how she would love to paint Lainey's captivating features.

The intercom on Eve's desk buzzed, interrupting her thoughts.

"Ms. Sumptor, Lainey Stanton is here to see you."

"Send her in, please," Eve said.

The door opened and Lainey walked in.

"Please have a seat," Eve told her.

Eve watched silently as Lainey looked around her office, enjoying the way she seemed to take it all in.

"It isn't you," Lainey said.

Interested, Eve raised an eyebrow and sat back in her chair. "Meaning?"

"I'm sorry. I shouldn't have..."

"No. Please, tell me," Eve encouraged her.

"I just meant...I don't know. The wood, the dark colors, the brown carpet, they're not you. But the painting. Van Gogh. Now that's you."

Eve's smile widened and she looked behind her at the colorful painting depicting two figures in the woods. She looked back at Lainey.

"Good eye. Why is it me?"

Lainey lifted a shoulder, and considered for a moment.

"The confidence, the strength. There's an air of independence, but there's romance, too."

Eve raised both eyebrows at that. "Romance? You get all of that about me from a painting?" There was a silence between them as Eve studied Lainey. "You know art."

Lainey hesitated, and then decided to tell Eve the truth.

"Yes," she said. "I majored in Art History in college. I've always had a love for it."

"Why?"

Lainey frowned slightly at what she considered to be a silly question, especially from someone who owned her own art gallery.

"Because it's fascinating..."

"No, why are you here?" Eve interrupted her. "Why apply for the accounting job when it's not what you want to do?"

"I thought it would get me closer to the gallery," Lainey answered honestly and waited for Eve's disapproval.

Instead, Eve picked up a piece of paper in front of her.

"Lainey Stanton," she read, and Lainey realized that it was her résumé.

"Thirty-seven."

She looked Lainey up and down and smiled approvingly.

"Married. Happily?"

A shadow crossed Lainey's face.

"I'm sorry," Eve said quickly. "It's none of my business."

"It's all right. Sometimes we're happy, but not always,"

Lainey answered grimacing. "I don't know why I told you that. Somehow, I just felt I could."

Once again, Eve smiled that bold and devastating smile and started reading again. "Two children, Kevin and Darren. I have a lot of information about you, Lainey. But nowhere here does it say art major. Why?"

"I didn't think it was necessary to mention it since I was applying for the accountant position," Lainey answered matter-of-factly.

"Hmm, I guess not." She liked Lainey's directness. Most people who dealt with Eve were intimidated by her, and almost always agreed with whatever she said, whether they had the same opinion or not. "Will you meet me at The Garden of Eve for lunch?"

It was an expensive restaurant nearby that Lainey and Jack had once gone to for their anniversary.

"I'd like that," she said.

"Good," Eve said with pleasure. "I'd like to get to know you a little better."

Eve had always wanted a good professional relationship with her employees, but she wanted more from Lainey, although what that more was, she wasn't quite sure. Why did she feel this way, Eve asked herself. "Don't tell anyone you're meeting me for lunch," she said as Lainey rose.

"I'm sure you've already experienced some animosity from a couple of people. If you tell them you're eating with the boss, it might get worse for you."

As Lainey left the office, she found herself trembling with anticipation, although why she should feel this way she had no idea. One thing was certain, however. This woman had brought something new into her life.

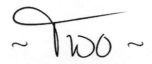

~ Two ~

Later, Eve waited for Lainey at one of the more secluded tables of the elegant restaurant. The aroma of gourmet food lingered with the sweet scent of the exotic flowers that surrounded her. It should have relaxed her. But she could feel men looking at her and knew what they were thinking, just as she had known since she was sixteen. A beautiful face, an exciting body. No substance, no brain. She had let them think that. Then. Now, it was Eve who made the decisions, and who chose the men she would share her time with, never letting them get too close, always shielding herself and her heart from hurt.

Although numerous people, including her employees, thought that she had many men, Eve never slept with any she had been seen dating, except for one. Adam. And her relationship with him was purely physical. She wouldn't allow it to be any more than that. Of course she cared for Adam, perhaps even more than she could admit. But she couldn't – wouldn't allow love to enter the equation.

"Hi," Lainey said quietly. As she had followed the waiter to the table, she had noticed the attention Eve was receiving from men and women alike, although Eve – clearly deep in thought – was oblivious to them.

Eve looked up and smiled brightly.

"Are you okay?" Lainey asked, sliding into the chair opposite her.

"Yes, of course. Why do you ask?" Eve replied cheerfully.

"You just looked so..." Lainey hesitated.

"So, what?" Eve asked.

"Lonely."

The silence that followed and the look that Eve gave her made Lainey uncomfortable. Why did she always have to open her mouth and say just what she was thinking?

Eve closed the menu that was in front of her. "I don't know why I look at this," she said, laughing. "I always get the same thing."

"You come here often?" Lainey asked, a little confused by the abrupt change in subject.

"Actually, I own it," Eve responded.

"Oh!" Lainey exclaimed. She couldn't have been more surprised if Eve had told her she owned the moon. The building that Sumptor Inc. was housed in certainly didn't look as though it were owned by someone who owned the busiest, most expensive restaurant in town. "I had no idea. My husband and I came here once for our anniversary. It's wonderful."

Eve chuckled, "Thank you. I'm glad you enjoyed your time here." She paused as the waiter came to take their order. "You were wondering why you're working in a closet if I own this restaurant, right?"

Lainey almost choked on her water at Eve's directness.

"Sorry," Eve said reaching across the table to pat Lainey's hand, deliberately ignoring the electricity she felt from the contact. She wasn't ready to analyze those feelings yet. "Are you okay?"

"Yes," Lainey said, after clearing her throat. She, too, had felt the electricity, and to say that it had confused her was an understatement. "To both questions. I didn't realize I was so transparent."

"You're not," Eve told her. "It was a logical guess. There was a fire, and I lost everything. Sumptor Inc., Sumptor Gallery, all of that beautiful art - all gone. I put all of the insurance money and much of my own into rebuilding, so when I found a place to work out of while the rebuild was being done, I didn't want to waste money on high rent. I know it's been hard on my employees to have to work in such conditions, and I apologize for that. But, the new place will hopefully make up for it. It's going to be beautiful. And the gallery...oh, Lainey, it's exquisite."

"I can't wait to see it," Lainey said with honest anticipation. "I'm so sorry about the fire. How did it start?"

She saw some emotion flicker in Eve's eye, but it was gone so fast that she didn't recognize what it was. Anger?

"I don't know," Eve said quietly. "No one seems to have that answer for me. 'Perhaps it was faulty wiring, Ms. Sumptor.' Perhaps."

"Were you an art major as well?" Lainey asked tactfully after the waiter brought their salads out.

"Yes," Eve told her, lifting a careless shoulder. "I studied in Europe mostly. Paris, Italy, Spain. You know, all the predictable places a young, art major should study."

Lainey frowned. "Your parents sent you to Europe to study? I would have loved that, but mine didn't have the money. You sound as though you didn't enjoy the experience."

"My parents didn't send me. I ran away. I ran all the way to Europe." Eve paused. "Does that shock you, Lainey? That I ran away? Eve Sumptor, the troubled teen?"

"How did you live?" Lainey asked her. In truth, it did shock her, but she wasn't about to pry into Eve's private life.

"I worked. I also sold my paintings and photographs. It's easy to get people to sit for you, to come up to your room, even take their clothes off for you if you're an attractive young woman."

It wasn't a lie, exactly, Eve thought, unaccustomed to the feeling of guilt for telling the edited version of the story. She had never had a problem with telling partial truths before, but then, she'd never met someone like Lainey. Maybe it was Lainey's sincere, soulful eyes that made Eve want to tell her everything. Because she believed it was Eve looked away.

"Did you..." Lainey began, and then caught herself. What had possessed her to want to ask such a personal question?

"Did I what, Lainey? Have sex with them?" Eve should have known the question would be there, but it still hurt. "No."

There was no hesitation, no uncertainty.

"I'm sorry, Eve."

"Don't be. I'm used to it. People look at me and see a beautiful woman. I suppose that means I should be a slut as well, but I'm not, contrary to popular belief. Not that it matters. It amuses me"

"It hurts you," Lainey corrected her. She watched, as Eve put down her fork.

"You see too much," she said quietly. "Tell me, why the accounting job."

Another abrupt change in subject had Lainey searching for an answer. "Why not?"

"Because, it's bound to be too boring for you," Eve told her.

"I'm a boring person," Lainey countered, staring down at the pristine, white table cloth.

"No. You're not." Eve was suddenly angry for reasons she couldn't explain. "Who told you that you were boring, Lainey?"

"No one has to tell me, Eve. I've always been boring. I was the good daughter. Now I'm the good wife and good mother. Nothing exciting happens in my life. Don't get me wrong," she continued quickly as she thought about what she had just said, "I love my children. They mean the world to me. And, I love my husband, though things could be a little better. They are who I am. I'm not like you."

"Like me? Hmm - And what exactly does that mean, Lainey?"

"I just meant - I don't know, Eve. You're beautiful, confident, successful, daring. Shall I go on?"

"What do you have on underneath that gray suit, Lainey?" Eve asked unabashedly.

"What?" Blushing, Lainey lowered her head again. Eve brought her hand to Lainey's chin and lifted her head.

"I didn't mean to embarrass you. I just want you to tell me what you have on. Humor me," Eve finished before Lainey could protest.

"A bra and panties," Lainey said in a low voice.

"What color?"

"Black."

"Lacy?"

Confused and uneasy about these unexpected questions, Lainey just nodded her head.

"See?" Eve declared triumphantly. "That's very sexy. The gray suit is your shield against the outside world. It portrays how you think everyone sees you. But underneath it all, there's a passionate, exciting woman just waiting to be set free. Actually, there's nothing boring about you at all."

Lainey thought about what Eve had said as she watched Eve turn her attention back to her salad. Even the way she ate was sensual.

"What are you wearing under your suit?" Lainey asked, surprising herself.

"Absolutely nothing," Eve answered boldly, lifting her glass to Lainey. "But we're talking about you. Children and a husband do not make you boring. They're the ones who should make you feel exciting. Especially your husband."

"Try telling Jack that," Lainey muttered. "Do you have someone in your life, Eve? Someone who makes you feel exciting?"

Eve remained silent for a long moment. "Yes," she said finally. "I'm seeing someone."

"How long have you been in the relationship?"

"I didn't say I was in a relationship, Lainey. I'm fucking him."

Lainey looked up sharply at Eve. "But..."

"Look, not all 'relationships' are fairy tales. I enjoy sex."

She paused as the waiter who was filling Eve's glass spilled the water. Apologizing profusely, the young man began mopping with a napkin. "It's fine, leave it," Eve said kindly, smiling devastatingly at him.

"I think you just gave that young boy his first orgasm." Lainey laughed.

"I hardly doubt it's his first unless he's twelve," Eve countered. "I'll leave him a nice tip. It's the least I can do to make up for embarrassing him like that. May I see your watch? I never wear one," she reached across the table and took Lainey's hand.

Her fingers were cool on Lainey's skin. "We should get going; you don't want to be late coming back from lunch on your first day."

As they left the restaurant together, Lainey was aware that every eye seemed to follow Eve. In the parking garage, they discovered that they had parked next to each other, Lainey's old, tan station wagon in dramatic contrast to Eve's sleek, black Jaguar.

Looking first at the cars and then at each other, they busted out laughing.

"See? Boring," Lainey managed between gasps of air.

"It's too much?" Eve laughed, disengaging the alarm.

"It's a beautiful car," Lainey commented.

"I'll give you a ride sometime," Eve slipped into the driver's seat and flashed Lainey a grin.

"I'm going to offer you something, Lainey, and I want you to think about it carefully." Eve paused for a moment, and then continued. "I want you to be my assistant at the gallery. Before you answer, I want to warn you. Being my assistant means you will have to be at my beck and call at all times, it means long hours with me and most of all it means putting up with my mood swings."

She reached over to the glove compartment and took out a pen and a card. After writing on the back of the card, she handed it to Lainey.

"Here is my home number. Talk to your husband, think about it and call me with your answer. As much as I would love to take you for a drive now, you should get back."

"Thank you, Eve. I don't know what else to say." Lainey's mind was racing. She couldn't believe what was happening to her.

"Don't say anything," Eve told her. "Just think about it and call me later." With that, she flashed Lainey that devastating smile, winked that charming wink and took off waving.

Lainey, having thought about nothing but Eve's offer throughout the day, could barely concentrate on anything else.

Now, as she sat at the dinner table with her husband and sons, she wondered how she would tell them and when. It had been so long since she had been this happy, and she wanted them to be happy for her.

"I was offered a promotion today," she announced and waited for a reaction.

Jack looked up, annoyed that she had brought up her job.

"A promotion? What moron offers you a promotion on your first day?"

"She's not a moron, Jack," Lainey answered. She knew how he felt about her working, but hadn't realized how much it would hurt not to have his support of something that she wanted to do so desperately. "I'll be working as her assistant at Sumptor Gallery. Art, Jack. You know how much I've wanted to do this."

"That's great, Mom!" Kevin exclaimed. He wasn't interested in art himself, but he knew how much she enjoyed it.

"Yeah, Mommy! That's great!" Darren chimed in.

Lainey placed a hand on each of her son's faces. "Thank you," she said. "It's going to mean longer hours for me. Do you think you can handle not having me around all the time?"

"Sure. I'm old enough to take care of myself, Ma, and I'll look out for squirt here, too," Kevin said with a grin ignoring Darren's argument that he was old enough to take care of himself, too.

"I know you are. Both of you. You'll be able to get in touch with me at all times, just in case." She glanced at Jack and saw his look of disapproval and anger. "Why don't you boys go up and get ready for bed. Leave the plates. I'll get them. I love you, both."

They each kissed her on the cheek, told their dad goodnight and bounded up the stairs, while Lainey waited for the argument she knew was coming.

"You're not taking it," Jack said with a finality that made it clear that, as far as he was concerned, that was the end of the conversation.

"Yes, I am." She rose and started to clear the dishes off the table. "You know I want this, and I'm going to do it."

"And what about us? Have you thought of that, Lainey? What about Kevin and Darren?" he said accusingly.

"Don't, Jack. Don't make me feel guilty about this. You heard the boys. They're happy for me. Why can't you be?"

"Why do you have to change things, Lainey? We were fine the way we were."

"No! No, we aren't fine, Jack." Her eyes pleaded for him to understand. "Things have to change. I'm your wife and yet you never touch me anymore. All I do is cook and clean for you. You see me as a mother, but goddamn it, Jack, I'm not your mother! I'm taking the job.

And things will change, because I don't know what will happen if they don't."

Eve sat on top of Adam, and he fisted his hands in her hair as she rode him. Sounds of lovemaking and the murmurs of unintelligible words filled the room. Eve enjoyed making love to Adam. He was not only amazingly skillful, but was also as uninhibited about sex as she was. If she wasn't careful, she could find herself having feelings for this man. Moaning, she reached down to take his face in her hands and kiss him. When her phone rang, she clung to him, letting the machine pick up.

"Eve?" The voice was uncertain. "It's Lainey. I just wanted to tell you that I'd take the job."

Riding Adam harder and faster, she cried out as she came. Breathing hard, holding Adam tightly to her, Eve closed her eyes and smiled slowly with satisfaction.

She couldn't explain why Lainey's decision had made her so happy, but Eve was determined to find answers for all of the feelings she was experiencing.

~ Three ~

"Do you know why Sumptor called this meeting, Meredith?" Katherine asked under her breath.

Each of them had found a memo on their desk this morning, requesting them to be in the conference room promptly at eight thirty.

"No. I have no idea," Meredith said, annoyed. She should have known, she thought. Eve should have told her what to be expecting, but instead she sat here just as much in the dark as everyone else.

Just then, Eve walked in the room dressed in fitted charcoal slacks and a pale, lavender cotton shirt that showed off her perfect figure. Every woman in the room felt a sense of envy as she sauntered in, sat down and crossed her legs, each movement filled with an underlying sexuality.

"Good morning," Eve began. "I know you're all wondering why I asked you here this morning. I thought you'd like to know that the new building is finished."

The room erupted with cheers and applause.

Eve chuckled. "I knew that would make you happy. You should pack all of your personal belongings and take them with you tonight. Everything else - will be thrown away. Seriously, all of the files that will be needed will be transferred from these computers to your new computers, which will be on your new desks with your new chairs."

The room buzzed with excitement.

"On another business matter," Eve began over the noise, "Lainey Stanton will no longer be supervising accountant."

A hush fell over the room, and Eve continued without skipping a beat.

"Katherine, that means you will take her place on a trial basis."

Surprised, Katherine could do nothing but stare. It was Meredith who broke the silence. "I don't understand, Ms. Sumptor."

Eve raised a brow. "Katherine is now supervising accountant. I trust that you will show her the ropes."

"Yes, of course. But, where will Lainey go?" Even though she was happy about Katherine's appointment, Meredith still found herself wary about Lainey. What was it about her?

"Lainey will be my new assistant at the gallery," Eve answered shortly. She rose. "Thank you. Don't forget anything when you leave for the night."

When they all started filing out of the conference room, each stopping to congratulate Katherine and Lainey, Meredith stayed behind.

"May I speak with you, Ms. Sumptor?"

"Yes, Meredith?"

"I appreciate you giving Katherine this opportunity," Meredith began.

"This is a trial basis," Eve interrupted her. "For Katherine and you, Meredith. I expect both of you to give each employee here equal treatment. If there are any problems, or complaints, I will personally look into it myself. Is that clear?"

"Yes ma'am. You won't be disappointed," Meredith said staunchly. She lowered her voice. "But do you think that Lainey is qualified for the position you've given her?"

"Yes. I do," Eve answered, annoyed. Meredith had always questioned Eve's decisions, but with Lainey there was more to it.

Was it jealousy, Eve wondered? She knew women could be catty, had seen it first hand before, but constantly being second-guessed on her decisions about Lainey was wearing on her nerves.

"You got my message," Lainey said as she replaced Meredith at Eve's side.

"Yes," Eve said, giving Lainey a wicked grin. "I'm sorry I didn't come to the phone. I was, shall we say, detained."

From the way Lainey flushed slightly, Eve knew she had understood.

"Come on," Eve said, taking Lainey's arm. "I want to show you the gallery."

"Something is going on here," Meredith said as Katherine followed her into her office. "I don't know what it is, but I don't like it."

"What are you talking about?" Katherine sat on the edge of the chair in front of Meredith's desk. "We got what we wanted."

"Yes, I know. But there is something going on with Lainey."

"Meredith, stop! Who cares about Lainey? She's not in our way anymore." Katherine leaned forward and lowered her voice, "Don't screw this up, Meredith. We've waited a long time for this opportunity."

"I'm not going to screw this up!" Meredith hissed. "But you need to understand, Katherine that we are going to be watched closely. Eve warned me. If we are not very careful, this could all blow up in our faces."

"All the more reason for you to not worry about Lainey."

"Don't you think it's odd that she's suddenly become Eve's assistant after working here just one day?" Meredith demanded. "Never mind. Let's just focus on what we have to do. And don't take chances. Whatever we do, let's not take any chances."

The alarm on Eve's car beeped as she pressed the button to disengage it. She opened the door for Lainey, walked around to the driver's side and slid in beside her. "Mind if I put the top down?" she asked.

"No, not at all." Lainey tried to relax. But now that she was alone with Eve, she found she was nervous. She thought of the explicit fantasy she had had the night before. Normally a dream wouldn't have given her such anxiety, but this one had been of Eve, and it had shocked Lainey to her core. With effort, she focused on here and now, and not the restless night before. She watched as Eve gracefully slid the car into gear, each movement fluid.

It was Eve who broke the silence between them once they got on the road. "How did it go with the family?" she asked, glancing over at Lainey.

"The boys are happy for me," Lainey told her. "Of course, they're just happy that they get to act like big boys now and take care of themselves."

"Good. And Jack?"

Lainey was silent for a long moment.

"That bad, huh?"

"He wasn't happy about me getting a job in the first place." Lainey sighed. "This just made it worse. He actually told me I wasn't going to take it."

"And yet you did," Eve said ruefully. "I don't mean to cause problems between the two of you, Lainey."

"It's not your fault," Lainey said quickly. "We had - problems before this. Now he just has a way to make me feel guilty."

"Why should you feel guilty?" Eve stopped at the red light and turned to Lainey. "Because of your children? They are more than welcome to come to the gallery to be with you if you have to work late, you know. That's not a problem. I love kids."

She saw the stunned look on Lainey's face and sighed.

"That surprises you? I guess I should have known that you would have felt that way. I should have prepared for the assumption that because I've chosen not to get married that I don't care for children."

She started to drive in silence when the light turned green.

"I'm sorry, Eve."

"No. Don't be. I'm used to everyone feeling a certain way about me."

"I'm not everyone."

Eve glanced at Lainey, holding her gaze for a moment.

"No, you're not," she said in a low voice. Lainey felt a flush creep up her neck and was glad when Eve turned back to concentrate on the road.

"I would love for you to meet Kevin and Darren," Lainey said. It was, she found, important that she made up for appearing to judge Eve. "They're great boys."

"I have no doubt they are. And I'd love to meet them. Jack, too."

"Getting Jack to do anything with me is practically impossible anymore," Lainey told her. "Knowing how he feels about me working, I don't think he would be too enthusiastic about meeting you."

She paused. It had been so long since she'd had anyone to talk to, and she felt so in tuned with Eve that she wanted to tell her everything.

"I haven't had sex in over two months," she said, blurting out the words and instantly regretting it.

"I can help you with that," Eve said quietly, and now it was Lainey who was shocked. "I mean with Jack," Eve went on, noting Lainey's embarrassment. "I can help you with Jack."

Before Lainey could respond, Eve pulled into a parking garage and stopped at the gate. The security officer came out of the small office and walked up to the car.

"Good morning, Ms. Sumptor," he said and tipped his hat to both women. He was in his thirties with sand colored hair and a plump belly that he sucked in as soon as he saw Eve.

"Good morning, Pauly," she said cheerfully. "How are you?"

"Better now that you're here."

Eve smiled a mind-boggling smile and winked at Pauly. "Hmm. And how are the wife and kids?" Pauly's triumphant smile faltered and he blushed.

"Um, they're good. Thank you."

"Good. Have a wonderful day, Pauly," Eve said and drove off into the parking garage, waving behind her.

"Does that come naturally?" Lainey asked with a giggle.

"What?" Eve responded with such an innocent look that Lainey couldn't help but to laugh.

"Flirting," she finally said.

"I wasn't flirting. He was flirting with me," Eve said with feigned indignation, and then smiled wickedly. "Men are funny. He sucks in his gut every time he sees me coming, and every time I ask him about his wife and kids, he lets it out. It amuses me."

"What's it like, having every man, and even women attracted to you?"

Eve pulled into the parking space and cut off the engine. She turned in her seat and fixed her eyes on Lainey's. "Are you attracted to me, Lainey?" She said abruptly. The two looked at each other in silence for a long moment, until Eve looked away, and slipping out of the car, waited for Lainey to join her. Neither of them said a word as they walked together to the elevator. Eve hadn't meant to ask that question and regretted it the moment it came out of her mouth. The best thing to do now, she thought, was just move on and forget it.

"You're going to love the gallery," Eve said stepping into the elevator and inserting a key to unlock the gallery floor. "It turned out much better than I imagined."

"I can't wait to see it." Lainey was grateful to Eve this time for the change in subject. She had been so close to giving Eve a truthful answer to her question and that might have spelled disaster.

When the elevator doors opened and the gallery was revealed, Lainey forgot everything. It was spectacular. There was no other word for it. Eve walked into the gallery with her arms spread wide and turning in circles.

"What do you think?" she asked, circling back to Lainey.

"Amazing."

And it was. The high ceilings and stark white walls were accented with bamboo wood floors. The entrance was a colossal space, with arch windows overlooking the crowded streets of artistic SoHo. The view in itself was a work of art.

Eve watched with interest as Lainey wandered around taking everything in. It was important to her what Lainey thought of the gallery. The realization intrigued and terrified her.

"Tell me what you see," Eve demanded.

Lainey spun around to stare at her. "But I'm only your assistant. I don't know if I have the vision..."

"And you won't know unless you try," Eve interrupted. "Don't worry, I'll have my input. But right now, I want to know what you see."

Lainey hesitated but for only a second. "There'll be sculptures and photographs as well as paintings, right?"

"I see you've done your homework," Eve's voice was amused.

"The sculptures will go here in the front room," Lainey said eagerly. "Not too many, because we don't want to overpower the simple beauty of the room itself."

The gallery was "U" shaped, separated by a thick wall in the middle and Lainey started on the left.

"The paintings, starting with the most bold, like the Cézanne's, will go here. The colors will catch people's eyes, and draw them here. As they go further, the paintings will mellow. The Norman Rockwell's will lead into the photographs. But, here," she said gesturing towards the middle of the walkway, "can be another small sculpture. It will give the viewer a sense of variety."

Lainey walked through the archway, Eve followed silently, intrigued.

"Color photos," Lainey said quietly, almost to herself. "We should begin with the color photography here, and, of course, scattered sculptures. Not enough to obstruct the walkway, but enough to charm the clientele. And then," she paused dramatically, "then we have the black and whites."

Eve raised her eyebrow questionably.

"Black and whites are my favorites," Lainey explained. "There's so much depth and emotion, but they also make you use your imagination. My favorite medium."

"Mine, too," Eve said softly. "I would love to photograph you, Lainey." She traced Lainey's cheekbone with her fingertip.

The moment was shattered by the buzz of the intercom. Eve broke the contact and walked to the door leaving Lainey behind, shaken.

Lainey's heart was racing as she watched Eve let the deliverymen in. She looked so calm, Lainey thought. As though nothing had just happened between them. Maybe it hadn't. Maybe Lainey had imagined the whole thing. Eve was a photographer, and a flirt. It meant nothing. Calming herself, Lainey went to join Eve as she told the men where to place various pieces, including a bronze of three children playing baseball, so real you could almost hear the crack of the bat.

Eve discovered that she was having difficulty concentrating on what she was doing. What in the hell had she been thinking? She hadn't been thinking, that was the problem. She had let her emotions take control.

Why? Eve Sumptor never let her emotions get in the way, or control her actions. The last thing she wanted to do was scare Lainey away, but if she kept this up, that's exactly what was going to happen. It was time to raise the wall around her heart that she had so foolishly let slip.

"Local talent," Eve explained to Lainey, all business now as burly, young men placed a chiseled stone figure of a nude woman by the alcove just where Lainey had suggested one should be placed. "I've decided to 'give back to the community' and give a few local artists some exposure during our grand opening."

"When are we opening?" Lainey asked amazed at how calm her voice was, and hating the tension and distance she felt with Eve now.

"In less than a week. Want to rethink taking this position now?"

"No." Lainey reached out to take Eve's arm, forcing Eve to look at her. "No, Eve. I don't want to rethink anything. And I don't regret anything."

"Good." Eve's amazing gray eyes darkened as they bore into Lainey's. "Because I'm not letting you go."

"Excuse me." A young man interrupted them with a paper for Eve to sign.

"Yes? Do you need me to sign these?" she asked.

"Y-yes ma'am," he stammered.

Eve took the clipboard from him, and signed her name in one fluid motion. Lainey watched, amused, as he flushed when she touched his arm. "There. Oh, and don't call me ma'am." Laughing, Eve hooked an arm in Lainey's. "Come on, I'll show you your office."

They walked up the stairs together arm in arm. As they reached the top, Lainey found herself just as impressed with what she saw upstairs as she was with the gallery itself. The doors of the offices had wooden frames with opaque, frosted glass giving them a very classy look. For accent, they were finished with beautiful brass handles.

Eve guided Lainey to the half wall that overlooked the expansive area, and for a moment they stood together, looking down on the entire gallery. Lainey caught a glimpse of Eve and what she saw in her face took Lainey's breath away. She could feel the pride and the love, peace and triumph coursing through Eve just by the deep breath Eve took and shivered with emotions herself.

"It's mine," Eve said in a low voice, almost as though she were talking to herself and then, becoming aware that Lainey was watching her, felt slightly embarrassed. Quickly gathering her thoughts, she smiled. "Let's go see that office now."

The moment Lainey walked in the door, she felt at home. It was such a strong feeling that it unnerved her.

"When I had this office decorated, I wasn't doing it for anyone specific. See the soft colors, and the lines of the architecture? There's a subtle sexuality here." Eve paused, considered. "This office was made for you."

And it was true. Eve had chosen muted colors and soft lines to accentuate the pewter carpet, which gave the room a full, rich look. The desk was big and modern, but very understated in a blonde oak. The sleek new, flat computer screen sat atop the desk, its only accessory besides a phone. Even the tan, leather chair looked as though it were made for Lainey, with its high back and delicate curves. Eve had also chosen a Monet to go on the wall behind the desk. Looking at it now, she knew she had made the right choice.

"You want to see mine?" She asked full of pride.

"Of course," Lainey replied. At the door, she paused to look back. My office, Lainey thought with a grin. Mine.

At the other end of the Berber carpeted hall, they came to a stop at double doors in the same style as the door to Lainey's office. "I'm narcissistic. I have to have everything bigger and better," Eve said, leading Lainey into the spacious loft style space.

"Now this is you," Lainey announced. The sexuality in this room was not as subtle as in Lainey's office. Although the tone was still muted, and the carpet was the same color, Eve had accented the space with bold colors. The couch at the far end of the office was white, seemingly unobtrusive, until you factored in the electric blue throw pillows. The rest of the furniture was modern, contemporary, without a hint of the antiquity that will fill the gallery. Eve's desk was made of frosted glass and steel, as fragile and yet as hard as the woman who would sit behind it.

The chair was oversized, but not overpowering and had the soft curves of a beautiful woman, a woman like Eve. Lainey noted that Eve had had the Van Gogh brought over from the other building. It suited this office, or maybe this office suited the painting. Lainey was sure of one thing and that was this space, the furnishings, the city around them, screamed Eve Sumptor. She had felt it the moment she walked in. She turned back to the painting.

"It is," Eve said, reading Lainey's mind.

"It must've cost..." Lainey caught herself.

"A small fortune? Yes. But it's worth it."

"I'm sorry; it was none of my business."

"It's ok, Lainey," Eve said quietly. "Feel free to ask me anything."

The ringing of Eve's cell phone broke the momentary silence. Taking out the phone, she walked to the huge bay window and sat on the sill. "Hello?"

"Hi." The sound of Adam's voice made Eve's pulse jump.

"Hi yourself."

"Did I catch you at a bad time?"

"No, not at all. What can I do for you?"

Lainey tried not to listen to Eve's conversation, but she had heard how Eve's voice dropped an octave to become a sensual whisper. She knew she had no right to be jealous, but she discovered that she hated the way Eve had smiled.

"Are you busy tonight?" Adam asked. Hearing Eve always excited him. She was beautiful, erotic and a spectacular lover, but to Adam, she was more. Although he had known since the beginning that Eve was not looking for a serious relationship or love, he had fallen in love with her the moment he saw her. But he had promised himself he would be patient, to wait for her to fall in love with him for he was sure she felt some of what he was feeling. But having to go home every night after being with her, not being allowed to wake up next to her in the morning to make love again was causing his patience to wear thin.

"I'm free tonight," Eve answered, smiling. "Meet me at my place? We'll order in."

"No," Adam said.

"No?" It was a word Eve rarely heard. She frowned.

"I want to cook for you," Adam said.

"You want to what?" she said tentatively.

"Cook for you. No take out tonight." Adam paused. Knowing he was taking a chance, he went on, "Let me stay tonight, Eve."

Eve's heart beat faster. God, she wanted so much to tell him yes. To stay with her, hold her. But she couldn't open herself up like that and let him in so she said the only thing she could say.

"No." She heard Adam's sigh and closed her eyes. 'I'm sorry,' she mouthed, never saying it aloud.

Putting her phone away after making arrangements, Eve sat there quietly, her eyes still closed. She knew, had always known, that Adam wouldn't wait forever. She had to think about that, and be prepared to lose him if she couldn't open her heart to him.

"Are you all right?" Lainey came to sit next to Eve, taking Eve's hand in hers. She felt the slight squeeze just as clearly as she felt the change take place in Eve. She's closing herself off again, Lainey thought. Building those walls.

"Don't," Lainey said quietly, taking Eve's chin in her hand. "Don't close yourself off to me like that. Let me be there for you. Please."

Eve stood up, bringing Lainey with her. "I'm starved," she said. "Let's order something to eat." And when Lainey held her steady, she added, "Not now. Not yet. I know I can talk to you. I feel it here," she said bringing Lainey's hand to her heart. "Just give me a little time. Now, about that food..."

They made a makeshift picnic on the floor of Eve's office, spreading the food out in front of them on the thick carpet. There were containers of pasta and marinara sauce, two loaves of Italian bread and salad that could feed an army with at least four different dressings. Because it was early, they settled for iced tea instead of wine.

"You weren't kidding when you said you were starved," Lainey said, surveying the feast. "How do you stay so thin?"

"I work it off every night," Eve replied with a sly grin. "I'm very - passionate about my workouts."

"Every night?" Lainey raised her eyebrows. She saw Eve lift a shoulder and smile sheepishly. "God. I wish it was like that with Jack."

"Why isn't it?" Eve broke off a piece of bread and offering it to Lainey.

"I guess that's what happens when you've been married for twelve years," Lainey said in an amused voice, looking down at her breasts. "Things start to fall...literally."

"Please, Lainey. You are an amazingly beautiful woman. If your husband can't see that then he's a fool."

Lainey smiled, embarrassed. "You're just being nice, I know, but it's good for my ego to hear a stunning woman tell me that."

"Hmm, honey, I never say things just to be nice. You'll find that out about me soon enough. You shouldn't hide your body, you know. Why don't you shock your husband by doing something outrageous?"

"Oh! I couldn't do that," Lainey laughed. "He's not the type that likes 'surprises'."

"Really?" Eve said and raised a brow. "So, if you were to walk in the room completely naked, he wouldn't get - excited?"

Lainey chuckled. "If I walked into the room completely naked, Jack would think I'd gone insane and I wouldn't blame him. Eve, I'm not twenty-three anymore, and I certainly didn't look like you or have your body when I was."

"First of all, honey, I'm not twenty-three," Eve told her. "I'm twenty-seven. And as for your body and your looks, I've said it before; you are an amazingly beautiful woman. Show it. Like this." Keeping her eyes level with Lainey's, Eve unbuttoned the top three buttons of her shirt. Lainey's pulse began to race.

"That's much better," Eve said huskily and reached for her iced tea. She looked at Lainey over the rim of her glass, "Go home tonight, put the boys to bed early and seduce your husband."

After eating, they spent the rest of the day unwrapping and unpacking statues, sculptures and paintings from local artists. The talent ranged from mediocre to brilliant, yet Eve gave all of them the same amount of time and attention, even going so far as to put the less outstanding in the most prominent spaces. Lainey observed, gave Eve her opinion when asked, and felt tremendously proud to be working for such a talented woman.

"It's really great what you're doing," Lainey told her.

"Placing statues?" Eve teased.

"No, silly," Lainey replied, giggling. "Opening your gallery to unknowns."

"Someone has to give them a chance," Eve said casually. "Why not me? Everywhere they go, these artists are going to be told that their work needs to be 'popular' and that they have to have sold so many in order to be shown in that gallery. If each gallery says that, how will these artists get popular and sell their art?" Eve picked up a small clay sculpture of an elderly man with a cane, turning it in her hands. "I know what it's like to want something," she said quietly. "The opening will give them the exposure they need."

"How big will it be? The opening," Lainey asked her.

"It's going to be huge, with press, art critics, and buyers. Then, of course, there are the artists, and the artists' families and friends." Eve stopped and looked over her shoulder at Lainey. "I hope you'll bring your family."

"I'd love to. I just hope they want to come."

"Tell them I insist," Eve said. "It's going to be the event of the year. It's the re-opening of Sumptor Gallery in New York City."

"You're excited about this."

"Yes. I am," Eve said and took a long look around her. "I've waited for this moment for what seems like an eternity. I have galleries in Italy, France, and different cities around the U.S., but this one means the most to me."

"What makes this one so special?" Lainey asked.

Eve didn't answer for a moment. "It was my first," she said at last. "When I learned of the fire, I knew that I had lost everything. I was devastated. I've never told anyone that before."

It was clear to Lainey when Eve bit her lip that she had said more than she had meant to say.

"The rest of the shipment will be here tomorrow morning," she said, continuing the unpacking. "I'll need you here early; will you be able to be here?"

"Yes, of course," Lainey answered, deciding not press Eve on the subject.

"Good. I'll give you a set of keys so you will be able to get in if you're here before me."

"Great. What time will you need me here?"

"Seven," Eve responded apologetically. "Is that a problem?" She asked when she saw Lainey hesitate.

"No! No, not at all. I just have to make sure Jack will get the boys ready for school," Lainey said. She wasn't going to let Jack ruin this for her. Kevin and Darren were his sons, too, and he would just have to help her out.

"Lainey? If this is going to cause problems for you, I can be here and you can just make it in later."

"I'll be here, Eve."

"Good. The deliverymen should be here shortly after seven. Being New York, you know how reliable that is, but we can hope," Eve brushed the dust off of her hands. "Now, let's get out of here. You have a husband to seduce and a gorgeous man is cooking me dinner. Good luck. I want details tomorrow."

"I want details, too," Lainey said with a grin. She was surprised to realize that she really meant it.

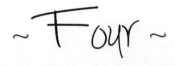

~ Four ~

Eve stepped out of the elevator and saw Adam standing at her front door, holding a grocery bag. She had always enjoyed beautiful things and men were no exception. Adam stood tall at just over six feet two inches, with jet black hair and the most amazing crystal blue eyes that melted her every time he looked at her. Every part of his body was perfect, from the muscles that rippled beneath her hands when she touched him, to his skillful hands that knew every part of Eve's body and exactly where she liked to be touched. But it was his mouth that drove her insane. The way he kissed her, the way he did everything with those full, sensual lips, amazed her.

"Hi," she said huskily, aroused just by seeing him, and was greeted in return with a staggering kiss.

"Ahem!"

Eve pulled away and greeted Mrs. Jenkins, an elderly neighbor who had just come out into the hall. Eve smothered a giggle when the old lady just huffed and went back into her apartment. Taking her own keys out, she unlocked her door.

"What was that for?" she asked Adam.

"Just because," he told her. "Why don't you go and change into something more comfortable while I start dinner."

Ten minutes later, Eve came back down wearing faded Levis and a white, cotton t-shirt that clung to her breasts. Barefoot, she padded to the kitchen.

"It smells incredible in here," she said, leaning around Adam's shoulder as he dipped a spoon into the mushroom sauce and turned to give her a taste. "Oh my God!" Eve said, closing her eyes and bringing her hand to her mouth. "That's amazing! Why didn't you tell me you could cook?"

"You never asked," Adam replied, then crushed his mouth to hers. When he picked her up she wrapped her legs around his waist and drowned in him. Just as quickly as it began, however, Adam ended it, abruptly setting her down and turning back to the stove. "Why don't you get us some wine?" he suggested shortly.

She frowned at Adam's back. She didn't understand why he was acting this way, but she didn't want to fight with him. "Do you want red or white?"

"Red," he responded without looking at her.

Selecting a light merlot from the wine rack, Eve took two glasses out of the cabinet. Filling each, she handed one to Adam.

"Is this how it's going to be tonight?" she asked.

"Why don't you help me out and prepare the vegetables for the salad," was Adam's answer.

Eve sighed and walked around to the other side of the island, separating herself from Adam. Grabbing a butcher knife, she began slicing a tomato with the grace and ease of a seasoned chef.

"You never told me you could cook," he said accusingly.

Eve glanced up at Adam. "You never asked," she said, throwing his words back at him.

"You never offered," he replied. "Why is that, Eve? Too intimate for you?"

"Don't," she said softly. "Why are you doing this, Adam?"

Adam was silent for a long moment. She saw the anger flash in his eyes a split second before he spun around, back to the stove.

"You're right," he said furiously. "Why am I doing this?"

He grabbed the sauce off the burner, setting it on the counter with a thump and spilling it.

"This isn't what you want, is it Eve?" he continued, coming around the island towards her. Before she had time to react, he caught the hand holding the knife and took it from her. Throwing it across the room, he dragged Eve to him, pressing her to him, ravaging her mouth with his, only to push her away from him and begin tearing off his shirt.

"This is what you want, isn't it?" he demanded, standing there, bare-chested in front of her, chest heaving. "Come on, Eve. Let's fuck. That's all I'm here for, isn't it?"

"Stop it," Eve told him voiding all emotion from her eyes as she looked up at him. "This isn't all I want from you."

"Then tell me what it is you do want, Eve," he said. "Because I'm not going to wait forever for you to make up your mind. I can't."

"I know," she whispered.

"Tell me what to do," Adam pleaded.

"What you have to do."

"And if that means leaving right now?"

Eve's heart stopped. Praying that her voice wouldn't betray her, she said, "If that's what you feel you need to do, Adam, I won't stop you."

"Would you be hurt?" Like I'm hurting now, he thought. Would you be dying inside like I am?

"I - I enjoy being with you, Adam," she went on gently. "Not just making love to you, but talking and just...being. I don't want you to go."

"Would you be hurt, Eve?"

"I would miss you," she said quietly, knowing it wasn't what he wanted to hear.

"But you wouldn't hurt, would you? There are no emotions with you are there, Eve?"

When he bent to pick up his shirt, Eve closed her eyes. Adam would never see the defeat or sadness inside her, would never know how she was dying inside just as much as he was. She would never let him.

"I'll never be that person," she said quietly after taking a deep breath. "If you want a wife, a mother for your children, a relationship - hell, a woman who isn't complicated, you don't want me. But if it is me you want, Adam, then here I am. No pretenses, no promises, just me. Take me or leave me." She wanted to beg him not to leave her, but instead she took a sip of wine and picked up the knife.

Lainey stood in front of the mirror in the bathroom trying to gather the courage to do as Eve said and seduce her husband. She squared her shoulders and untied her robe. Letting it fall to the floor, she caught her reflection in the glass and remembered what Eve had said to her. 'You are an amazingly beautiful woman.'

Lainey's pulse quickened as she thought of how Eve had reached over and unbuttoned her shirt. Eve had made her feel beautiful and desirable in a way that even Jack had never made her feel. Lainey closed her eyes and ran her hands down over her breasts, her stomach. Lower.

She took a deep breath and walked into the bedroom where Jack was sitting in bed reading. He was still attractive to her, maybe now more so than before. His brown hair was accented now with a sprinkling of gray at the temples making him look distinguished. His eyes were a gilded brown and Lainey could remember a time when he would look at her with such love and desire.

"Jack," Lainey said in a low voice.

Vaguely annoyed at being interrupted, Jack looked up and was astonished to see Lainey standing before him completely naked. "Lainey?" he exclaimed. "What are you doing?"

Taking his book from him, she climbed on the bed and straddled him. "I want you, Jack," she whispered in his ear. "Make love to me."

"Lainey the boys are in the other room," Jack said, pushing her away.

"And we're in here and the door is locked," she told him. "Make love to me."

"What's gotten into you?" he demanded, shifting uncomfortably beneath her.

"Jack, it's been months since you've touched me." She hesitated. "Are you having an affair?"

"Don't be ridiculous, Lainey. I'm home every day by five o'clock. When would I have the time to have an affair?"

"Then it's me? You don't want me anymore?"

"Lainey, I'm tired. It has nothing to do with you."

"You're still mad about the job," she accused him. "You're still pissed off that I'm going in early tomorrow and you have to get the boys ready."

"*Who's going to get the boys ready for school, Lainey?*" he had said when she had told him that Eve needed her to come in early. And when she had told him that he would simply have to do it, he had reminded her that she was their mother. That was when she had lost her temper and reminded him that it was time for him to be around for them, too.

"I said I'm tired, Lainey," Jack said now. It's been a long day and yet he had to admit she was exciting him. Why not, he thought. He was only a man after all. With a sigh he shifted his position until he was on top of her. Pushing aside his boxers, he entered her. She felt good, he thought. Better than he remembered. He began to pound inside her, breathing harder, moaning her name and Lainey knew that it was almost over. When he had finished, Jack rolled off of her.

"That was great," he said. Then, turning his back on her, he fell asleep.

They laid in bed, one alone, one lonely and both thinking of the other. If Lainey's evening had not gone as expected, neither had Eve's. When she and Adam had made love she could feel a difference. He was slipping away from her and there was nothing she could do about it. Adam wanted more than she could give him and no matter how much she cared about him, she would never be able to give him what he needed. Eve knew he wouldn't wait forever, and she prayed she had the strength to watch him walk away.

As the sleepless night had gone on, Eve's thoughts had turned to Lainey. Eve could admit that Lainey intrigued her. What confused her was this inexplicable attraction she felt. Rarely had Eve met someone to whom she had felt so drawn. Adam had been the first, and the only until now. As she lay there alone, Eve thought of Lainey and wondered how far she would go to satisfy her curiosity.

Lainey arrived at the gallery at precisely seven after stopping to get coffee and donuts. She was waiting for the elevator when Eve strolled up beside her.

"Good morning," Eve said and smiled.

"Good morning. I brought you some coffee." Lainey handed Eve a cup.

"Mmmm. Thank you. This is exactly what I needed, but it's not in your job description, Lainey." Both women stepped into the elevator as the doors opened. Eve glanced at Lainey. "Why don't you try your key? I want to make sure it works for you." Eve took the donuts from Lainey as she brought her keys out.

Lainey inserted the key and turned it. "Works perfectly," she announced with pride, and turned to Eve, "I know it's not in my job description, but I don't mind bringing you coffee. Besides, you look like you could use it. You look tired."

Eve chuckled. "Thank you. That was exactly the look I was going for."

"I didn't mean that in a bad way," Lainey explained laughing. "I just meant you must have had a long, hard night."

Eve's smile faltered ever so slightly, but Lainey had noticed.

"Oh! How did your night of seduction go with Jack?" Eve asked Lainey cheerfully as the elevator doors opened up to the gallery.

Lainey rolled her eyes.

"That good?"

Lainey paced over to the window and stared out, and watched silently as people started filling the sidewalks. Eve walked up behind her and placed a hand on her shoulder.

"Want to talk about it?"

"I did what you said," Lainey began. "I walked into the bedroom completely naked."

"And?"

"And nothing. He looked irritated and confused." She laughed shortly. "I don't think it excited him at all."

"It would have excited me," Eve said quietly.

Lainey felt the flush creep up her neck. "Um, well...it didn't faze Jack much," Lainey went on. "Even when I got into bed and straddled him."

"Wait! You straddled him? While you were naked? And he didn't grab you and make mad passionate love to you? He is a fool."

"I had to practically beg the fool to make love to me. He was 'too tired'. It had been over two months and he's too tired? I even asked him if he was having an affair."

"What did he say?"

"What else? No."

"Do you believe him?"

"Yes." She paced away from the window, away from Eve so she could think. "He's home every day at the same time, has the same routine. Day in and day out."

She hadn't really realized it until she said it, but that was what her marriage had become. Day in. Day out. Everything was always the same.

"Anyway, after rejecting me, making me feel like the fool, he was suddenly on top of me and inside me. Before I could even catch up or register what was happening to me, he was finished."

She looked at Eve, tears brimming in her eyes. "After that he said, 'that was great' then rolled over and fell asleep."

"Bastard," Eve said with vehemence. "So you didn't...?"

Knowing exactly what Eve meant, Lainey laughed mirthlessly. "No. I haven't for so long, I've forgotten what it feels like."

"How long?"

"Since we were first married."

"Twelve years?" Eve asked in amazement.

"It seems that long. It was wonderful in the beginning. We couldn't keep our hands off each other. Then after Kevin was born it just seemed to go downhill. I thought it was the woman who was supposed to lose interest, not the man."

"I'm sorry," Eve said softly.

Lainey shrugged. "What can you do?"

"Hmm, a lot," Eve said with a grin. "And I certainly wouldn't have turned over and fell asleep before pleasuring you."

The intercom buzzed.

"Damn it," Eve whispered. "Today they show up on time."

"I'll get it," Lainey said. She needed to do something, to clear her head. What would she have said if they hadn't have been interrupted? Lainey's heart jumped when she thought about it.

Eve laid her forehead against the cool window. How could Jack treat Lainey like that? And why was she thinking about what she would have done for Lainey instead of thinking of how to fix Lainey's marriage? Why did she care so much?

"Eve?"

She turned when she heard Lainey call her. "Yes?"

"Where do you want all of this?" Lainey asked and watched as Eve walked towards her. Eve had worn faded jeans and a matching button up shirt with the sleeves rolled and the top three buttons undone. Her hair was up in a ponytail and she had minimal make-up on. Lainey had never seen anyone quite so beautiful. She had no idea that her own jeans and t-shirt had Eve thinking the same thing about her.

"Just put them here in the front room."

Eve was all business now, Lainey noticed, directing the movers where to place the sculptures and paintings. It was time, despite what was happening between them, for their work to begin in earnest.

"We have to do this before the opening of the gallery," Katherine said. "Sumptor will be preoccupied enough not to notice anything, but we have to cover our tracks. Meredith? Are you listening to me?"

Katherine sat in Meredith's office trying to go over their plans, uncomfortably aware that Meredith was not really listening.

She had been on the computer the whole time looking up God knows what while Katherine did all the work on their plot.

"What are you doing?" she demanded.

"I'm listening to you, Katherine," Meredith answered irritably. "I know exactly what we have to do. Why don't you just go and finish the adjustments on those reports. We shouldn't be discussing this here anyway."

Katherine rose and looked over Meredith's shoulder just as her friend shut down the monitor. "Why are you looking up the name Stanton? My God, are you insane? What does Lainey have to do with this, Meredith? Why are you wasting your time?"

"I'm not wasting my time," she assured her. "There's something going on with her, and I want to know what it is." It troubled Meredith that Eve had taken Lainey under her wing. She had been with Eve for over four years and had never been treated as anything more than an employee. So what was it about Lainey that fascinated Eve?

"Lainey is not our problem, Meredith," Katherine said, pushing a hand through her dark, curled hair impatiently. "But you will be if you don't pay attention to the task at hand. We've come too far to screw everything up now, so forget about Lainey and let's do this."

Meredith heaved a sigh and gave up on her search on Lainey Stanton. For now.

Eve and Lainey spent the morning and part of the afternoon carefully unpacking the priceless and pricey art. Lainey observed that Eve examined at each piece with the eye of a professional, an artist and a critic. They ordered a pizza for lunch and sat in the middle of the hard wood floor, shoes kicked off, laughing and talking. It was the first time Eve could remember sitting down and having a real conversation without someone wanting to either sleep with her or scratch her eyes out. She had had girlfriends, of course. Okay, one girlfriend, who once she got married, kept telling Eve that she needed to settle down and get married instead of remaining a lonely business woman. With Lainey she felt more complete. She sensed that they could trust one another, tell each other things they would never tell anyone else.

Lainey had been a mother and a wife for so long that she had forgotten what it was like to just be Lainey. With Eve she felt like an individual with her own dreams. As much as she loved her sons and Jack, Lainey realized now that she needed to find herself before she was gone forever. From the moment she had met Eve, Lainey had started her journey back to herself.

Eve took a bite of pizza and glanced over at Lainey. "I haven't talked this way with anyone for a long time," she said. "Truth or dare?"

"Truth," Lainey shot back, amused. She felt as though they were two girls together, sharing secrets.

"How old were you when you lost your virginity?" Eve laughed and reached over to pat Lainey on the back when she choked on her pizza. "Sorry. Too personal?"

"No, no," Lainey replied, clearing her throat. "I'll learn not to be surprised by you soon. I hope. Actually, I was twenty-two. Don't look at me like that, I was!"

"Twenty-two? Was Jack your first?"

"And only, yes."

"Do you ever feel that you've missed out on something or maybe picked the wrong person?"

"I didn't before. I'm not so sure anymore." Lainey lowered her eyes. "Or maybe he's the one that thinks that way."

"You love him." Eve would never have dared go so far but something told her that Lainey badly wanted advice. "I've never met Jack, Lainey, but I can't imagine anyone falling out of love with you. Have you talked to him about how you're feeling?"

"He doesn't want to talk. He thinks everything is fine. That's the biggest reason we fought about me taking this job. He is afraid it's going to change things between us. I hope it does, because I can't do this anymore. I need more. More passion, more romance, more attention, more excitement. Just. . .more."

"I know absolutely nothing about love, Lainey," Eve said, twisting her hair into a knot at the back of her head. One of her high cheekbones was streaked with dust. "But I do know about passion, romance, attention and excitement. The direct approach didn't seem to work last night, but we could try a different approach. That is, if you want my help."

"I do want your help, but not only with Jack, Eve," Lainey said sincerely. "*I* need help. When I look at you, I see a woman who knows who she is and what she wants. I want to be that kind of woman."

Now that she had started to talk, she couldn't stop until it was all out.

"I was only two years younger than you when I got married," she went on, "and Jack is the only man I've ever been with. I don't want to think that I've missed out on anything, but I can't help it. I'm not saying that I would have wanted anything different if I could do it all over, but maybe I would have waited to get married and found myself first. Maybe then, my marriage wouldn't be falling apart now. Maybe I'm the problem, Eve. Not Jack."

Eve saw tears brimming in Lainey's eyes and felt her heart break a little. She reached over and took Lainey's hand in hers.

"I'll do everything that I can to help you, Lainey. Maybe we can help each other."

"What could I possibly help you with?" Lainey said in amazement. "You have everything. You know exactly who you are. I'm ten years older than you, for crying out loud, and I'm more lost now than I was when I was younger. You – you're a beautiful, young woman who has it all."

"Looks can be deceiving, Lainey," Eve said softly, and then took a deep breath. "Come on. We have less than one week to get this gallery presentable. Let's work on that, and while we do that, we'll work on finding Lainey Stanton." She pulled Lainey to her feet. "We'll discover the woman inside of you, Lainey. I promise." With that, Eve let Lainey go suddenly and walked away.

"You take the right side, I'll take the left."

Lainey stood there for a moment, trying to understand what was happening to her. Because something was. But there was no time now. She had work to do, and she was going to make sure that Eve realized that she had made the right choice when she had hired her.

They worked non-stop for the next three hours. With less than four days until opening, Eve became more anxious and energized. A young, beautiful woman had to do more work to prove that she was worthy of the respect that the art world had to give. She was determined not to let anything go wrong, and she would certainly keep the esteem and prestige she deserved. She had agreed with Lainey's vision of how the art should be arranged, and now with only minimal changes created a display only a true artist could have conceived of.

"You are brilliant at this," Lainey had to say finally. "You have an amazing vision, as though you were born to do this."

"Thank you, Lainey. I believe I was," Eve responded. "Would you help me with this?" She turned to Lainey with a colorful rendition of a man with a cigarette painted by Picasso in hand. "I want it here."

She motioned to the middle wall separating the two walkways of the gallery. Eve waited as Lainey brought the ladder over to her.

"Would you mind getting up there and placing it while I make sure that it is aligned from down here?" she said.

Not about to let Eve know she was afraid of heights, Lainey agreed and started up the ladder. Eve handed her the painting and stood back to get the best view.

"A little higher on your left. Good. Now, bring the entire painting up a few inches. Good, a little more and that should do it. Lainey?"

Suddenly aware that Lainey was swaying slightly, Eve hurried to catch the painting in one hand and support Lainey with the other. "You scared me," Eve whispered into Lainey's ear. "How are you feeling? Do you want to sit down?"

"No, I'm...I'm fine. I just feel stupid."

"Why? Here, please sit down. You're still shaking." She eased Lainey down to the floor and sat next to her.

"I didn't want to tell you that I was afraid of heights." Lainey laughed softly. "I guess you know now." Lainey didn't add that the real reason she was shaking was because she was in Eve's arms.

"You could have really hurt yourself," Eve scolded her. "Why didn't you say something? Did you think I wouldn't understand?" Eve wasn't certain whether she wanted to laugh or cry.

"It's silly. I should have been able to get up there with no problem. I just didn't want you to think I couldn't do it."

"*That's* silly, Lainey. You want to know the truth?" Eve grinned guiltily. "I'm afraid of heights."

Lainey laughed. "You are not!"

"Yes, I am. That's why I asked you to do this for me. Had I known that you felt the same way, I would have done it myself. It's one of my deepest, darkest secrets, so if you tell anyone I'll deny it!" Eve reached over and tucked a strand of hair behind Lainey's ear. "Don't be afraid to tell me anything, Lainey, and please, don't put yourself in danger like that again. I don't want anything to happen to you," she finished softly.

"Thank you. For catching me."

"My pleasure," Eve replied with a wink. "I think it's time for a break. We accomplished a lot today on the gallery. Let's work on you now." She smiled apologetically when her cell phone rang.

"Can we start over?" she heard Adam say. "Let me make last night up to you. I was a jerk, Eve. I know that now. I'm sorry, let me make it up to you, baby, please."

"It wasn't your fault." Eve got to her feet and started pacing. "I know this is hard for you, and I don't blame you for being upset. I'm sorry, Adam."

For not being the woman you deserve, Eve thought, and for not giving you what you need.

"No, Eve. You've told me what to expect from the beginning and you've never pretended with me. I knew what I was getting in to. I should have never pressured you, or said the things I did. Tell me what I can do to make it up to you."

"You don't have to make it up to me. It's okay."

"Eve. Please."

Eve could hear the fear and hurt in Adam's voice and it touched her to know how much he felt for her. She wanted to soothe him, and have him soothe her. But she also wanted to show him that sex wasn't the only thing she was interested in with him.

"I have something that I have to take care of tonight," she said. She knew he would be disappointed, but she needed this time to think. "Wait, please. I have to do this tonight, but meet me at the club tomorrow at nine. I think it's time we had a date, Adam. Can we do that?"

Adam had been disappointed and a bit jealous when Eve had told him she had other plans. But he would do as she asked and take her on a date. She deserved it. She deserved everything. "We can do that. But Eve?" he told her. "Just tell me it's not another man."

He knew in his heart that she would never hurt him that way, but he needed to hear it from her.

"Baby, you know the answer to that." Eve deliberately dropped her voice to a sultry whisper. "No one can do to me what you do. There's not another man, Adam. Only you."

"I wasn't trying to listen," Lainey said as Eve slipped her cell phone in her pocket. "And I certainly don't want to pry into your personal life, Eve..." Lainey began.

"It's fine, Lainey. I don't mind."

"How long have you and Adam been seeing each other?"

Eve began tidying the gallery before leaving for the night. "Hmm, almost two years, I think."

She knew what was coming next. She had heard it many times before. 'Why aren't you married?' 'Where is the relationship going?' As a result, what she heard Lainey say next was so unexpected that it sent her into fits of laughter.

"Do you realize that your names are Adam and Eve?"

"I like you, Lainey. I really do. Come on, let's get out of here."

They were still laughing when they stepped out of the elevator and into the parking garage. Disarming the alarm Eve hesitated before getting into her car. "Hop in," she said to Lainey.

"What?"

"Hop in. I want to take you somewhere. Unless you need to get home."

"No. I mean, no, I don't have to get home right away. Jack is there." Lainey settled into the passenger side next to Eve. "Where are we going?"

"You'll see. Don't worry, Lainey. I won't keep you out too late."

As they drove down the quiet, tree lined street, listening to a Marc Anthony CD, Lainey wondered how she could be so at ease with Eve and at the same time so nervous. She stole a glance at Eve out of the corner of her eye, and saw her tapping her long, slender fingers to the beat of the music. Lainey was absolutely stunned at the thoughts she had about Eve's fingers. Flushing, she turned her head to stare out the window.

Eve smiled to herself. Lainey was like an open book sometimes, and Eve found the reading intriguing. She pulled up to the curb in front of her apartment building.

"Where are we?" Lainey asked.

"Come on," was Eve's only answer as the doorman came to open her door for her.

"Good evening, Henry," Eve said as he tipped his hat. "How are you tonight?" He was a wonderful black man in his late fifties with graying hair and a tender smile, and he had come to seem like a sort of father figure to Eve. Somehow it comforted her to see him every night when she returned home.

"Mighty fine, Miss Eve," he replied. "Mighty fine. The missus told me to tell you 'Hi' and to thank you for the photos of little Stevie. She's shown everyone on the block. They're her new pride and joy!"

"Well, I'm glad she enjoys them. Tell her 'hi' for me and she's very welcome," Eve said as they got out of the car. "This is Lainey Stanton, Henry. She's my new assistant at the gallery, and a very good friend of mine."

"Well, how do, ma'am? Any friend of Miss Eve's is a friend of mine." Henry saluted Lainey and went to hold the door open for the two women.

"I expect you and Trudy to be at my opening, Henry," Eve said. "It wouldn't be the same without you."

"Yes, Miss Eve. We'll be there for sure."

"He's sweet," Lainey commented as they rode the elevator up to the thirty-first floor.

"He's a doll," Eve told her. "His wife Trudy makes the best cornbread I've ever had, and Stevie is one of my favorite subjects. He's such a little ham. He's going to be a heartbreaker when he grows up."

As Eve dug her keys out of her pocket, her neighbor's door opened and then snapped shut when she said hello. Eve laughed quietly. "Home sweet home."

"Is she always that nosey?" Lainey wondered aloud.

"Mrs. Jenkins? Yes. It's fine, though. She's like a watchdog. At least she'll know if anything is wrong," Eve told her leading Lainey down the hall and into the living room of her spacious loft style apartment.

"Wow!" Lainey stopped abruptly and looked at her surroundings. The apartment was decorated in stark white furniture and carpet with the paintings that dotted the walls providing the only color. The cathedral ceiling gave the room an open and airy feel, and yet even being exceptionally pristine it was inviting and cozy. White marble surrounded the fireplace that was the centerpiece of the beautiful room. To the left of the fireplace was a spectacular white grand piano, and to the right was a white oversized chair that Lainey could imagine Eve curling up in with a good book and glass of wine. The thing that struck Lainey the most was the lack of family photos to grace the beautiful place. It was as if Eve had no past, no family. The thought saddened Lainey for reasons she couldn't explain.

"This is the real you," Lainey said quietly. "White. It's classy, though others would probably mistake it for purity. But that's not what you were going for, was it? This is more of a sanctuary for you, a safe haven. The only colors you've chosen are those in the paintings. But everything else is quiet, which is what you need."

"You see way too much, Lainey," she said quietly. "I don't invite many people here, because it is my sanctuary, but no one has been able to see what you have in just a few moments. I'm not sure how I feel about that."

She paused and bit her lip as though she was about to say more, but then she moved toward the kitchen.

"Would you like something to drink?" she asked. "Tea? Wine?"

"Wine would be wonderful, thank you," Lainey told her.

"Do you mind if I use your phone? I should call Jack and let him know I'll be late."

"Of course, please," Eve called over her shoulder. Lainey took a deep breath, preparing herself for the fight she knew was coming with Jack, and picked up the phone.

"Hello?"

Lainey's mood lifted immediately after hearing Darren's voice on the other end of the line. "Hi, sweetie, it's Mommy."

"Hi, Mommy! Guess what I'm doing!"

"What are you doing?"

"I'm eating hot dogs!" Darren giggled. "Daddy said it was okay!"

"Did he? Well, then I guess it's all right. Where is daddy, sweetie?"

"He's in the kitchen. You wanna talk to him?"

"Yes, please. Darren, Mommy loves you."

Eve walked into the room at that moment and smiled to herself. It was endearing, seeing this side of Lainey. She handed her a glass and sat, cross-legged, on the couch.

He giggled. "I love you, too, Mommy. DAD! Mommy's on the phone! She wants to talk to you!"

"Hello? Darren, go wash up and tell Kevin he better be doing his homework! Sorry."

"It's fine. Hot dogs, Jack?" She sighed. "Never mind. I'm going to be a little late tonight; I just want to let you know."

"How late?" He was annoyed. It irritated him that he was resentful of her new job.

"I don't know. I shouldn't be too long."

"Fine. Just be careful coming home."

"I will. Tell the boys I love them." Lainey hesitated. "You, too, Jack."

"Me too. Er, don't stay out too late. Please."

Lainey hung the phone up momentarily confused. She had expected Jack to be angry and instead he had been concerned.

"Everything all right?" Eve asked.

"Yes. Everything's fine." She nervously twisted the stem of the wine glass around.

"Relax," Eve said in a low voice. "I didn't bring you here to seduce you. Come on."

"Where are we going?"

"To my bedroom." Eve hooted with laughter when Lainey stopped dead in her tracks. "Are you afraid of me, Lainey?"

"No! I'm sorry, I don't..."

"I don't bite - unless I'm asked to."

Lainey's cheeks turned rosy. She couldn't remember the last time she felt so young and inexperienced. She was acting like a fool. She barely managed not to flinch when Eve took her hand in hers and led her up the curved stairs.

Eve's room was a vast and immaculate space, and Lainey's jaw dropped as she stepped into the sitting room which adjoined it.

"You have a sitting room in your bedroom?" Lainey asked in amazement. "I barely have room for more than a chair or two in mine."

A white couch that looked comfortable and big enough to sleep on centered the room and to its left sat an oversized chair that reminded Lainey of the one in the living room, positioned in front of one of the two fireplaces. She guessed from the complicated remote control sitting on the table that a full entertainment center lay hidden behind the white cabinet walls and that the curtains, lights and alarms were all at Eve's fingertips.

Lainey ran a fingertip lovingly across yet another piano, this one a white baby grand. "Do you play?" she asked. And when Eve nodded, "Will you play for me sometime?"

Eve smiled in response saying neither yes nor no. She had never played for anyone. Perhaps that would change soon, Eve thought.

Eve's bed was mammoth sized, and stood upon a platform three steps high. The pristine white of the comforter and sheer white veils that hung from the canopy surrounding the bed only served to make it look as if it had came out of a fairytale.

"You sleep there?" Lainey demanded.

"I told you I was narcissistic and needed everything bigger and better," Eve said with a shrug. "Besides, it's a great 'sex' bed."

She led the way to a vast closet. Lainey noted that each shoe was in its place and the clothes were separated in likes. Shirts, skirts, jeans, dresses and slacks all had their own area.

"There is a reason I brought you here, Lainey," Eve said as she rummaged through the dresses. "As you know, Adam and I are going dancing tomorrow night. I would like it if you – and Jack, of course - came too."

"Jack?" Lainey exclaimed. "My Jack? Dancing? I don't see that happening. Besides, wouldn't you and Adam want to be alone?"

Eve found the dress she was looking for, a black cocktail dress with a plunging "V" neckline. "That's exactly what I don't want," she said, dropping it on the bed. "Look, there are two motives for me asking you to go, Lainey. Number one, I think doing something new and exciting will help you and Jack find that spark, again. I saw, when you were talking to him, how much you love him and how much it hurts you that you two have grown apart. I believe that if you just spent some time together, maybe do something that you've never done before, it would help."

Eve paused, and then decided to be honest with Lainey.

"My second reason is much more selfish," she confessed. "Adam and I...we have no problems in bed. As a matter of fact, things there are incredible, phenomenal. It's outside of the bedroom we have problems. And it's not his fault. He's perfect. It's me. I'm great in the bedroom. It's everything else that I'm horrible at and terrifies me. So I'm asking you to go because what I don't want is to end up back here. I want you to help me understand what it is I have to offer Adam other than sex. Do you understand?"

Strangely enough, Lainey did. Eve wanted to be in a situation in which sex wouldn't be thick in the air. Most likely she thought that being around Lainey and Jack would help her.

"How am I going to convince Jack to go?" she asked. "And how can I really help you not end up back here, Eve?"

"You have to keep reminding me that I don't want to end up having sex with Adam tomorrow which, believe me, will be an achievement in itself. It's going be one of the hardest nights of my life as I truly enjoy being with him. As far as Jack is concerned, you could just tell him that you would like to spend some time with him. Which is true. But, that you would like to try something a little different. Dinner and dancing, with his wife, how can he resist?" Eve gave Lainey a charming, hard-to-resist grin. "Will you go?"

"Yes, of course. Just tell me when and where and we'll be there."

Eve smiled that devastating smile, "Good. Tomorrow night, nine o'clock at O. Do you know where it is?"

"Yes."

"Fantastic. Take this dress. You'll look beautiful in it."

"What? Oh, no, Eve I can't take this."

"You don't like it?"

"It's beautiful! I love it, but I can't..."

"Lainey, I never say anything I don't want to say. And, I never do anything I don't want to do. I want to give this to you. Take it. Please?" Eve paused, astonished by what she was about to do. "Can you spare a few more minutes, Lainey? I'm not sure why, but I would like to show you something."

"Of course."

"Good," Eve replied. "Follow me." In the sitting room, she picked up the remote control, pressed a button, and a panel in the wall opened revealing a short hallway.

"I've never shown this to anyone, and I'll confess that it unnerves me that I want to show you," Eve said leading Lainey to a thick, metal sliding door.

Lainey didn't even try to hide her amazement. She had read of secret passageways in books before, but never had she actually seen one. "Are all of the apartments in this building like this?"

"I had my place renovated to suit my needs," Eve told her. She slipped a gold chain out from under her shirt and removed a key. In a moment, the door slid open and she motioned for Lainey to go in.

The moment Eve opened the door Lainey was awestruck. The smell of paint and paint thinner hit her first, but was forgotten the moment she saw easel after easel of beautiful oil paintings, primarily portraits. There was a magnificent study of an old woman with a weathered face and wise eyes, and another of a young woman whose haunted eyes seemed to hold the secrets of a life of sorrow.

"Oh my God, Eve. These are magnificent! Did you paint these?"

"I just finished that one this morning," Eve said gesturing to an image of an old man smoking an old fashioned briar pipe.

"This morning?" Lainey exclaimed. "You were at the gallery at seven this morning. When did you have time to do this?"

"I don't sleep much," Eve said matter-of-factly. "And when I'm restless I paint."

"Are you going to display them in the gallery?"

"No."

"Why? They're amazing."

"They're mine, but thank you for the compliment."

Lainey walked around the enormous studio taking in each painting, each color, each stroke, until she came to one that was covered with a paint stained sheet. "May I?" she asked and Eve nodded.

It was a nude painting of an extraordinary looking man. A man whose body could have been chiseled by Michelangelo himself.

"Is this Adam?" Lainey asked, not sure how she knew it was the man Eve was seeing, but certain that he was perfect for her.

Eve nodded.

"What a beautiful man. You're a lucky woman." Lainey's eyes wandered down the length of Adam's breath-taking body with its muscular chest, and rippled stomach. It was clear that Adam and Eve belonged together. Their bodies were made for each other.

Lainey's eyes didn't stop at Adam's stomach. "Oh my!" she exclaimed, turning red. "You're a very, very lucky woman. Does he know how to use it?"

Eve laughed aloud at Lainey's bold question. "Oh yes," she said. "Extremely well!"

"Did he pose for this?"

"No," Eve admitted reflectively. "He doesn't even know it exists. He's never been in here. I'm a photographer as well as an artist and I have a photographer's memory. More to the point, he's a fabulous subject and I've had a lot of time to study him."

"I bet you have," Lainey murmured. Tearing her eyes away from the painting, she noticed some of Eve's photography on the other side of the room.

Eve stayed with the painting of Adam for a while longer as Lainey crossed the studio and stopped to touch Adam's painted face before she replaced the sheet over the canvas. Mortified by her sudden vulnerability, Eve quickly replaced the cover and went to join her friend who was studying her work intently.

"Eve," Lainey said. "These photos are incredible. Just amazing. Do you develop them yourself, too?"

"Yes. My dark room is in there, through that rotating door," Eve answered, indicating a tall canister looking entryway.

"I've always wanted to learn how to do that."

"I'd love to teach you sometime."

"That would be wonderful." Lainey tried not to think of the thrill that moved through her. "And these photos of the little boy, they're fantastic. Is this..."

"Little Stevie? Yes." As Lainey gazed at the photos, Eve picked up her Nikon off of the table, and quietly snapped a photo.

"Oh! Eve, don't!" Lainey said raising a hand to shield her face.

"Sorry. Occupational hazard," Eve told her. "Adorable isn't he? He's going to steal a lot of hearts when he gets older. You're beautiful." She aimed her camera again and Lainey raised a hand to cover her face. "You're even more beautiful when you blush," Eve told her. "Okay, okay. No more photos. For now."

"I love this photo," Lainey said of the black and white of Stevie, needing to get Eve's focus off of her. "No wonder it's Trudy's pride and joy." She hesitated, debating whether or not to ask someone as talented as

Eve, someone who has already given her so much, for a favor. "Would it be possible for you to, um..."

"Take some of Kevin and Darren?"

"Yes, I'm sorry. I didn't want to ask."

"No. Please, it's fine. I'd be more than happy to. Would you like one of the whole family, as well?"

"If it's no trouble, that would be wonderful."

"No trouble at all. Now, I've shared quite a bit of myself with you tonight. Something that I didn't do intentionally, but actually I think I'm glad I did."

Eve smiled and hooked her arm through Lainey's and started out of the loft.

"I'll take you back to your car," she said. "Or, I could just take you home."

"Eve, it's too far. Besides how would I get to work tomorrow?"

"I'll pick you up, silly. And anyway, I like driving, so it's fine."

"It's not too far out of your way?"

"Lainey, I don't mind. Really. Let me take you home. It just doesn't make sense to drive all the way back to the gallery when it would be easier to just drive you home and pick you up tomorrow."

"If that's the easiest thing for you, then let's go!" Now Jack and the boys could meet Eve. Maybe then Jack would understand why she wants to do well at her new job.

~ Five ~

Eve pulled up to the curb in front of Lainey's two-story house of off white stone and russet shutters, surrounded by colorful azaleas and a well kept lawn.

"Beautiful," she said simply.

"Thank you." Lainey opened her door and paused before getting out. "Would you like to come in for a minute?"

"I'd love to if you're sure it's not too late."

"Not at all. I want to introduce you to my boys before they go to bed. And, I know Jack would like to meet you as well."

Eve released her seatbelt and stepped out on the curb. She took a deep breath smelling the air which was so clean compared to the exhaust fumes of the inner city. She looked up and down the street of the neighborhood.

"You've picked a lovely place to raise your sons," she said as she fell in step with Lainey on the walkway to the front door. "Maybe if I decide to 'settle down' I'll look for a place around here. Don't look at me that way, Lainey. It could happen."

"I never said it couldn't," Lainey said grinning.

The first thing that hit Eve was the sound of two young boys having what seemed to be a heated argument over who was the better superhero, Spiderman or Superman.

"Come on in. Welcome to my zoo," Lainey said laughing.

As soon as she closed the door behind them, the youngest of the boys came racing into the foyer.

"Mommy, Mommy! Tell Kevin that Spiderman is a better superhero! He doesn't know nothin'!"

"Anything," Lainey corrected. "And Kevin is allowed to have his own opinions, just as you do. Now, come and give me a kiss." Darren ran and leapt into Lainey's arms. To Eve, it was the sweetest thing she had ever seen. "Darren, this is my boss, and friend, Miss..."

"Eve." Eve extended her hand to Darren. "It's nice to meet you, Darren."

"You're pretty!" Darren exclaimed with an honesty only children possess and took Eve's hand, shaking it with energy.

"Why, thank you. You're very cute," Eve replied which set Darren giggling just as Kevin dashed into the foyer to join them.

"Hi," Eve said. "You must be Kevin. I'm Eve." Again, she extended her hand in greeting, chuckling when Kevin only stared at her. "It's nice to meet you," she said, taking his hand.

"She's pretty isn't she, Kevin," Darren chimed in to his brother's humiliation.

"Mom! Darren's been bothering me all night. Will you tell him to leave me alone?" Kevin said, clearly trying to sound as grown up as possible in front of Eve.

Lainey tried, unsuccessfully, to hide her amusement at what she knew was a little crush that Kevin had on Eve. "Now, Darren, leave your brother alone. And you, young man," she added, crooking a finger at Kevin. "Come here and give your mom a kiss hello."

"Mom!" he began, but knew better than to argue with her and obeyed.

"Thank you. Now where's your father?" Lainey set Darren down and both boys took off running.

"Dad! Mommy's home! And there's a pretty lady with her!" Darren shouted.

"Adorable," Eve said chuckling, as she followed Lainey into the living room. "They really know how to boost a 'lady's' ego."

Unlike Eve's home, Lainey's looked thoroughly lived in. Photos graced the mantle above the fireplace and lined the pale yellow walls of the hallways. Eve had known that Lainey was a proud and loving mother and the photos only substantiated the fact. Toys were scattered on the floor of navy carpeting and traditional furniture. The house was full of color and life and Eve didn't know whether to feel comfortable and welcome or extremely alone.

"You have a lovely home, Lainey."

Lainey watched as Eve studied the photos, and thinking of how Eve had none in her own home, had to fight the urge to reach out and console her. She could feel the sadness inside Eve no matter how much Eve tried to hide it. Just then, she heard Jack walk into the room and turned to him quickly.

Eve turned in time to see Lainey kiss Jack quickly on the mouth and hook her arm in his. "This is Eve Sumptor," she said pleasantly. "Eve, this is my husband, Jack." She nervously watched as the two shook hands. She saw Eve deliberately tone down her devastating smile and was grateful for her efforts. She didn't believe Jack would fall for Eve's charm, but she didn't want to find out if she was wrong.

"Lainey has told me a lot about you and the boys," Eve said. "It's nice to finally meet you all."

"It's nice to meet you as well. I hear the gallery is coming along just fine."

"Yes it is. Thanks to Lainey. She's been a tremendous help to me, and her visualization is remarkable."

Eve saw Jack swell with pride.

"She always did have a good eye," he said, draping an arm around Lainey. "Please, won't you have a seat?" Jack gestured to the couch on the far side of the room.

Catching Darren peeking around the corner at her, Eve beckoned for him to join her. In an instant he was at Eve's side, Kool-Aid in hand and a big red grin, propping himself next to her when she sat down.

"Can I get you something to drink?" Jack asked her. "Wine?"

"Actually, that looks refreshing," Eve said, pointing to Darren's Kool-Aid.

"I'll help you, Jack," Lainey said, smiling at Eve. She was Darren's first crush and Lainey couldn't blame him.

After Jack and Lainey disappeared into the kitchen leaving Darren and Eve alone, Kevin, doing his best to look cool by playing his Game Boy, joined them.

"Move over squirt," Kevin said, trying to wedge himself between Eve and his brother.

"No! I was here first! Eve, tell him I was here first."

"Kevin, why don't you sit next to me over here?" Eve said sweetly and patted the couch on the other side of her. "What are you playing?"

"Baseball. Do you want to play?"

"Sure. Will you show me how?"

"This is homerun derby," he told her eagerly. "So when the pitcher pitches the ball to you, you swing at it and try to hit a homerun. Okay? Use this button to hit."

"Sounds easy enough. Are you going to cheer for me, Darren?" she said, bumping his shoulder with hers.

"Yes!" He giggled and settled in to watch this beautiful grown up, play video games.

In the kitchen, Lainey took down three glasses while Jack got the Kool-Aid out of the refrigerator. "She's great isn't she?" she asked.

"What? Oh. Yes, she seems very nice." In fact, Eve seemed a little too nice to Jack. It had been his experience that women who looked like that were never that nice unless they had an agenda. He wondered what Eve's was with his wife.

"Do you think she's pretty?" Lainey pressed him.

"She's gorgeous. But then you're gorgeous, too."

He bent his head and met Lainey's lips with his for a rare tender kiss. "Is she really going to drink this stuff?"

Lainey laughed. "She never does anything she doesn't want to do, so I guess she is. Come on, let's hurry and get back out there before the boys drive her nuts."

The boys and Eve had their heads together and were cheering when Lainey and Jack came back into the room. Lainey had never seen Eve so relaxed and carefree. The transformation was fascinating. She was even more amazed by the way her sons were acting. Normally shy with new people, they were talking and laughing with Eve as though they had known her all their lives.

Even Jack had to admit that, even if Eve was pretending, she was great with Kevin and Darren.

"The boys were just teaching me how to hit homeruns," Eve said proudly. "I'm pretty good."

"Yeah, Mommy, she's good!" Darren chimed in excitedly. "She got more homeruns than Kevin!"

"I think Kevin was just letting me win to make me feel better," Eve told Darren.

"Next time, I'm gonna play my best," Kevin warned her.

"I'll expect nothing less."

"Boys, it's time to go upstairs and finish your school work," Jack announced.

"Sorry about that," Lainey apologized after the boys disappeared.

"No. Don't be, they're wonderful. It's been a very long time since I've played video games. It was fun." She turned her attention to Jack. "While I have this opportunity with you, Jack, I'd like to ask you something. I wanted to invite you and Lainey to my club tomorrow night for dinner and dancing. Would you be interested in joining us?"

"Us?" Jack inquired. He didn't see a ring, and didn't remember Lainey mentioning anyone special in Eve's life.

"Me and my date, Adam. We'd love for you to join us."

"I'd like to go, Jack," Lainey told him. "Let's get out and have some fun."

Inside she was thanking Eve for being so smooth and saving Lainey from an argument. Jack could resist Lainey when they were alone, but he was far too polite to ever turn down an offer given by someone else. Later she would ask Eve why she hadn't told her that Eve owned O. For now, she waited, holding her breath for Jack's answer.

"Well, Eve, if we can find a babysitter we would love to go," he said finally.

"I'm sure we won't have a problem finding a babysitter," Lainey said to Eve giving her a discreet wink that Eve found endearing. "Count us in for tomorrow."

"Wonderful." Eve turned her smile up a notch and took a drink of her Kool-Aid.

"Eve! Look!" Eve set her glass down and turned her attention on Darren who came running into the room with what looked like a toy fire truck in his hands.

"Darren! Don't bother Ms. Sumptor," Jack scolded. "You're supposed to be doing school work."

"It's okay, really. He's not bothering me. And please, call me Eve. Ms. Sumptor was my mother." Turning back to Darren she said, "What do you have there?"

"It's my fire truck," Darren responded with a shy smile. "It's my favorite toy. I wanted you to see it." He held the toy out to Eve with a mixture of pride and trepidation. Lainey knew that he'd never shared his favorite toy with anyone and watched in astonishment as her youngest son handed over his pride and joy to Eve.

"Oh! It's beautiful, Darren," Eve said with genuine admiration, turning the toy over and examining it as carefully as if it were a work of art.

"It used to make noises. It had a siren and everything, but Kevin broke it." Darren sniffled and stuck out his bottom lip as Eve wrapped a consoling arm around him.

"Tattle tale," his older brother said, putting in his own appearance.

"It's bed time boys." Lainey stood up, shielding the emotions in her eyes. "Say goodnight to Eve, and go up and get ready for bed. I'll be up in a minute to tuck you in."

"But, Mommy, I'm not tired," Darren complained, yawning. "I want to stay up with you and Eve."

"Darren, sweetie, you can barely keep your eyes open. Come on, now, it's time for bed."

"I'm getting tired, too," Eve admitted to Darren in a whisper.

"Are you going to stay here with us?" he whispered back.

"No, honey. I'm going to go home."

"But, I want you to stay with me. What if I never see you again?"

Eve laughed softly. "You'll see me again." Eve all but melted when Darren leaned in to give her a hug and a sweet kiss on the cheek.

"Promise?"

"Cross my heart," she pledged, making an X over her heart with her finger. "Goodnight. Sleep tight. Goodnight, Kevin."

"'Nite, Eve. You're pretty cool," he said quickly and then bounded up the stairs without another look back, missing the flattered smile Eve gave him in return for his compliment. But Lainey didn't.

"Jack, why don't you go up and help the boys get ready for bed," she said. "I'll see Eve out."

"Fine. Eve, it was a pleasure." Jack extended his hand once again. "We'll see you tomorrow."

"Fabulous," Eve replied. "It was wonderful meeting you. Goodnight."

The look Lainey gave her when Jack and the boys were gone staggered Eve.

"Every minute I find out something new about you and it never ceases to amaze me," Lainey told her quietly. "My sons are the most important things in my life, and I can't tell you how it made me feel to see you relate to them the way you did. I may never fully know you, Eve, but I'm enjoying the learning process."

As Lainey walked with her to the car, Eve realized that if she didn't take control of her feelings, people were going to get hurt. Gathering up every ounce of strength she had in her, Eve turned and faced Lainey. "I'll pick you up tomorrow around eight. All right?"

"That's fine," Lainey said, confused and disappointed by the change in Eve. She had wanted the intimacy of the moment to continue. She wanted Eve to say something, anything that would give her more insight into the depth of Eve's heart.

"Be careful what you wish for, Lainey," she murmured. "You might just get what you want."

She let her gaze fall on Lainey's mouth and linger there.

That night, lying next to her husband, Lainey dreamt of Eve and smiled in her sleep.

While Lainey was dreaming, Eve sat alone in her apartment with only a glass of wine to keep her company. She tried sleeping, but couldn't turn off her mind long enough to relax. She couldn't focus long enough to paint and she was becoming frustrated.

Slipping on one of the shirts that Adam had left behind, she padded downstairs barefoot looking for something to occupy her. Finding that her CDs could produce nothing that satisfied her, Eve sat down at the piano and tinkered with the keys with one hand, holding her wine glass in the other until, becoming suddenly inspired, she set the glass down on the piano and began playing, her long, slender fingers moving gracefully and skillfully over the keys. Closing her eyes, she let the music flow through her, fill her.

Anyone who heard Eve play would have thought she had been classically trained and she would let them believe that, for the truth gave too much insight into her life. She had taught herself how to play to keep from going insane, because sometimes the only way to escape the harsh reality of life was to lock herself away and drown herself in the sound of the piano.

While she played, she thought about Adam and Lainey and what they meant to her. Both had touched her as no one else ever had. Somehow or other they had unwittingly found a place in a heart that had been so cold for so long. She thought of the re-opening of the gallery here. She had known from the moment she heard about the fire that it had not been an accident, and someday she would prove it.

Her playing became more passionate as it did when she became angry. She took a deep breath, and turned her thoughts back to Lainey. She remembered the photos decorating the house and the happy boys running around. Her hands froze on the keys as she looked around her apartment. It was so devoid of emotion, she thought, just like her. She had closed herself off completely years ago, and made a vow never to let anyone in.

"What am I doing?" she asked herself. Was it possible that she was considering opening the door to her heart? And what would happen if she did?

The next morning, Eve pulled up to the curb in front of Lainey's house at precisely eight o'clock. Satisfied with her appearance after checking her reflection in the rearview mirror, she stepped out of the car onto the sidewalk and was nearly run over by a morning jogger who stopped to watch appreciatively as she started toward the house, in her skin tight Levis and clinging, white cotton shirt. She wore her hair up, exposing a long, slender neck.

Eve knocked on the front door and waited. She thought she heard barking from inside the house, although couldn't remember seeing a dog the night before. When Lainey opened the door, a not so little golden lab came hurtling towards her.

"Oh!" Was all Eve had time to say before the animal had all but jumped up into her arms.

"Rufus! Down!" Lainey scolded, grabbing him by his collar and pulling. "I said down! I'm so sorry, Eve."

"Rufus is it? Hey boy." Eve took the dog's ears in her hands and began scratching. "Aren't you a cutie?" Giving him a little shove, she muscled her way into the house. "I don't remember meeting him here last night."

"He was sleeping, thank God," Lainey told her. "Rufus! Get down or I'm taking you to the vet for shots!"

To Eve's amusement, Rufus sat down with a thump, tail wagging behind him and whined.

"I'm running late! I am so sorry," Lainey said. "I woke up late and then had to get the boys ready for school. And, of course, Jack was no help at all..."

"Lainey," Eve interrupted. "Relax. I'm not in a hurry."

Lainey took a deep breath and chuckled. "In that case, would you like some coffee?"

"I'd love some, thank you." Eve watched Lainey hurry off to the kitchen, admiring how the flannel shirt she had on stopped at mid-thigh giving Eve a great view of Lainey's legs. She found herself wondering what exactly Lainey had on underneath the shirt.

She reached down and scratched Rufus' head.

"Find another admirer?" Lainey asked, returning with two cups of coffee. "Cream and sugar, right?"

"Right." Eve smiled, taking a sip of the coffee and peering at Lainey over the rim. "Perfect."

Lainey cleared her throat. It always made her pulse jump when Eve looked at her like that, and she was beginning to enjoy the feeling more and more.

"Come on upstairs and talk to me while I change," she suggested.

Eve lifted one perfect eyebrow and smiled slowly. "Sure."

"Sorry about the mess," Lainey said self-consciously when they reached the bedroom.

"Don't apologize," Eve told her. "You have two kids, a husband and a dog. Your house is supposed to look like it's lived in."

"'Lived in'. That's a nice way of putting it. Compared to your place, it looks like a hurricane had just come through here."

"I have a maid," Eve said simply. "And I live alone. How much of a mess can one person make?"

"Ask Kevin or Darren. They'll tell you how."

Eve laughed. "Okay, how much of a mess can one adult make?"

"You'd be surprised," Lainey murmured and when Eve looked at her questioningly, she dismissed the subject with a shrug.

"Would you like to sit? I could clean off the chair for you."

"No, you don't have to do that," Eve assured her. "I can sit on the bed."

Lainey turned towards the closet to decide on what to wear, not wanting to admit that seeing Eve sitting on her bed made her heart beat a little faster.

"Jeans are okay?" Lainey saw that Eve was studying the wedding photo of Lainey and Jack that they kept on the stand beside the bed.

"Yes, fine. Until the gallery opens," Eve said looking around with an artist's eye. Lainey certainly had good taste, she thought. The walls were white here, and the carpeting a deeper blue than downstairs. It was a room decorated to suit both a man and a woman with its picturesque landscape paintings, and bold antique furniture. She imagined that the armoire that stood against the opposite wall housed a TV for late night entertainment. Two plush chairs upholstered in the same off white as the bedspread sat in front of a bay window overlooking the backyard, a most sought after commodity in the city.

"It's very cozy here," Eve commented.

"It's a matchbox compared to your room," Lainey replied.

Eve looked Lainey in the eye. "Don't make comparisons to me," she said softly. "Sometimes bigger isn't always better. Sometimes, it's just bigger."

Lainey saw something flicker in Eve's eyes then, that same loneliness that she had seen before. But as quickly as it appeared, it was gone again.

"Darren asked about you this morning," Lainey said, finding the pair of jeans she wanted and taking them down off the hanger.

It warmed her to see Eve's face light up. It had been wise to change the subject.

"Yeah? What did he say?"

"He wanted to know when he was going to see you again."

"Hmm. What did you tell him?"

"I told him soon."

"Good," Eve grinned. "Tell him I look forward to seeing his handsome face again."

"You know, you're his first crush," Lainey told her. "I always knew he had great taste."

"You are a wonderful mother, Lainey," Eve watched as Lainey turned away and pulled her jeans up, shimmying them over her hips, and giving Eve a quick glimpse of Lainey's nice, round butt. "They're marvelous young boys. It reflects well on you."

"Thanks," Lainey said, zipping up the jeans. "It's scary sometimes. Being a mother. I'm always worried that I'm doing something wrong, or that they'll grow up and not want to be with me anymore."

It was the first time Lainey had talked about her fears of motherhood aloud, and she found she was happier than she would have imagined to finally be able to talk to someone openly like this.

"I'm sure that it is very scary being a mom, but I can't imagine those two sons of yours not wanting to be with you," Eve told her genuinely. "They love you very much, and know you love them just as much. Stop worrying. You're doing a brilliant job."

"Are you close with your mother?"

Eve's smile faded. "My mother is dead," she said quietly.

"Oh, God, Eve. I'm so sorry."

Eve held up her hand. "It was a long time ago."

"Do you have any other family?" Lainey risked asking, going into the bathroom and beginning to brush her hair in front of the bathroom mirror.

"None to speak of."

"No brothers or sisters?"

"I'm an only child." Eve came to stand behind Lainey.

"What about your father?" Lainey's pulse had quickened when Eve walked in.

"What about him? I'd rather not talk about this right now, Lainey. Okay? Mind if I do something with your hair?"

"Sure." Lainey's already quickened pulse jumped as Eve and ran her fingers gently through her hair.

"You should wear it up," Eve murmured. Lainey could feel Eve's warm breath on her neck as Eve reached around her for a barrette, her soft breasts pressing against her back and discovered that she was violently aroused. "You look beautiful."

Lainey turned until she was face to face with Eve, so close they could feel each other's breath. They stood there like that for what seemed like an eternity until finally Eve took a step back.

Going back to sit on Lainey's bed, she picked up her coffee to take a drink and saw Lainey pause in the act of taking off her flannel shirt.

"Do you want me to turn around?" Eve asked. When Lainey didn't answer, Eve stood up and turned her back to Lainey, smiling to herself. It was amusing that one minute Lainey looked as though she wanted to jump Eve and the next she was shy about changing in front of her.

"Okay," Lainey said when she had her shirt on.

"Don't button them all. Leave the top three undone," Eve told her, unbuttoning one of the buttons herself.

Lainey nodded and held her breath. She wanted so much for Eve to make a move, because Lainey didn't know if she had the courage to do it.

"Ready?" Lainey heard Eve say.

"What?" Oh, yes. Lainey was ready.

"Are you ready?" Eve said. "To go?"

"Oh! Yes. Yes I'm ready." Embarrassed, Lainey cleared her throat and went to put on her shoes. How could she have thought that Eve meant anything else?

Eve smiled at Lainey's back. She had wanted so much to touch Lainey in a way Eve knew Lainey had never been touched.

It was for that reason that Eve resisted. She didn't think either one of them were ready for the consequences that would bring.

As they went downstairs, Eve appreciated the way the faded jeans clung to Lainey's curves, showing off her very fine backside.

She waited by the door as Lainey took Rufus out to the backyard, then they walked out to Eve's car side by side. Slipping into the car, Eve put the key in the ignition and her Jaguar purred to life.

"Would you mind if I put the top down and turned the music up?" Eve asked Lainey. "It's sort of a tradition on a beautiful morning like this."

"Well, I wouldn't want to get in the way of a tradition," Lainey teased. "Of course I don't mind."

"Thanks. By the way, you should wear jeans more often. You have a great ass."

As the buoyant sounds of Shania Twain washed over them Lainey stared at Eve not believing what she just heard. When it finally hit her, she turned to look out her window, covering her smile of pride and pleasure with her hand. Eve was full of surprises. She wondered what would come next.

~ Six ~

Meredith was sitting at her desk going over the altered reports when her phone rang. "Sumptor, Inc. this is Meredith," she answered. Her blood froze when she heard the voice on the other end.

"Is the plan in motion?"

"Yes, sir. I'm working on it now. The reports have been changed and we've covered our tracks."

"Take more. The preliminary reports you gave me are unsatisfactory."

"More? But we're being cautious..."

"Who is paying you to do this?" he interrupted.

"You are, sir," Meredith answered timidly.

"That means you do what I say. Take more. Do you understand?"

"Yes, sir, I understand. But what if she notices? The more we take, the more the risk."

"She's preoccupied with the gallery, is she not?"

"That's true, but..."

"Then she won't notice anything," he snapped. Dealing with little people like Meredith annoyed him. Unfortunately he had to put up with her for now. Later, he would deal with her for even thinking of questioning him.

"I'll take care of Eve. You just do as you are told. I thought the deal was to get you into the gallery with Eve while your friend took over there."

The glitch in his plan displeased him and it was just one more thing Meredith and Eve needed to be punished for, but at the present time, he needed to rework his plan and find another way to get to Eve through the gallery.

"Yes, sir, it was," Meredith said apologetically. "I don't know what happened. This Lainey person came out of nowhere and before I knew it, she was assisting Eve. She was hired to be an accountant, but after the first day, everything changed."

"Who is this Lainey person?"

"I don't know. I've been trying to find out more about her, but I haven't come up with much. All I know is she's married with two sons."

"What's her last name?"

"Stanton. But I don't think..."

"I'll take care of it," He told her irritably. "Do your job. That will be all."

Meredith sat with the phone in her hand for a moment, and then carefully hung it back up. This man frightened her as no one had. Thankfully she had never met him, but the phone calls were enough to give her nightmares. Meredith was almost sorry that Eve had such an enemy. She didn't dislike Eve and didn't know why this man hated her so much, but the money was too good to turn down what he had suggested or question his motives. Besides, Eve had insurance, so it wasn't like Meredith was doing much harm to her directly. Meredith focused on the reports again, sighing.

Where the hell was she going to pinch the money from and not get caught, she wondered, and settled in to work it all out one more time.

"Where should we put this?" Eve called out to Lainey, turning the painting she held around so that Lainey could see it.

"Oh my God! That's hideous."

"Lainey! Where are your manners?" Eve teased her. "It's not that bad."

"Are you serious? Even Darren could do better than that."

"Ouch. You are a harsh woman, Lainey," Eve replied, laughing. "Remind me to not show you any of my paintings from my 'earlier' years. Okay, so it's no Picasso..."

She studied the painting again. "You're right. Darren could do better. Have him draw me something and I'll put it up. In the meantime, we have to find a place for this."

"You have a storage closet, right?" Lainey said as seriously as she could.

"Lainey!" Eve's cell phone rang. "Hmm. Saved by the bell," she said. "This is Eve."

Lainey watched the amusement fade from Eve's face.

"I see. Yes," she said finally. "I understand. No. I'll take care of it. Thank you." Eve found that she was more resentful about being interrupted than she would have imagined. Somehow, right at this moment, nothing seemed more important than what was going on between her and Lainey. "I have some things I need to take care of," she said. "Do you think you could do a little more here and then lock up for me?"

"Of course," Lainey replied, concerned. There had been a note of irritation in Eve's voice just now that she had never heard before. "But - is everything all right?"

"Yes. Everything is fine. But that's not what you want to ask, Lainey. What is it?"

"Nothing. Really. I thought we could..." she sighed. "I'll lock up. Will I still see you tonight?"

"You thought that we could what, Lainey?" Eve said softly. "Say what you want to say to me. Don't ever be afraid to tell me what you want."

"I-I just thought we could have lunch together." Lainey said quickly.

Eve smiled brilliantly. "I'd love to have lunch with you."

"But I thought there was something you had to do now."

"It can wait," Eve told her. "I have to eat, right? And I'd much rather have you as company than eat by myself. There's a little deli on the corner downstairs. They have great burgers." She hooked her arm in Lainey's. "Come on. Let's go stuff ourselves."

Two hours later, Eve stepped out of the elevator at Sumptor, Inc. and headed to Meredith's office. She was glad she'd had lunch with Lainey. It had done a lot to lift her mood. She enjoyed their conversations, and even the sexual tension she knew they had between them. It was exciting for Eve, even if a little bewildering.

"Good afternoon, Ms. Sumptor."

"Good afternoon, Jackie," she said to the small blonde woman who had appeared beside her. "How are you?"

"I'm just fine, thank you." Jackie replied more than a little surprised that Eve knew her name. "How is everything at the gallery?"

"Great. Thank you for asking. Could I ask you something?"

"Yes, ma'am. Of course."

Like everyone that came into contact with Eve, Jackie was struck by the mere presence of her. There was something about Eve's eyes, and the way it looked as if Eve could read every thought in a person's mind.

"How is everything here?" she asked. "Are you being treated well?"

"Yes, ma'am. I love working here."

"Jackie, don't call me ma'am. Call me Eve."

"Oh, I couldn't," the young woman said shyly. "My mother always taught me respect. It would be disrespectful of me to call you anything but ma'am or Ms. Sumptor."

"Ms. Sumptor then," Eve replied. "So, you're not having any problems with anyone?"

Jackie shifted her eyes away for a fraction of a second, just long enough for Eve to be alerted to something she already expected.

"Jackie," she said thoughtfully. "I'm not asking you to get anyone in trouble and whatever you say will stay between us. But if you are having any problems, I want you to know you can come to me. I want you to keep loving working here," she paused long enough to give Jackie a chance to respond. "Okay. If you ever want to talk to me, you can get a hold of me either at the gallery or through my assistant."

"Thank you, Ms. Sumptor." It was clear to Eve that the young woman felt relieved.

"My pleasure, Jackie," Eve told her. "Have a great day."

Jackie headed back to her own office, feeling horrible for lying to Eve. She would get the courage to tell Eve everything one day, she thought, and closed her office door behind her.

Eve opened Meredith's door and found Katherine sitting there with her having what looked to be a very important discussion.

"Ms. Sumptor!" Meredith stood up so quickly she almost knocked her chair over. "I-I wasn't expecting you today. Did we have a meeting scheduled?"

She looked down at her calendar, wondering how she could have forgotten that Eve was coming.

"No, Meredith," Eve replied crisply. "We didn't have a meeting. Good afternoon, Katherine."

"Hello, Ms. Sumptor," Katherine replied, hoping she sounded calm. How much had Eve heard?

"Could you excuse us, please?" Eve said. "I need to speak with Meredith."

Eve waited until Katherine closed the door behind her, before taking a seat in front of Meredith's desk and crossed her legs.

"To what do I owe this pleasure?" Meredith said with feigned cheerfulness, praying she sounded sincere.

"I own the company, Meredith. Do I need a reason to just drop in?" Eve could see that Meredith was nervous and she was glad of it. "Can I see the quarterly reports?"

"I'm sorry?"

"The quarterlies. I want to see them," Eve repeated calmly.

"Th-they're not, um, done yet," Meredith stammered.

"Not done?" Eve repeated incredulously. "Why, exactly, aren't they done, Meredith?"

Meredith searched her mind for a plausible excuse while a line of cold sweat trickled down her back. Suddenly, inspiration hit her and she looked up at Eve with an almost triumphant smile.

"I had to show Katherine the ropes, so we haven't had time to do the quarterlies, yet."

"Hmm. There are nine other people in this department, Meredith. Now, tell me again, why aren't the quarterlies done yet?"

Eve's eyes never left Meredith. It was Meredith who faltered. Her 'triumphant' smile faded.

"Well, Ms. Sumptor," she explained, clearly flustered. "I just felt that...that I wouldn't be able to give it the attention it needed or that one of the less experienced employees would need, if I were busy training Katherine."

"I see," Eve countered. "And Katherine needed a lot of training? That's a bit disappointing considering she's been here going on three years now."

"No, she didn't need a lot of training, but..."

"Let me see that report there on your desk," Eve interrupted.

"What report?" Meredith felt her hands go wet and clammy.

"That one, there." Eve pointed with a perfectly manicured finger. "The one that says Quarterly Report."

Meredith placed a hand over the report, panicking now. "It's not finished."

Eve leaned forward and raised an eyebrow. "Is there a reason you are not following directions, Meredith? Hand it to me." Eve held her hand out. "Now."

With great reluctance Meredith picked up the altered report and handed it to Eve. She held her breath as Eve took it and studied it silently.

"Hmm. It seems I have some house cleaning to do, doesn't it?" Eve finally said.

"What?" From Meredith's terrified expression, Eve knew that she had struck gold.

"Well, I can't keep these people on if they are doing such a horrible job," Eve said simply. "I'm losing quite a bit of money compared to last quarter according to these figures, so either you've made a mistake, or, my employees are not doing their jobs."

Holding on to every ounce of control she had, Eve reached for a pen off of Meredith's desk and began writing on the report. When she was finished, she laid the pen back on the desk and handed the report back to Meredith.

"Your math is wrong here," she said mirthlessly. "Not a good sign for the manager of accounting, is it?" Rising, she placed both of her palms on Meredith's desk. "Be careful, Meredith. I can be a very nice woman, but if you cross me, I guarantee you'll see just how much of a bitch I can be." She leaned closer. "You don't want me as an enemy. I promise you that. Fix it."

Eve had made her point. That was clear from the distress on Meredith's face. "Have a nice day, Meredith," she said sweetly and left, closing the door with a snap that made Meredith jump. As Eve walked towards the elevator, she saw Katherine out of the corner of her eye. Changing directions, Eve stopped in front of Katherine startling her.

"Ms. Sumptor. You scared me."

"Where are you going, Katherine?"

"I-I was just going to see Meredith."

"Meredith is busy. I believe you have work to do, too."

As much as Katherine hated to admit it, she was afraid of Eve. "Yes, ma'am, but..."

"Go back to your office, Katherine."

"Yes, ma'am."

Eve turned her head then and locked eyes with Jackie, who jumped at the contact. Deliberately, Eve softened her gaze, nodding once to Jackie before turning to leave.

Meredith nervously picked up the phone, still shaking from Eve's visit. She dialed and took a deep breath to calm herself as she waited for him to answer.

"You are not to call here," he answered angrily.

"Yes, sir, I know," Meredith said quickly. "I didn't know what else to do. I think Eve is suspicious."

The mentioning of Eve's name renewed his interest. "Is that so? Why do you say that?"

"She just came here wanting to look at the quarterlies. She wasn't happy, sir."

"Did she notice anything?"

"I'm not sure. But she did threaten me."

"Eve threatened you? What did she say?"

"That if I crossed her I'd be sorry and that I didn't want her as an enemy," Meredith said defensively.

"Ahh, yes. She's right about that. Little Eve can be very nasty."

"What do I do?" Meredith asked, now even more frightened by Eve's threat.

"Do what I told you to do," he said sharply. "As I said before, I'll take care of Eve. Don't ever call here again."

Tony Sumptor sat back in his chair and smiled. His hair was darker than his daughter's and he wore it slicked back away from his face. He was striking and unforgettable, with eyes a darker gray than Eve's and a stubborn jaw, but most saw him as arrogant and shady. That jaw twitched as he thought of Eve. "Yes, Eve," he muttered to himself. "Make it a challenge for me. You know how I love playing games with you. Soon, it will be time for a little family reunion."

~ Seven ~

Eve joined the two men waiting for her in the coffee shop. "Could you two be any more obvious?" she said as she slipped into the booth. "The car, the suits, hell the coffee shop all scream cop."

"Hello to you, too, Ms. Sumptor." Detective Harris was in his mid-thirties with sandy blonde hair and a full beard to match. His eyes were compassionate, Eve thought. They were a warm, golden brown and always just a little too serious, the eyes of a man who had seen the horrors of police work day in and day out.

Detective Carter was a few years younger than his partner. His hazel eyes held more humor and mischief and his red hair, always unruly, reminded Eve of someone who just rolled out of bed. Eve liked both of the men although Detective Carter raised her warning flags for reasons she didn't understand.

"Some coffee, Ms. Sumptor?" Harris asked.

"In this place? No, thank you. I enjoy my health."

Eve sat back and watched as the younger man filled his cup with enough sugar to create an instant cavity. "Why did you ask me here?" she asked. "I'm a busy woman, detectives, with a gallery opening in a couple of days."

"You weren't too busy to pay Meredith Lansky a visit today after my call," Harris told her.

"I own the company, Detective. I have to go there every once in a while," Eve responded with a smile.

"You could have jeopardized the investigation!" Carter reminded her.

"Did I?" Eve asked him.

"That's not the point, Ms. Sumptor."

"That's precisely the point, Detective Carter. Do you honestly think the person that is after me is going to stop just because I go to check on a few altered reports?" She leaned toward them, resting her elbows on the table. "Surely you can't be that naïve. They're decoys, detectives. Meredith and Katherine are mere pawns in this game of chess. Nothing else. What they're up to is simply a distraction."

"If you knew that, why did you play into it?"

"Because, Detective Harris, I know how to play the game. This person wants to destroy me and will stop at nothing to do it. But he also wants it to be a challenge for him. Where's the fun if it's easy?"

"You know who's doing this to you, don't you, Eve?" Harris asked her.

Eve looked him in the eye. "I have a feeling."

"And you didn't tell us?" Carter whispered heatedly. "Why would you keep that little bit of information from us Ms. Sumptor?"

Eve turned her gaze on him. "Because, Detective Carter, you have a feeling about who it is, as well. Why haven't you told me?"

Harris leaned in, interrupting the rant he knew his partner had on the tip of his tongue. "Who do you think is after you, Eve?"

"My father," Eve said shortly.

"Do you have any proof?" Harris asked.

"Well, that would be your job now wouldn't it, Detective." She grinned sardonically and stood up. "Now, if you'll excuse me, I have a date to get ready for." And giving the two men a last, radiant smile, she left them.

"Lucky man," Carter mumbled and sighed. "Is it me, or do you want to go home and jump your wife every time you see that woman?"

"It's just you," Harris told him and took a sip of his coffee, watching Eve disappear into the crowd.

"Right. I forgot. You want to jump her."

"Get out of here," Harris said slugging his partner on the shoulder. "We have work to do."

Eve sat in front of her vanity mirror, wearing only a robe, with her legs crossed. With the touch of a fingertip to the remote, energetic dance music filled the room. Taking her hair in both hands, she twisted it into an attractive hairstyle and securing it with a diamond encrusted barrette. She pulled a couple of strands down to frame her face that was still bare of any cosmetics and thought about the events of the day as she prepared for her night out.

When Eve had received the phone call at the gallery, she had known that the game had begun. It annoyed her, but she would play. And this time she would win. But she had left the detectives even more frustrated than before. They knew who was after her, had leads but never told her, and of course couldn't do anything without evidence. But Eve was not about to sit back and let her father try to ruin her again. She would fight to protect everything she has worked so hard for and didn't give a damn what the cops told her. They didn't know him. They didn't know the lengths he would go to, to defeat her. But Eve did and she had set her own plan in motion to ensure that she comes out on top this time.

A shower had relaxed her and now the music pumping through the speakers lifted her mood even more. She vowed not to let this get in the way of a wonderful night with Adam.

Eve patted a minimum amount of powder onto her face and added color to her eyelids before applying mascara. But, it was when she got to her lips that she chose to be bold, deciding on a deep shade of red to accent her full lips. Letting her robe fall to the floor, she strolled naked to the bed and slid into the black, satin thong, so tiny that she wondered why she even bothered.

Next, she put on the matching black satin bra, running her hands over her breasts and down her flat stomach, stopping at the edge of her panties. Her thoughts ran between Adam and Lainey and the way each one of them aroused her.

"Stop it, Eve," she told herself. "You're coming home alone tonight."

The black fitted pants that zipped up from the back, fit her like a glove and she chose a long, sheer black shirt that went down to her knees to wear with it. She buttoned the two buttons in the front leaving an 'X' to show her cleavage and toned belly.

Checking her appearances in the full-length mirror, she slipped on her heels and headed downstairs.

Lainey stood in front of the mirror, in just her panties and bra, studying her image. She had decided on black lace to wear underneath her clothes, knowing Eve would have approved of her choice. She had always been comfortable with her looks, but it hadn't been until she had met Eve that she actually felt beautiful.

Jack had desired her, loved her, but no one had ever looked at her the way Eve Sumptor had. What was it about Eve's eyes that made it feel as though she were looking at the very soul of a person?

Why did it feel like she was seeing the person Lainey wanted to be instead of who she really was?

Lainey heard Jack in the other room and closed her eyes. She loved him very much and didn't want to hurt him, so why couldn't she get Eve out of her mind? She dreamt of Eve, thought of Eve and she couldn't stop. Maybe it was just curiosity, she thought. But what if it were more? She remembered how Eve had taken her hair in her hands and how it had felt when Eve had ran her fingers through it. Then she recalled Eve's body pressed to hers.

"Stop it, Lainey," she whispered to her mirror image. "You know nothing can ever happen between you two."

Putting her hair up again the way Eve had arranged it this morning, she began the task of applying her makeup choosing neutral colors, except for her lips which she painted a rich shade of scarlet. Taking the little black dress Eve had given her from its hanger with care, she held it up to her. It smelled of Eve. Lainey closed her eyes.

"I have got to stop this," she warned herself.

Stepping into the dress, she pulled it up over her hips and breasts. A perfect fit, she thought, surprised. She turned to look at herself and for the first time she saw what Eve saw, the woman she wanted to be instead of who she really was.

When Eve stepped out of the elevator into the lobby of her apartment building, Henry was there, ready for her with the door held open.

"You look beautiful tonight, Miss Eve," he said, tipping his hat. "Hot date?"

Eve laughed. "Very hot. Don't wait up."

Lainey stepped out of the bathroom and waited for Jack to turn to her. When he did, his heart almost stopped.

"You look great," he said, walking up to her. "Where did you get this dress?" he asked and ran a finger down the strap. The touch of his hand had Lainey pressing herself to him.

"It was a gift." Her lips were a breath away from his. "Kiss me, Jack."

"We're going to be late, Lainey," he told her, but he closed his eyes and breathed her in. After twelve years, she could still excite him.

"So? I'm sure Eve will understand. Kiss me. Just once."

"What if I can't stop, Lainey?" he said, his voice hoarse with desire. It was exactly what Lainey needed to hear.

"Later tonight you won't have to stop," she whispered and stood on her tiptoes to kiss him gently on the lips. "Ready to go?"

"We could always stay home. Say we couldn't find a babysitter."

"Jack!" Lainey laughed. "We have to go. We promised. I'll make it up to you."

In true Eve fashion, Lainey winked seductively and slipped on her black spiked heels. If Jack's reaction was any indication, it was clear that Eve's advice was already starting to work.

When Eve pulled up to the curb in front of O, Adam was waiting for her. Her heart skipped as she noticed how his black jeans and tight black shirt showed off his incredible body. Aroused by the way Adam looked at her, she wrapped her arms around his neck, taking no notice of the onlookers watching them.

"Hi," she said, her voice thick.

"Hi," he said, his voice rough with emotion as Eve pressed her body to his. "You look amazing."

"So do you." She reached up, took his face in her hands and brought his lips to hers for a mind-boggling kiss.

"How about we forget the club and go back to your place?" he whispered in her ear. "I want to be inside you, Eve."

"God, Adam." Eve moaned, kissing him again, and then placing her fingers over his mouth. "I want that, too. But no sex tonight. This is a date. We've never been on a date, Adam. Can we do this without ending up in bed?"

"Of course, Eve." He kissed her palm. "If that's what you want, that's what we'll do."

"Yeah?" God, his mouth was driving her crazy. This was going to be harder than she imagined. "Mmm. Let's go in before I change my mind."

Eve was pleased to see people lining the block to get into the club as she walked up to the bouncer. "Hey, Bruce," she said.

"Good evening, Ms. Sumptor." Eve had chosen Bruce originally because of his size. He towered over her, standing at six five and had to be at least three hundred pounds. But, it was when he spoke to Eve that she knew she had made the perfect choice. His voice was deep, yet soft, and he was very respectful, although when he was angry, his voice boomed loud enough to scare even the manliest of men.

Unhooking the velvet rope, he ushered them into the marble foyer of the club. "Damn, she's hot," he mumbled to himself and then turned back to do his job.

Inside the club, the music pumped loud and the lights blazed to the rhythm of the beat. Eve and Adam made their way through the crowd, towards the dance floor.

"Ms. Sumptor?" Eve felt a hand on her shoulder and turned.

"Hi, Ashley," she yelled over the music.

"Your table is ready in the VIP area. Would you like me to get you something to drink?"

Ashley was a voluptuous red head wearing a mini dress made of red spandex. Eve liked her because, despite Ashley's appearance, she was a very sweet young girl from the Midwest.

"Two club sodas," Eve told her. "Ashley, there are two more joining us tonight. Please be sure they get whatever they want on the house. I invited Lainey and her husband," she explained to Adam. "I'm sorry, I should have told you."

"It's okay," he grinned, kissing her gently on the lips. "You really don't want to end up in bed with me tonight do you?"

"I really do want to," she corrected him. "That's why I invited them."

Eve ran a fingertip down Adam's cheek and stood on her tiptoes. "Dance with me," she whispered in his ear, driving him wild.

Eve led Adam to the dance floor, and felt the beat flowing through them as she moved her body with his. He pulled her closer, loving the way she felt against him. Eve brought her arms up and wrapped them around Adam's neck and they swayed together in an erotic dance as if only the two of them existed.

Lainey and Jack pulled up to the curb and waited for the valet. "This doesn't look like our scene, Lainey," Jack said as he observed the crowd lining the block.

"Give it a chance, Jack," Lainey told him and linked her arm through his. "Let's be young again. It'll be fun."

"Fun," Jack mumbled as he took the ticket from valet and walked up to the bouncer. "Do we have to wait to get in?"

"Name?" Bruce asked looking down at Jack.

"Stanton. Jack and Lainey Stanton," Jack replied.

"You're on the list," he told them and spoke briefly into his headset. "Someone will be out to take you to the VIP area."

Only a moment had passed before the voluptuous red head opened the door to the club. "Mr. and Mrs. Stanton?"

"Yes," Lainey answered.

"Right this way. Ms. Sumptor is expecting you."

"Do you think those are real?" Lainey whispered in Jack's ear.

Jack chuckled at his wife and leaned down to kiss her temple. "Hush."

Ashley led them to the luxurious VIP area of the club. It was decorated in white, which Lainey now thought of as Eve's signature color, with glass tables and modern V back chairs. The tables sported thin monitors in the center, but no keyboards that Lainey could see. Lining the railing that separated the area from the rest of the club were white plush couches that club goers could relax on while they watched the dance floor on any one of the fifty-two inch TVs surrounding them.

"What can I get you two to drink?" Ashley asked.

"I'll take a beer, whatever's on tap," Jack told her.

"A wine spritzer for me, please," Lainey said.

"Very well. Ms. Sumptor said to treat you with whatever you wanted," Ashley said, guiding them to a table. "I'll be back with your drinks. If you would like something to eat, just press your selection on the monitor and it will be brought to you. Enjoy your time here at O. If you need anything, my name is Ashley and I will be happy to help you."

"Excuse me, Ashley," Lainey asked. "But where is Eve?"

Ashley pointed at Eve down on the dance floor. "Dancing," she responded with a smile.

Lainey caught a glimpse of Eve and Adam on the crowded dance floor. They looked so right together, she thought, and so exotic. They were two of the most beautiful people Lainey had ever seen. No wonder they were together. The way they were dancing was so sensual and passionate that Lainey could only imagine what they were like when they made love.

"You call that dancing?" Jack said.

"Yes. What do you call it?"

"Fucking with clothes," he said. "Although Eve isn't wearing much."

"Stop it," Lainey protested, annoyed. "She looks beautiful. And they don't look like they're fucking. Just having fun. Let's dance, too."

"I'm hungry," Jack told her. "Let's get something to eat instead."

Just then, Eve's eyes locked with Lainey's and the jolt of the contact made her catch her breath. She watched as Eve crooked a finger, beckoning Lainey to join her.

"I'm going to go dance," she told Jack. "Are you coming?"

"No. I'll wait for you here. I'm going to order something to eat, you want anything?"

"Order whatever," she told him impatiently. "I'll be back."

When Eve left Adam's side and pulled her onto the dance floor, Lainey's first impulse was to retreat. But then Eve danced around her until her back was against Eve's breasts, and she knew there was nowhere else she'd rather be. She felt Eve lean into her, felt Eve's breath on her ear.

"You look wonderful," Eve whispered. "I knew you would."

"I don't know how to dance. Not like this," Lainey replied and felt like an idiot. It wasn't what she had wanted to say. She wanted to tell Eve how incredible she looked and to thank her again for the dress. But, all of that escaped her as soon as Eve touched her.

"It's okay. Just relax." Eve slipped her hands down to Lainey's hips and began swaying them with hers. "Follow my movements. Relax, Lainey. Feel the music. Feel me." Eve pressed closer to Lainey, feeling that great ass against her as Lainey started moving to the rhythm of the music. "Mmm. Yes, Lainey. Like that," Eve whispered, arousing Lainey.

Taking Lainey's hands in hers, she raised them over her head. She glanced seductively at Adam as she and Lainey swayed together. He would enjoy this, Eve thought. A small moan escaped from Lainey when Eve pressed even closer and started singing quietly in Lainey's ear. Eve danced in front of Lainey then and pulled her until she was sandwiched between Adam and Lainey. She felt Adam's arms come around her waist and she brought Lainey's arms around her neck. She was in heaven. She felt incredible having the two of them so close to her, rocking with her in an erotic dance.

Lainey had never felt more alive and turned on than she did at this moment. All she could feel was Eve's body close to hers. All she could see was Eve looking into her eyes with that bewitching smile of hers.

As for Adam, he held Eve tight, loving the way she felt as she moved that beautiful body of hers against him. Lainey was a beautiful woman, he thought, though no one could compare with Eve for him. And the way she danced with Lainey was amazingly arousing. This was only a date, he reminded himself. He had told Eve there would be no sex, but he hadn't realized just how difficult that would be.

Jack ordered a steak and baked potato for himself and Lainey and waited for her to return. What in the hell did Lainey want to come here for, he wondered. This was not their scene. The dance music was too loud and the clientele too young. Although he had to admit the ambiance was incredible, it just wasn't for him. Sipping his beer, he walked to the railing. He watched, shocked as much as intrigued, as Lainey danced with Eve.

The music changed seamlessly and Eve felt Lainey pause.

"Come on," Eve said. "Let's take a breather."

"You go on ahead," Adam told her. "I'll be right there."

Being that close to Eve had made him rock hard and he needed to calm down before meeting anyone else and making small talk.

Eve rubbed against him. "Don't take too long," she purred in his ear, and then gave him suggestions on what she would like to do to him in his current state.

"You're not helping," he groaned and reluctantly pushed her away. "Be good."

"Where's the fun in that?" she teased. "Do you want something to eat?"

It was Adam's turn to make Eve groan when he leaned in and told her exactly what he wanted to eat.

"Thank God you're here," Eve said, linking arms with Lainey. "This is going to be harder than I thought." Eve's mind was still reeling from seeing Lainey in the little black dress. "You really do look beautiful, Lainey. The dress looks amazing on you."

"Thank you. I love it." Lainey felt the heat from Eve's eyes. "You look incredible, yourself."

"Hello, Jack," Eve said as they reached the table. "I trust you're being served well." Eve picked up her club soda and took a sip, watching Jack over the rim of glass.

What was it about the way Eve looked at him that left him feeling just slightly uncomfortable, yet slightly excited?

"I hope you ordered whatever you wanted," she told him. "It's on the house tonight."

"That's very kind of you, thank you."

"My pleasure," Eve said and took another sip of her drink. "You didn't join us on the dance floor, Jack. Why was that?"

"He said that what you and Adam were doing wasn't dancing," Lainey answered before Jack could respond. He had annoyed her when he had said what he had and now she was getting retribution.

"Oh?" Eve smiled. "What were we doing?"

Lainey knew Jack would be upset with her, but she was too interested in Eve's reaction to stop now. "He said it looked like you two were fucking."

Eve's reaction was a radiant smile. "Really? And what's wrong with fucking, Jack?" When Jack didn't answer, his face flushed with embarrassment, Eve grinned. "Hmm. Well, if you're not going to - dance with your wife, I will," she told him and taking Lainey's hand, she strolled off, leaving Jack staring after them.

"I think you shocked him," Lainey said, delighted despite herself.

"Good." Eve chuckled. "He'll watch us together and either get jealous or turned on. Either way, you're in for a treat tonight."

"Is that why you're dancing with me now?" Lainey asked her, disappointed. "So I can get lucky tonight?"

"I'm dancing with you because I enjoyed the way your body felt next to mine," she said boldly. "What it does to Jack is just an added bonus."

Lainey's heart raced. Not only has Eve shocked Jack, but she had done a hell of a job at shocking Lainey as well. When Eve pulled Lainey to her, she could only think of the other ways she wanted to be with Eve.

Adam made his way to their table and, noticing that Eve and Lainey were not there, spotted Eve immediately on the dance floor. Just seeing her and the way she moved was exciting him again, so he turned away and joined Jack at the table.

"Hi. I'm Adam." Adam extended his hand and shook Jack's in greeting.

"Jack. Nice to meet you." The man was handsome enough, Jack thought. No wonder he was with Eve. Jack couldn't imagine someone like Eve being with anyone less than perfect.

"Nice to meet you." Adam took a sip of his club soda and placed an order for food on the monitor. He glanced down at the two dancing women. "Your wife is quite beautiful," he commented.

Jack followed Adam's gaze. "Yes, she is thank you. And, your..." He paused, not sure what Eve was to Adam.

"Eve? She's not mine," Adam said simply as he stared at Eve. "Eve doesn't belong to anyone. Yet." He looked back at Jack. "Amazing isn't she? I hear Lainey is helping out quite a bit at the gallery. It means a lot to Eve."

"Lainey seems to love doing it," Jack said and took a drink of his beer.

Adam heard the edge in Jack's voice. "You don't approve?"

"I'm just not used to her not being around," Jack explained. "We have two sons who need her and Eve keeps her pretty busy."

"I'm sure Eve has told Lainey that if she ever needed to leave early it would be fine," Adam told him, not appreciating Jack's accusatory tone. "She's pretty understanding. Besides, I believe Eve sees Lainey as more of a friend than an employee, otherwise you wouldn't be sitting where you are now."

He leaned forward and fixed his stare on Jack. "Eve is a very generous and kind-hearted woman, Mr. Stanton. Don't let the tough exterior fool you. If Lainey is ever in need, Eve will be there. Your wife is a lucky woman."

Jack's attempt at an apology was cut short when Adam raised his hand and waved at the two women.

"Hey, beautiful," Adam said as Eve slid gracefully on the seat next to him.

"Hey, handsome," Eve said back and leaned over to kiss Adam gently on the lips. She saw the spark of anger in his eyes. She would ask Adam about it later, but, for now, for Lainey's sake she let it go. "Did you order something to eat?" she asked him.

"Yes, I did. I ordered you a Caesar salad, is that okay?" Adam ran a finger down Eve's spine and sent chills coursing through her body.

"Perfect," she answered, not meaning the salad. "I'm sorry, I haven't formally introduced everyone."

"It's fine. We've met." Though Adam's voice was pleasant, Eve heard the tension in it. What could Jack have said to have upset him? "We've danced together but I don't believe we've actually said a word to each other," Adam said to Lainey.

"Eve has told me a lot about you," she said sweetly.

Adam's lips quirked, "Eve talks about me? How interesting. You'll have to let me know what she says one day."

"No, she doesn't." Eve shot a look of feigned hurt and betrayal over at Lainey. "She's said enough already."

Lainey giggled. "Oops. Was I not supposed to say that?"

"Come on, baby, give me a little hint," Adam teased.

Eve ran a hand up Adam's thigh and leaned over to whisper no in his ear, nipping the lobe between her teeth as she did.

Lainey saw that Jack was trying his best not to watch the two lovers tease each other. Why can't it be like that for us, again, she wondered sadly. All I want is more excitement. She took a long drink of her wine spritzer and sighed inwardly. If she wanted a change, she was going to have to make it herself.

Later, Eve and Adam returned to the dance floor, leaving Lainey and Jack at the table.

"I'm having a good time, Jack," Lainey said, moving to sit beside him on the plush banquette. "We should do this more often."

"Not with them. And not here," Jack replied dryly.

"Why? What's wrong?"

"They're not like our other friends, and this place is not like the places we go to. I don't like it, Lainey."

They were silent for a moment, watching the TV screens as the cameras panned over the club, turning the crowded scene into a sea of lights that bounced off of the mirrors on the wall.

"That's exactly what I like about them, and this place, Jack," Lainey said in a low voice. "I like Eve, and I'm going to continue this friendship I've started with her. I'm sorry if you don't like that, but that's how it's going to be."

"So, you're choosing her over me?"

"I don't want to choose between anyone, Jack, because I shouldn't have to. Don't make me," she added, praying that he would leave it at that.

"What is it about her, Lainey?" His hair was tousled from running his hands through it and he looked worried. For a passing moment, Lainey felt sorry for him. But she needed things to be different. "How did she change you?"

"She didn't change me. All Eve did was give me the courage to make those changes that I needed to make." Lainey took Jack's hand in hers. "Jack, I love you, but I had lost myself in being your wife. I want to find that woman you fell in love with again."

Glancing up at the TV screen, she saw Eve and Adam kissing passionately in the center of the dance floor. "Excuse me. I'll be right back," she said before Jack could respond to what she had just told him.

Eve had completely forgotten all about her plan not to end up in bed with Adam tonight. She wanted him. Needed to feel him inside her. They would just have to try this dating thing some other time, she thought, as she fisted her hands in his hair and kissed him deeply. "I want you," she breathed against his mouth.

Adam's hands found their way underneath Eve's shirt and she moaned when he touched her skin.

"Ahem!" Lainey cleared her throat and waited for Eve to break the kiss. "Sorry, Adam. Could I borrow Eve for a moment? Thank you." Without waiting for an answer, Lainey took Eve's arm and dragged her away from Adam to the ladies room. "What are you doing?" she demanded, relieved that they had a corner to themselves.

Eve stifled a grin. She wondered what the repercussions would be if she told Lainey that she looked like a cross between a jealous lover and a mother standing there with her hands on her hips and a stern look on her face. "I'm standing in the bathroom with you, Lainey," she replied, straight-faced, deciding not to risk it.

"Ha, ha, very funny, Eve. What happened to not wanting to end up in bed with Adam tonight?"

Seeing Eve kiss Adam that way had upset Lainey more than she cared to admit.

"Oh, that," Eve shrugged. "Yeah, I don't think that's going to work tonight."

"Yes it is!" Lainey insisted. "You told me to help you through tonight and I'm going to do that. I don't want you sleeping with Adam tonight, Eve."

Eve stepped closer to Lainey and wrapped a strand of her hair around her finger. "Tell me something, Lainey, and be honest with me," she said in a low voice. "Are you doing this for me? Or are you jealous?"

"I'm doing this for both reasons." If she wanted the truth, she'd give her the truth. "I'm jealous, Eve."

"Now you know how I feel knowing you're going home with Jack, and that he'll be making love to you." Eve's eyes dropped to Lainey's mouth. "Hmm. This isn't helping me." She couldn't risk doing what she wanted to do here.

"What's happening between us, Eve?" Lainey demanded.

There had been a time, not long ago, when she would never have believed she could be this open with another woman. But things were becoming incredibly confusing.

"I don't know, Lainey. Scary, isn't it?" Being alone with Lainey in the aroused state she was in wasn't a good idea. "I think we should get back out there."

"What about Adam?" Lainey didn't want to ask because she didn't know if she could handle the answer. But she'd made a promise and she intended to keep it. Besides, she had to know.

"I'm going home alone," Eve said.

Two hours later, Eve laid her head back against the tub and tried to let the whirlpool relax her. As soon as she had arrived home, she turned on melodic music, lit candles, shed her clothes and sunk into the tub filled with aromatic bath oils. No matter how hard she tried to clear her mind, she couldn't help thinking about Adam and how much she wanted him with her now. Then her mind would switch to Lainey. *"I'm jealous, Eve,"* she had said.

Jealous.

Eve shut her eyes tightly, but couldn't get Lainey's face out of her head. "What is wrong with me?" she said aloud. She took a deep breath and began to hum along with the music, but nothing was helping her. She was aroused and alone.

She ran her hand over her firm breast, feeling the nipple grow taut. Eve moaned softly as she let her hand roam further down to her stomach. She had never been aroused enough to do this to herself before and the thoughts it conjured up stunned her.

Thoughts of Lainey.

Frustrated, Eve sat up in the tub and ran a hand through her hair. "And this is supposed to help you get sex off your mind, Eve? My God, I'm in trouble. Snap out of it!" she ordered herself, and stepped out of the bathtub and into her terry cloth robe.

Retreating to her bed, Eve found herself focusing on Lainey. There was so much tension between them. She knew Lainey wanted her as much as she wanted Lainey. But, Lainey was married, Eve reminded herself. She loved her husband, and Eve wouldn't jeopardize their friendship for a quick roll in the hay to satisfy her curiosity.

Eve began stroking herself, determined to do anything to get some rest and forget about all of this. Again, she massaged her breast and lightly trailed down until, just as she became daring enough to actually touch herself, her phone shrilled making her jump. It was one in the morning.

"Eve?" Lainey's voice was barely a whisper, but hearing her had made Eve's pulse quicken. "Did I wake you?"

Lainey couldn't believe she had actually called Eve after sitting in front of the phone for over an hour gathering the nerve to pick it up and dial.

"No, you didn't wake me. Is everything okay?"

"Yes. I just wanted to..."

Wanted to what? Lainey thought. Was she going to tell Eve that she wanted to know if Adam was there?

"You wanted to know if I was alone." It wasn't a question. Eve smiled to herself. "Yes, Lainey. I'm alone."

"I'm sorry. I shouldn't have called."

"Don't be sorry. I'm glad you called. I was having trouble sleeping anyway." Eve lay back on her pillows and for the first time since being home, began to relax. "How did things go with Jack?"

"They didn't." Lainey sat back in her chair and propped her feet up on the ottoman. She hadn't been able to sleep either. Every time she closed her eyes she would see Eve.

"Why? What happened? I thought for sure..."

"I couldn't," Lainey interrupted her. "Jack was tired and half drunk anyway, so I didn't even pursue it."

"Hmm. I'm sorry." In reality, Eve was happy that Lainey hadn't been with Jack tonight, but she wouldn't tell Lainey that.

"Well, maybe tomorrow we can leave the gallery early and go to your house. We can set up a whole seduction scenario for the two of you."

"Eve. I don't want to talk about Jack right now." Eve's soft voice was driving Lainey wild and she found herself wanting to touch herself while talking to her. Before she even knew what she was doing, Lainey slipped a hand into her panties and began a gentle massage.

"I'm sorry. I thought that was what you wanted, Lainey. To bring that spark back into your relationship."

"I do. I just don't want to talk about it now." A moan escaped Lainey's lips as she started moving her hand faster.

"Lainey?" Eve heard the moan and closed her eyes. "What are you doing?" Lainey never answered, but her breathing came faster. "Where are you?" Eve asked her.

"He can't hear me," Lainey breathed.

"Oh, God. Lainey." Eve slipped her own hand between her legs and began stroking as she listened to Lainey. "We shouldn't be doing this." But all she could hear from Lainey were small, incredibly sexy moans. Eve struggled to keep her own response quiet as she touched herself, afraid that hearing them, Lainey might stop. "Lainey," she whispered.

"Eve."

Eve heard her whispered name and then a sharp intake of breath as Lainey came. Not being able to hold back anymore, Eve arched and came quietly as she listened to Lainey's labored breathing.

"Oh, God. I'm sorry," Lainey said, mortified by what she had just done, and hung up the phone quickly.

"Lainey! Wait!" Eve's attempt at keeping Lainey on the phone was answered by a dial tone.

"Damn it!" she swore, throwing the phone across the bed. Pushing a hand through her hair, she stared up at the ceiling. She wanted to call Lainey back, to tell her that there was nothing wrong with what she had done. That Eve had enjoyed it, too. But, Lainey wasn't alone like Eve was, and Eve knew she couldn't take that chance.

Lainey had already been at the gallery for over an hour before Eve came in, busying herself with cleaning and unpacking, trying not to think of the night before. But it haunted her every minute. What had she been thinking? Calling Eve in the middle of the night and doing what she had done. Making no secret of it. How would she ever be able to face Eve again? Lainey felt her whole body tense when the elevator door opened.

"Good morning, Mikey," Eve greeted the young intern who would be helping at the gallery for the next couple of months. He was twenty-two and awkward, with his thick glasses, second hand clothes and squeaky voice that sounded as though he hadn't hit puberty yet. But, he was also extremely intelligent and had a lot of heart, and Eve liked him.

"Good morning, Ms. Sumptor." Mikey sniffed and pushed his glasses up on his nose. "The Dalis came in this morning. Mrs. Stanton has been unpacking them." He lowered his voice to a whisper. "She's not in a very good mood this morning. She's been extremely quiet."

Eve saw Lainey slip up the stairs without even giving her a glance. "Hmm, so I see," she said. "I'll see if I can make her feel better."

She found Lainey standing over by her office window, staring down at the crowded city streets.

"Are you ever going to look at me again?" Eve asked her. "Please, Lainey. Look at me. Do you feel guilty for doing what you did? Are you embarrassed? Because you don't have to be."

Eve moved closer to Lainey and put her mouth close to Lainey's ear. "I did it, too," she whispered and felt Lainey shiver.

"But why didn't I..."

"Why didn't you hear me?" Eve finished the question for her. "Which reason would you like to hear first?"

She took Lainey's chin in her hand and lifted Lainey's face to hers. "I was enjoying listening to you so much that I didn't want to interrupt you," she said slowly. "That's one reason. The other reason is it was all very unexpected, and I was afraid that if I made any noise you'd stop and I didn't want you to stop, Lainey. I'm sorry. I should've told you."

Lainey was amazed at the full force of the relief that swept over her.

"I would have loved knowing that you were doing it, too," she said, reaching out for Eve's hand just as someone knocked at the door.

Eve groaned. "It's your office," she said when Lainey hesitated.

Lainey took a step back from Eve. "Come in," she called out.

Adam opened the door and stuck his head in. "Hey. Sorry to interrupt. Your intern told me I could find you up here. Good morning, Lainey. I just wanted to see you before I went in to work, Eve. Can I talk to alone you for a moment?"

This was the first time Adam had come to see her here at the gallery. Was it possible that he felt jealousy, too? It was an interesting idea.

"I missed you last night." Adam pulled Eve into his arms when they were alone in her office. "I almost called you."

Thinking about the call she had received, Eve smiled. "I missed you, too." She met Adam's lips with hers and kissed him deeply. "Mmm. Don't get me started. Is that why you're here? To tell me you missed me?"

She sat on the edge of her desk and studied Adam. He looked great in his tailored suit, and Eve knew he looked even better out of it.

"Yes, and to tell you that I enjoyed our date last night. It was nice."

Adam was having a hard time concentrating. Eve looked amazing in her jeans and stretch button up shirt that was, in true Eve fashion, unbuttoned enough to give Adam a great view of her cleavage.

"Yes, it was." Eve took a hold of Adam's tie and pulled him to her, spreading her legs so that he fit in between them. "We should do it again sometime."

"We will." He wrapped Eve's legs around him and pressed his body to hers. "How many dates do I have to take you on before I can get you back into bed?"

"Mmm. Keep doing that and you won't have to wait too long," she told him. "Let's just take it one day at a time, okay?"

"Okay. Whenever you are ready. I have to go. Call me tonight?" Adam tucked a strand of hair behind Eve's ear and kissed her cheek.

How was it possible that she could feel this overwhelming desire for two, very different people? More importantly, what was she going to do about it?

Eve knocked on Lainey's door and once again received no answer. But this time, when she looked in she saw that Lainey was not there. Sighing, Eve walked down to the gallery.

"Is she in a better mood?" Eve asked Mikey as she found Lainey unpacking paintings in the further room.

Mikey shrugged. "She still hasn't talked, but she seems to be doing a little better."

Eve reached into her front pocket and brought out some money. "Would you do me a favor? Run down to the deli downstairs and get me a coffee. No, make that two coffees and two donuts. Glazed. And whatever you want."

"Need some help?" she asked Lainey as soon as he was gone.

"The Dalis look wonderful," Lainey said, keeping her distance.

"I'm sorry about Adam."

"Why should you be? He's your boyfriend, right?" She glanced over at Eve. "What are you laughing at?"

"Nothing. It's just that "boyfriend" sounds so high school." Her smile faded. "It bothers you that I'm seeing Adam."

"No. Why should it?" Lainey lied. Studying the painting she had just unpacked. "Dali is one of my favorites," she said quietly. "His work is ever changing. Every time you look at them you see something different."

"Yes, you do," Eve said, looking at Lainey not the painting. "Don't do this, Lainey. Don't close yourself to me now," Eve pleaded softly.

Lainey turned to Eve. "I have to take a step back, Eve. I can't breathe when I'm this close to you."

Eve closed her eyes. "If that's what you need."

What she needed was Eve. Instead Lainey said, "Last night you offered to come to my house and help me with Jack. Is that offer still open?"

Eve took a deep breath. "Of course it is."

She built the wall around her heart as a defense to the hurt she was feeling. If Lainey needed to space, that's what Eve would give her.

"Where do you think this should go?" she asked Lainey, pointing at a small piece that featured the twisted figures that was signature Dali.

Lainey walked over to the wall next to the arched window overlooking the streets which were, like Dali's paintings, ever changing. "I think it should go here. The view would be a nice compliment to complexity of the piece."

"I agree." Eve walked up behind Lainey and placed a hand on her arm. "I think we should let Mikey put it up for us. We don't have to let him know we both have a fear of heights. He's getting us coffee right now."

With perfect timing Mikey stepped out of the elevator, hands full. He handed the women their coffee and donuts.

"Your change is in my pocket, Ms. Sumptor."

"Keep it," Eve told him. "Thank you for the coffee."

"But, you gave me a twenty," he protested.

"Keep it," Eve repeated. "He's a good kid," she told Lainey as he strutted off with a toothy smile. "I have a few things I need to take care of in my office. If you need anything, just come and get me. Have Mikey help you with that painting."

Eve read the confusion and emotions on Lainey's face.

"I'm stepping back, Lainey, but I'm not going anywhere," she said as she looked into Lainey's eyes. "I'll be in my office."

Eve sat behind her desk with her head in her hands. If she didn't figure out what was going on between her and Lainey soon she was going to go crazy. Taking a deep breath, she pushed Lainey out of her mind, picked up the phone and dialed, tapping a finger on her desk as she waited for an answer.

"It's me," she said when the other end picked up. "The game has begun. Are you ready to play? Good. I need you to be my eyes and ears for right now. I want to know everything that Tony is doing. I also need you to find out everything he's been doing since he's been released from prison. I want to know if he's violated any rules of his parole. Anything. If he's littered by throwing a gum wrapper on the ground I want to know about it. If I can get him put away again that would be a point for me. I'm not going to lose this time." She paused and thought of Lainey. Eve wouldn't put her at any risk. "If he comes near the gallery I want to know about it," she continued. "He may keep a low profile, but he'll come up soon and make his presence known to me. I'm counting on you to keep me informed on everything that goes on where Tony is concerned. I know we couldn't get everyone to play on our team, but I know I can do this with those we have. As soon as we have any kind of evidence that can put him away again, without implicating you or anyone else in the process, we will move on it. I'll wire the money to the account I had set up for you tomorrow morning. If anything happens, contact me. Until then, I'll be in touch."

Hanging up, she opened a file and took out a surveillance photo of Meredith. "Now. What to do with you and Katherine," she said aloud. "Maybe I should just let Tony deal with you himself. It would save me the trouble and be less messy for me."

She sighed and rubbed her temple where the beginning of a headache was brewing. "We'll see," Eve said, putting the file away. Now that the ball was in motion, she could go back to focusing on the grand opening of the gallery. Putting everything else out of her mind, Eve set in to making arrangements for the big event.

Lainey was putting the finishing touches on a display over which Eve had given her full creative control. When she stood back and critiqued her work, she knew it wasn't her best, but she hadn't been able to concentrate. Thoughts of Eve kept distracting her every time she let her mind wander for inspiration. She hadn't seen Eve since that morning and was beginning to think that she was avoiding her. Not that she blamed her. She had basically told Eve to leave her alone and Eve was just doing as she asked.

Irritated, she busied herself with making changes in the display, and didn't hear the elevator opening or the man walking towards her until he was right behind her.

Eve descended the stairs just in time to hear a man's voice raised in anger, and felt her own temper rising with each step that she took.

"Look, you little nothing bitch," he shouted. "I don't know who you think you are, but if you want to keep your job, I suggest you go and get Ms. Sumptor for me now!"

"Mr. Palmer." Eve's voice was as icy as her stare as she walked up and stood toe to toe with the short, pudgy man wearing a bowtie. "My gallery is not open yet. What are you doing here?"

"Ms. Sumptor. I came for a sneak peek," he told her, exasperated. "But this woman tried to stop me."

"There are no sneak peeks, Mr. Palmer," Eve told him. When the man tried to move past Eve, she moved with him, her eyes never leaving his.

"I'm the most influential art critic in this city, Ms. Sumptor, as you well know," he threatened her. "If you want a good review, I suggest you let me take a look around."

Eve could feel her temper snap, but she kept her voice cold and under control. "What you are, Mr. Palmer is an arrogant son of a bitch," she said icily. "If you want to see the pieces so you can write your little column, then you will have to wait until the opening. And, if you want to keep writing that little column of yours, then you will give the gallery a fair and just review because I will not tolerate fallacious reviews of any kind. Do you understand? If you come back here before the opening, I will have you thrown out." Eve took a step closer to the man and dropped her voice. "And if you ever talk to my assistant like that again, I will personally throw your ass out. And I won't be gentle. Is that clear?"

The art critic opened his mouth to say something and shut it again when Eve raised an eyebrow. On a less than confident huff, he spun around and stalked out.

"Are you okay?" Eve asked Lainey.

"Yes. Thank you. What an asshole," Lainey said, trying to check her own anger. "I'm impressed with how you handled him."

In fact, Lainey had been a little frightened by the coldness of Eve's voice, and more than slightly aroused by her pure authority. It was an odd combination of feelings, one she had never felt before.

"Don't be," Eve told her indifferently. "He's just a small time art critic who has an ego the size of Texas. He's more of an idiot than I thought since he knows that I'm friends with his boss and I could have him fired with one word."

Eve looked past Lainey at the display she was working on, frowning slightly.

"It's not done," Lainey said hurriedly. "I was just re-doing it." Her voice trailed off when Eve walked past her.

"Is this how I make you feel, Lainey?" Eve asked.

"I-I don't understand. What do you mean?"

"Frustrated. Confused. Sad. The colors you've chosen don't compliment one another. You've created a sense of chaos instead of serenity and the pieces you've chosen represent repression. Sexual repression. There's anger and sadness in this display. Is this how I make you feel?"

A single tear slid down Lainey's cheek. "Lainey," Eve whispered, but didn't go to her.

"That's what you see?" Lainey studied the display again herself. It was exactly how Eve had described it. It was as clear to her now as it was to Eve. "It's not your fault, Eve," she said. It was all true. Since the moment she met Eve her emotions were uncontrollable. It scared her. It excited her. "It's me."

Turning away, she walked to the stairs to sit down.

Ignoring the voice that told her to stay away, Eve went to Lainey and sat next to her. "Talk to me, Lainey," she murmured. "Tell me what you want from me."

"I don't know." Lainey crossed her arms on her knees and laid her head down. "Maybe this is all too much for me. Life was so much simpler when all I had to do was be a mother and a wife. Now, I'm more confused than I was when I set out to 'find myself'. I don't know what to do, Eve."

"Do you want to quit?" Eve asked her quietly. "Do you want to go back to being a mother and wife and forget about this? And me?"

Her heart was racing with the fear that Lainey would say yes. But she couldn't let what was happening between her and Lainey destroy Lainey's talent or her peace of mind.

"No. I can't go back," Lainey told her. "And, I could never forget about you, Eve. You are in me now. In here." She placed her hand on her heart. "I just don't know what to do about it yet, and it scares me to think about what I could, and want to do."

"Lainey, look at me." Eve waited until Lainey focused on her. "Whenever and whatever you decide, I'll be there for you. I'll never pressure you to do anything, never expect anything from you. I'll just be here. If you need time to sort out what's going on inside, I'll give you that time. I'm sorry that I've put you in this position and made you feel this way, Lainey. That was never my intention. I'm just as confused about this as you are."

"I don't want you to be sorry, Eve," Lainey said quietly. "You didn't do this to me. Things happen and we have to deal with what comes our way. But, I'm glad you are as confused as I am. That makes me feel a little better." She gave Eve a small smile, then it disappeared again. "You don't have to come over tonight. I never considered your feelings about helping me with Jack. I'm sorry. That was selfish of me."

"No," Eve said. "You did nothing selfish. I told you I wanted to help you. If that means I have to help you fix your relationship with your husband, then so be it. I'm willing to do that. All I want, Lainey, is for you to be happy, and I'm ready to do anything to make that happen."

Eve stood up and held out her hand to Lainey. "Come on. Let's get you home and get you laid," she teased with a wink. "Tomorrow you can work on that display again and see if you can come up with something a little less - repressed."

"What if it doesn't work? What if Jack isn't what I need right now?"

"Then you'll tell me what you do need," Eve told her. "And what you want from me. I'll do my best to give you everything."

Eve didn't pull up in the drive way behind Lainey, opting instead to park on the curb. She turned the car off and sat for a moment, her head resting back against the seat. "You can do this," she told herself. "Do it for Lainey. Are the boys here?" she asked as they met at the front door.

"They're staying next door with friends," Lainey told her. "I made the arrangements so that I could have tonight to be alone with Jack."

"It's okay Lainey," Eve said when Lainey stumbled over the name. "I'm perfectly aware that you are married and that you love your husband. Let's go make you irresistible. It shouldn't take that long," Eve said with a wicked grin.

Lainey opened the door and readied herself for the attack she knew Rufus had in store for her. But, instead he jumped on Eve, hard enough to make her lose her breath.

"Rufus! Down!" Lainey took Rufus by the collar.

"Déjà vu," Eve laughed.

"I'm sorry," Lainey told her. "And actually, I'm a little pissed off. He usually does that to me, but now that you're here he picks you. I'm the one who feeds you and takes care of you, damn dog."

When Lainey returned from letting Rufus out into the back yard, she found Eve grinning. "Sorry," Eve said. "Must have been that bacon scent perfume I wore today."

"Shut up," Lainey laughed. "You can't help it that you're alluring to every living soul on this planet."

"Including you? Sorry. I didn't mean to say that," Eve said as she followed Lainey upstairs to her bedroom.

Lainey stopped midway on the stairs to turn back and look at Eve. "Including me," she answered honestly, and then continued up to her bedroom. "Now, where do we begin?"

Eve smiled at Lainey. "Well, let's see. Let's start with what you're going to wear. We want something that is going to give Jack easy access."

"Eve!"

"What? We don't want to make this complicated, right?" Eve said innocently. "Show me what you've got."

Lainey opened the top drawer of the dresser and began digging through it. When she pulled out old, ugly flannel pajamas and held them up in front of her, Eve gave in to a fit of hysterics.

"Please tell me you're kidding," she managed to say while trying to catch her breath. "Keep digging." Eve took the flannel pajamas from Lainey and threw them over her shoulder. "These we're throwing away."

"But, I like them. They're comfortable," Lainey protested.

"You know what else is comfortable? Sleeping in the nude. That thing is going in the trash," Eve told her.

"Is that how you sleep?" Lainey asked, envisioning the image of Eve completely naked in her huge bed.

"Every night."

Lainey looked at Eve. She knew how sexy Eve was with clothes on and could only imagine how incredible she looked naked. Lainey cleared her throat and looked away, not catching the knowing look on Eve's face. "So, why am I not just doing that?" Lainey asked. "Why not just be naked?"

"Hmm. Well, I, myself, would enjoy that if I were sleeping with you. But, you've tried that with Jack. It didn't work. At least not how you wanted it to. So, we're going to try something a little more subtle."

"How about this?" Lainey said and turned holding up a black lacy teddy.

Eve raised a brow. "Why Lainey, I didn't know you had it in you to buy something that slutty."

"Slutty? Why do you say that?"

Lainey turned to examine herself in the mirror with the teddy held up to her. She noticed that the hem of the thing didn't even go down far enough to cover anything.

"Okay, never mind. It's slutty. Don't ask me where that even came from," she said as she threw it over her shoulder to join the flannel PJs on the floor. "What about this one?"

She dug a long, white flowing gown out of the drawer and held it up to her for Eve to assess critically.

"That's the one," Eve said quietly. "Put it on."

Lainey saw the look of appreciation and desire in Eve's eyes and her pulse began to race. Instead of leaving the room or making Eve turn around, Lainey began to undress there in front of Eve.

As much as she wanted to watch, Eve turned around. "Let me know when you're ready," she said, closing her eyes to imagine what was happening behind her.

"You don't have to turn around."

"Yes. Believe me, I do." *For your sake, and mine,* Eve thought.

Lainey sighed, knowing why Eve wasn't looking at her. Part of her was disappointed while the other part was grateful. If something were to happen between them right now, she was not sure she would have the courage to see it through.

"Ready," Lainey said softly.

Eve caught her breath at the sight of Lainey standing there in a satin gown that clung to Lainey's body like a second skin. "My God, you're stunning," she murmured. "Absolutely stunning."

Eve ran a fingertip across Lainey's bare shoulder and leaned closer, her lips a breath away from Lainey's. "Tell me to stop, Lainey." At that exact moment, they heard the front door slam shut.

"Shit! He's early. You have to hide, Eve," Lainey said to her in an urgent whisper. *Damn it, why did he have to be early? Just when she was about to fulfill the dream that had invaded her sleep every night since meeting Eve.*

"Hide? Why?" *She had been so close to getting everything she wanted. Instead, she was being told to hide like a mistress. Eve supposed it was a sort of poetic justice.*

"He can't know that you're here. Especially with me looking like this. Just, please, trust me."

"Where am I going to go, Lainey?"

Lainey looked around frantically. "In the closet."

"How cliché," she mumbled closing the door of the closet behind her.

"Lainey?"

"Hi," she said breezily. "You're home so early that I didn't get to finish getting ready for you."

"What is this? What's the special occasion?"

"No special occasion, Jack. I just wanted to surprise you."

It was an impossible situation. What had she thought she was doing with Eve? What would have happened if Jack had arrived five minutes later? And what kind of chances was she taking with her marriage?

"Well, I'm certainly surprised. You look great." He turned towards the closet.

"Wait!" She yelled and then laughed. "I mean, come here."

"Let me hang up my clothes, Lainey. You know I like to change as soon as I come home."

"Can't you just, for once, do something spontaneous?" she asked him. "Throw your damn clothes on the floor, Jack. I want to make love to you. Now."

Lainey took his hand and pulled him to the bed, making sure his back was to the closet as she pushed him down on the bed and straddled him. When he made a move to position himself on top of her, she stopped him. "No. Like this," she said and unbuttoned his shirt. She undid his pants and pulled them off, taking his boxers with them. "Close your eyes," she told him.

Through a crack in the closet door, Eve's eyes trailed down and back up the length of Lainey's body, and felt herself get wet when Lainey looked back at her. She watched as Lainey straddled Jack again and took him inside her, dropping her gaze when they both moaned and Lainey began rocking her body back and forth.

She shielded the emotions in her eyes when Lainey looked up at her, riding Jack faster, her moans becoming louder. She slipped a hand into her jeans as Lainey watched.

Lainey was so close, but she heard Jack calling out her name and knew that if she didn't come now, she wouldn't at all. Lainey tried slowing the pace of their lovemaking, but Jack only moved faster, reaching up to grab her breasts.

"Lainey."

"Jack, wait. Not yet," she told him. She looked back up at Eve and noticed that she had removed her hand from her jeans.

"Jack, slow down."

"No, Lainey. Now." With one hard thrust, Jack emptied himself into Lainey until he collapsed, exhausted and out of breath.

"Wow!" he said breathlessly. "Let's do that more often." He patted Lainey's ass and lifted her off of him. "I'm going to take a shower. What's for dinner?"

"I don't know yet," Lainey answered miserably and shrugged into her robe. "What are you doing?" She ran up to him and stopped him just before he opened the closet door.

"I'm getting my clothes. What is wrong with you?" He asked, looking at her strangely.

"Nothing is wrong with me. Go take your shower. I'll bring your clothes in to you," she told him and stood her ground in front of the closet door.

"I can get my clothes myself, Lainey."

"Will you just let me do this for you, please? Go. Take your shower. Relax."

Jack sighed heavily. "Fine," he said and disappeared into the bathroom.

Lainey waited until she heard the running water of the shower before opening the closet door. "I'm so sorry," she told Eve. "I never meant for you to watch."

Eve gave Lainey a small smile. "I'm going to get out of here before he comes back out."

Lainey ran after her and grabbed her arm. "Eve."

"Lainey, its fine," Eve said. "I know my way out. You don't have to walk me down." Eve took two steps and turned back. "I'd never treat you the way he did, Lainey," she said. "You'll know what pleasure is when you're with me."

"I know I will," Lainey whispered to herself as she watched Eve hurry down the stairs. "I can't wait."

Eve pressed her forehead against her steering wheel. She was angry, angry that she had had to watch Lainey make love to Jack, and angry that Jack didn't know how to please Lainey. She swore and started the car. "Someday, Lainey," she said aloud and drove off.

Half an hour later, she found herself at Adam's front door, not exactly remembering driving there. She knocked, the need to have him becoming more urgent with each passing second. He answered the door, bare-chested, wearing jeans.

"Eve!" he said, clearly surprised and delighted to see her.

Eve stopped dead when a young brunette appeared next to Adam, wearing only boxers and a tank top.

"Who is it, Adam?" she asked and then, apparently feeling the heat radiating from Eve's angry eyes, stepped back.

"Eve! Wait!" Adam cried as she turned and ran down the steps. "It's not what it looks like. Damn it!"

"I guess that was Eve," the brunette said as he threw on a shirt.

"You guessed right," Adam retorted putting on his shoes. "Tell Jill to lock up. I don't know when I'll be back."

Eve's hands were shaking violently when she got to her front door and tried unlocking it. "Damn it!" she swore vehemently and took a deep breath to calm herself. Finally, she got the door open and hurried inside. Once inside, she leaned back against the door and tried to control her breathing.

"Son of a bitch!" she whispered heatedly. "Son of a bitch!"

She slammed her closed fists against the wall. How could he do this to her? If he wanted out of the damn relationship all he had to do was tell her. Eve paced the living room cursing Adam, until she finally gave up and sank down on the couch. Head in hands, she massaged her temples to relieve the headache that was beginning to pound. Just then, she heard the banging on the door.

"Eve! Open up!" She heard Adam shout. "I know you're in there! Henry told me he saw you coming up! Eve, open the door. Please."

Giving up, Eve put the chain on the door and opened it.

"What? You're going to wake up the damn neighbors," she said through the crack of the door.

"It wasn't what it looked like, Eve," he protested.

"Wasn't it? How old is she Adam? Twenty?"

"She's nineteen, but..."

"Oh! Even better! Goodbye, Adam," Eve retorted, attempting to shut the door.

"Will you listen to me?" Adam demanded, pushing one foot in the door. "It's not what you think."

Eve gave him a humorless laugh. "And, I suppose next you're going to tell me that she was your sister."

"No, but she's a friend of my sister's. It's true, Eve. Jill is in town. She's staying with me and the girl you saw is a friend of hers. You have to believe me, Eve. I would never do that to you."

From the corner of her eye, Eve saw Mrs. Jenkins peeking out of her door.

"What was I supposed to do?" Adam continued. There was desperation in his voice. "My sister just showed up with her, I couldn't just put them out on the street."

"Will you let me close the goddamn door so I can take the chain off?" Eve said, her voice emotionless. "I don't particularly want to talk to you right now, Adam, but obviously you're not going anywhere, and I don't want an audience." Eve gestured irritably for him to come in and shot Mrs. Jenkins a look before closing the door. "Start talking," she said folding her arms across her chest.

"Can we sit down?"

"No," Eve told him and stood her ground.

"Her name is Megan," Adam said wearily. "She and my sister have been friends since kindergarten. Jill brought her here to show her the city and they ended up on my doorstep. I swear to God, Eve, that's the truth."

"Do all of your sister's friends walk around half naked when they're visiting you?" Eve asked him. "And, you. You were half naked yourself when you opened the door. What was I supposed to think, Adam?"

"I know it looked bad, Eve." He pushed a hand through his hair in frustration. "I had just gotten out of the shower before you showed up. As for Megan, that's just how she is, I guess. Look, they ordered a pizza and when you knocked on the door, they must have thought the pizza had arrived and that's why she came to the door."

He picked up Eve's phone. "Call my place. Ask for Jill. She'll tell you that what I'm saying is the truth. Call." He reached out for her, but Eve backed away.

"Don't," she told him.

"Eve, I would never hurt you that way," he said quietly.

"I don't hurt, remember?" she said, walking into the living room and sinking down onto the couch, pushing a hand through her hair. "But, I do get pissed off."

"Tell me you believe me, Eve," he begged, falling to his knees in front of her.

Eve searched his face and found only sincerity there. "Fine," she said simply.

"Fine?" he exclaimed. "What's that supposed to mean? I beg you to believe me and all you can say is 'fine'?"

"What do you want from me, Adam?" she asked exasperated. "I told you I believed you, what more do you want?"

"At least tell me why you came to my apartment, Eve."

"To fuck you."

He moved closer to her and took her hands in his. "We could still do that."

"Don't you get it, Adam?" Eve said impatiently. "I came there to use you. Today has been a very frustrating day, and I came over for a release."

"And, you think I should be mad at that?"

"Why aren't you? Adam, I didn't go there to talk or to be comforted. What I wanted was sex. Nothing more."

"And you thought of me. It's perfectly normal to want to be with the person you..." He trailed off.

"You what?" She gave a mirthless laugh. "You can't even say it when you're talking about me, can you, because you know there's nothing in here." She raised one hand to her heart.

"That's not true, Eve," he protested.

"It is!" She closed her eyes for a moment. "The whole point of last night was to show you, to show myself, that there was more between us than sex, that I could give you more than sex."

She looked at him again. "But, I can't. I'll never be able to give you what you want. Adam, I can't be who you need me to be."

"Eve, you are what I want, what I need. I told you from the beginning that I would wait for you as long as I had to, and I meant it."

"You also told me the other night that you didn't know how much longer you could wait," Eve reminded him. "And, when we made love that night you felt the difference just as I did. I know you did."

It was dangerous to press him. She knew that. But they couldn't keep ignoring what was happening. Did she really have the right to keep holding on to him, knowing she couldn't give him more?

"Things haven't changed for me," he told her. "Yes, that night it was different because I tried to pull back from you. What I found, Eve, was that I don't want to pull away from you."

He touched her cheek and leaned in to kiss her.

Eve put her fingers to Adam's lips. "You can't stay," she whispered. Adam lowered his head and sighed. "I'm sorry," Eve told him. "I'm just not ready for that."

"What happened to you, Eve? Why can't you open up to me?"

"Don't. Don't try to analyze me. I'm not going to talk about my past. This is who I am, Adam." She lifted his chin so that he would look at her. "Why are you with me?" she asked.

"Because I love being with you."

"You love having sex with me."

"No, Eve. I'm in love with you."

Eve felt her entire body go rigid. "You don't even know me, Adam," she whispered.

"I know enough about you to know that the thought of not being with you is unbearable to me," he told her, reaching out to trace the outline of her face. "I don't want to be without you. I know that when I'm with you it kills me to know that you can't open up to me. And," he continued before Eve could say anything, "it kills me to walk out that door every night and leave you alone. I hate not being able to wake up with you in the morning and feel your body next to mine. I want to be able to roll over in the middle of the night and touch you, to make love to you."

"Adam."

"You don't have to say anything, Eve. I just wanted you to know how I felt. I'll try my best to give you the time you need because no matter how much you want to hide the fact from me, I know you care."

"I do care," she said softly. "I care very much for you. I just don't...I can't give you more. I don't know how."

"Then for now, this is enough."

Adam took Eve's face in his hands and brought his mouth to hers, kissing her passionately. Burying her hands in his hair, Eve moaned as his tongue merged with hers and he started unbuttoning her shirt. Eve lifted Adam's t-shirt over his head and ran her hands over his chest as he slipped her shirt off her shoulders and bent his head to roll his tongue over her skin. Eve tipped back her head and groaned as his hands traveled across her stomach, around to her back. His fingertips trailed down her spine, giving her chill bumps.

Adam stood up and held his hand out to Eve, but she remained seated and reached up to undo his jeans. God, she loved Adam's body. The way his muscles rippled when she touched him or the way he trembled when her mouth was on him. She took him into her mouth then, and heard him groan as he fisted his hands in her hair.

She was driving him insane with the things she was doing with that perfect mouth of hers and he fought to stay in control. When he couldn't take anymore, he brought Eve up to him and undid her jeans. "You're so beautiful," he whispered, his voice rough with desire, while his eyes roamed over her naked body.

Eve crushed her mouth to his and wrapped her legs around him when he picked her up.

"No," she said when Adam started for the stairs. "Down here. In the chair."

Sitting her down in the oversized chair in front of the fireplace, he got down on his knees in front of her. Adam took Eve's nipple in his teeth and gave it a gentle tug, nipping and licking his way down over Eve's stomach, loving the way she moaned and moved into him. His hands gently parted Eve's legs further and he dipped his head to taste her. Eve let out a cry as Adam's tongue probed her.

"Adam," she moaned, her breathing coming faster as she neared that first peak. Adam took her over the edge with his mouth, groaning as he felt her body tremble after the orgasm. Still gasping, her body gleaming with sweat, she pulled Adam to her and in a deft movement, was on top of him as he sat in the chair.

Eve leaned her body back, putting her legs over Adam's shoulders, resting her feet on the back of the chair, and took Adam inside her.

The position gave Adam a wonderful view of Eve and he let out what could only be described as a primitive growl as she rocked her body. He feathered his hands up her legs and turned his head to kiss the inside of her knees.

"God." Eve moved her body faster, taking Adam's hands in hers.

"Eve," Adam breathed. He wouldn't be able to hold back much longer, he thought. She was driving him mad. "Oh, Eve."

"Inside me, Adam. Now, now, now." They both cried out as the orgasm washed over them. Adam felt Eve tighten around him her body convulsing and he let himself empty inside her.

"My God, Eve," he groaned, his own body still trembling.

Eve brought her legs down, straddling Adam so that she could kiss him. "I'm not done with you," he whispered.

"Mmm. I hope not," she told him and kissed him again.

Adam stood up with Eve's legs locked around him and took her to the couch where he brought his body down on top of hers and moved slowly inside her.

"Am I hurting you?" he asked when she cried out, sharply.

"No! Don't stop," she told him and murmured his name, as he started moving again. "You feel so good," Eve whispered in his ear, flicking her tongue out to tease it.

"Wrap your legs around me, baby. Hold on to me."

"Make love to me, Adam," she begged him, moving her body under his, matching his rhythm. "Don't stop." Eve was desperate for him. The need, the pure lust for him, staggered her.

The sound of flesh against flesh, moans, and whispers filled the room as they brought each other to that peak again. Adam thrust inside her faster and faster as Eve tightened her legs around him.

"More, more. Give me more, Adam. Yes!" She raked her nails down his sweat slicked back as he obeyed. She wanted so much more than she deserved. Wanted to give so much more than she had.

"Eve." He buried his head against her shoulder. I love you, he mouthed, and came, taking her over with him.

They lay there together, spent and satisfied, Eve's fingertips roving over Adam's back. "Don't move," she told him when he stirred. "Stay inside me. Just for a little while longer."

"I'll stay inside you forever if you want me to, Eve." He kissed her mouth gently and played with her hair, hoping against hope that she would tell him to stay. Everything he ever wanted was right here beneath him, and yet she always held him at arm's length. He was never allowed to give her everything, or take more than she permitted.

"I should go," he said finally.

"Not yet. Please? Stay a little longer." Eve wanted to tell him to stay the night, to take her to bed and sleep with her. Why couldn't she? Why, every time when she opened her mouth to say those words, did nothing come out?

"As long as you want," he told her. "How is the gallery coming?" he added in an attempt to get his mind off of leaving. "It looked great when I was there earlier."

Eve smiled radiantly, and Adam's heart almost stopped at the pure beauty of her. "Thank you. It's coming along great. I think we'll actually be done ahead of schedule." She kissed his cheek and neck, her tongue tasting the salty residue of sweat.

"Lainey is doing a great job."

Eve's eyes fluttered closed when she heard Lainey's name.

"Yes, she is."

"I like her."

Eve thought of Lainey and the attraction they had to each other. "So do I."

"Jack is another story," Adam said, adjusting a throw pillow behind Eve's head.

"Why do you say that?" She remembered how upset Adam had been at the club then. "What did he say to you last night?"

"It was nothing," he told her, trying to brush it aside.

"Obviously it was something if you were upset. Tell me, baby."

"I don't think he likes you very much, Eve."

"Really? I'm heartbroken," she replied with dripping sarcasm. "Why do you feel that way?"

"I don't think he likes Lainey working, and he thinks you're a slave driver. I believe he thinks you're changing Lainey."

God, I hope so, Eve thought to herself.

"I took up for you," Adam went on, and earned another heart stopping smile.

"My hero." Eve brought Adam's mouth down to hers and kissed him fervently, her tongue dancing with his. She gasped and arched to him. "Mmm. I love it when you grow hard inside me," she said breathlessly.

Eve woke up in the middle of the night and reached for Adam. The bed was empty beside her and for the first time, Eve felt completely alone, and sorry that she had made him leave.

~ Eight ~

"Meredith!" Katherine burst into Meredith's office and slammed the door closed behind her. "The talk around the office is that Jackie was seen talking to Sumptor."

"Will you calm down? You scared the hell out of me!" Meredith sat back in her chair and put her hand over her pounding heart. Eve's warning had Meredith on edge with nerves. "What are you talking about?"

"Jackie. She was talking to Sumptor."

"So what?" Meredith asked irritably as she watched Katherine pace her office. "Sit down, you're making me nervous."

Katherine sat with a thump. "So what? So, maybe she's the reason Sumptor just showed up. It's just too much of a coincidence, Meredith. You need to call whoever it is you're dealing with and tell them that Jackie is endangering the plan."

"I can't call him. We're going to have to deal with Jackie ourselves until he contacts me."

"And, how do we do that?"

"We fire her," Katherine said simply.

"If we fire her what's stopping her from going to Eve and telling her everything?" Katherine demanded. "We have to do something to keep her quiet." Katherine began to pace again. Too much was riding on this and she couldn't let anything go wrong. Not only was there money at stake, but Katherine's freedom as well.

"Stop pacing. You're going to wear a hole in the floor, and I can't think with you distracting me," Meredith told her impatiently. "Look, I think I know exactly how to get rid of her and keep her from telling Eve anything."

Ten minutes later, Jackie sat nervously in Meredith's office, her hands neatly folded in her lap. "You wanted to see me, Ms. Lansky?"

"Yes, Jackie." Meredith's face was stern. "I've been checking some of your accounts today and have come across some discrepancies."

"I don't understand," Jackie protested. "I double check all of my accounts to make sure they're correct. Surely there's some mistake."

She took the papers that Meredith handed to her and studied them.

"This can't be right," she said in a low voice. "This isn't my work."

"Oh, I assure you, it's yours," Meredith told her. "And, what this tells me is that you are pinching from the company."

"No! That's not true! I would never do something like that!" Jackie's heart was racing. Why was this happening to her?

"I'm sorry but that's not what it looks like here," Meredith said, her unpainted fingernails tapping on her desk. "How do you think Sumptor will feel when she learns you've been stealing from her and her clients?"

"But, those figures are wrong! They're not mine! I'll just tell Ms. Sumptor..."

"Who do you think she's going to believe, Jackie? You or me? Particularly since the evidence is here in black and white."

Jackie started to panic. If she could just explain to Eve that she would never steal from her, Eve would know she was telling the truth. "What are you going to do?" she asked Meredith. "Well, I've decided that I'm not going to tell Sumptor about this little incident. That way no charges will be made. However, I'm afraid I'm going to have to let you go."

As Jackie started to cry, Meredith almost felt sorry for her. But, she's getting what she deserves for running to Eve, she told herself.

"Jackie, if I hear that you have gone to Sumptor after this discussion," she continued. "I'll have to show her this evidence. Charges will be made, and you'll be prosecuted for this. You don't want that do you?"

Jackie shook her head dejectedly.

"Good," Meredith told her, satisfied. "You can clean your desk out and leave quietly. We don't have to make a big deal about this. I'll just tell Ms. Sumptor that you found a new job and that you had to start right away. It's a simple as that."

Jackie rose slowly. "I don't know why this is happening, but I want you to know that I didn't do this. I won't let you get away with this. I'll find a way to prove my innocence."

"No, Jackie. I don't think you will," Meredith said quietly as the young woman left the room. She picked up the phone and dialed. "I need to leave a message. It's important," she said firmly.

There was nothing that she liked better than decisive action. Now that Jackie was out of the way, she and Katherine were home free.

"I need you to do something for me," Eve said to Mikey as she stepped out of the elevator. "I had a painting restored and they just called me to let me know that it's ready. Here's their card. Could you go and pick it up for me? Take a cab, it will be faster. Just tell them Eve sent you."

As soon as he was gone, she joined Lainey in the further room. Lainey's welcoming smiled faded when she saw Eve's face.

"You fucked him," she said accusingly.

Eve raised an eyebrow. "Excuse me?"

"You fucked Adam last night, didn't you?"

"Yes." She sighed when Lainey whirled away from her. "Lainey."

"I know we're opening tomorrow night," Lainey said, fighting back the tears. She had no right to feel jealous. Did she really expect Eve to never be with Adam again? It was unrealistic of her to believe that, so why did she feel so horrible. "But I need to ask you for the rest of the day off today."

"I'm sorry, Lainey," Eve said helplessly. She hated to see Lainey hurting this way, but the gallery had to come first. "That won't be possible."

"I have things I need to do."

"And, I need you here. This is a critical time for the gallery and everything needs to be perfect."

"Things are already perfect here!" Lainey snapped. "Everything about you is perfect. Some of us are not that lucky. All I'm asking is for today. I thought you told me you wanted to see me happy."

"I do." Eve tried to control her rising anger. "And I'm not perfect, Lainey. You're pissed at me because I had sex with Adam last night."

"No. I'm not."

"Don't lie to me, Lainey," Eve said sharply. "Did you ever stop to think about what it did to me when I had to watch you fucking Jack?"

She hated reminding Lainey of what had happened in her bedroom the night before, but it wasn't fair for her to be blamed for making love to Adam.

"Take the day," she said quietly and walked away.

Eve was sitting at the computer when Lainey knocked on the door an hour later.

"Come in," she called out, keeping her voice steady and professional although she ached inside. She hadn't been expecting Lainey to treat her with such resentment, and it hurt more than she ever imagined. She didn't look up when Lainey came into her office.

"Eve," Lainey said quietly. "I'm sorry. I don't know why I acted that way."

"I thought I told you to take the day off, Mrs. Stanton," Eve said as she continued typing.

It cut Lainey like a knife to hear Eve call her that. "Eve, please. I'm sorry. Will you look at me?"

Lainey didn't know which was worse; the cold shoulder Eve was giving her or the look that was completely void of any emotion. "Don't look at me like that."

"Make up your mind, Mrs. Stanton."

"Stop it!" Lainey cried. "Say my name damn it! And, don't look at me that way, as though we were strangers." She rounded Eve's desk and pushed Eve's chair back. "I said I was sorry. I have no explanation for how I just treated you."

"Back off, Lainey." Eve's voice was low and as cold as ice. She couldn't bear to have Lainey that close to her. It was dangerous to feel this much.

Lainey stepped back. "I'm sorry," she whispered and turned to run out, but was stopped by Eve's hand on her arm.

"I never meant to upset you, Lainey," Eve told her. "I just needed him last night."

"Just tell me that you didn't do it to get back at me for what happened."

"No! How could you think that? I didn't intend to tell you, but I guess I underestimated how observant you really are. I didn't do it to hurt you or get back at you. I did it for me, because I needed it. Do you understand?"

"Yes. Yes, I understand. I can't tell you that I like it, Eve, because I don't. But, there's nothing I can say about that. I have no right to say anything."

Eve rose and saw Lainey tense. "Don't worry. I'm not going to kiss you."

"What if I want you to?" Lainey whispered.

Eve lowered her forehead to Lainey's and tightened her grip on Lainey's arm. "Lainey, if I kiss you, I'm afraid I won't be able to stop there."

The intercom on Eve's desk buzzed and she swore. "Next time we do this, let's make sure we're alone and can't be interrupted."

"Yes?" she said into the intercom.

"Ms. Sumptor, there are two detectives here to see you," her secretary said. "Shall I send them up?"

Eve frowned. "Yes. Show them up please."

"Why are the police here?" Lainey asked, concerned.

"I have no idea." She turned to Lainey. "I noticed that the display isn't much different. Do you still feel that way?"

"Yes. A little, I guess. I'll leave you alone and go work on it."

"Thank you. Lainey, when you are working on the display," she called after her, "don't think about what hasn't happened yet. Think about things that you want to happen. Who knows? Maybe they'll come true."

"Another beautiful woman," Carter muttered as he watched Lainey descend the stairs.

"Yes, she is," Eve said, startling them by showing up at the door unexpectedly. "Come in, Detectives. What can I do for you?" Eve strode away from them, incredibly beautiful, even in jeans and a t-shirt. Harris cleared his throat and sat down in the one of the chairs in front of Eve's desk while Carter took the other.

"Ms. Sumptor," he said. "Do you know a Jackie Sawyer?"

"Yes, of course. She's one of my accountants at Sumptor, Inc. Why?"

"Is this Miss Sawyer?" Harris handed Eve a photo.

Eve felt a sinking in her stomach. "Yes," she said. "This is Jackie. What's going on, Detective?"

"Did you know that Miss Sawyer was embezzling money from the company, Ms. Sumptor?"

Eve registered disbelief.

"That's impossible," she said matter-of-factly.

"That's not what these say," Carter said and handed Eve copies of Jackie's accounts. "According to these records, she's been stealing from you for a few months now."

Eve focused her gaze on him. "Then those records are wrong, Detective Carter."

"Why are you so sure?" Harris asked her.

"Jackie has worked for me for two years, and I have never had any problems with her," Eve told him confidently. "She's a good worker and enjoys what she does."

"If you're so sure she wasn't embezzling, why did you have her fired?" Carter asked.

"I didn't," she told him. "This must be the work of Meredith and Katherine to get the attention off of them. You're falling into their trap, Detectives. Tell me you're not investigating Jackie."

Eve tried to relax, but couldn't get the rid of the sick feeling in her stomach.

"We have no choice but to investigate her, Eve," Harris said. "She was found in her apartment this morning, an apparent suicide."

A range of emotions flashed across Eve's eyes before they became flat again. Eve fought the wave of nausea that washed over her. Jackie was dead, she thought, sick with sorrow, an innocent young woman who had nothing to do with this little game that was being played. Sorrow was fast turning into anger.

"She didn't kill herself," she said her voice low and dangerous.

"This was found with her body," Harris said gently and handed Eve a letter that was bagged for evidence.

Though it took a tremendous amount of effort, Eve's hands were steady as she reached for the bag and read the note inside. '*I can't live with what I've done anymore. I'm sorry, Eve. Please forgive me.*' The muscles in Eve's jaw worked as she fought to keep her composure.

"She didn't kill herself," Eve repeated and handed the bag back to Harris.

"All the evidence..."

"I don't give a damn about the evidence, Detective Carter!" She interrupted with a burst of anger. "That young woman was not stealing from me and she did not kill herself." She pointed to the bagged note. "If you are using that as evidence, let me tell you one thing. Jackie never called me Eve."

"Eve, we can't base our investigation on that alone. This looks to be an open and shut case. But," Harris went on before Eve could protest. "I tend to agree with you and I'm not going to sweep this under the suicide carpet. This young woman had too much to live for. Did you know she was getting married in the spring?"

Eve closed her eyes and mourned for Jackie and her family. When she opened her eyes again they held grief, but the detectives would never know to what extent.

"No. I didn't know that," she said sorrowfully. "Tell me how she died."

"Ms. Sumptor..."

"Please," Eve pleaded with Harris.

"It was an overdose," Harris told her. Eve's eyes darkened so quickly that it almost scared him. And then, suddenly, she was expressionless again.

"I see. Have you notified her family yet?"

"We're going there next," Carter told her. "We wanted to talk to you first."

"Do you think I killed her, Detective Carter?"

"No, we don't think that, Ms. Sumptor," Harris answered for his partner. "We just wanted to see what you thought about this before going to her family and having to tell them their daughter killed herself. I believe now we have to tell them that foul play is expected and that we will do everything we can to get to the bottom of this."

"Thank you for coming to me with this," Eve said, rising, her voice dismissive. She badly needed to be alone to absorb the reality of what had happened. "If there is anything I can do to help you, please do not hesitate to ask."

"We'll be in touch," Detective Harris told her. "We trust that you will not try to take this matter into your own hands. Let us handle it."

"Detective Harris," Eve said as they reached the door. "Please tell Jackie's family that if they need anything at all to call me. I'll contact them myself, soon."

When they were gone, she slid down the wall and buried her head. "He's not going to get away with it again, Mama," she whispered in the empty room. "I swear he will pay."

Lainey turned from her display to see Eve descending the stairs. She couldn't pinpoint why she felt a chill when she saw Eve, but something was different.

"It's looking better," Eve said when she reached Lainey's side. "You must have a good imagination." Her smile didn't quite reach her eyes.

Lainey laid a hand on Eve's arm. "What is it, Eve?"

"Hmm? Nothing. You know, I'd change this sculpture. Perhaps use something less bulky. I'm sorry. This is your display, and you should choose what you want to use."

"It's all right. I want your opinion. Actually, I agree. I just haven't gotten there yet."

"Oh. Okay. Well, I'm sure you will have it done by opening tomorrow," Eve said distractedly.

"Yes, I will. Eve? Talk to me. Tell me what's wrong." Lainey felt more than slightly troubled by Eve's mood. She had never seen Eve be so disconnected from her surroundings.

"Where's Mikey?"

"He came back with the painting you sent him for and then went for a late lunch. Do you need him to do something for you? Can I do it?"

"No, I don't need him." Eve's voice trailed off as she walked to the window, resisting the urge to lose herself in Lainey's arms.

"Does this have something to do with why the police were here?"

"Lainey." Eve sat down on the windowsill, the backdrop of artistic buildings behind her, and waited for Lainey to take her place beside her. "I know that you weren't at Sumptor, Inc. for very long. But do you remember Jackie?"

Lainey remembered the young girl that had spoken to her on her first day at Sumptor, Inc. "Yes," she said. "I remember her. She was very nice to me. Why?"

Eve inhaled deeply.

"What is it?" Lainey demanded, a feeling of dread settling over her. "Is something wrong?"

"Jackie's body was found this morning in her apartment," Eve said quietly. "She died of an apparent overdose."

"Oh my God." Lainey leaned forward, resting her elbows on her knees and covering her face with her hands. "I-I don't know what to say. She didn't strike me as the type that did drugs."

"She didn't." Eve turned to Lainey. "She was murdered."

Lainey gasped. "I don't understand. I thought you just said..."

"It was made to look like a suicide," Eve said. Something in her voice turned Lainey's blood to ice. "I have reason to believe that this happened because of me."

"Why would you say that?" Lainey protested. "This can't be your fault, don't blame yourself."

"It is my fault," Eve said. "I'll have to live with that for the rest of my life."

The death of this innocent young woman made Eve fear for Lainey's safety. She would be damned if she would let her father take someone else so important in Eve's life.

"I don't want you coming here alone," she continued slowly. "As a matter of fact I don't want you going anywhere alone. I've hired more security, but promise me you'll have someone with you at all times."

"You're scaring me, Eve."

"I don't mean to frighten you." Eve took Lainey's chin in her hand. "Or maybe I do, I don't know. I just need to make sure you won't get hurt. If anything ever happened to you, I don't know..."

"Nothing's going to happen to me," Lainey told her with unconvincing confidence.

"You're right, because I won't let it," Eve assured her vehemently. "From now on, I'm going to pick you up and take you home. When you're not with me, you'll be with Jack."

"Eve, you don't have to do this."

"Yes, I do, Lainey," she murmured. "It would be safer for you if you weren't even working with me." Eve paused. "But, I don't want to let you go even though I know I'm being selfish."

"I don't want to go. I want to be here with you."

Eve ran a hand over Lainey's hair. "Good, because I want you here with me, and I'll do everything I can to protect you. He got past me this time," she added in such a low voice that Lainey barely heard her. "I let my guard down and he got past me. I never expected it. Never saw it coming. I won't let it happen again. I swear to God, I won't let it happen again."

"Eve! You're bleeding!"

Eve looked down at her fisted hand, her nails digging into her skin. "I'm fine."

"I'll go get something," Lainey said. "Stay here."

"I said I'm fine."

"And, I told you to stay here. I'll be right back."

"Who were you talking about?" Lainey asked when she had returned with a wet paper towel.

"What do you mean?"

"You said he got past you. Who's he?"

"I said that?" Eve frowned. Although she was tempted, she couldn't tell Lainey what was going on, not yet. "I guess I meant the person who did this. Everything is ready for tomorrow night," she said, changing the subject. "The champagne is ordered and will be here in the morning. The caterer will be here in the afternoon."

Eve's entire mood changed in the blink of an eye and had Lainey trying to catch up.

"I have interviews in the morning, and a photo shoot. Be ready to answer some questions. I'm sure the reporters will want to talk to you, too."

"Why me?" Lainey asked, suddenly nervous about tomorrow.

"You did a lot of this, Lainey," Eve told her. "Of course they are going to want to talk to you. I would wear something a little less casual though. But not that gray suit!"

"I'm sure I can find something else to wear," Lainey assured her. She still mourned for Jackie, but was glad that Eve was getting back to being Eve.

"How long do you think it will take you to finish the display?" Eve asked. It was important just now to get Lainey's mind off of Jackie's death. She was sure of it. Lainey was much too vulnerable at the moment. Eve could bear the weight of the grief she felt herself. For now.

"I don't know, maybe an hour or less."

"Good. How about after you're done, we go shopping? Tomorrow's a big day! We need to knock them dea..." Eve stopped abruptly. "We need to blow them away tomorrow. So, we'll need to dress to impress."

"Shopping sounds like a great idea!" Anything to get this tragedy off their minds, and at the same time allow her to spend more time with Eve, Lainey thought.

"Good. Just think of me as your muse while you're finishing the exhibit." Eve's mouth was a breath away from Lainey's. "Do me a favor?"

"Anything," Lainey told her.

"Put your arms around me."

Lainey took Eve in a tight embrace, and Eve did what she had wanted to do since coming downstairs. She lost herself in Lainey's arms, holding her there until the pain started to subside.

They both heard the elevator at the same time and broke away from one another as she watched Mikey come into the gallery.

'Thank you', Eve mouthed to Lainey, smiling.

"You're welcome." Lainey turned her attention back to her display. She could still feel Eve in her arms. With newfound inspiration, she knew exactly what she wanted to do with the display.

"Mikey!" Eve called. "Could you come over here for a minute, please?"

"Yes, ma'am?" Mikey sniffed, pushing up his glasses.

"Did you call the florist?"

"Yes, ma'am. The white roses will be here in the afternoon. Also, the limo service has reserved four white stretch limos for you and they'll be available to you all day."

"Very good," Eve said approvingly. It was a relief to be able to lose herself in the details of the gallery opening. Lainey's embrace had helped as well. She would never be able to push Jackie's death to the back of her mind. She didn't want to. But she needed to keep her mind sharp. "Why don't you take the rest of the day off? I think we're ready for tomorrow, and I'll need you here early, is that okay?"

"Yes, ma'am! I'm probably going to be too excited to sleep anyway!"

Eve chuckled. "Well, try to get some rest. It's going to be a very long day tomorrow. Have you thought about what you're going to wear? This is a big day for you, Mikey. Take this," she said, handing him some money. "And buy you something nice."

"No, ma'am. I couldn't..."

"That was an order from your boss," Eve interrupted. She slipped a pen from his shirt pocket and took his hand in hers. "Go here," she said, writing an address on his palm. "Tell them you need a blazer and some grey slacks for tomorrow, and a tuxedo for the opening. Tell them I sent you." Eve looked up at Mikey. "Are you bringing anyone?"

"I thought I'd bring my mom," he told her. "She's never been to anything like this before."

"Well, she should have the time of her life," Eve told him. "A limo will pick you up in the morning, and it's yours all day. I hope that you and your mom will have a wonderful time tomorrow."

"That was very generous of you," Lainey said after Mikey left. "I never knew you were such a softy."

"Get to work," Eve said with authority. "Hurry. We've got some shopping to do ourselves."

It was great to see the display transforming from sad and frustrated to joyful, sexy and seductive. Lainey's imagination must be working overtime, Eve thought.

Just then, Eve felt a chill course through her body and her smile faded. She turned her head slowly to look out the window and spotted him down on the street immediately. Eve lifted a hand and formed a gun with her thumb and forefinger. With a vicious smile she pulled the 'trigger' and watched him retreat quickly. "See you soon...Daddy," she whispered sardonically.

It infuriated him that she could make his heart pound painfully. The bitch, he thought. How had she known he was there? She had looked right at him, threatened him and he had run away like a scared little boy. I just wasn't prepared, he thought to himself, trying to soothe his ego. After all, it was the first time he had seen her since he had been released from prison and he hadn't known what an exquisite beauty she had become. As a girl she had been very pretty, but as a woman, her pure radiance had knocked the breath out of him. And those eyes, burning him with their heat. He would have to be more careful next time. And, seeing her now had him changing the plans he had for her. She would die, of course, but there was no reason he couldn't satisfy his craving for her first.

~ Nine ~

"Oh, Eve, I can't afford this place." Regretfully, Lainey looked at all the beautiful gowns around her. The cheapest one so far had been over twenty-five hundred dollars. Jack would have a fit if she'd bought a dress that expensive.

"Don't worry about it. It's on me," Eve told her as she picked out a red floor length gown and held it up to Lainey.

"No, I can't let you do that." Lainey caught a glimpse of her reflection in the mirror and sighed. "It's beautiful, but I just can't let you do that."

"You're not letting me. I'm doing it. Do you like this one?" Eve studied the dress critically and then put it back. "Maybe something a little less vibrant."

"You don't like red?" Lainey asked her.

"Yes, I do, and I'm sure it would look great on you. But, let's see what else they have."

"Your gown is ready for you to try on, Ms. Sumptor."

Eve turned and smiled at the short, hefty woman that spoke with a Hungarian accent. She wore glasses on the tip of her nose and a measuring tape around her neck.

"Thank you, Miss Hannah," she said, taking the garment bag from the older woman. "This is Miss Hannah. She's amazing. Give her some ideas of what you're looking for and she'll be able to help you. This is Lainey, a very good friend of mine. Will you help her find something special?"

"Yes. Come along." Miss Hannah grabbed Lainey's arm and pulled her with her. "You go try on that dress, Ms. Sumptor and you better not have lost any more weight. I've already had to take it in twice. Go, now. Hurry up."

Eve gave Lainey an apologetic smile, knowing what she was in for with Miss Hannah. The woman was amazing enough with clothes; her people skills were not as pleasant. "I'll be right out," she told Lainey and disappeared behind the curtain to change.

"Tell me what you are looking for," Miss Hannah said to Lainey.

"I'm not sure. Something elegant, I suppose."

"Yes, yes. Elegant. You are Ms. Sumptor's assistant, no?"

"Yes," Lainey answered, confused as to what that had to do with her choice of a dress. She let out an 'oh!' when Miss Hannah lifted Lainey's arms roughly and began measuring Lainey's waist.

"Take off your shirt," she told Lainey briskly.

"Excuse me?" Lainey crossed her arms in front of her.

"Take off your shirt, I need to measure you. Don't be silly, girl. There is no one here but me." Miss Hannah placed her thick hands on her hips and tapped a toe. "The opening is tomorrow night, no? We don't have time for you to be modest. You don't have anything I haven't seen."

Lainey looked around to make sure they were alone and slipped her shirt over her head, feeling self-conscious as Miss Hannah placed the measuring tape around her breasts.

"Mmm hmm," Miss Hannah said to herself, measuring Lainey's arms and her waist again. "I think I have something for you. You'll want sexy as well as elegant if you are going to be standing next to Ms. Sumptor tomorrow night. Ahh, Ms. Sumptor. It fits good, no?"

Lainey completely forgot about being half naked. Eve looked dazzling. The white gown flowed down the length of her slender body, barely touching the floor, and a slit ran all the way up to Eve's hip on the right side leaving one incredible leg completely exposed. The neck was a plunging 'V' that stopped at Eve's belly button and when Eve turned around exposing the entire length and breadth of her smooth, tanned back, Lainey almost moaned.

"Yes. It's perfect," Eve told Miss Hannah, but her eyes were on Lainey.

"I'll be right back with a dress for you, young lady. You can put your shirt back on now unless you want to wait since you'll have to take it off again."

She marched away, her short, brown hair swaying with each step.

"I think you should wait," Eve told Lainey, placing her hands on Lainey's trembling ones as she began to fumble nervously with her shirt. "No need to get dressed when you'll only have to take it off again. Besides, I'm enjoying the view."

"So am I," Lainey said. "You look incredible."

"Would it scare you to know that I want to kiss you right now?" Eve asked her in a low voice.

"Yes. And, no," Lainey answered. In fact, it was what she wanted. She had never felt this way before, and no matter how scary it was it was also exhilarating. "Would it shock you to know that I want more?"

They should stop doing this to one another, Eve told herself. These startling verbal encounters were becoming harder and harder to step away from. And that was dangerous. "We should remember we're not alone," she said, defusing the situation with a grin. "So? You like it?" She did another turn for Lainey, the white silk skirt billowing around her.

"Very much," Lainey told Eve. "Can I ask you something?"

"Anything."

"What is it with you and the color white?"

Eve laughed. "You know, I don't know. It's just my favorite color I guess."

"Well, it definitely works for you."

"Thank you. And, being half naked definitely works for you," Eve said with a flirtatious wink. "I can only imagine what you're like completely naked."

"Eve. You're embarrassing me."

"I'm turning you on," Eve contradicted her.

"I've found the perfect one." Miss Hannah ambled back into the room holding the same red dress Eve had picked out earlier. Eve and Lainey looked at each other and laughed.

"She's the expert," Eve said with a shrug. "Why don't you try it on?"

Lainey took the dress and disappeared behind the curtain, while Eve studied her image in the mirror.

"How does it look, Miss Hannah?" Eve asked, smoothing her hands over her hips.

"You lost more weight," she said accusingly. "But, not enough to ruin the dress." She turned Eve around and fiddled with the dress. "It looks good. Your young man will be wanting to get it off of you as soon as he can."

Eve laughed. "He does that anyway."

"Ahem." Both Eve and Miss Hannah turned to look at Lainey and Eve's smile broadened. "Do you like it?"

Even though it was not as daring as Eve's, the red suited Lainey and the material clung to her body revealing her curves.

The neck dipped low enough to show Lainey's cleavage, and the straps left her shoulders mostly bare. Eve let her gaze rest there for a moment before meeting Lainey's eyes. 'You look beautiful', she mouthed behind Miss Hannah. No single word could have affected Lainey any more than those unspoken words.

"She'll take it," Eve said aloud.

Lainey began to protest. She couldn't let Eve spend this kind of money on her. But she knew that, in the end, she would let it happen. Just as, in the end, she might just let a good deal more happen.

They walked out of the little shop with two bags each and headed for Eve's car. "Is Jack coming tomorrow?" Eve asked Lainey as they put their purchases in the back and slid in the front, next to each other.

"He's being a brat about it," Lainey told her, "but he'll be there."

"What about Darren and Kevin?"

"Oh, no. They wanted to see you, but they didn't want to go to some 'boring art thing'." Lainey quoted. "Jack's mother is going to keep them for the night."

"'Boring art thing'," Eve chuckled. "I guess when you're that age, art is boring unless it's done with crayons. I'm going to take you home," she added, pulling out into traffic.

"What about my car?"

"If you're lucky, someone will steal it and take it off your hands," Eve joked. "It'll be fine where it's at, but if you want, I can have someone drop it off at your house tonight."

"Eve, you don't have to baby-sit me."

"Lainey let me do this. Please? Besides, I like spending time with you."

They drove the rest of the way in silence, enjoying the cool night air and each other's company.

"Give me the keys to your car," Eve said as they pulled up in front of Lainey's house. "I'll have someone bring it out here to you in case you need it." When Lainey handed her the keys, Eve kissed her on the cheek. "If I'm not here to pick you up in the morning," she said, "wait for the limo. It's yours for the day. Get some rest, tomorrow is going to be hell."

With her garment bag over her arm, Lainey came to Eve's side of the car and, leaning in the window, kissed Eve gently on the lips. "Thank you," she said, and ran up the driveway.

"Wow!" Eve said to herself as Lainey disappeared into the house. Gathering her senses, she took one last look at the house and saw Lainey standing at the living room window. Eve wasn't sure how much longer she would be able to put up with this tension between them before acting on it. And if she did act on it, would she be risking the best friend she ever had?

"An innocent woman was killed today." Eve spoke into the headset as she paced her home office. "He will pay for that. He was also at the gallery today. I told you I was to be notified if he came anywhere near there."

"We don't know how he got around us, Ms. Sumptor," a man's voice replied. "We've been watching him and he hadn't budged."

"Apparently you're not watching close enough," she said icily. "You know him. You're aware of how clever he is. Don't let him fool you again. I've hired more people to watch his goons, so I want you to focus on him. Understood?"

"Yes, ma'am. We won't let it happen again. We've recruited a couple more guys ourselves."

"Do you trust them?"

"Yes, with our lives."

"You'd better. Or it will be your lives. He'll never let you get away with this if he finds out you're working with me, so watch your back."

"We'll take care of ourselves, ma'am. You just be careful. Word is he's coming after you with a vengeance now. He wants more than just your death."

"I know what he wants," Eve told him. "He'll have to kill me to get it."

"We're not going to let that happen. Do you want us to take care of Meredith and Katherine?"

"No. I'll take care of them. You just focus on Tony. Tomorrow is a big night for me and I don't want anything to mess it up. I don't think he's dumb enough to try anything with all of those people and the press there, but keep your eyes open. I'll be in touch."

Disconnecting, she took the headset off and tossed it on her desk. She picked up a dart and rolled it in her fingers. Spinning quickly she threw it at the target. "Bull's eye, you son of a bitch," Eve said with disgust as it hit Tony's photo right between the eyes.

Eve slipped into bed naked. After her last phone conversation, she had taken a long relaxing bubble bath to clear her mind. She had so much to do tomorrow and needed sleep to be sharp and on her toes, but she had to make this one last call before shutting her mind down for the night.

"Hey, baby," Eve said, her voice a seductive whisper.

"Mmm. Hey, yourself," Adam replied, his deep voice making Eve smile. "Where are you?"

"In bed. I thought I'd give you a call before I went to sleep."

"Are you ready for tomorrow?"

"Everything's set," she told him. "The gallery looks great, and everything has been checked and double-checked. I don't see anything going wrong."

Eve fluffed her pillows up behind her and lay back to unwind, with Adam's voice soothing her.

"But are you ready, Eve? This is a big night for you. I know the reopening of this gallery means a lot to you."

Adam loved just listening to Eve breathe. If they never said a word to each other on the phone, he would be happy to just listen to the soft sexy sound of her drawing breath.

"I'm ready. I've waited for this for a long time. It is a big night for me." Eve paused. "I'm glad you're going to be there with me, Adam," she said quietly.

"I'm glad you want me there with you, baby," he replied, his voice raw with emotion.

Eve closed her eyes and thought of the night before with Adam. "Last night was wonderful," she said aloud.

"Yes, it was." He had thought about last night every minute of the day. The only thing that would have made it better was if he could have stayed. He'd awakened in his own bed wanting to take her in his arms.

"When I woke up this morning, I could still feel you inside me," Eve whispered. "I wished you were here to make love to me."

"Eve..."

"Adam," she interrupted wondering why had she told him that? The need for him was growing more and more each day. She just wished she knew why, and if it had anything to do with her unexplored attraction to Lainey. She couldn't be falling in love with him. Could she? Whatever the reason, she had revealed too much to him. "I should go. It's going to be a long day tomorrow. I have to be at the gallery early, so I've hired a limo to pick you up. Is that okay?"

"Yes, that's fine." Hearing Eve tell him that she had wanted him there that morning had made Adam's heart soar. It was a step, Adam thought. He knew it was hard for her and that she needed more time and he was determined to give it to her.

"I'm sorry we can't show up together," she told him. "But, I think I'm going to enjoy seeing you arrive alone."

"Oh? Why is that?"

"So I can see you step out of the elevator, the best looking man there, knowing that you're there for me. Adam..."

Eve hesitated. What was she about to say to him?

"Yes, Eve?"

"Sweet dreams, l'amant."

"You're making it hard for me to hang up," he told her.

She heard the frustration in his voice and knew he wanted more. But her attention was being pulled in so many directions.

She wished she knew which route it would take.

Eve read the paper and drank her coffee as she rode the elevator up to the gallery. She had decided to wear black slacks that were made for her body, and a white button down long sleeve, silk shirt that was unbuttoned enough to expose the swell of her breasts. The look was stylish and sexy, and exactly what Eve wanted for the photo shoot. When the doors slid open, she stepped out of the elevator and into chaos. The gallery was full of florists and deliverymen, one of whom was leaning against a bronze statue of a boy holding a dolphin.

"That's a $500,000 piece you're using as your personal leaning post," she told him. And as the young man bolted upright, "Stand up straight. It's better for your posture."

"Ms. Sumptor?" A young, slender brunette stepped in front of Eve.

"Yes?"

"I'm Molly Burke with Ava's Exotic Flowers," the young woman announced nervously.

"Is something wrong?" Eve demanded.

"I'm sorry to have to tell you this, but only half of your order arrived." Whatever response the girl expected, it was most likely not the one that resulted.

"Do you expect the other half anytime before the opening?" Eve asked pleasantly.

"I don't know," the girl stammered. "They didn't say. I'm sorry, Ms. Sumptor." It was clear that she was waiting for yelling to begin.

Eve took another sip of her coffee. "Well," she said, "We'll just have to compensate by alternating the roses with orchids. If the rest of my order comes in before the opening, I'm sure you'll figure out what to do with them."

"Ms. Sumptor?" A lanky man replaced the young woman. He too, looked extremely nervous.

"Yes?"

"One of the cases of Dom Perignon was accidentally dropped and destroyed," he told her.

"Of course it was," Eve answered, amused. "Then this is what I would suggest you do, Mr.?"

"Banks. William Banks, ma'am."

"I would suggest that you go to every liquor store in the city and buy every bottle of Dom you can find, Mr. Banks," Eve said easily. "And if you can't locate enough Dom, buy Cristal."

"Yes, ma'am."

"Ms. Sumptor?"

"Don't tell me," Eve said as a middle-aged woman wearing a blue serving outfit stepped up to her. "The caterer has come down with a case of food poisoning."

"She has? But, I just spoke to her..."

"Calm down," Eve said, laughing. "I was joking. What is it?"

"Oh!" The woman put her hand to her heart and let out a relieved laugh. "The caterer wanted me to tell you that four of her people wouldn't be able to show up tonight. She wanted to know if eight servers would do instead of twelve."

"Tell her I expect her to find four more people," Eve said amiably. "I want twelve servers here tonight."

"Ms. Sumptor?" A familiar looking blonde holding a microphone and followed by a camera man blocked her way. "Lisa McBride, Channel Four News. I was wondering if you'd like to do your interview now."

"Could you hold on for just one moment?" Eve asked her. "I need to speak to my assistant. It will only take a minute."

She hurried towards Lainey before anyone else could stop her.

"Good morning," Lainey said, trying to hold back her amusement.

"Has it been like this all morning?"

"Pretty much. I think Mikey is going to have a nervous breakdown. He's been arguing with a woman from the flower shop about where the floral arrangements should go."

"I'm sure he can handle it," Eve told her, noticing that Lainey, too, had chosen to wear black slacks and a powder blue blouse, the top three buttons undone. "You look great," she told her, flattered with being imitated.

"So do you," Lainey told her.

Remembering the gentle kiss of the night before, Eve grinned and handed Lainey her coffee. "Finish it for me," she said. "I have to go and do interviews now. There's a blurb here in the newspaper about the opening. Your name's in it, too."

Lainey took a sip of Eve's coffee and smiled. Since graduating with a degree in art history, this was what she had wanted to do. She was part of one of the most prestigious galleries in the city, and she couldn't be happier despite all of the pandemonium around her. Today was going to be a long and wonderful day she thought.

Two hours, a dozen interviews and what seemed like thousands of photos later, Eve found her way back to Lainey.

"Thank God I don't have to do this every day," she said and positioned herself behind the display to hide. Lainey handed Eve a Diet Coke. "I stole it from the caterer. I think she's out for my head now," she joked and felt heat course through her body when Eve let out a throaty laugh.

"Well, thank you for risking your life for me. I'll make it worth your trouble. I promise." Eve's voice was raspy and sexy from talking all morning. "How are you holding up?" she asked Lainey, taking a sip of her stolen Diet Coke and studying Lainey over the rim.

"I think I'm doing pretty well," Lainey answered proudly. "Not bad for an old mother who hasn't worked in years."

Eve raised her brow. "An old mother?" She leaned forward slightly and lowered her voice. "You're too beautiful and exceptionally sexy to be called an old mother," she said softly, satisfied when Lainey flushed slightly.

The gallery was still in chaos, and would be until right before the opening, but there was something Eve needed to take care of and thought now would be the best time. Besides, she knew Lainey would be safe here until she could get back to her.

"I have to leave for a little bit," she told Lainey. "Do you think you can take care of things here until I get back?"

"I won't have to do interviews will I?" Lainey asked hesitantly.

Eve chuckled. "No. That portion of the day is over for now. There'll be more photographers and journalists tonight at the opening, but I'll take care of them. You'll be able to just enjoy the night."

"What about you? You should be able to enjoy yourself, too."

"I will. But, it all comes with the territory." Eve took another sip from her can and handed it back to Lainey. "I have to go. I shouldn't be too long. Don't leave the gallery. If you need something, have Mikey go get it for you."

"Eve..."

"Lainey. Do this for me, please?" Eve's eyes pleaded with her.

"Okay. I won't go anywhere. I promise."

"Thank you. If you need me for anything, you have my cell number. If you can't reach me on the cell, I'll be at Sumptor, Inc., so you'll be able to catch me there."

"Sumptor, Inc.? Oh, God, Eve. Do they know about what happened to Jackie?"

"Don't think about it," Eve told her. "Just focus on what's going on here and what has to be done before tonight. Okay? I'll be back soon."

Eve passed a deliveryman as she stepped into the elevator. "Watch out for her," she said without turning her head. "I want her safe."

Eve walked into Sumptor, Inc. and headed straight for Meredith's office. It didn't surprise her to find Katherine sitting there with Meredith.

"Ms. Sumptor!" Meredith exclaimed as Katherine stood up, ready to leave.

"Sit down, Katherine." Eve's voice was cold. "Don't say a word. Either of you. You will listen to me and you will remain silent."

Eve slammed the door shut behind her and positioned herself between it and the two women. "Yesterday," she said, "you fired one of my best employees."

"Ms. Sum..."

"I said you will remain silent, Meredith!" Eve shot the nervous woman a scathing look. "You'll explain to me why you let Jackie Sawyer go later. But, right now you'll listen. As of this moment, you do not have the authority to fire anyone. The only thing you two will be able to do is come in here, do your job, and go home. All of your security clearances have been revoked."

"But..."

"Shut up, Katherine!" Each word was said with a crisp iciness and Katherine shrank back in her chair. "Say one more word and I'll have you demoted to janitor by the end of the day. I want to know what happened. I want to know why Jackie isn't sitting at her desk today."

"Actually, Ms. Sumptor," Meredith said, obviously thinking fast, "Jackie found a new job."

"Bullshit," Eve interrupted quietly. "I detest liars, Meredith. Try again."

"Ms. Sumptor, I hate to have to tell you this," Meredith said stiffly. "I was hoping it wouldn't come to this, but, Jackie has been stealing money from the company and its clients. I let her go to protect you."

"Bullshit," Eve repeated, her eyes burning.

"I have all the evidence here in black and white," Meredith said hastily, shuffling papers on her desk trying to find the tainted accounts.

"What you have is nothing," Eve told her. "Do you have any idea who you are dealing with? Any idea what you've done? Jackie Sawyer's body was found in her apartment yesterday."

Meredith and Katherine gasped.

"You're both in way over your heads," Eve continued. "I could fire both of you right now, and I should. But, I won't. Not yet. But I swear to you, I will get to the bottom of this. Until then, I'm watching you. Don't think that I'm too busy with the gallery not to know what's going on here, I know more than you could ever imagine." Eve turned her icy stare to Katherine. "Get back to your office, now."

"Yes, ma'am." Katherine rose.

"Don't let me catch you here in Meredith's office again," Eve said with quiet fury, stepping aside to let her pass. "Do you understand?"

"Y-yes, ma'am," Katherine stammered.

Once Katherine was gone, Eve went to the desk and looked Meredith in the eye.

"Do you think this can't happen to you?" she demanded. "Do you think you're so important in this game that you're indispensable? You're not."

It gave her more than a little pleasure to see the sheer terror in Meredith's eyes, Eve discovered.

"You have no idea what you've gotten yourself into," she went on. "I told you not to cross me. I could be the only one that can save you."

Leaning her hands on the desk, she saw Meredith's hand move to the telephone.

"Who do you want to call, Meredith?" Eve said contemptuously. "Hmm? Who do you think is going to help you? Be careful who you trust your life with. You wouldn't want to make the wrong decision, would you?"

Eve straightened. She wanted so much to punish Meredith severely for what she had done. But Eve wasn't her father.

Meredith would suffer the consequences, the lawful way.

"Don't show up at the opening," she said. "The press will be everywhere, and I don't think you'll want a photo of me throwing you out in tomorrow's paper. Have a pleasant day, Meredith."

Eve stepped into the elevator and pressed the ground floor button. Reaching into her pocket, she brought out a small earpiece, fitting it into her ear. "Okay, ladies. Give me something to work with," she said to herself and listened.

"Jackie is dead!" As Eve expected, Katherine practically ran into Meredith's office the moment Eve was gone and slammed the door behind her.

"Jesus Christ, Katherine!" Still shaken by Eve's visit, Meredith jerked dropping the bottle of aspirin she had been fighting to open. "Are you out of your mind? Sumptor could come back."

"She's gone. I made sure she had left before coming in here." Katherine paced nervously around the office. "She scares me, Meredith, and, now this? You never told me he'd kill Jackie."

"I didn't know!" Meredith gave up on the bottle and threw it across the room. She pressed her fingers to her temples to try and relieve the pressure that was building up there. "All I did was leave a message that she should be watched. I didn't know he was going to kill her!"

Nausea threatened to take over as Meredith struggled to get back in control.

"Say his name, Goddamnit," Eve swore as she slipped behind the wheel of her Jaguar. "Give him to me."

"I want out!" Katherine said. "I didn't know murder was going to be involved!"

"There's no way out, Katherine. If we try to leave now, the same thing could happen to us." The sickness washed over Meredith, almost overpowering her. "We have to see this through."

"I didn't sign up for this, Meredith. We were supposed to just alter the books. Sumptor would lose money and possibly the company and we would get paid. No one was supposed to get hurt." Katherine sat down in the chair and covered her face with her hands. "No one was supposed to get hurt," she repeated.

Katherine looked up at Meredith. "She knows, doesn't she?"

"I don't know what she knows!" Meredith replied angrily. "He said he'd take care of her. Instead she's breathing down our necks." She sighed heavily. "I need to think. We've come too far, and now we could be accessories to murder."

"I had nothing to do with that! I don't even deal with − with whoever it is you are dealing with! I'm not going down for this, Meredith. You find a way to get us out of this or I'm going to Sumptor and telling her everything!"

Meredith watched Katherine storm out of the office before she picked up the phone.

"Eve! Where are you?" Relief flooded Lainey's voice when Eve called. The rest of the day had been a nightmare. Everything that could have gone wrong did, but Lainey had no intention of telling Eve that. She wanted Eve to know that she could count on her to take care of the gallery when she wasn't there. "How did things go?"

"As expected," Eve answered, deciding not to upset Lainey with any details. "I'm in the car, on my way home to change for tonight. I called to tell you to have the limo take you home so you can get ready, too."

"What about all of the people here?"

"Tell Mikey to stay there. I'll be there as soon as I can to relieve him."

"Are you sure? I can stay until you get here."

"Lainey. Go home and relax for a while. You don't need to be there early, so just come at eight. Jack will appreciate not having to be there any longer than necessary."

"If you're sure," Lainey said, slightly disappointed, but didn't know why.

"I'm sure," Eve said. "Are you alone?"

People surrounded Lainey, but she could have been alone since no one was paying attention to her. "As alone as one person can be in a room full of people. Why?"

"I just wanted to make sure no one would see you blush when I told you I can't wait to see you tonight," Eve said, her voice turning seductive. "It's going to be very hard for me to keep my eyes off of you."

"God, Eve," Lainey whispered.

"I'll see you tonight, Lainey," Eve said softly. Despite everything that had happened, Jackie's death, the confrontation with Meredith and all the rest, she could not get the picture of Lainey as she would look tonight out of her mind. She knew if she acted on her feelings it would complicate her life further than it already was. She was beginning to not care about the consequences.

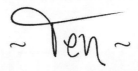

~ Ten ~

It was only a quarter to eight and already the gallery was full of people. Eve had been there for over an hour, ready to make an impact from the moment the first guest arrived.

She had chosen a sleek French twist for her hairstyle tonight, leaving her neck and shoulders bare except for a single diamond necklace. Diamonds also dripped from her ears, the only other accessory Eve wore to accent her white gown.

The look worked, as everyone had their eyes on Eve as much as the art she was presenting. Sipping champagne, Eve greeted everyone from artists to buyers to critics with the same congeniality and enthusiasm, answering questions, posing for photos, and charming those patrons who just didn't know if they wanted to spend that much money for art.

"It's simply fabulous, dear. I think you've outdone yourself." Mrs. Durham was in her fifties and married to one of the wealthiest men in the city. But, coming from old money, Mrs. Durham knew excellence when she saw it, even if she was a little eccentric herself. She was certainly a contrast to Eve's elegant beauty in her gaudy, multicolored gown and enough jewelry to light the midnight sky, but Eve liked her courage to go outside the norm.

"I saw you eyeing the Renoir over there," she said. "It's beautiful isn't it?"

"Don't give her any ideas now, dear." Mr. Durham appeared next to his wife wearing a traditional tuxedo. The two were complete opposites, and perfect for each other, Eve thought noticing his wife's input on his suit by the multicolored tie and cummerbund. "We're only here to look." He raised his champagne glass to Eve. "And to drink to your success, of course."

"Now, Mr. Durham, that is a great piece," Eve persisted teasingly. "Just imagine how it would look in your home. Could you really deprive yourself, or your wife, of such beauty?" She leaned closer to him, dropping her voice. "And, I do hear that your anniversary is coming up soon. What better way to say 'I love you' than an original Renoir?"

"You're good, young lady," Mr. Durham said with a chuckle. He shook his head in mock defeat. "Fine. We'll take it."

"Very good." Eve lifted her glass to him and gave Mrs. Durham a wink. "I'll make sure it's reserved for you." Just then, Adam stepped out of the elevator and caught Eve's eye.

"Now *that* is a work of art," Mrs. Durham told Eve under her breath.

"Yes, he is," Eve replied, aware that her pulse had quickened.

"Hi." As usual, the moment he saw Eve, he was hard and wanting her. The way her gown dipped so low in front made him want to trace his tongue over every exposed part.

Eve read Adam's mind and felt every inch of her heat with desire. "Hi." She kissed him sensually on the mouth.

"You look incredible," he said in her ear as he picked a glass of champagne from a passing waiter.

"Thank you, so do you. Mr. and Mrs. Durham, you remember Adam."

"Yes, of course. How are you?" Mrs. Durham said, holding out her hand.

"I'm well, Mrs. Durham. You're looking lovely as usual."

Dipping his head, he kissed the back of her hand. "Mr. Durham. Keeping in shape I see."

The older man shook Adam's hand heartily. "Just as charming as your young lady here, aren't you? It's good to see you again, Adam."

"Ms. Sumptor?" Mikey interrupted hesitantly.

Eve was pleased to see that the young intern was extremely prompt. Now here he was dressed sharply in an understated tuxedo. She made a mental note to thank Miss Hannah again for making him look wonderful and confident.

"Lizzie Chapman from The New York Times is looking for you," Mikey said, his eyes shining with what was clearly a new appreciation for Eve's beauty. "She would like to ask you a few questions for her column."

"Fine." Eve turned to her party with an apologetic smile. "Excuse me, please. Duty calls. Join me, Adam?"

As they crossed the crowded gallery, arm in arm, Eve felt a sense of pride. The turn-out was a tremendous success, and having Adam here with her meant more to her than she had ever imagined possible.

"Look at this photo, Mikey," his mother, a tall, thin woman with a mane of black hair, wearing a simple black dress which accented her still youthful figure, said to him. "Look at how the photographer uses the light."

"It's great, Mom," Mikey told her. He was so excited that she could be here, and so proud to be with her. Because of Eve, he knew that he fit in with all of the other people at the gallery with their expensive clothing. And his mom, thanks to her innate fashion sense, might have bought her clothes at the consignment shop but looked, as usual, like a million.

"These are the kind of photos I want to take, Mikey," she said dreamily.

"You will, Mama. You're doing so well."

"I don't know mi hijo. The artist who took this is muy talentoso."

"Thank you," Eve said from behind them. "This is one of my favorites, as well."

"Ms. Sumptor!" Mikey wondered how long she had been there. "Um, Mama, this is Ms..."

"Eve." Eve offered and held her hand out to Theresa.

Mikey had told her that Eve was beautiful, but Theresa had never imagined that his employer possessed the stunning quality of the woman she saw standing before her. Suddenly nervous, Theresa fiddled with the crucifix around her neck.

"I can't thank you enough for everything that you've done for my son, Ms. Sumptor," she said.

"Your son is an asset to Sumptor Gallery and we're lucky to have him," she told the proud woman with her hair pinned back in an inexpensive, rhinestone butterfly clip. "He's extremely intelligent and knows his art."

"Ella es casi demasiado buena ser verdad, Mikey. ¿Ella es verdadera?" Theresa said to her son and was surprised when Eve answered herself.

"I'm real," Eve said with a chuckle. "I live on the theory that good people deserve good things in life. Mikey tells me that you are a photographer yourself. I'd love to see your work sometime."

"Oh, I just play around," Theresa said humbly. "I don't have your talent."

"I don't believe that," Eve replied. "Art and talent are not learned, Theresa, they're something you are born with."

When she introduced Adam to Theresa, he kissed the back of her hand charmingly, and Eve found that she was overjoyed having a man as wonderful as Adam on her arm.

Their conversation ranged from art and photography, to Mikey's schooling and what he was like as a boy – much to Mikey's embarrassment and Eve was sincerely enjoying her time with them.

It was a welcome break from all of the commotion around her. Though Eve's attention was occupied by her company, she was still aware of the people surrounding them. She was also aware that someone was missing. Eve lifted Adam's arm to look at his watch.

"That's the hundredth time you've checked the time, Eve," Adam said curiously.

"Sorry. It's just that Lainey's not here yet. Have you seen her, Mikey? Has she called?"

"No, ma'am."

"I'm sure she'll be here soon," Adam told her.

"Yes, I'm sure she will. It was wonderful meeting you, Theresa," Eve said, trying to ignore the gnawing sense of uneasiness that was beginning to overwhelm her. It wasn't like Lainey to be late for something like this, not when she knew that the opening meant so much to Eve. "Please, enjoy the rest your evening. I will talk to you again, I'm sure, before the night is over." Eve looked at Mikey. "If Lainey calls come and get me please."

"Yes, ma'am." Mikey agreed and watched as Eve walked away arm in arm with Adam. He knew he would never be able to compete with Adam, so settled with if Eve was happy, Mikey would be happy for her.

"Are you worried about Lainey, baby?" Adam asked Eve.

Her nails have been biting into his arm and that was unlike Eve.

"I'm sure she just got held up," Eve told him, frowning. "It's just not like her to not phone."

"Do you want to call her?" Adam began to reach for his cell phone.

"No. I'll give her a few more minutes." Knowing that an experienced undercover bodyguard was protecting Lainey, Eve tried to tell herself that there was no real reason for her to be worried. But that didn't mean she wasn't. She would just feel much better when Lainey got there.

"Miss Eve." Henry, looking very stylish in his suit and tie called to her.

"Henry. How are you, handsome?" Eve smiled, joining him.

"I'm great. You're looking mighty fine tonight."

"Shall we leave these two alone?" Adam came to Trudy's side and kissed her on the cheek.

"If it means I get to spend time with you, then let's go." Trudy, a dark, petite woman with streaks of gray in her black hair that was done up in a bun, patted Adam's face and linked her arm with his.

"Sorry, Trudy. This one is not up for grabs," Eve said playfully and pulled Adam to her. "How are you tonight, hun. You look wonderful."

"Thanks to you and that Miss Hannah. That woman is a miracle worker with clothes," Trudy said and smoothed her hands over the purple velvet dress Miss Hannah had made her.

"Ms. Sumptor?" Lizzie called from in front of Lainey's display. "We were wondering if you could tell us a little more about this display. It's very ingenious. Wherever did you come up with the idea?"

As if on cue, the elevator door opened and Eve turning, locked eyes with Lainey with a disgruntled looking Jack beside her, feeling relief and joy flowing through her. "I agree," Eve said to the reporter. "It is very ingenious, but I didn't do it. You would need to ask Lainey Stanton."

"I'm sorry I'm late," Lainey told Eve under her breath, taking a flute of champagne from a passing waiter.

"It's okay. Ms. Chapman from The New York Times was just commenting on your display."

"I was just telling Ms. Sumptor how creative it was. It's so full of intrigue and sexual energy," Lizzie told Lainey. "What was your inspiration?"

"I suppose inspiration for something like this comes naturally when you work with someone like Eve," Lainey said, sipping her champagne.

Eve raised an eyebrow, surprised by Lainey's bold and honest answer. "Well, what a wonderful compliment," she said aloud when everyone else remained in stunned silence.

"I agree," one of the art critics said finally. "Ms. Sumptor definitely inspires this kind of feeling and I believe Ms. Stanton captured it beautifully."

"Just make sure you spell Lainey's name correctly in your article," Eve teased, and then turned to Jack. "I know you've just arrived, but I need to steal your wife for a moment. I have to bring her up to speed on what's been going on." Smiling pleasantly at Jack, who frowned in return, she turned her attention back to the rest of the group. "Excuse us. Please, eat, drink, buy." When a photographer shot her kissing Adam, she shook her head and led Lainey upstairs to her office. She needed desperately to know what was going on.

Eve opened the door of her office for Lainey and motioned her inside.

"I'm so sorry I'm late," Lainey began hastily.

"Lainey," Eve interrupted. "Are you okay?"

"Yes. Yes, I'm fine." Lainey took a deep breath, trying to hold back the tears. "I just can't believe I was late."

"What's wrong?" Eve asked softly. From the moment Lainey had stepped out of the elevator, Eve had known something was not right.

"Nothing," Lainey lied and tried to make her smile sincere.

Eve sighed. "Lainey, if you don't want to talk to me about it then you don't have to, but please don't lie to me."

"I just don't want to ruin your night," Lainey told her, not meeting her eyes.

"Honey," Eve said, her voice quiet. "You're not going to ruin anything. Talk to me."

Lainey saw the genuine concern in Eve's eyes and knew she could tell Eve everything.

"Jack and I have been fighting all evening," she said. "I don't know what his problem is. He just started in on me when we were getting ready, all of a sudden saying he wasn't going. I told him I needed to be here, that I couldn't be late, but he just didn't care. I had to practically beg him to come."

"Why didn't you just come alone?" Eve was becoming tired of Jack's attitude with Lainey, but kept her opinion to herself.

"I should have," Lainey said with a sigh. "He's not speaking to me anyway. It's never been this bad, Eve. We've had fights before, but not like this."

"I'm sorry."

"It's not your fault."

Eve came close to Lainey and took her champagne from her setting both glasses on the desk. "We both know it is my fault," Eve said softly. "I know that Jack doesn't like me."

"That's not true!"

"That is true," Eve replied with a shrug. "He thinks I'm changing you."

"You are," Lainey whispered.

Eve gently pulled Lainey even closer. "It looks as though I'm not helping you very much with your marriage."

"You're helping me find myself," Lainey told her. "Until I figure that out, my marriage will stay the same. Jack will get over this working thing. Things will be normal again. Boring, but normal. But I don't want normal anymore, Eve. I want excitement and passion."

Eve lifted her hand to Lainey's face and feathered a finger across her cheekbone. "You look beautiful," Eve murmured.

"You're the first one to tell me that tonight." Lainey could barely breathe with Eve so close. Why couldn't she just gather the nerve to kiss Eve, as she wanted?

Eve sighed heavily and shook her head. "Has anyone ever told you that you are married to a fool?"

Lainey laughed. "I believe you may have mentioned that before."

Eve smiled. She trailed a finger down Lainey's cheek, and then on impulse, she touched Lainey's mouth lightly with her fingertip. Lainey's lips parted in response. The urge to kiss Lainey was almost irresistible. "I'm sorry." Eve cleared her throat. "We should get back. I'm sure everyone is wondering where we are." She tucked a strand of hair behind Lainey's ear. "Don't let Jack get you down. You've worked hard for this. I'm proud of you."

Lainey's heart swelled. Hearing Eve say that she was proud of Lainey meant more to her than Eve would ever know.

"Come on," Eve said gaily, taking her hand. "Let's go sell some very expensive art."

Eve and Lainey were rarely able to exchange more than a few words with one another for the remainder of the evening. Eve was pulled in so many directions by so many people that Lainey could barely keep up. As for Jack, his attitude didn't improve any to Lainey's dismay. And the more he drank, the worse it became.

The secret looks Eve would give her when no one else was looking were the only thing that kept Lainey sane. She tried to avoid Jack for as long as she could by talking to Mikey and his mother, and getting to know Henry and his wife.

Meanwhile, Lainey overheard Eve breeze through conversations that ranged from art to politics. She watched Eve charm clientele into buying art they didn't even know they wanted, laughing at the men's awful jokes, and winking surreptitiously at the wives who got what they wanted. Lainey herself sold a few paintings by following Eve's example, which only seemed to piss Jack off even more. Whenever he had the chance, he told her that she was flirting too much, or acting too much like Eve.

"I'm leaving, Lainey," Jack told her for the umpteenth time. "You're either going with me or you can find your own ride home."

"The limo is mine, Jack. *You* find your own way home," she whispered angrily at him. "Why are you doing everything you can to ruin this for me?"

"I'm not doing anything," he told her in a low voice. "I came here didn't I? I came to support you when I don't even like this sort of affair. You know that."

"You are not supporting me. You have been bitching all night." Lainey smiled momentarily while the Durham's passed them. "Why are you doing this?"

"I'm not going to discuss this here, Lainey. If you want to talk then you'll go home with me now." He set his glass of champagne down on the lap of a bronze figure of a seated woman that was worth over a quarter of a million dollars and walked away from her.

Picking up the glass, Lainey went to find Eve. She just needed to talk to her, hear her say that everything would be all right. Then she saw Eve with her arm around Adam's waist, saw him bend to kiss her and, with tears threatening to fall, she walked quickly to the elevator.

"Mrs. Stanton?" Mikey called after her.

Lainey willed the elevator to open. "I'm sorry Mikey. I have to go," she told the confused intern before the doors slid shut, hiding her falling tears.

~ Eleven ~

Adam followed Eve out of the limo in front of her apartment building, and took her in his arms.

Unaware that she was being watched, Eve reached up and kissed Adam passionately, moving her tongue in an erotic dance with his.

"Are you sure you don't want me to come up?" Adam asked against her mouth.

"No." Eve laughed quietly and kissed him again, this time less passionately. "Mmm. Rain check?"

"Soon," Adam answered and kissed her. "Dream of me."

"Dream of me," Eve told him and disappeared. This was the way it had to be for now, she told herself.

Across the street, Lainey wiped away her tears and laid her head on the steering wheel. She should have stayed home, but she needed to see Eve. It had been hell watching Eve with Adam, and Lainey had been relieved when he had left instead of going up with Eve. Now she sat there trying to find the courage to go up to Eve.

Once inside her apartment, Eve walked into the living room and threw her keys on the coffee table along with the diamond earrings she had removed in the elevator. She thought about calling Lainey as she had wanted to all night long. But, there was Jack to consider. It would only make things worse for Lainey if she were to call and that's the last thing she wanted to do. But she had been worried ever since she had looked around the gallery and found that both of them had gone. When Mikey had told her they had left separately, she had become increasingly concerned. But, she reminded herself now as she went upstairs to shower, their quarrels were none of her business – unless, of course, Lainey wanted them to be. All she wanted was for Lainey to be happy.

"Damn it! Just go up there," Lainey scolded herself as she sat alone in her car. She had told Jack that she was leaving two hours ago and not to wait up because she didn't know if she would be home, thanking God that the boys were at their grandparents and wouldn't have to hear their parents fighting. But that was in the past. What Lainey was thinking about now was Eve and how she would react to Lainey being there. She didn't think Eve would turn her away, not when she needed a friend. So why was she too scared to get out of the damn car and go up to her apartment?

"Coward," she said with disgust and laid her head on the back of her seat. What would Eve do if she were in her place?

Eve wouldn't be afraid. She wouldn't be sitting in the car at almost one thirty in the morning debating about what to do. She would be doing what she wanted to do. Lainey took a deep breath and made her decision.

Eve splashed water on her face and looked in the mirror.

"Coward," she said to her reflection and snatched up a towel to dry her face. Why hadn't she just kissed Lainey tonight in the office?

She tried to tell herself that it wasn't what Lainey needed, that kissing her would only cause problems. But she knew that wasn't her reason. It was only an excuse so she wouldn't have to think of how it frightened her to know how much she really wanted to kiss Lainey. Of course she had thought about the consequences, knew that in the end it would turn out badly. She just didn't know how long she could want Lainey and have the strength to keep turning away.

Eve shook her head and walked out of the bathroom, still naked from her shower. Picking up Adam's shirt, she slipped it on, and went into the sitting room. With a groan, she plopped down on the couch and contemplated calling Lainey again. She pushed her hands through her hair and frowned when she heard the doorbell. The only person that it could be was Adam. Oh God, she didn't know if she could deal with him at this hour. But it wasn't Adam standing on the other side of the door.

"Why are you out alone?" Eve demanded. "Especially at this time of night?"

"Do you want me to leave?" Lainey asked. Her heart was pounding so hard. Eve's reaction wasn't the one she had been hoping for.

"How did you get here?" Eve asked as she closed and locked the door.

"I drove."

"Alone? Lainey, I told you not to go out without someone with you. I thought you understood."

"Eve, please. I'm here and I'm fine. Stop treating me like a child."

"I'm not," Eve protested. "I'm sorry, Lainey. It's just that with everything going on, I can't help but worry. Just like I was worried when you were late tonight."

"I explained that," Lainey said, angry now. How could she have known how Eve was going to react? One minute she acted as though she wanted to be with her more than anything, and now Eve seems as though she doesn't even want her there. She probably wanted Adam to be here instead. "You said you understood."

"I do! I didn't mean that. I'm just trying to tell you that I worry. That's all. I care about you, Lainey. I don't want anything to happen to you."

"Well, I'm fine."

You're pissed off, Eve thought. "What happened to you tonight?" she said aloud. "Why did you leave without telling me?"

"I tried to telling you but you were busy." Lainey remembered Eve clinging to Adam's arm, lifting her lips to his.

"You could have come to me. I'm sure I wasn't that busy with a client that you couldn't say goodbye to me." Eve felt her own temper rising.

"I didn't say you were with a client. You were busy with Adam. I didn't want to disturb you."

"That's the most ridiculous thing I ever heard!" Eve exclaimed in disbelief. "Is that why you're mad? Because I was with Adam? Lainey, you know I'm seeing him, that's not going to change." She paused. "What makes you think he's not here now?"

"Because I saw you kiss him goodnight," Lainey told her, flushing. "I've been here for the past two hours."

"You've been out there, alone, for the past two hours?" Eve said. "When I distinctly asked you to not be alone, to always have someone with you? What if something had happened to you?"

"I've just told you that I've been waiting and watching for you for hours and all you are worried about is if something had happened to me?" All at once, the events of the night hit Lainey brutally and she realized that she was emotionally exhausted.

Eve saw the weariness in Lainey's face and her heart broke for her. Taking her coat, she noticed that Lainey had changed into Levis and a large t-shirt that made her seem younger and more fragile than ever.

"You wouldn't be here if you weren't upset, and I don't think it has everything to do with me being with Adam," Eve said. "Lainey, tell me what happened."

"He left me. Jack. He left me at the gallery. Just walked out."

"Son of a bitch," Eve whispered.

"My choice of words were a little harsher," Lainey said with a little laugh.

"Why didn't you come and get me?"

"I told you why."

"Goddamnit, Lainey. You should have come to me. I would have been there for you. You didn't even give me a chance."

Eve was right. Lainey hadn't given her a chance and the shame of it only brought more internal fatigue.

"I'm sorry," she said, her voice trembling with threatening tears. "I didn't know what to do. When I saw you, you were smiling at Adam, kissing him. I just couldn't handle it with everything that was going on, so I left. I went home, tried to just forget it all, but ended up fighting more with Jack."

"About me?" Eve asked softly.

"Yes. And everything else."

"Sit down, honey." Eve took Lainey's arm and guided her to the couch, and sat in front of her on the coffee table. "Talk to me."

"It's all the same thing, Eve. He doesn't want me to work. He doesn't think you're a good influence on me. He doesn't think I'm being a good mother."

"He said that? The fucking bastard," Eve whispered vehemently. "Don't you ever let anyone tell you that you aren't a good mother, Lainey. I've seen you with your sons. What Jack said to you was just plain stupid. He only said it to make you feel bad. Do not give him that satisfaction, honey."

Lainey tried holding in the tears, but it was becoming increasingly difficult.

"You don't care what he says about you?" she asked.

"I don't give a shit what he says about me," Eve told her. "He doesn't know me, and what he says is based on ignorance. But, he says what he does about you because of some asinine jealousy. He's trying to hurt you, Lainey. He knows you're a great mother, sweetie, and he also knows how much it means to you. If you let him, he will push your buttons until you give him what he wants." Eve took Lainey's hands in hers and squeezed them. "Don't give in to him," she said. "I know it seems to be the easiest thing right now. You're tired of fighting and you just want it to stop. But, honey, you lose that way. You lose more of yourself, you lose self-respect and believe it or not, you lose part of him. The part that respects you and loves you for who you are."

Lainey just stared at Eve. "For someone who claims to know nothing about love, you sure have the right things to say."

Eve gave Lainey a small smile. "I've never been in love, Lainey, but I've seen how it works. I've seen too many people take each other for granted, or expect things that are simply not possible. I've seen people get hurt when they couldn't deliver the impossible, when they were too intimidated to fight back. I won't sit back and watch that happen to you." Eve said it so quietly, so intensely it made Lainey frown.

There was something more in Eve's words, a mixture of anger and sorrow that made Lainey wonder what had happened to make Eve feel that way. Before Lainey could ask anything, Eve continued.

"What was it about tonight that made him this way? Was it just the opening and your part in it? Or was there something else?"

Lainey lowered her eyes. How could she tell Eve the truth without making her feel miserable? She could lie and tell Eve that it had just been the opening. After all, it wasn't really a lie; she would just be leaving parts out.

"Don't even think about lying to me," Eve said, taking Lainey by surprise. "You're like an open book sometimes. Every emotion, every thought is written across your face. Tell me the truth. What did I do to provoke him?"

There was no use in arguing with her, Lainey realized. She had had enough of arguing anyway.

"It was the dress," she said softly. "He didn't understand why you bought it for me. He said that he didn't know why you were flaunting your money, that you must have some secret agenda."

To Lainey's surprise, Eve chuckled. "Secret agenda? Like what? To get you into bed with me?" They looked at each other then, their unspoken attraction growing with each second. "Do I need to buy you dresses for that, Lainey?" Eve asked softly.

How could Lainey tell her that that was exactly what she wanted? And, she certainly didn't need gifts to do it.

"I'm so confused," Lainey said touching her forehead. "I don't know what the hell is going on in here anymore. Or here," she added, putting a hand to her heart. Before Lainey knew it, she was crying the tears she had fought so hard to keep inside.

"Oh, Lainey." Eve got to her knees in front of Lainey and put her arms around her and held tight. "It's okay, baby. Let it out." Eve gently rubbed Lainey's back, trying to soothe her.

Instead of soothing, Eve was arousing. Feeling their bodies pressed against each other's was more than either woman could take. Eve brought her hand up to Lainey's hair and stroked softly.

She felt Lainey's heart pounding against her chest and closed her eyes. She knew what she was about to do would change everything, but Eve just didn't have the strength to back away this time. She turned her face into Lainey's neck and breathed her in.

She smells so good, Eve thought. Gradually she backed up until her face was inches from Lainey's. Very slowly Eve leaned in and kissed Lainey gently, sensually on the mouth, and heard Lainey moan softly. Eve kissed her again, bringing her hand to Lainey's face and touching her cheek.

"Do you want me to stop, Lainey?" she whispered.

All Lainey could do was shake her head. She couldn't believe what was happening although she'd dreamt about it since she first laid eyes on Eve. Now it was happening and Lainey was petrified and incredibly excited at the same time.

Eve saw the fear in Lainey's eyes, but also saw the yearning. This time, instead of the kiss Lainey was expecting, Eve licked Lainey's lips from the bottom to the top. The sensation of Eve's tongue made Lainey tremble and sigh with longing. Eve touched Lainey's lips with her fingertips and looking into Lainey's eyes, gently parted them. Moving to Lainey, she kissed her again, touching her tongue to Lainey's. Both of them made a sound of pure pleasure at the contact and Eve moved closer, urging Lainey to give her more. Lainey deepened the kiss, boldly intertwining her tongue with Eve's and feeling a devastating thrill of pleasure when Eve moaned in her mouth.

Eve trailed her hand down Lainey's arm, taking her hand in hers. Slowly, Eve brought Lainey's trembling hand up to her breast, pressing until Lainey squeezed gently. Then Eve's hand left Lainey's and reached over to cup Lainey's breast.

Lainey gasped and backed away suddenly. The sensation was too intense. She had never felt the way she had when Eve's hands touched her, and it was more than she could handle. "I'm sorry," she said and stood up, walking away from Eve.

"No. It's okay." Eve touched her lips with her fingers. Heart pounding, she struggled to get back in control before turning to Lainey. "It's okay. I shouldn't have taken advantage of the situation."

"You didn't! Please don't think that, Eve."

"I did. Look, I should have known better. The moment just got the best of me." She saw the hurt in Lainey's eyes. "There are so many reasons why this shouldn't happen, Lainey."

"Are you telling me you didn't want this?" The pain in Lainey's heart was too much to bear.

"That's not what I said," Eve said softly. "Lainey, every time I've been near you, alone with you, wanting to kiss you, wanting you, I've stopped. If we went as far as we want to go with each other, it could only turn out terrible in the end."

"That's not true," Lainey told her.

With tremendous effort, Eve kept herself from putting her arms around Lainey. "It is. Honey, you're married. If we do this, you will regret it..."

"No! I wouldn't!"

This time Eve did embrace her. "You will," she promised. "You'll start to feel guilty about what we are doing, about hurting your husband. Eventually, you'll start to resent me and I would lose this friendship that I've come to cherish so much."

"I would never regret that, and I could never resent you."

"Yes, you would. It's inevitable," Eve said gently, and then, before Lainey could object again, "It's late. I don't want you to drive home alone, so you're staying with me tonight."

"I'm so glad you said that. I told Jack I wasn't coming home. I told him I would be here if the boys asked for me."

Eve took Lainey's hand. "Come on. You're exhausted. We're going to bed. What's wrong?"

"I can just sleep down here on the couch," Lainey demanded. Now that the opportunity to be with Eve had come, Lainey was terrified.

"No, you can't. Come on." Eve led Lainey to her bedroom, up the platform to the bed and began the process of taking Lainey's shoes off. "Relax, honey."

Lainey was torn between continuing to protest and just giving in to the need. She was exhausted, even though just being on Eve's bed made her want Eve even more. And Eve had practically told her that nothing would happen, or should happen between them.

"I'm going to sleep on the couch in the sitting room," Eve said.

"No. I can't let you do that."

"Lainey, it's okay. Do you want something more comfortable to sleep in?"

"No, this is fine."

Going to her dresser, Eve took out a white silk nightshirt.

"Just in case you change your mind," she told Lainey as she turned down the bed and tucked Lainey in. Fighting the urge to get in with her, Eve sat on the side of the bed and pushed Lainey's hair back with a fingertip. "Get some rest. You've had a long day today; hopefully you'll sleep well. We'll talk more in the morning. Good night."

"Good night. Thank you," Lainey said even though she knew she wouldn't be sleeping. She needed Eve too much. "Thank you, for everything."

Eve sank onto the couch with a sigh. She touched her lips, thinking of Lainey's on hers. The taste of Lainey lingered on Eve's tongue. She wouldn't get any sleep tonight, she knew. Not with Lainey so close and wanting her the way she did. Restless, she propped her feet up and settled in for a long, sleepless night.

"Eve?"

Eve looked up abruptly, dropping her fingers from her mouth, and saw Lainey standing at the entryway between the bedroom and the sitting room. She had changed into the silk nightshirt and looked at Eve with a pleading desire. Eve rose from the couch fighting the battle between what she desired and the inescapable loss that she will ultimately face. And then, Eve made her decision and began kissing Lainey passionately. Lainey responded with more fervor than Eve had dared to imagine.

Reluctantly, Eve broke the kiss and led Lainey back into the bedroom and once again climbed the steps of the platform to the bed. She turned Lainey to her, never saying a word, and began unbuttoning her own shirt. As Lainey watched, Eve ran her hands down, parting the shirt slowly, and then slipped it off her shoulders letting it fall to the floor.

Lainey let out small sound of pleasure as she took in the magnificence of Eve's bare body. She had known, without doubt, that Eve would look wonderful naked, but she wasn't prepared for the exquisite beauty. Nervously, Lainey reached up to unbutton her own shirt, but Eve stopped her.

"Eve..."

"Shh." Eve put a finger to Lainey's lips. Reaching down, she slowly unfastened the buttons of the nightshirt and slid it off. Lainey's heart raced, and her blood pounded in her ears as Eve's eyes roamed over her body, covered now only by the thin material of her bra and panties. And then Eve was tracing Lainey's lips with her tongue, moving to her chin, teasing with her lips and teeth.

Lainey angled her head when Eve got to her neck and groaned when Eve's teeth nipped her. She put her hands in Eve's hair, pulling her closer and felt Eve's movements become more eager.

"If you want to stop, just tell me," Eve whispered her mouth close to Lainey's ear.

"Don't stop," Lainey told her, her voice hoarse with need.

Eve nudged Lainey onto the bed and lay next to her, their bodies touching. She brought her lips to Lainey's and kissed her deeply, letting her hands explore her trembling body. She traced the lacy edge of Lainey's bra, loving the satiny, smooth feel of Lainey's skin. Eve lowered her head to replace her fingers with her tongue, rolling it over the swell of Lainey's breast, moaning when Lainey arched her back. She took the edge of the bra and lowered it, exposing Lainey's breast, and caught the taut nipple between her teeth. Lainey cried out in ecstasy as Eve's teeth and tongue worked wonders.

Eve sat up, bringing Lainey with her, sliding the straps of Lainey's bra off her shoulders. Lainey fell back against the bed, gasping as Eve's lip traveled down over her stomach. Her body shook uncontrollably and she gripped the sheets, arching her body as Eve's hands cupped her breasts and Eve's tongue worked lower on her stomach, outlining her panties at the waist. She felt Eve slipping off her panties and felt as though her body would explode at any moment.

Eve saw Lainey close her eyes and took a moment to just look at her. Such an amazing body, Eve thought, so soft, so beautiful. She marveled at how steady her hands were as she touched Lainey. Inside, she was feeling anything but steady. Each kiss, each touch was a new sensation for Eve, and she loved the learning process. As much as she wanted Lainey's hands on her, Eve wanted to please Lainey more, to show her how it felt to be cherished. She lay next to Lainey again, their naked bodies meeting and fixed her eyes on Lainey's.

"I don't know what to do," Lainey whispered.

"Just relax," Eve told her. "Let me please you." She lowered her mouth to Lainey's and kissed her gently. "This is for you, don't think about anything. Just feel."

Eve spread Lainey's legs gently. Running her fingertips up Lainey's thighs, she felt Lainey tense.

"You can tell me to stop at any time, honey," she murmured, her voice hoarse with desire.

Lainey shook her head. "I don't want you to stop." She gripped the sheets above her head as Eve continued her journey up her thighs.

Eve touched Lainey, feeling her soft velvety wetness and let out a guttural sound of pure pleasure from the sheer thrill of finally knowing what it was like to feel Lainey.

Lainey cried out, her body convulsing as the orgasm rocked her.

"I'm sorry." A tear rolled down Lainey's cheek. She hadn't expected that to happen and was embarrassed and disappointed at letting Eve down.

"It's okay, baby." Eve licked the tear from Lainey's cheek. "It's only your first one. I'm not done with you."

"You don't understand," Lainey said sadly. "I've never had multiple orgasms. I don't think I can."

As soon as the words were spoken, she realized that Eve was arousing her again, massaging her gently and teasing Lainey's ear with her teeth.

"You've never been with me before. You can, and you will," Eve vowed. "I promise." She felt Lainey move her body as she urged her up again.

"Eve." Lainey moaned, stunned by what was happening to her. She became aware of Eve moving and watched in bewilderment as Eve positioned her body over Lainey's. Then Eve brought her head down to kiss Lainey's breasts, moving lower to her stomach. When Lainey realized where Eve was going her pulse jumped, her body shook and her breathing quickened.

"I'm not as confident as you think I am," Eve told her, reading Lainey's mind. "Tell me if I'm doing something wrong."

Lowering her head, she tasted Lainey.

"God!" Lainey arched her body, as Eve probed her with her tongue.

Moaning, Eve pulled Lainey closer, their movements becoming faster and more desperate. She brought Lainey to the edge with her mouth, and then sent her tumbling over by using her hands.

"Oh my God!" Lainey opened her eyes when she felt Eve's warm body next to hers again. "What did you do to me?"

Eve frowned slightly. "You didn't like it?"

"Are you kidding me? I loved it! I've never felt anything like that before."

Eve gave Lainey a shy smile. It was the first time she had seen Eve be anything but confident, and she found it endearing.

"I'm certainly not a virgin, but what you just did to me made me feel like it was my first time."

Eve propped herself up on one elbow. "I'm glad you enjoyed it." She bent down and kissed her playfully.

"What about you, Eve?" Lainey said, blushing. "How was it for you?"

"I've dreamt of doing these things to you since the first moment I saw you," Eve confessed. "You're surprised. Well, it surprised me, too. No one has ever had that effect on me."

No one except Adam. Eve didn't want to ruin the moment by mentioning his name.

"Especially another woman."

This moment was so surreal to Eve. Just days ago, she would have never imagined that she would be in bed with anyone other than Adam. Now, with Lainey beneath her, she can't imagine being anywhere else.

"I don't know what it is about you," Eve continued. "It's more than your amazing beauty. Don't do that. Look at me." She waited until Lainey looked at her, then bent down and kissed her passionately. "Believe me when I tell you that you are beautiful."

Lainey's breath caught when Eve's hand found its way back between Lainey's thighs. "Eve. I can't possibly do that again." She buried her hands in Eve's hair as Eve proved her wrong all over again.

Eve made love to Lainey until they were both spent. They fell asleep in each other's arms, a first for Eve, each dreaming of the incredible time they just experienced.

Eve woke to Lainey's head on her breast, her legs wrapped around her. She was immediately aroused as well as a bit unsettled by Lainey's presence. She felt Lainey stir and stretch her body. The movement was so sensual, the contact to Eve's naked body so unbelievably rousing that she had to control the urge to wake her. Suddenly awake, Lainey tensed and tried to move away without waking Eve until she felt the other woman's arm tighten around her.

"Mmm. Don't move. I like you like this," Eve told her sleepily. "Are you okay?"

Lainey relaxed considerably when she felt Eve's arms tight about her. "I'm not so nervous anymore," Lainey said, snuggling closer.

"You were nervous?"

"A little." Lainey shrugged, adding sheepishly, "I didn't know what to expect, the morning after."

"I understand," Eve said and brushed a finger down Lainey's nose. "This is all very new to me. I mean waking up with someone next to me. No one has ever stayed the night before."

"Not even Ad..."

"No one," Eve interrupted.

"So, I'm your first?" Lainey teased.

"Yes, in more ways than one," Eve laughed.

"I like being your first," Lainey said with a note of quiet seductiveness.

Eve raised an eyebrow and bent to kiss Lainey's waiting lips. The kiss turned passionate, both women moving closer to deepen it. Eve felt Lainey's hand lightly caressing her breasts and felt her nipples harden in response. Then Lainey's touch traveled timidly to Eve's stomach, inching lower. God, she wanted Lainey to touch her so badly that it took all of her strength to stop her.

"Mmm. Not yet," Eve whispered hoarsely, covering Lainey's hand with hers.

"You don't want me to touch you?" Lainey asked, baffled.

"I do. Just not yet." She brought Lainey's hand up to her breast, holding it there. "Touch me anywhere but there. Touch me everywhere but there, Lainey."

"Okay." Lainey didn't understand, but she would give Eve all the time she needed. When Eve was ready, Lainey would try to please Eve as much as Eve had pleased her.

Eve turned, pushing Lainey down against the bed and bent her head to kiss her. She slipped her hand between Lainey's thighs. "Soon," she whispered. "Very soon." Eve worked on Lainey, arousing her lazily, teasing Lainey's tongue with her own.

Lainey had begun to move her body with Eve's rhythm when the phone rang startling them both.

"Don't stop," Lainey begged Eve. Obediently, Eve ignored the ringing of the phone, letting her machine pick up.

"It's Eve. You know what to do."

"This is Jack Stanton." Eve froze. "Could you tell my wife to call me, please? Tell her, her sons are wondering why their mother didn't sleep at home last night. Thank you."

He hung up the phone with a distinctive click and Eve and Lainey just lay there for a moment, speechless, both of them motionless.

Lainey put her hand on Eve's and began moving it again. "Don't stop. Make me forget, Eve. Make me forget everything."

Eve rolled on top of Lainey and positioned herself between Lainey's legs, bringing Lainey's knees up. She placed her hand between their bodies and slowly put her fingers inside Lainey.

"More, Eve. Please," Lainey pleaded breathlessly.

Eve moved faster, deeper, harder until both of them forgot everything except each other.

Only when she woke up, stretching and reaching for Lainey did Eve find her gone. It was nearly ten in the morning, and she realized that she had been asleep for two hours.

"Lainey?" She listened for an answer or the sound of the shower, anything to indicate that Lainey was still there. As she tossed her legs over the side of the bed, she saw Lainey's jeans and t-shirt on the floor. Blowing her hair out of her eyes, she let out a small laugh. Never before had she been afraid that someone wouldn't be there when she woke up. Picking up Adam's shirt, she slipped it on. She felt incredible. The night, and morning, she had just shared with Lainey was more beautiful than she could ever have imagined. But it infuriated her that Lainey was able to slip past the bodyguards she had hired, and now she had to attend to those matters. Looking at the door to make sure she was alone, Eve picked up the phone and dialed.

"It's me," she said. "I'm not alone so I don't have much time. First, is Katherine safe?"

"Yes, ma'am."

"Is she cooperating?"

"Not yet."

"Convince her that she needs to work with you. I don't care how you do it, just do it. Listen, Lainey Stanton showed up at my apartment last night. Alone. I told you to watch her."

"We did ma'am. She went home. We just assumed that she would stay there."

"Never assume anything. If anything happens to her..."

Eve's voiced trailed off. She didn't want to think about that because she knew now that she couldn't bear it if something happened to Lainey. "Don't slip up again. Understood? She's with me now. I'll be in touch when I need you."

Lainey's with me now, Eve thought to herself, but for how long? She picked up Lainey's shirt and held it to her nose. Eve closed her eyes and breathed in Lainey's scent. What in the hell was it about Lainey that had such a hold on her? She folded the shirt and put it with Lainey's jeans, then went in search of Lainey.

She found Lainey downstairs standing in front of the stove, wearing Eve's silk nightshirt, cooking.

"You're cooking for me?"

"Oh!" Lainey jumped and dropped the spatula. For a long moment they looked at one another and remembered the way it felt to be in each other's arms.

"Sorry. I didn't mean to scare you. Smells good." Eve bent and sniffed Lainey's neck. "Smells even better."

"There's bacon and scrambled eggs," Lainey said, tucking her hair behind her ear. "I didn't know what you liked, but I took a gamble since all of this was in your refrigerator."

"Are you nervous again?" Eve asked her, putting her mouth to Lainey's ear. "Don't be nervous with me ever again." She turned Lainey until they were face-to-face and kissed her. "Please?"

"I promise," Lainey said. "Now, go sit down. It's almost ready. I made some fresh squeezed orange juice for you."

"I had oranges?" Eve picked up the glass and took a drink.

Lainey laughed. "Yes. Don't you know what you buy at the grocery store?"

"I don't usually shop." Eve took another sip of the orange juice. "This is really good. Thank you. You know you didn't have to do all of this."

"I wanted to." Lainey transferred the eggs and bacon, together with pancakes on to a plate for Eve and set it down in front of her. Her husband's call that morning had upset her, but right now she didn't want to think about him. Right now, all she wanted was to have this time with Eve. "What do you mean you don't shop?"

"I have someone that does it for me," Eve told her. "I just can't seem to find the motivation to go to the grocery store." As Lainey reached for the coffee cups Eve was rewarded with a glimpse of Lainey's bare ass.

"You look great in my shirt," Eve told her. It felt wonderful to wake up and have someone there to do something as simple as have breakfast together. It felt amazing to have that someone be Lainey.

"I feel great in your shirt," Lainey told her, reaching over the island to kiss Eve as she set the coffee cup in front of her.

"How do you know where everything is?"

"What?"

"The knives and forks, the plates, the coffee cups. How do you know where to find them?"

"Oh. I had to search for them, but I did that before you came down." Lainey chuckled. "I should have just told you that I'm just good."

"I would have believed that," Eve said and winked wickedly.

"Eat," Lainey ordered with a giggle and handed Eve a fork.

"Hmm, that would be my pleasure. But, can you wait until I have some food?"

"Eve!"

Eve laughed. "I'm joking. But, only a little. You know, usually I don't eat breakfast, but after last night, I'm famished. Another first for me." She took another forkful of eggs. "Mmm. These are very good."

"Thank you. They're my sons' favorite." Lainey's voice trailed off as she thought about Kevin and Darren and the phone call Jack had left.

"Lainey? Honey, are you okay?" Eve reached over and took Lainey's hand.

"Yes. I can't stand it when he does that to me. Like it's all my fault that we're fighting. He always tries to make me feel guilty about the boys."

"Do you? Feel guilty?" Eve asked and held her breath for the answer.

"Not about being with you, Eve. But, what am I going to tell my sons? Daddy and I are fighting so I went over to Eve's house to sleep with her?"

"Is that why you slept with me?" Eve asked her, suddenly wary. "Because you are fighting with Jack?"

"No! God, Eve, I didn't mean it that way. I'm sorry."

"It's all right. I just needed to make sure that wasn't the only reason."

"It's not even a reason. I was with you because I wanted to be, because I needed you. You must know that. I've needed you since the moment you said hello to me, even though I don't know why because this has never happened to me before."

She walked around the island to Eve and touched her cheek.

"Last night meant so much to me. And, this morning. And the next time we make love."

"The next time?" Eve teased, pulling her closer, between her spread legs. "Will that be soon?"

"I hope so." Lainey ran her fingers through Eve's hair, tugging Eve to her and kissing her sensually.

"Mmm. So do I." Eve wrapped her legs around Lainey's waist. "But, first, let's work out this guilt you have about Kevin and Darren. I don't think you should give them too many details about what you've been doing. But, tell them the truth."

"The truth. It's not that simple with kids, Eve."

"Yes, it is." Eve sighed when Lainey looked unconvinced. "I don't have kids, baby, but, I do remember what it's like to be one and have your parents tell you that everything is fine. My mother tried to tell me every day that nothing was wrong. And every day, I knew she was lying and I hated her for that, that she didn't love me or trust me enough to tell me the truth. She died before I had the chance to forgive her, or help her.

Don't do that to them, Lainey. Kids are more perceptive than you want to believe. Tell them the truth."

Lainey touched Eve's cheek with her fingertips. It was the first time Eve had told her so much about herself. Lainey's heart opened even more.

"So, I tell them the truth," she said. "But what happens if they think it's my fault that Jack and I are fighting? What if they blame me because I'm working just like Jack does? What if they think I'm angry at them or that I'm here instead of at home because I don't want to spend time with them?"

Eve took Lainey's face in her hands. She hated seeing her worry so much and she hated what Jack was doing to her. "Then we prove them wrong."

"How?"

"We take them somewhere. Do something fun with them."

It was, Lainey discovered, an idea that excited her. Something about it seemed so right. "Where?"

"I don't know." Eve chuckled. "We can take them to Coney Island, or the zoo, or rollerblading around Central Park. We can take them anywhere you want, baby."

"We?"

"Yeah." Eve lowered her gaze, unsure. "Unless you don't want me to go."

"I do!" Lainey traced Eve's lips with her finger. "You want to spend time with my kids?"

"Of course. Honey, I like Kevin and Darren, very much. I would like the opportunity to get to know them better."

Lainey stared into Eve's eyes. "What is it about you, Eve?" she asked quietly, still tracing Eve's mouth. Suddenly she crushed her mouth to Eve's and kissed her deeply, as their bodies fused.

Eve moaned, fisting her hands in Lainey's hair. Reluctantly she broke the kiss, and pressed her forehead to Lainey's. "Hmm, why don't you call them and see if they'd like to go do something with us. You can use the phone in here if you want." She kissed Lainey gently on the lips again. "I'll just finish eating – my breakfast."

Lainey laughed and playfully pushed away from Eve. "You do that. Just leave room for dessert." Lainey took a deep breath as she picked up the phone. "I hope Jack doesn't answer," she said.

"So do I," Eve mumbled and took a bite of her pancakes.

"Hi, honey," Lainey said when Darren answered. "It's Mommy."

"Hi, Mommy! Where are you?"

"I'm over at Eve's house."

"I wanna be at Eve's house, too! Daddy said you didn't come home. Why not? Did you want to have a sleep over with Eve?"

Lainey looked over at Eve who was watching her as she ate. "Something like that, honey," Lainey told him.

"We don't got to go school Monday, Mommy. Are you going to be here?"

Lainey heard the uncertainty in his voice. "I'll be there, Darren," she promised him. "Or, you can come to work with me. Would you like to do that?"

After all, she told herself, Eve had told her to bring them any time.

"Yeah! I wanna go! Okay. Do you want to talk to Daddy?"

"No. I want to talk to you and Kevin, honey. Is your brother there with you?"

"He's upstairs. Do you want me to go get him?" She heard him drop the phone before she could answer. "Kevin! Mommy's on the phone! Here he is, Mommy. He told me to stop yelling at him."

Lainey realized that, although Eve had taken up nearly every waking moment for the past twenty-four hours, she had still missed the boys with all their clamor, all their enthusiasm. And love.

"Tell him I asked him to get on the other phone, please."

"Where are you?" Kevin demanded. "Daddy said you didn't want to be here so you left. What happened, Mom? Did we do something wrong?"

Eve watched Lainey slam her hand to the wall and was immediately up and beside her, taking Lainey's hand in hers.

"No, honey. You didn't do anything. I'm not upset with you, either of you. Darren are you listening?"

"Yes, Mommy."

She squeezed Eve's hand for support. "I want to talk to you both about what's going on, but not on the phone. So, Eve and I wanted to know if you guys would like to do something fun today. We could all hang out and talk. Just be together. Would you like that?"

"Yeah!" Both boys yelled in unison. "Is Daddy going to?" Darren asked.

"No, honey. Just you two."

"But, Eve will be there right?"

"Yes. Is that okay?"

"Yes! I wanna see Eve. Kevin, don't you wanna see Eve, too?"

"Yes. I don't mind if she goes, Mom. I like her."

"Can we stay the night at Eve's, too, like you?"

Lainey laughed. "Well, I don't know. Let me ask." She moved the receiver away from her mouth. "They want to know if they can stay the night at Eve's, too."

Eve smiled that devastating smile of hers. "Of course," she said, and then dropped her voice to a whisper. "As long as mommy stays, too." She ran a finger down the front of the nightshirt, between Lainey's cleavage.

Lainey closed her eyes, her heart pounding. She grabbed Eve's hand to stop her, but ended up bringing it to her wetness between her thighs. Lainey covered the mouthpiece of the phone again and moaned quietly. *Don't stop*, she mouthed to Eve, then cleared her throat.

"She said yes." Lainey held the phone away from her ear and chuckled when both boys shouted in delight. "Why don't you boys go and pack..."

"Make sure they pack a bathing suit," Eve whispered, her hand still working Lainey slowly.

Lainey frowned slightly, confused, then shrugged. She was having a hard time concentrating on anything but Eve's fingers.

"Eve said to make sure you pack your bathing suits."

"We're going swimming?" Darren asked, his voice excited.

"I guess so. Go pack and we'll be there to pick you up soon. Don't tell your daddy where you're going. I'll tell him when I get there. I love you both."

"Love you!" They said together, then hung up and ran to get packed.

Lainey hung up the phone and arched into Eve's hand. "More," she whispered.

Eve pushed Lainey back against the wall and drove her up, making her cry out as she came. She brought her lips to Lainey's and kissed her gently. "Mmm. Wonderful." She stepped back. "Why don't you go up and take a shower. I'll clean up down here."

"You have a maid, why don't you come up with me," Lainey said, reaching out to tug Eve back to her.

"I'd love to, but she knows my habits. I think she would have a heart attack if she saw two plates and the remains of breakfast. I wouldn't want to do that to her." She kissed Lainey again, longer and deeper. "I'll be up soon. I promise."

Eve waited until Lainey was out of hearing range before picking up the phone. "Hi, it's Eve," she said in a low voice. "Get the plane ready. I'll be there with three guests in about an hour. Destination is Orlando. I know I don't have to tell you that discretion is key. Oh, and make sure there are fun snacks on the plane, and some video games." She hung up and turned to look at the dishes and thought of Lainey, naked in the shower upstairs.

"What am I? Insane?" she asked herself and, forgetting about the dishes, she ran up the stairs.

Eve pulled her Jaguar into Lainey's driveway and cut the engine. "Are you ready for this?" she asked Lainey, glad that her uneasiness was hidden behind her sunglasses.

Lainey took a deep breath. "I think so."

"How do you think Jack is going to take this? You and the kids staying with me?"

Lainey let out a cynical laugh. "Not well. Now, ask me if I care. I need this, Eve. To be with my sons. To be with you." She wanted so much to reach over and take Eve's hand. Instead she opened the car door. "Let's do this," she said.

Eve followed Lainey to the house determined not to let her emotions show, especially to Jack.

"Prepare yourself for getting jumped on," Lainey warned her as Rufus began to bark.

"Mommy!" Instead of Rufus, Darren ran up and jumped into Lainey's arms. Rufus had his sights on Eve again and bounded towards her.

"Hi, honey!" Lainey planted a kiss on the top of Darren's head while Rufus attacked Eve. "Should we help her?"

Darren giggled. "Nah. Eve can take care of herself, Mommy. She's so cool."

"Why thank you, Darren," Eve said, taking Rufus's ears in her hands and giving him a little shake.

"Where do you think you're taking my sons?" Jack came up behind Lainey and gave Eve an unhappy look.

"Now they're your sons," Lainey murmured before turning to face her husband. "I'm going to spend the weekend with them, Jack," she said. "Do you have problem with that?"

"Yes. If you want to spend time with them, then you can do it here. At home."

"Honey, why don't you go upstairs and get your stuff for this weekend," Lainey told Darren and set him down.

"Daddy wouldn't let me pack. He says we're not going anywhere."

Lainey gave Jack a nasty look over Darren's head. "We're going, honey. Go upstairs and tell your brother to get ready, too. Okay? I love you."

"I love you, too." Darren looked up at his father with uncertainty, but seeing that Jack wasn't paying any attention to him, he made a break for it and ran upstairs. Lainey waited until Darren was out of sight before turning on Jack.

"How dare you undermine me and tell the boys they're not going with me?"

"How dare you make plans for this weekend without asking me first?" Jack countered. "I will not discuss this while we have - company." He inclined his head to Eve.

"We will not discuss this at all!" Lainey hissed. "I'm taking the boys and we're spending the night at Eve's house. We're going to have fun spending time together, and then we're going to talk about what is going on between us." Spinning on her heel, Lainey started upstairs just as Jack caught her arm.

"What is going on between us, Lainey?" he said angrily. "Ever since you started working with this woman, you've changed. What's happening to you?"

"Careful, Jack," Lainey said with quiet fury. "Let go of me."

"You're not taking them."

"I am! Let go, Jack! You're hurting me!"

Eve put her hand on his arm. Her touch was light, but he could feel the heat radiating from her. And there was rage in her eyes.

"I'm parched, Jack," she said, her voice expressionless. "I don't suppose I could trouble you for a glass of water."

For a moment he looked as though he might say something none of them would ever forget and then, releasing Lainey, he slammed his way into the kitchen.

"Go get ready, honey," Eve said softly. And then, as Jack appeared holding a glass, "Why don't you keep me company while Lainey gets ready?"

"This is all your fault," Jack told her. "She would have never done something like this. Everything was fine before you came along."

"If that were true, Lainey wouldn't be so desperate to change now." Eve moved closer until her face was inches from his. "If you had made Lainey happy, Jack, she wouldn't have come to me."

"Hi, Eve!" Kevin said, jumping from the third step to the bottom of the stairs.

"Hi there. You all set to go?"

He glanced quickly at his father then back at Eve. "Yes. Hey, where are we going?"

"Yeah! Tell us!" Darren chimed in, shifting a small backpack on his shoulders. They were both dressed in chino shorts and t-shirts, and looked ready for fun.

"Ah, ah, ah. That's a surprise," Eve told them. "Wait and see."

"Aww, come on!" Both boys chorused.

"If I told you, it wouldn't be a surprise," she winked. "Your dad was just telling me that he hopes you have a great time."

"Really, Daddy?" Darren squealed as he ran to embrace his father's waist. "You're not mad anymore? You won't be angry at me because I wanna go with Mommy?"

Jack looked at Eve, taken aback. "Of course I'm not going to be angry with you, Darren," he said.

Lainey came down stairs, carrying to small suitcases in time to see Jack sink to his knees in front of Darren.

"Kevin, come here, please." He waited until Kevin joined his brother. "I'm not mad at you. I was just – well, I was upset that I wouldn't be spending time with you this weekend. But, Eve is right. I hope you have a wonderful time with your mommy, and I want you to tell me all about it when you get back. Okay?"

"Okay. I think we're going swimming!" Darren said with a giggle.

"Really? Well, be careful." Jack hugged both boys. "I'll see you when you get back. How long will you be gone, Lainey?"

"I'm not sure. I'll call you later, or have the boys call you." Lainey paused on the way to the door. For the first time in her twelve-year marriage to Jack, she was leaving him and, to her surprise, the thought was more than a little daunting. When she turned to look at him, she found she didn't know what to say. "Goodbye, Jack," she finally murmured.

It sounded so final that Jack's heart sank as he watched as his family walked out the door.

"You guys ready for an adventure?" Eve asked looking at the boys in her rearview mirror.

"Yeah!" they yelled in agreement. Kevin and Darren had never been in a convertible before and made sure Eve knew just how awesome her car was.

"When are we going to find out where we're going?" Kevin asked. "Will you tell us, Mom?"

Lainey looked back at them. They looked so happy being there with her and Eve, the top down, the wind blowing their hair as they drove down the rural street. It almost made her forget everything else. Almost. "I don't know. Eve won't tell me either. All she will say is that it's a surprise."

Eve gave all of them a beguiling smile and said nothing.

"I bet we're going to the zoo!" Darren guessed.

"No. We've gotta be going somewhere with water. Eve told us to bring our swimsuits, remember. Are we going to the beach, Eve?"

When Eve just shrugged her shoulders, both boys laughed.

"You're not gonna tell us anything, are you?" Kevin shouted.

"I'm sure wherever Eve takes us will be fun," Lainey told them. "Where are we going?" she asked as Eve turned onto the airport access road.

Eve only grinned as she turned on to a street that led behind the terminal.

"Where are we going, Mommy?" Darren asked, his little voice getting more excited by the minute. "Wow! Look at that one over there!" Darren pointed excitedly to one of the small planes.

"No, look at that one, squirt!" Kevin cried. "It's awesome!"

All Lainey could do was look around in complete bewilderment. When Eve came to a stop in front of a Boeing Business Jet, she let out a gasp.

"Wow!" both boys said in amazement and Darren added, "Are we getting on that?"

A man wearing black slacks and a white shirt with pilot's wings clipped on the left pocket approached them as Eve got out of the car. "Good morning, Ms. Sumptor," he said. His eyes were hidden behind dark sunglasses and his thick crop of brown hair was topped with a captain's hat.

"Good morning, Steve." Eve smiled. "The bags are in the back." She popped the trunk for him and turned to Lainey. "Surprise."

"I don't understand. Kevin! Darren! Stay here with me!" she called to the boys who were already out of the car running around, wild with excitement. "Where are we going?"

"Steve. Could you take the boys on board and show them the cockpit? Is that alright Lainey?"

"Yeah, can we go, Mommy?" Darren jumped around her, tugging on her shirt.

Lainey hesitated and looked at Eve then back down at Darren. "Okay, but don't touch anything and be good."

"Yes, Mommy! C'mon, Kevin!" Both boys took off like a shot, Steve following them, carrying the bags, including the Gucci suitcase Eve had managed to put in the trunk without Lainey seeing her before they left her apartment.

"Are you going to tell me what's going on now?" Lainey asked Eve when they were alone.

"Honey, I just wanted to do something special for you and the boys. I thought taking them to Disney would be fun."

"Disney? We're going to Florida?" Lainey asked incredulously. "Eve, we can't just fly to Florida on a whim."

"Why not?" Eve answered calmly. She hadn't expected this reaction from Lainey and was a bit disappointed.

"Why not?" Lainey tried thinking of a good reason why they shouldn't be going to Florida, and found she couldn't. She had already told Jack that she didn't know when they were coming back. The boys did have Monday off of school. And this would be fun for them.

"There's not a damn reason why not," Lainey said quietly. "I'm sorry, Eve. I was surprised and I overreacted. This was the last thing I ever expected you to do."

"It's fine," Eve said, clearly relieved. "I suppose I should have cleared it with you first. But I wanted to surprise you. To do something spontaneous, you know?" It was difficult, she discovered, to be in a situation where she couldn't do the natural thing and touch someone she cared about. If this had been Adam, nothing would have prevented her from showing her affection.

"You don't have to do this, Eve," Lainey reassured her. "I don't need to be impressed. You've already impressed me enough."

Eve laughed. "I'm not trying to impress you, honey. Honestly, I just thought the boys would have fun, and we could just get away from everything for a couple of days. I need a vacation," she said, thinking of the multiple times she had tried to call Jackie's parents, to console them and offer them help, only to be turned away. "What better way to spend a weekend away than with you and the boys?"

Eve tucked Lainey's arm in hers as they walked towards the plane.

"Who knows, if you're lucky maybe I'll impress you some more this weekend."

Lainey grinned. "I won't forget you said that. I just have three questions."

"Well, good thing today is your lucky day. I'm in the mood to answer you."

"Just as long as I'm not using up that luck for these answers," Lainey said, laughing as followed Eve into the plane.

"Oh my God," Lainey said as they entered the plane. The carpet was plush, a rich ivory color that matched the leather of the luxurious seats. There was a couch on the far right side, and on the left, four extremely large, extremely comfortable looking seats surrounding a cherry oak, gloss finished table. The entertainment center included everything from a DVD player to the latest in video game consoles. Lainey could only imagine what the rest of the plane looked like.

"Do you own this plane?" she asked Eve.

"Is that one of your three questions?" Eve asked her playfully.

"Mom! You gotta see this!" Kevin popped out of the cockpit and tugged on his mom's arm. "C'mon. This is so cool!"

"I'm coming. Wow," Lainey said in awe as she looked at the highly complicated control board. "This is very cool. Darren you're not touching anything are you?"

"No, Mommy. Steve said we could come up here when we're born in the air!"

"Airborne, dummy," Kevin corrected with a sigh.

"Kevin. Be good and be nice to your brother. This weekend is for nothing but fun. Okay?"

"Yes, ma'am. Sorry, squirt. This is so great, Eve. Are you going to tell us where we're going?"

Eve smiled back. "How about you'll see when we get there. Now, why don't we go get seated so Steve can take off? I'm sure he'd be happy to have you come back later."

"I sure would, ma'am. We're clear for takeoff any time you're ready," Steve told her.

"Great. Let's go. Go pick a seat, guys." The boys filed back into the cabin, so excited they could hardly see straight.

When they were out of earshot Eve turned back to the pilot. "No one is to know where we're going," she said in a low voice. "Is that clear?"

"Yes, ma'am. Your destination is not being released to anyone," Steve told her. In fact, Eve knew that only the crew on the plane and Christine, who had taken her original call, knew the destination and that she could trust all of them. Otherwise they wouldn't be working for her.

"Good. Thank you, Steve. You were great with the boys. I bet they'd love to be taught how to fly this thing."

Eve's plane was another private sanctuary that she rarely shared with anyone and it mystified her that she was sharing it with Lainey? What made things so different with her than with Adam? And why was it that being this open with Adam scared her? Eve joined Lainey, sitting next to her in one of the four seats surrounding the table. The boys were situated on the couch in front of the entertainment center eyeing the game console.

"Have they ever flown before?"

"No, and I haven't been on a plane in years. I'm a little nervous."

"Don't be nervous. I'm here with you," Eve told her with a smile. "I'll be right back." She got up and went towards the boys. "Seatbelts on," she told them, getting down on her knees in front of them, helping them. "Your mommy tells me you've never flown before. Are you scared?"

"No. I think it's going to be great!" Darren told her.

"I'm not scared, either," Kevin said, sounding unconvincing.

"Hmm. Okay, well, listen, do you like rides?" she asked Kevin.

"Yeah, they're fun."

"This is just one big ride. In the beginning, when we're going up, it'll feel a little funny here." Eve patted Kevin's stomach with her hand. "But, once we level out you won't even know we're moving, okay?"

"Okay." Kevin nodded.

"If you start to feel sick at anytime for any reason, there's a bag on the side of the couch right here, that you can use. But I think both of you are going to be just fine. You're going to love the ride. Keep your seatbelts on until I'll tell you it's okay to take them off, alright?"

"Okay," they answered together.

"Once we're settled, someone will be out here to get you drinks and snacks and you can play that game you've been eyeing."

"Can we go up there again?" Darren asked gesturing to the cockpit.

"Of course. If that's what you want," Eve said as the plane began to move. "I have to go sit down now and put my own seatbelt on."

"You're really great with them," Lainey told her.

"They make it easy. They're great kids. Are you ready?" Eve asked as she snapped her seatbelt together.

Lainey let her breath out slowly. "I think so. Is there an airsick bag on my seat, too?"

Eve chuckled. "Please don't get sick. I can handle just about anything but that." She took Lainey's hand under the table and gave it a squeeze. "Everything will be fine. Just relax. It's a little different than being on a commercial airline, because it's a little steeper on the ascent. But, don't think about it."

"What am I supposed to think about?" The plane began to move faster and Lainey's grip on Eve's hand tightened.

"Well, let's talk about those three questions," Eve told her. "Let's see, your first one was do I own this plane. The answer is yes, I do."

"Exactly how rich are you?" Lainey asked in disbelief.

"Don't waste one of your three questions on a question I won't answer. Are you okay?"

Lainey closed her eyes and tried nodding but couldn't move. She didn't remember being this terrified of flying.

"Kevin are you okay over there?" Eve called.

"No sweat!" Kevin said with glee.

"How about you, Darren?"

"This is fun!" Darren said and clapped his hands together.

"Good. The remote to the TV is right next to you. You can go ahead and turn it on if you want." Eve turned her attention back to Lainey. "Baby, are you going to be sick?" she whispered.

Lainey shook her head weakly. "Talk to me. Get my mind off what's going on." She felt Eve switch hands under the table and thought it was because Lainey was squeezing the life out of Eve's left hand. But, as she squeezed the right hand, Lainey felt Eve touching her thigh and moving up. Lainey's eyes flew open.

"Eve!"

"Shh. They're watching TV and they can't see under the table. Relax." Eve moved her hand more until she was at the hem of Lainey's shorts.

When Eve slipped a finger inside her shorts, Lainey was thankful she had thought to change into them. Of course, she had only been thinking about what a wonderful day it was outside, but now, she was thinking so many more wonderful things were happening inside. She muffled a moan as Eve's fingers worked her up.

"I bought the plane because I'm spoiled," Eve said suddenly.

"What?" Lainey began moving her body slowly, looking over to make sure they weren't being watched.

"I'm spoiled." Eve repeated thinking of how good Lainey felt. "I hate flying commercial and being surrounded by so many people, and the food, disgusting. I was flying to Europe and around the country so often that I decided to buy my own plane. In the end it's well worth the investment." She probed deeper, stifling a moan herself. "What's your next question?"

"I can't think," Lainey whispered.

"Sure you can," Eve replied quietly.

"Um. Oh God. Uh, okay, why...God, Eve!" Lainey bit her bottom lip to keep from crying out.

"Why what?" Eve's fingers moved faster inside Lainey. She felt the plane begin to level out. "Go over, baby," she whispered to Lainey.

Lainey brought her hand to her mouth and bit her knuckle to stay quiet. She closed her eyes tightly and came.

Eve removed her hand and brought it up to her lips. "Why what?"

"You expect me to think after that?"

"Did I take your mind off of flying?" Eve asked her.

"Yes. I couldn't think about anything but what you were doing to me," Lainey responded quietly.

"Good. We're going to have company soon, so stop smiling like that," Eve said with a wink.

"Company? And, I'm not smiling." Lainey giggled.

Eve laughed. "The flight attendant. She waits until the plane is airborne before putting in an appearance. It's a requirement of mine." She glanced over at Lainey. "And, you're still smiling."

"You guys can unbuckle your seatbelts now," she said to the two boys who were sitting quietly on the couch watching cartoons.

"Good morning, ma'am. Your coffee." A young, strawberry-blonde appeared next to Eve and set a tray in front of them. She wore the same black and white uniform as the captain with a black scarf around her neck.

"Thank you, Rachel," Eve said to her.

"I can see why you're spoiled," Lainey teased Eve.

"Ah, so you were listening," Eve teased back and grinned at Lainey. "You never did ask me that second question."

"Can I save my last two questions for when we're alone?" she said in a low voice.

Eve smiled. "Absolutely."

"Where is she?" Tony pounded his fists on the desk in front of him. The morons, he thought. Ask them to do one simple thing and they botch it.

"We don't know, sir," one of the men sitting in front of him answered nervously. "She got on a plane this morning with a woman and two kids."

"Where did she go?" Tony pronounced each word precisely. The two goons in front of him were sweating and that was the way he wanted it. It had been his experience that fear was better than respect any day.

"We don't know, sir."

"You keep saying that. I can't stand ignorance. I don't want to hear the words 'we don't know' coming from your mouth again. Do you understand? Now, find out what her destination is! It can't be that hard to find out where the goddamn plane is going."

"But, sir, it was a private jet. They won't give us that information."

"A private jet?" His rage came to the point of boiling over as he picked up a crystal vase full of white roses, Eve's roses, and threw them across the room. The bitch, he thought. She thinks she can just get away with using his money like that? He would show her what it's like to have nothing soon. Very soon.

"Find her," he snarled. "I don't care what you have to do to get the information, but find her. If you don't, you will deal with me, and I won't be in a good mood. And where is this Katherine woman? She couldn't have just disappeared off the face of the earth."

The two henchmen looked at each other.

"Don't tell me. You don't know." He leaned forward, tapping his fingertips together. "I suggest you find her, too. She has information that could hurt me. And if I get hurt, you get killed. Do I make myself clear?"

"Yes, sir. We'll find them both, sir."

"You better, and I want more information on Eve's guests. Get out."

When they were gone, he picked up a sheaf of photos of Eve taken at her gallery opening. "You think you can hide from me, little Eve? Think you can just spend my money any way you want? Well you're wrong, my pretty. I'm going to enjoy punishing you."

~ Twelve ~

The flight was smooth and uneventful, thankfully. The boys enjoyed playing games and received flying lessons from Steve. Lainey was given a tour of the jet by Eve. She was amazed by everything she saw, from the bathroom of gold and cherry wood with a full shower, to the bedroom that sported a queen size bed. Seeing the bed, she found herself wondering if she'd get the chance to become a member of the 'mile high' club, and even after the night she just spent with Eve, the thought shocked her.

The shock for Lainey didn't end with the aircraft. When they stepped out of the plane, a stretch limo that had Kevin and Darren oohing and ahhing, was waiting. Eve's lifestyle was unquestionably different than what Lainey was accustomed to, but Lainey found she enjoyed being waited on hand and foot. Then, another shock came when they got out of the limo in front of a huge house instead of a hotel. It was a white stucco mansion with dual pillars framing the entrance of the expansive home and was bordered by splashes of color from beautiful roses of multiple shades.

"Is this yours?" Lainey asked Eve, though she already knew the answer.

"Wow! Mom, are we staying here?" Kevin asked in wonder. Darren couldn't speak, he just ran ahead of everyone looking at everything in sight, the palm trees that lined the driveway, the impeccable green lawn that seemed to go on forever, and the magnificent rock pond that featured a small waterfall.

"Yes," Eve said. "To both questions." She winked at Kevin and chuckled at Darren who was too interested in the fountain that centered the roundabout driveway to pay attention to anyone. She walked up to Darren and handed him a penny. "Make a wish," she told him.

"Yeah?" Darren looked up at Eve and gave her a toothy grin.

"Yeah." She grinned back and watched as Darren closed eyes tightly making a wish and threw the penny in.

"You wanna know what I wished for?" he asked Eve, taking her hand as they walked to the house together.

"Well, if you tell me, it won't come true," Eve told him. "How about this? When you get your wish, then you can tell me all about it. Deal?"

The massive white double doors opened and a gray haired woman, wearing a navy and white uniform greeted them. "Thank you for having everything prepared, Alison," Eve said after she introduced them. "That's all. I'll take care of everything for the next three days."

"Welcome," Eve said and bowed, extending her arm to gesture Lainey and the boys in. "You can put the bags here."

It was like stepping into paradise, Lainey thought. The home was done in intense white, just as Lainey might have expected. White marble with hints of gold flecks covered the floor of that front entrance until it reached the spacious living room where it turned to white plush, sculpture carpeting. The furniture reminded Lainey of the furniture that decorated Eve's New York home, all of it looking luxurious and comfortable. Beyond the living room was a spotless sliding glass door that spanned the length of the room and opened to a beautiful, unusually shaped pool with crystal blue water glittering in the sunlight. A white Baldwin baby grand piano, adorned with elegant candles in soft pastel colors, sat in the far corner of the living room, forming a striking picture with the pool as the backdrop. Everything was so flawless that Lainey was worried about the boys messing something up.

"It's beautiful, Eve," Lainey said quietly. Kevin and Darren had already made their way across the house to look out at the pool. "Every time I see white, I think of you now."

"Is that the only time you think of me?" Eve teased.

"Can we go swimming, Eve?" Darren asked as he stared out at the pool with wide, excited eyes.

"If it's okay with your mom, yes," Eve answered and laughed as Darren ran to his mother.

"Mommy! Eve says we can go swimming if it's okay with you. Can we?"

"Yeah, Mom! Can we?" Kevin demanded.

Lainey realized suddenly that she couldn't remember having been happier. Her sons were in heaven and so was she. And the woman who was responsible for it all was looking at her with desire in her eyes.

"Yes. After," Lainey said over their 'hoorays', "you put your things away. And, we have to eat."

"But, Mom..." The boys complained.

"No buts," she told them and turned to Eve.

"I'll show you to your rooms," Eve said reading Lainey's mind. She put her arms around each of the boys. "So, do you guys want separate rooms or would you rather bunk together?"

"Together!" they said at the same time.

"Perfect. I don't have a room with two beds," Eve told them apologetically. "But, I can give you a room with a huge bed. Is that all right?"

"Yeah, we don't mind. Do we squirt?" Kevin told her trying to look as grown up as possible. He knew that Darren was always scared in new places and that he would end up in his room anyway. It was just easier to do it this way, he thought.

"Nope," Darren said cheerfully.

Eve grinned at both of them. They walked up the curved staircase and Eve stopped in front of one of the first doors in the long, open hall. "Here we go then," she said and opened the door. The room was huge, and in the center stood a colossal bed with a white goose down bedspread. For color, Eve had had the room accented with bold, deep red throw pillows. The view was of the fountain and gardens surrounding them. It looked, to Lainey, like a beautiful painting.

"Wow!" Darren whispered and ran to jump up on the bed.

Lainey took Kevin's arm to hold him back and bent down. "Thank you," she whispered in his ear. She knew what he had done for Darren and loved him for it. Kevin shrugged a little and grinned.

"Why don't you guys get unpacked while I show your mom to her room?" Eve suggested. "You can put your stuff in any of the drawers in the dresser. The bathroom is right through that door and if you need anything else, just let me know. Oh, by the way, the TV is hidden." Eve picked up a remote and pushed a button. Like magic a screen appeared at the foot of the bed.

"That's neat!" Darren squealed. "Did you see that, Kevin?"

"Yeah! Cool! What did you press?" Kevin asked Eve.

"Just press this button here," Eve showed him. She looked over at Lainey. "They can put their suits on right? We'll change, too, and if you guys like cheeseburgers, then we'll have that for lunch." Eve smiled.

Eve led Lainey further down the hall and stopped in front of a door on the opposite side of the hall than the boys' room. There were double doors at the end of the hall.

"Your room?" Lainey asked with amusement.

"How did you guess?" Eve replied as they entered a room even bigger than the boys'.

"It's amazing." The bed was covered with the same goose down comforter with hunter green accents. A beautiful landscape painting by Sisley made the room even warmer. Lainey's view was of the screened in pool below and a walkway that led beyond the picturesque flowering trees. "I can't wait to see yours," she said quietly to Eve.

Eve shut the door softly behind her and turned the lock. "I've been wanting to do this for the longest time," she said, turning Lainey to her. She lowered her mouth to Lainey's and kissed her gently.

"The boys are…"

"In the other room unpacking and changing," Eve finished. She tucked Lainey's hair behind her ear. "But, I'll stop if it makes you uncomfortable."

"No," Lainey told her. "I've been wanting to do that for the longest time, too. Kiss me again, Eve. More," she said against Eve's lips. Eve's tongue mingled with Lainey's and, in that moment, both of them knew they wanted nothing more than to lose themselves in each other.

It was Eve who finally broke the kiss. "I should leave you to unpack now," she said softly. "I'll see you downstairs. If you need anything, you know where my room is."

"Careful, Eve. You're not alone here with Lainey," she whispered to herself, leaning against her bedroom door. Eve's room was decorated exactly like the one in New York. All of her homes were decorated alike. It gave her a sense of belonging, a sense of stability she had never known before. No matter where she went, she was home. The only thing missing here was Eve's secret loft full of paintings and photos. Her sanctuary in Florida was the pool and the complete solitude. Changing out of her jeans and t-shirt into a white bikini and sarong, she went downstairs to join her guests.

"Why are you just sitting in the hot sun?" Eve asked as she joined them by the pool. "Go swim."

"Can we, Mom?" Kevin asked. She had told them that they had to wait until after lunch, but it was hard waiting when all they wanted to do was swim.

Lainey lifted her hand to shield her eyes and lost every thought she had in her mind. Eve was simply magnificent, her tanned body a spectacular contrast against the sheer white of her bikini and sarong. The exposure of the swells of Eve's breasts down to her toned stomach was almost too much for Lainey to bear. The only thing Lainey found disappointing was that the sarong covered most of Eve's amazing legs.

Eve caught the desire in Lainey's eyes and felt every inch of her body heat. She was thankful for the dark sunglasses she had on because not only was she aroused by Lainey's reaction, but also by Lainey's appearance lying, as she was, on the white lounge chair, her arms above her head, one of her great legs stretched out with the other bent at the knee. Lainey had chosen a sleek black one piece. The neckline dipped low, giving Eve a great view of Lainey's cleavage, and the right side was cut out to expose half of her waist and back. Though only a moment went by, it seemed like they had been staring at each other for eternity. Eve glanced over at the boys who were still waiting for an answer. "Lainey?" She smiled. "Is it all right for the boys to swim while I make lunch?"

"Oh, um, sure. Yes, I guess that would be fine," Lainey said distractedly. Her thoughts came back as she heard the boys cheer. "Be careful! Kevin, keep an eye on your brother."

"Yes, Mom!" Kevin jumped in the pool with a splash with Darren following behind him. Lainey rose and confronted Eve. "My God, you look incredible," she whispered. "How am I supposed to keep my composure when you come down here looking like that?"

"The same way I do when I come down here to see you looking like that," Eve replied, her breath warm on Lainey's cheek. "We bottle it up and take it out on each other later."

"I can't wait," Lainey said, so quietly Eve barely heard her.

Eve moaned softly and took a deep breath letting it out slowly. "Okay. Now that I'm aroused, I guess I'll go start on lunch."

"Wait, you were serious?" Lainey asked.

"Yes, I was serious. Why are you so surprised? You don't think I can cook do you?" She put her hand to her heart and feigned pain. "I'm hurt. My heart is now broken. Actually, I took classes at the Cordon Bleu while I was in France."

"I don't know how much the boys will appreciate Cordon Bleu cooking," Lainey said hesitantly. She was uncertain what to say or do. Eve had surprised her once again by sharing more about her life and it was obvious she was doing it because of the boys. But this wasn't the art world they were talking about now. This was a world in which two children were involved and Lainey wasn't sure how much experience Eve had with this.

"There's more," Eve assured her. "When I came back to the states, I was in Arizona, I think, in the middle of nowhere. I stopped at this diner and met this woman named Flo."

Lainey laughed in disbelief. It was this playful side of Eve that she enjoyed so much.

"I kid you not," Eve continued. "Her name was Flo, and she made the best cheeseburger I'd ever tasted. It was unbelievable. The spices were perfect. It was thick, juicy, and messy, everything a great burger should be."

"And, 'Flo' taught you how to make it?" Lainey asked amused.

"Hmm. She was a tough cookie," Eve said, lighting the grill. She hadn't intended on telling Lainey any of this, but she was taking pleasure in the fact that Lainey was entertained by it. "It was supposed to be an 'old family recipe', but you know me. It's time to get the burgers ready."

"Eve!" Lainey laughed.

"Don't worry; I'll be right through that door," Eve teased, pointing towards the kitchen entrance. "If you start to miss me too much, you can come and visit me. The boys are good swimmers right?"

"Will you stop? Tell me how you got the recipe!" Later, when Lainey thinks back on this conversation, she will remember how free and happy she felt.

"Honey, the boys are probably starving. I know I am." Eve winked and pulled away from Lainey.

"Eve. Are you going to tell me how you got the recipe?" Lainey laughed.

Eve glanced over her shoulder and grinned at Lainey. "Is that one of your three questions?" she asked, and then disappeared inside the house.

Lainey could only stare after Eve and laugh. She would get Eve to tell her the rest of the story no matter what it took, but she'd be damned if she would waste a question on it. Eve would see later just how persuasive she could be, too. "Are you guys okay?" Lainey called to Kevin and Darren.

"Yeah! Are you going to come in, Mommy?" Darren asked as he dog-paddled around Kevin.

"Maybe after we eat. I'm going to help Eve with lunch first. Now, Kevin, I'm going to be right through there, okay? I can see you from in there and can be out here in no time if you need me," Lainey told him. She knew the boys had taken swimming lessons since they were barely old enough to walk, but she was a mother and still worried about them. She made sure she had easy access to get back out to the pool in a hurry if, God forbid, she needed to. "Stay in the shallow end until we come back out, understood?"

"Yes, Mom," Kevin obeyed. "We'll be fine. I'll watch squirt."

"I can swim!" Darren said with pride. "Mommy, can we have something to drink? And, is Eve gonna swim with us, too?"

"I'll bring some soda out for you, but you can't drink in the pool. I'm sure we can convince Eve to come in, too." She stood by the door and watched Eve work for a moment before saying anything. Just observing Eve move expertly around the kitchen was arousing Lainey.

"Did you come to help or to watch?" Eve said, startling Lainey.

"To help," Lainey said. "How did you know I was here?"

"I could feel you," Eve answered when Lainey was beside her. "There's a spatula in the second or third drawer over there. Could you get it for me, please?"

Lainey opened one of the drawers and found nothing but matches and other miscellany. She also found a pack of cigarettes, the same kind she had found when she had cooked Eve breakfast that morning. "You don't smoke, do you, Eve?" Lainey asked, smiling. "There's another pack of Newports here like the one I saw in your kitchen this morning."

"I used to smoke, a long time ago," Eve said, shrugging. "I keep a pack, sort of as a reminder of why I quit. Disgusting habit."

"There are so many things I don't know about you," Lainey told her, putting bottles of coke on a tray. "You ran away from home. You lived in Europe, making a living through your painting and photography. You smoked. You own Sumptor, Inc., Sumptor Galleries, The Garden of Eve, O. By the way, what does O stand for?"

"Orgasm." Eve laughed at Lainey's shocked expression. "Oasis. It stands for Oasis, though most people like Orgasm better." Eve listened to everything that Lainey knew about her and found it was more than most knew. "Are you writing a book?"

"It's just that you never talk about yourself." And it was true, she realized. Ever since she had met Eve, she had been intensely attracted. Intrigued. Yet she knew so little about her.

"You forgot the part where I attended cooking school in France, then bullied some poor woman named Flo in Arizona for a burger recipe," Eve joked, and Lainey laughed.

It felt so wonderful to be here like this, to have Eve talking about herself for once, if even just a little. Lainey wished that time would stand still and they could be like this forever with the boys splashing in the pool and being intimate in this new way. It told Lainey that, just possibly, she meant more to her than she had realized.

Lainey laid her hand on Eve's cheek. "I also know that you're a very generous, extremely beautiful woman, and an exceptional lover."

Eve turned her face and kissed Lainey's palm. "What more do you need to know?" she teased. "Come on, let's go make some burgers."

Lainey sighed when Eve pulled away from her. "Are you ever going to let me know who the real Eve is?" she asked quietly.

"You know more than anyone, Lainey," Eve said after a long pause during which time for Lainey seemed to come to a halt. "That's scary enough for me. Don't push me to open up. Please." And, without another word, she picked up the tray and walked out onto the patio.

Lainey felt let down. There was no use pretending that she didn't. But the time would come when Eve would trust her with the story of her life. She would let things come naturally.

They sat around the table by the pool and ate Eve's special cheeseburgers.

"These are good, Eve!" Darren took a big bite of his burger and ended up with most of the condiments on his face.

"They're better than dad's, Mom. Don't tell him I said that," Kevin grinned, picking up a fry and dipping it in his ketchup.

Lainey had been dreading the conversation she needed to have with the boys about her and Jack. "Speaking of dad, do you remember me telling you that I wanted to talk to you about why I wasn't at home last night?"

"Are you getting a divorce?" Kevin asked quietly. "Justin's parents just got divorced. His dad moved to Connecticut and he gets to spend the weekends there with him."

"What's a divorce?" Darren asked.

"It means that Justin's mommy and daddy won't live together anymore," Kevin explained.

"I don't want you or daddy to move to 'Netticut," Darren protested.

"Honey, that's not going to happen," Lainey assured him. "Come here and sit on my lap. Your daddy and I are having a couple of problems right now and I just needed a little time to myself. Neither of us is going anywhere." She didn't know what else to say. How could she tell them that she didn't know what was going to happen? Divorce was the furthest thing from her mind, but how could she be sure that was not where they were headed?

"That's why you spent the night with Eve?" Darren asked, sniffling now.

"That's one reason," Lainey told him and glanced at Eve who was watching her silently. "Eve is very special to me."

"She's your best friend? Like Justin's mine?" Kevin asked.

"Yes, she is." She saw Eve lower her eyes, and caught the small smile that lit up her face. A shiver ran through Lainey's body. "Eve has helped me very much with everything I've been going through. I hope you guys don't mind if you see more of her."

"We don't mind, Mommy. Eve's great!" Darren said, stealing one of his mother's fries.

Eve cleared her throat. "I think I'll go get another coke. Anyone else want something?" She stood up and cleared some of the dishes off of the table before leaving.

Lainey chuckled. "She's shy," she said, almost to herself. It was one more thing she had learned about Eve.

Eve leaned against the counter and looked out at Lainey and the boys. For the first time in her life she felt as though she had a family. The thought was not only glorious, but also terrifying. Eve knew they weren't her family, never would be, but she would cherish the moments she had with them. She watched as the boys got up and hugged their mother, then jumped in the pool. Eve waited for Lainey to come to her, carrying plates in from outside.

"Everything okay with them?" Eve asked, taking the dishes from Lainey.

"Yes. They don't understand why Jack and I are fighting, but then, neither do I," Lainey said with a small laugh.

Eve, loading the dishwasher, looked over at Lainey. "You don't understand why you're fighting?" Eve could think of so many reasons, but opted not to say anything.

"I just don't know why he has to be this way." Lainey shrugged. "I hope he understands that I'm serious about needing things to change between us. Not just the way we make love," her voice trailed off as she saw Eve paused. "I'm sorry," she said.

"For what?" Eve tried to make her voice casual all the while seeing Lainey making love to Jack as she had been forced to do that terrible night.

"I didn't mean to say anything that might hurt you," Lainey told her.

"Listen," Eve said quietly. "No matter what happens between us, I know you are married. I know that when this weekend is over, you'll be going back to Jack. I don't want to think about it," she continued, "but I know it's going to happen. If he's smart he'll fight for you."

"What if he doesn't?"

"Then he's a bigger fool than I ever imagined." She didn't want to think about any of this. She just wanted to have this weekend with Lainey. "Why don't you go swimming with the boys? I'll be out soon."

"You're very good at that," Lainey murmured.

Eve looked over her shoulder. "At what?"

"Turning your emotions on and off in the blink of an eye."

The ringing of her cell phone interrupted Eve's answer.

"Could you get that for me, please?" Her hands were full of dishes and she needed a minute to digest what Lainey had said to her.

Lainey gave a little sigh and picked up the phone. "Eve's phone," she said.

"Hello?" It was Adam's voice. "Is Eve around?"

"Adam, hi. It's Lainey. Hang on a moment, Eve will be right with you."

As much as she liked Adam, Lainey didn't want to be talking to him. She couldn't help but feel jealousy whenever he was concerned; no matter how hard she tried not to feel that way.

Eve took the phone from her and mouthed *I'm sorry* before taking Adam's call. "Adam?"

"Hey, baby. Do you know how much I love hearing your voice?"

"Why are you calling?" Eve asked him. "Is something wrong?"

"Sorry. Am I disturbing you?" His voice was terse. It wasn't the response he was hoping for and it hurt.

"I'm sorry, Adam. I didn't mean it the way it sounded."

"I stopped by the gallery, you weren't there," Adam said after a brief silence. "I stopped by your place; you aren't here, either, so I thought I'd call you."

"You're at my place? Why didn't you call first?" Eve shut her eyes. Why was she being such a bitch to him? She couldn't think straight with Lainey watching her with hurt in her eyes. "I'm sorry," she said before Adam could say anything. "Did you need me?"

"No. I just thought we'd go out tonight. Or, I could fix you dinner, since it has been two years for us." It wasn't only disappointment in his voice, she realized. There was something more, a mixture of anger, hurt and frustration.

"Oh God, Adam, I'm so sorry. I forgot."

"It's fine," he said. "Listen, I have to go. Maybe I'll catch up with you later."

"Adam." But he had already hung up and Eve was answered with silence.

"I should have left."

Eve looked at Lainey and gave her a small smile. "Don't worry about it. It wouldn't have made a difference anyway."

The phone rang again and Lainey went outside. Whatever Eve's problem with Adam might involve, she didn't want to be a part of it. She didn't want thoughts of him to ruin this beautiful time she had with Eve, and she only felt jealousy where Adam was considered.

"I just want to know one thing. Where are you?" His tone was detached and Eve knew that she wouldn't be able to say anything to change the way he felt. Not until she could put her arms around him and tell him nothing had changed between them. So many things were happening to her, but she couldn't deny what she still felt for him.

"I'm out of town," she said.

"I see. And, Lainey is with you?"

"Yes. She's been having a difficult time, so I took her and her sons away for the weekend."

"Why did she answer your phone? You never let anyone answer your phone."

His questions were beginning to annoy her, but she kept her anger in check. "We just finished lunch and I was cleaning up the dishes," she said. "My hands were full."

"You cleaned? Did you cook as well?"

She heard the accusation in Adam's voice and sighed. "What are you more upset at Adam? That I didn't tell you I was leaving or that I cooked for someone?"

"Why didn't you tell me you were going away?"

"First, it was a spur of the moment decision that I made this morning. Second, I don't normally justify my actions or have to get permission to go anywhere from anyone."

"I see. I didn't realize I was just anyone."

"This conversation is getting us nowhere, Adam," Eve said softly. "I'm sorry I didn't talk to you first before leaving. I'm sorry that I cooked hamburgers for two little boys." She paused for a moment and then continued. "I'm sorry that I forgot about today being two years for us. I don't know what else to say."

"I'm sorry, too." Adam's voice was barely above a whisper. "I guess we have nothing else to talk about. Goodbye, Eve."

"Damn it!" Eve swore softly. She knew Adam was hurting, but as much as she wanted to call him back and soothe him, she couldn't. She didn't know what to say to him, couldn't say what he wanted to hear. Eve decided that she would have to worry about Adam and their relationship later. Right now, there was Lainey to consider.

Someday soon she was, she knew, going to have to decide what to do about the situation she was in. But just as she was about to go back out to the pool, her phone rang again. Weary of fighting more with Adam, Eve checked the caller ID before answering.

It wasn't Adam this time. "Yes?" Eve answered.

"Christine is in the hospital."

"Goddamn it! When did he get to her?"

"This afternoon after you left. He was pissed that you took off, and even more pissed that no one knew where you went. He wanted answers no matter what it took to get them."

"Is Christine going to be okay? What happened to her?" The people around her were either getting hurt or killed and the burden was weighing heavy on her.

"She was beaten pretty badly. A few broken bones, but she should recover fully."

"You couldn't have stopped them?"

"No ma'am, not without blowing my cover. I did the best I could. I kept her alive."

"At least she's alive. Did he find out what he wanted?"

"Not unless you're in Las Vegas. That was the destination Christine gave us."

"What hospital is she in?" She jotted down the information he gave her. "I'll take care of everything else as far as she's concerned. Anything else I need to know?"

"Katherine is coming around. I think she's finally starting to believe that we are the only ones that can save her."

"Good. And Meredith?"

"I don't think he's going to put up with her much longer. Since you've rescinded her security clearance, she's not much use to him."

"Get to her before he does. Make her understand that You are the only one that can save her now."

"Yes, ma'am. That's all from this side for right now."

"Fine. Thank you for the information. I'll be in touch."

"You guys having fun?" Eve asked as she joined them.

Lainey was sitting at the edge of the pool with her feet emerged in the water as the boys splashed around her.

"Are you going to swim with us, Eve?" Darren asked as he swam up to the edge of the pool. "If you come in, Mommy will, too."

"Well..." Eve took off her sunglasses and began untying the sarong. "Let's go swimming then." Striding to the middle of the pool, she dove in gracefully, her long, slender body barely making a splash, not surfacing until she had swum the length of the pool.

"Your turn," she called to Lainey, who hadn't taken her eyes off of Eve since she had shed the sarong.

"I can't dive like that," Lainey called back when she finally was able to think again.

"Try, Mommy!" Darren squealed.

"Okay, okay. I'll try." Lainey stood up, feeling Eve's eyes on her with every move she made. The muscles in her belly tightened in response. "Are you going to stay there?" she called to Eve.

"Yes. Swim to me, l'amant."

After her heart stopped hammering, Lainey took a deep breath and dove in. With her eyes closed, she swam underwater towards Eve. Her lungs began to scream as she swam the length of the pool, and she wanted to surface. Just when she thought she couldn't hold her breath any longer, her hand brushed against Eve's bare stomach. Lainey emerged from the water, sucking in air. When she opened her eyes she was close enough to Eve to feel their legs touching.

"Hi." Eve smiled. She wanted to lean in and kiss Lainey, but knew the boys were watching. "Catch your breath yet?"

"How do you do that so effortlessly?" Lainey was practically panting, but not only because of the swim. Behind her, Lainey could hear Kevin and Darren cheering and turned to wave at them. "I need to exercise more."

"I could help you with that." Eve ran a finger down Lainey's back and sent chills coursing through Lainey's body.

"I bet you could." Lainey propped her arms on the edge of the pool next to Eve to rest and watched Darren and Kevin play in the shallow end. "What did you call me?"

"Hmm?" Eve's eyes were closed, her wet hair slicked back off of her face. She was enjoying the sun, the sound of the boys having fun and having Lainey next to her.

"When you said 'swim to me' you called me something. It sounded, I don't know, French. What was it?"

Eve opened one eye and peered at Lainey. "It is French. L'amant. It means lover."

"Oh." Lainey blew out a breath. "I like that. Are you fluent in French?"

"Is that one of your three questions?" Eve teased.

Lainey chuckled. "No. Make this one a freebie, please?"

Eve smiled. "Yes. I'm fluent in French and a couple of other languages. It came in handy when I lived there."

"You never cease to amaze me," Lainey said quietly.

Eve shrugged a little. "It's nothing special. I've always had a love for language, so I studied. Nothing anyone else couldn't do."

Lainey looked over at Eve, who had closed her eyes again. *She is so humble. And, so beautiful,* Lainey thought. At this moment, Eve looked so at peace, a far cry from how she had looked when she had come out from the kitchen. Lainey wondered what Adam had said to her to upset her. "Do you want to talk about it?" she said now.

"Talk about what?"

"Adam, and what he said that troubled you." As soon as she said it, Lainey felt the tension seep back into Eve and regretted it.

"Nothing to talk about." Eve pushed off the side of the pool and dove under before Lainey could say anything.

"Damn it!" Lainey swore and kicked away from the side.

Eve kept her distance from Lainey for the remainder of the afternoon, making sure that they weren't alone. When she wasn't swimming with Kevin and Darren, she was floating by herself, or lying out in the sun. Her whole demeanor told Lainey that she didn't want to talk. After they were done swimming, they played video games, made dinner, and watched a movie.

While the boys got ready for bed, Eve locked herself away in her bedroom. Standing under the hot spray of the shower, she tried to let the tension wash away. She knew that Lainey was only trying to help, but talking about Adam had only made Eve feel guilty and despondent. Seeing Lainey disheartened only made Eve feel worse, but if there was anything she didn't need right now it was to feel responsible for Lainey's moods. Granted it was her fault that Lainey was unhappy right now. She had withdrawn when they had all been so close. Almost like a family. But that was the thing, of course. None of this was real. Lainey had her own family, her own husband. What did she think she was doing, making that beautiful woman emotionally dependent on her because of her own needs?

Stepping out of the shower, she began to dry her hair and heard a knock. Wrapping a towel around her and trying to calm her nerves she went to answer it.

"Can I come in?" Lainey said. She was wearing a thin t-shirt and shorts that accentuated her wonderful curves that Eve was so attracted to.

"Are the boys in bed?"

"No. They're playing video games." The sight of Eve almost naked made it difficult for her to keep her mind on what she had come to say. Why was it that even now, after they had shared so much, she should be taken by surprise by the electrifying effect this woman had on her. "I just wanted to apologize to you..."

"There's nothing to apologize for." Eve interrupted, going back into the bathroom. She was combing her hair when Lainey stepped in after her.

"I obviously upset you. I never intended to do that."

"I'm not upset with you, Lainey," Eve said softly, looking at Lainey in the mirror. "Let's just forget it, okay?"

Lainey sighed. "Fine. The boys would like to know if you would come and play another video game with them before they go to bed."

"Sure. Tell them I'll be right there."

When Lainey started out the door, Eve grabbed her arm and pulled her close. "I told you I'm horrible outside of the bedroom," she said by way of her own apology. "I'm just not good at any of this." She kissed Lainey gently. "Forgive me?" she whispered.

"If you forgive me," Lainey told her. It had been torture having Eve be so distant towards her. Eve was just beginning to open up to her, but she had pushed too hard.

"Deal." Eve deepened the kiss before letting Lainey go. "Let me get dressed and I'll be in to play a couple of games."

"Can I watch?"

"Me get dressed, or us playing games?" Eve asked her.

"Both." As usual, talking to Eve made her feel sexy and exciting. Alive.

"Mmm. Yes." Eve walked out of the bathroom, letting her towel fall to the floor.

"Is this where you get that?"

Eve glanced over her shoulder with a questioning look. "Get what?"

"That perfect no line tan."

"It's one of the places," Eve told her. "One day, I'll take you to another place without the boys, and I'll show you exactly how I have no tan lines."

"I'd love that." Lainey cupped Eve's breasts.

"Don't do that."

"Why?" Lainey scraped her thumbs over Eve's nipples and Eve's back arched in pleasure.

"Because." She gripped Lainey's wrists. "I have to play games with your boys before I can play games with you, honey."

Lainey found it hard to believe that someone like Eve would actually enjoy sitting with her legs crossed, on the floor and playing with two kids. At the same time, she couldn't help but remember Eve standing naked before her. She wanted so much to touch Eve, to please her, as Eve had pleasured her.

Eve glanced at Lainey and smiled. She knew what Lainey was thinking, could feel it deep inside her. Tonight, Eve wanted to give herself to Lainey. It has been so incredibly difficult for her to not have Lainey touch her, not to feel Lainey's hands satisfying her.

Eve tried telling herself that it was because she wanted Lainey to know what it was like to be pleasured, but was she scared as well? She would find out later tonight she hoped.

"Okay, guys," Eve said finally. "Time to get some sleep."

"Aww, but we want to play some more!" Darren protested.

Eve looked over at Lainey and winked. "Well, I'll give you a choice," she said, pulling both boys to their feet. "All right?"

"Okay!"

Eve waited until both boys were sitting on the bed in front of her. "Ready for your choices? You can keep playing video games until you fall over or go cross eyed. Or..." Eve paused dramatically. "You can go to bed now and get some sleep for our big day tomorrow at Disney."

"Disney!" They both jumped up off the bed and danced around.

"We're going to Disney, Mommy!" Darren ran over to Lainey and jumped up in her arms. "Are we going to see Mickey Mouse?"

"I'm sure he'll be there with everyone else," Lainey said laughing.

Kevin was still doing his little happy dance, and before he could stop himself, he threw himself into Eve's arms. Lainey didn't know which one of them was more surprised, Kevin or Eve, and tried to conceal her grin.

"Um, sorry," Kevin said bashfully and let go of Eve's neck, trying to slide back down to the floor.

"It's okay," Eve told him quietly and kissed him on his cheek. Kevin turned bright red and bowed his head so that Eve couldn't see the big grin on his face before he ran to his mom.

Darren saw the kiss and wanted one, too. Wiggling out of his mother's arms, he ran to Eve.

"Can I have a kiss, too, Eve?" He held his arms up so that Eve could pick him up, and giggled when she tickled him before lifting him up to her.

"Of course you can have a kiss." Eve pressed her lips to Darren's cheek and gave him a loud kiss making him giggle more.

"I guess this means that you guys are done playing games and want to go to bed."

"Yeah! Which Disney are we going to?" Darren was still hanging on to Eve's neck as she bent down to pull the covers back.

"Disney World, dufus. We're in Florida," Kevin said, climbing into the bed.

"I know that, dufus. Which one though?"

"You mean which park?" Eve asked.

"Yeah. Which park are we going to?"

"We can go to all of them if you want. Why don't we just play it by ear tomorrow and see what happens. All right?"

"Okay." Darren yawned as Eve as she laid him down in the bed. "You're the greatest, Eve!"

Eve smiled back and brushed his hair off his forehead. "I think both of you are great." She tapped Kevin on the nose. "Get some sleep. We'll wake up early in the morning and have all day to play."

Lainey came over and tucked both of the boys in bed, kissing each of them. "Goodnight. I love you both. Sweet dreams."

"'Nite, Mommy. Love you." Darren sunk his head into the plush pillow and was almost immediately asleep.

"'Nite, Mom." Kevin lifted his hand to Lainey's cheek. "You have sweet dreams, too. Don't worry, everything will be okay."

Lainey bent and hugged Kevin. "Thank you, honey," she whispered in his ear, and kissed his cheek again.

Wanting to give Lainey and the boys a little privacy, Eve waited at the door until Lainey came toward her, her eyes shining with unshed tears.

"Are you okay?" Eve asked her.

"Yes. I'm fine." Lainey turned to Eve. "I want to be with you," she whispered.

"Then be with me," Eve told her as she led her toward her room.

"I don't know if I can. They are pretty heavy sleepers, but this is a strange place for them. What if they wake up and they're scared? They'll come looking for me."

Though she was disappointed, Eve smiled at Lainey. "I guess I'll just have to dream about you then."

Lainey sighed. "I'm sorry."

"It's okay. I understand." Eve touched Lainey's cheek. "I want you, but I understand." Leaning in, she kissed Lainey gently on the lips, before turning reluctantly toward her own bedroom. "Get some rest, honey. We have a long day ahead of us tomorrow."

"Eve." Lainey waited until Eve looked back at her. "I don't know if I can stay away."

"If you can't, my door will be unlocked and I'll be waiting."

Leaning against the closed door of her bedroom, Lainey fought the urge to follow Eve. She had to think about her sons.

Eve had told her to get some rest, but Lainey knew that wouldn't be happening.

Eve lay naked in bed, awake, thinking of Lainey. She had wanted to be with her so much tonight, but she knew that the most important things to Lainey were her boys. Eve would never do anything to jeopardize that relationship. So, she would lie alone and restless and hope that she would make it through tomorrow.

She closed her eyes and took a deep breath to relax, then began to hum, then sing softly to herself the way she had when she was a little girl and wanted to forget everything. There were those nights when she had hidden deep in the closet with Mr. Snuffles, her stuffed teddy bear and best friend, rocking back and forth, singing to herself to drown out the shouting downstairs. Singing began to unwind Eve's mind, as she sank deeper into her pillow, unaware that Lainey had come into the room.

In the soft glow of the moonlight, she could see Eve's arms thrown above her head, her eyes closed. The sheets barely covered her breasts and one leg lay bare on top of the sheets. She had tried to stay away but every time she closed her eyes she would see Eve. Feel her. After making sure the boys were sleeping peacefully, she came to fulfill her own needs.

She wanted to touch Eve, but didn't want to disturb the peaceful state Eve was in, so she just listened and watched. Lainey told herself that she shouldn't have been surprised that Eve's voice was as beautiful as she was. It was sweet and serene and just a little haunting, Lainey thought. Eve shifted slightly and the sheets moved, baring her breasts to Lainey.

She had seen Eve naked before, but still went weak at the sight. As much as she didn't want to disturb Eve, there was no way she could keep her hands off of her now.

Eve was half asleep and thought she was dreaming when she felt Lainey's hands on her breasts. She moaned softly when Lainey tweaked Eve's hardened nipple and arched to offer more. When she felt Lainey's mouth brush hers, Eve opened her eyes. "Lainey?" She whispered, confused. "I thought..."

"I couldn't stay away." Lainey stood up straight and stripped away her t-shirt and shorts. When Lainey was naked, Eve tossed the sheets off. When she straddled her, and cupped her breasts, molding them, Eve was amazed. She had always thought of Lainey as shy, unable to make the first move, and now she was discovering how much she was enjoying this new side of Lainey.

"Are you sure you want to do this?" she said.

"Yes." Lainey gasped as Eve pinched and tugged her nipple. "The boys are deep asleep. They must be comfortable here. With you."

"Good. I'm glad. Now, kiss me."

Lainey bent down and kissed Eve passionately, feeling the heat of the kiss course through her body. "I can't stay," she whispered.

"I know. We'll make the best of the time we have together."

"I want to touch you, Eve."

Eve's heart pounded inside her chest and she hesitated.

"Don't you want me to touch you?"

"I do. God, Lainey, I do."

"Do you think I won't be able to please you?" It suddenly occurred to her that the reason Eve had been reluctant might not have been because she was nervous, but because Lainey was inexperienced at this.

"No! Oh, honey, that's not it at all. I know you can please me." Eve sighed softly. "Every time I've thought about being with you – since the beginning - there was always one thing I'd wanted to do. To please you. I never expected anything in return. I don't want you to feel as though you have to give me anything in return. It satisfies me just to be able to give you pleasure."

"I know I don't have to, Eve. I want to. I've wanted to from the very beginning as well. I don't know if I'll be any good at it, but I at least want to try."

Eve looked into Lainey's eyes for a moment, not saying a word. "Do what you want to me," she whispered.

Lainey hesitated, then laughed nervously. "Now that I'm here, I don't know what to do."

Stretching her arms above her head, Eve said, "I want you to do what you want to do to me. What you have been dreaming about doing to me. You don't need my help for that."

Lainey took a breath and very slowly, very timidly rubbed her hand across Eve's stomach, feeling her tremble inside.

"It's okay, take your time," Eve said in a low voice. "I'm not going anywhere." She kept her eyes on Lainey's and saw all of the emotions passing through Lainey. She was scared, excited, shy and so full of want that Eve felt herself wet and ready before Lainey even touched her.

Lainey's pulse was pounding so hard in her ears that she didn't know whether it was her body trembling or Eve's below her. She inched her hand down even further and felt Eve's soft skin beneath her fingers. Needing more, wanting more, Lainey finally touched Eve, feeling her silky wetness.

Eve arched her back. "Oh, God!" she cried.

"Am I doing something wrong?"

"No!" Eve groaned. "No, you're not doing anything wrong."

After only a moment's pause, Lainey slipped her fingers inside Eve.

"My God!" Eve had never imagined it would feel like this.

Lainey felt drunk with power. Eve's body quivered with passion and pleasure, the passion and pleasure that Lainey was giving her. She drove Eve faster, loving how Eve's body moved beneath her, how Eve felt so hot and wet.

"Don't stop, Lainey! Please, don't stop!" Eve gripped the pillow with one hand as she buried the other in Lainey's hair, bringing her down to kiss her. She spread her legs further and lifted her hips giving Lainey more. Eve's moans became louder and she felt Lainey's movements hesitate. "No! Don't stop!" She looked up at Lainey. "They can't hear, baby. It's okay," Eve told her, reading Lainey's mind.

"Are you sure?"

"I'm positive. Please, don't stop."

Lainey relaxed and her hand began to move again. Eve moved her body in a small circular motion and Lainey followed.

"Does it feel good?"

"Oh, yes." So good, Eve thought. Just when Eve didn't think it could get any better, it did. She didn't know what Lainey did, but whatever it was, it was spectacular. "There! Oh, God, yes!" Eve fisted her hand in Lainey's hair, almost painfully. "More, more." Her breath was sobbing, her fingers digging into the pillow. The orgasm came fast and hard, drowning her in a wave of pleasure. She moaned Lainey's name, as she relaxed.

"Now I know why you enjoy this side so much," Lainey said a little breathless.

"This side is pretty great, too." Eve's smile was slow. "You're wonderful."

"So, I did okay?"

Eve chuckled. "You did fantastic." She rolled over until Lainey was pinned underneath her. "Now, it's my turn."

They lay spent, their bodies slick with sweat, holding each other. Every thought, every worry had disappeared while they were in each other's arms. No one existed but them. Not Jack, not Adam, not Tony, no one. It was only after the pleasure, when they were coming down from the high of being together, that each of them thought of the consequences of their actions. Though they both felt a bit of guilt about what they were doing, neither of them would have changed a thing. They needed this. They needed each other, to find themselves.

Eve felt Lainey shift beside her and held her tighter. "Don't leave yet," she whispered.

"I have to." Lainey tried to move again, but Eve stopped her.

"Eve."

"Just a little longer, baby, please?"

The lazy plea had Lainey snuggling closer. "Don't let me fall asleep." She ran her hand over Eve's naked body, taking pleasure in the fact that she could make Eve tremble with just a touch.

"Keep doing that and neither of us will sleep." Eve trailed a fingertip down Lainey's bare shoulder. "Are you cold?"

"No." The chill bumps on her skin were not because of Lainey's naked body being uncovered. "It's you," she told Eve softly. I can't be falling in love with you, Lainey thought to herself, but if I'm not, what am I feeling?

Don't fall in love with me, Eve pleaded silently, I don't deserve your love. Eve tried hardening her own heart against what she was feeling for Lainey. She didn't love, didn't feel. Hadn't she already proven that with Adam? And, wasn't it just like Eve to be selfish enough to want to be with someone who was already taken and confused? You really are that much of a bitch aren't you Eve, she scolded herself.

"Eve!" Lainey rolled out of bed and rushed to put her clothes on.

"What is it? What's wrong?" Eve rubbed her eyes and tried focusing on Lainey. "Where are you going?"

"I told you not to let me fall asleep!" Lainey snapped. "What if the boys had woken up? What if they're awake now and looking for me?"

"I'm sorry, honey. I didn't mean to fall asleep." Eve pushed herself up into a sitting position and glanced over at the clock. "It's only five o'clock. I doubt they're up yet."

"That's not the point, Eve. I told you I couldn't stay."

Eve raised an eyebrow. "I said I was sorry, Lainey. And, this is not all my fault. You fell asleep, I fell asleep, no one else is awake, and we haven't been caught. Let's take a breath, okay?" She reached up and took Lainey's hand. "Sit. Calm down." Eve tugged Lainey down on to the bed. "I understand why you're so upset. I do. But, honey, don't ever use that tone of voice when you speak to me again."

Lainey heard the edge in Eve's voice and saw the warning in her eyes. "I'm sorry," she apologized, pulling her t-shirt over her head. Lainey has seen Eve in a temper before and certainly didn't want to be the brunt of it now. Especially after the time they just spent together.

"Lainey, I'm sorry," Eve leaned forward and kissed Lainey. "I didn't mean to snap at you."

"It was my fault. I shouldn't have blamed you for me falling asleep."

To Lainey's surprise, Eve looked amused. "I'm not going to argue with you about who was at fault. We fell asleep. Let's be thankful the boys didn't wake up." She reached up and tucked hair behind Lainey's ear.

"I overreacted," Lainey admitted. "I was just worried that the boys would find I wasn't in my bedroom and get scared."

"I understand."

"So, you're not mad at me anymore?"

"I was never angry with you, Lainey."

"I've seen that look before, Eve. It scares me." Lainey let out a little laugh. "Remind me to never do anything that makes you look at me that way again."

Eve embraced Lainey suddenly, holding her tight, so tight that she could feel her shaking. "I would never hurt you," she murmured. "Never!"

Suddenly Lainey was afraid. This was not the Eve she knew. The woman clutching her had nothing in common with the self-possessed, confident, playful Eve she knew. There was even something childlike about her voice when she repeated, 'I'd never hurt you. Never.'

"Eve? Honey, look at me." Eve was, trembling, holding on to her as though she were afraid to let go. "Eve, please." Eve finally loosened her grip and Lainey framed her face in her hands. "I know you would never hurt me."

Eve heard the familiar screams now. "Don't hurt her!" Eve cried, pulling her knees up to her chest. "Don't hurt her!"

Alarmed, Lainey took Eve's wrists in her hands and held them. "Baby, please. Look at me." Not certain what to do, Lainey put her arms around Eve as she would one of the boys and kissed her closed eyelids.

Eve laid her forehead on Lainey's shoulder as though she were exhausted.

"Eve? Honey, are you okay?"

"I'm fine." She gave Lainey a small smile. "You should go back to your room before the boys wake up."

"I'm not going anywhere. Do you want to talk about this?"

"Talk about what?" Eve's voice was expressionless. She had hoped this would never happen when she was with someone, particularly someone she cared about.

"Eve, you really zoned out there for minute." Lainey held Eve's ice cold hand in hers. "You were so scared."

Eve couldn't think, not with her head pounding the way it was, not when she was vulnerable enough to possibly say something she didn't want Lainey to know.

"There's some aspirin in the medicine cabinet in the bathroom," she said. "Could you get me a couple, please?" Eve waited until Lainey disappeared into the bathroom, then buried her head in her hands. "Damn it!" How was she going to explain this?

When she opened the medicine cabinet, the prescription bottle caught Lainey's eye first. Eve Sumptor. **Pentobarbital**. A sedative? Why would Eve have a sedative? It's none of your business, Lainey, she told herself as she tapped three aspirin into her hand and filled a glass with water.

Eve raised her head from her hands when Lainey came back into the room. When she looked up, it was clear she was confused.

"Do you feel better?" Lainey set the tablets and water on the side table. She wanted to make everything all right again. But she had no idea what to do to help Eve.

"I'm getting there." Eve reached up and brought Lainey's palm to her lips. "You can go back to your room now. I'll be fine."

"I told you, I'm not going anywhere."

"Lainey..."

"Eve. Don't argue with me. You're so pale. I've never seen you like that before."

Lainey suddenly remembered the episode in the gallery the day Eve found out about Jackie's death. She recalled the way Eve had looked as though she were somewhere else, digging her fingernails into her hands until they bled. And afterward she had spoken about 'him' getting past her, that she wouldn't let it happen again. But, this time was different. Clearly Eve was still in the grip of whatever had happened to her, trembling as if she couldn't get warm.

"Talk to me," Lainey said. "Tell me what happened."

"I'm tired Lainey," Eve told her. "I'm sure the boys will sleep for a couple more hours. I'd like to get a little more rest myself."

"Eve." Lainey was torn between wanting Eve to open up to her, and wanting to let her rest knowing she still hurt.

"I don't know what happened, Lainey," Eve said quietly.

"You don't remember anything?" Lainey didn't understand. She trusted Eve, gave herself to her, felt safe with her, but there was so much more under the surface that she didn't know.

"No." Eve rested her pounding head on her knees again.

"You said 'Don't hurt her'. What did you mean?"

Eve's head snapped up, a stunned look on her face. "I said that?" How could she have been so careless? "I...I have no idea what that means," Eve lied. "I don't know why I said that." She took the glass from the nightstand and, still naked, rose from the bed and walked to the bathroom. She turned on the faucet, letting the cold water run as she leaned on the counter, her eyes closed. Idiot. She cupped her hands under the water and splashed water over her face. And then, reaching for a towel, she stopped cold as dread washed over her.

"Fuck." Opening the medicine cabinet, she grabbed the prescription bottle and hurled it across the bathroom, pills scattering everywhere.

"I wasn't going to ask you about them."

Eve spun around at the sound of Lainey's voice.

"He hit her," Eve said, her voice harsh. "My father. He used to hit my mother. I tried to stop him once. He hit me so hard, I lost consciousness."

Lainey's heart broke for Eve. Never once had she imagined that Eve had grown up with such pain in her background. She wanted to go to

Eve, to hold her, but didn't know if that was what Eve wanted right now. Instead, she found Eve's robe and wrapped it around her.

"Thanks." Eve went back to the bed and pulled a blanket around her. She didn't want to be telling Lainey these things, but couldn't seem to stop.

"After he hit me, I never defied him again. My nights were filled with screams and yelling, the sound of glass breaking. I'd hide deep in the closet, singing to drown out the screams." Eve gave a humorless laugh. "I had a teddy bear, Mr. Snuffles. He'd keep me company. I wouldn't come out of the closet until my mother coaxed me out."

Eve closed her eyes, her chest tightening at the memory. "Her face would be battered and bloody," she went on. "She would try to cover it with make-up, but I saw. I saw everything. Yet every night when I heard her screams, I would hide." Eve bowed her head. "I didn't help her," she whispered. "I didn't do anything."

"You were only a child, Eve," Lainey told her. Tears were running down her face, but Eve's eyes were dry. "What could you do?"

"I used to sit in there, in the closet, and make plans to run away," Eve continued. "But, I couldn't leave her with him. I would never hurt you. Never. When you said that you were scared, it triggered something inside that I try to forget. But I'm not like him, Lainey. I can't be."

"I know, baby." She had been frightened, but she knew, deep inside, that Eve would never do anything to harm her. Otherwise, she never would have gotten this involved. She had to believe that. "I know."

"You should go before the boys wake up." Eve saw the disappointment in Lainey's eyes and was sorry for being the one to put it there. "No one knows what I just told you, Lainey. I'm not sure how I feel about you knowing. Not that I don't trust you. But I'm a strong woman. You have to believe that. And now I'm tired. I really just need to be alone."

Lainey was half way across the room when Eve called out for her. She turned and the need in Eve's eyes made her rush back and take Eve in her arms. They held each other tightly for a moment in silence.

"I wish there was more I could do for you," Lainey whispered.

Eve touched her finger to Lainey's lips. "You have no idea how much you've done for me already," she said. "No idea at all."

Once she was alone, Eve took a deep breath releasing it slowly. She rubbed her temples to relieve the pressure before picking up her cell phone.

"Hello?" The voice on the other end was groggy with sleep.

"It's me."

"Eve? Is something wrong?" he said suddenly alert.

"No. I'm sorry to call so early. Where is he now?"

"He's been holed up. Still sulking because he doesn't know where you are."

"Have you persuaded Meredith yet?"

"No, she's not budging. I have to be careful, but I'll get to her."

"And Katherine?"

"Still nothing. I'm working on it, Eve. You don't have to worry about it."

"I do have to worry about it!" She snapped. "I want him off the streets now. If the police can't do it soon I will. I'll be in touch."

Taking a steadying breath, she dialed again.

"Hello?" Adam answered sleepily.

"Hi." Eve realized she was nervous. After their last conversation, she wouldn't blame him if he never wanted to speak to her again.

"What...why, why are you calling?"

Eve could imagine him, the way he looked. His hair mussed from sleep, his body naked and warm. "I..." She hesitated. "I'm sorry."

Adam closed his eyes, his heart pounding in his chest. "Sorry? For what?"

"For everything."

"Could you be more specific?"

"We're always fighting about something, Adam," she said. "I know that it's my fault. I just wanted to tell you how sorry I am."

Adam tapped the phone on his head with disgust. Eve had already hung up. There were so many things he could have said. He could have told her that it was his fault as well, or that he was sorry, or that he was happy to hear her voice. But, he said none of that and now it was too late.

"Stupid, stupid, stupid." He dialed her cell and hoped that she would answer. She didn't.

"Shit." Adam tossed the phone down and sank back down into bed.

"When are we going, Mommy?" Darren sat on the stool at the island in the middle of the kitchen and swung his feet.

"I told you, honey. Soon." Lainey stood at the stove, cooking breakfast for the two boys. They hadn't slept for much longer after Lainey left Eve's room, but Lainey wouldn't have been able to sleep anyway. She couldn't get what Eve had told her out of her mind. There was so much more there that Lainey didn't know. One thing she was sure of, she would be there for Eve, if and when she needed her.

"Is Eve still sleeping?" Kevin ruffled his brother's hair before stealing a sip of his juice. "Did we wear her out yesterday?"

"I think you might have," Lainey told them. "She's not used to having two boys running around like I am. Now eat. We'll let Eve sleep as long as she needs to."

"What's Eve going to eat?" Darren demanded.

"I'll make her something when she comes down."

"She can have some of my eggs and shosheges if she wants," Darren said. "I'll share with her."

Lainey chuckled. "You eat your eggs and sh...sausages. But that's very sweet of you, honey."

"Yes it is." Eve leaned over Darren's shoulder. "Smells great. Good morning, boys. Good morning, l'amant. Sorry to keep everyone waiting."

How confusing it was, Lainey thought. One moment she was being pushed away and the next she was l'amant. Who was this woman she desired so passionately? Would she ever really know her?

"Did you rest?" Lainey asked her.

"Don't make anything for me," Eve replied, avoiding the question. She filled a cup with coffee. "I'm not hungry."

Lainey studied Eve from the corner of her eye. She looked rested. Certainly there were no signs of the hysteria that had shaken her a couple of hours before.

"You guys ready for some fun?" Eve asked, hopping up onto the counter.

"Yeah!" They both yelled simultaneously, their mouths full of food.

Darren looked over at Eve. "Do you know Mickey Mouse, Eve?"

"Hmm, maybe. Why? Do you want to meet him?"

"Yes! And Goofy, too! Can you 'troduce us?"

Eve chuckled. "I'll make some calls and see what I can do. How's that?"

"Cool!"

"Cool." Eve repeated and took another sip of her coffee. "As soon as you guys are finished eating, we'll be ready to go."

"I'm finished! Can I be excused, Mommy?"

"May I, and yes you may. Go put your shoes on and use the bathroom before we leave. You too, Kevin."

Eve was dressed in black short cotton shorts and a hooded shirt that was unzipped to show the tops of her perfect breasts cupped in a bikini top rather than a bra. "You look great, Eve," Lainey said after the boys raced out of the room. "I've wanted to tell you that since you came in here. You have great legs." She ran her fingertip over Eve's bare thigh. What was it about Eve that made her yearn to be in her arms?

"You look great, too." Lainey's Levi shorts were only slightly longer than Eve's, showing off much of her shapely legs and she wore a white t-shirt that clung to her breasts. "Lainey, you're arousing me. You know, we're probably going to get wet today." Eve shot Lainey a wicked grin. "There'll be at least a couple of water rides. As much as I'd love to see you in a soaking, white t-shirt, you should think about wearing a bathing suit underneath."

"I'll go put one on." Lainey gasped when Eve squeezed her breast, pinching the hardened peak. "Now who's arousing whom?" She backed away reluctantly. "Tell the boys I'll be right down?"

Eve noticed the concern in Lainey's eyes. It was the last thing she had ever wanted to see. Especially from someone she was so intimate with. If she wanted to continue this relationship with Lainey, she would have to be more careful in the future.

Eve pushed open the front door with her hip, her arms full of a sleeping five year old. Lainey followed her inside, holding Kevin who was fast asleep as well. The boys were completely exhausted after their full day at Disney. It had been one of the most wonderful days, not only for Darren and Kevin, but for Eve as well. She felt like a kid herself, or perhaps the kid she was never permitted to be. They rode such rides as Space Mountain and Test Track, and even tested their fear level by braving The Tower of Terror. But it was just being with Lainey and the boys that had given her the biggest thrill.

Lainey had been overjoyed watching her sons laugh and run around, looking at everything in absolute awe. Everything was so new to them, and larger than life. And, seeing Eve with them, laughing and playing or holding the boys hands, had filled Lainey's heart with so much happiness that it stunned her. They rode as many rides as they possibly could, and as promised, Eve had made some calls with the result that Darren and Kevin got to have lunch with their favorite characters, including Mickey, Donald and Goofy. They went to every one of the parks, trying not to miss anything, and stayed until the last firework had exploded. Too tired to even stand during the parade, they had had to sit on Eve's and Lainey's shoulders and they were asleep before they even got to the car.

Taking the sleeping boys up to their room, Eve and Lainey tucked them in and kissed them. Seeing Eve be so tender and generous with the boys deepened her longing for the woman. The power of it staggered her.

After closing the door to the boys' room, Lainey grabbed Eve's hand and walked quickly to Eve's bedroom. Once the lock was turned, she pounced on Eve, pushing her back against the door, devouring her mouth with a hunger that neither of them had expected while she unzipped her shirt and peeled it off.

"God, I want you so much." Lainey's voice was hoarse with need, her eyes darkened with desire. She had been patient all day but now they were alone, and the yearning erupted in her, kindling the heat between Eve's thighs, hot and lusty.

"Take me," Eve whispered. "Now!"

Lainey's breath hitched as she slipped a hand inside Eve's shorts and cupped her, feeling the heat and wetness.

"Go inside." Eve placed her hand over Lainey's and pressed. Her eyes rolled back when Lainey slipped inside her. She fumbled with the button on Lainey's shorts, swearing when her fingers couldn't perform the simple task of unfastening a button.

Lainey's laugh was hoarse. "Hurry!"

"I'm trying. Mmm, Lainey. Don't stop." Finally, she got the shorts unbuttoned. "Did you have to wear such complicated clothes?"

"Sorry," Lainey giggled. "I'll go naked next time."

"No you won't, because then I'd have to kick everyone's ass for looking at you. Ahh, there," she breathed, yanking Lainey's shorts down, cupping her hand between Lainey's naked thighs, sighing when at long last she touched Lainey's sweet wetness.

Together they stumbled to the floor, kissing, touching, nipping at each other and laughing.

"You feel so good." Lainey's breathing was fast and rough as she tried to match Eve's rhythm.

"So do you." Eve could feel herself get closer to the peak, felt Lainey tighten around her fingers like a vise. "Now, baby," she whispered roughly, driving Lainey up and over the first peak.

"Now, now, now." They both arched, crying out as the intense orgasms swept over them.

"Jesus!" Lainey blew out a breath. "Incredible!"

"Absolutely." Eve kissed her gently. "Think we can make it to the bed?"

"I don't know. I don't think my legs are working."

"Hmm. Damn. I was hoping you would carry me."

"Oh, well in that case, give me a couple of minutes." Lainey laughed.

"How about we carry each other." Eve dragged herself up, and held out a hand for Lainey, almost losing her balance as she pulled her up. "Okay. I think we can make it."

They staggered to the bed and fell face first when they got there. "Will you set your alarm?"

"You want me to move?" Eve teased. "Why? Do you want to leave early tomorrow?"

She had been dreading having to take Lainey and the boys back to Jack, but right now she could only live for the moment. Tonight there was no tomorrow.

"No. I want to sleep with you."

Eve's eyes narrowed. "Afraid I'll lose it again," she said. "So you can be here to take care of me?" It was the first time either of them had mentioned what happened the night before.

Lainey lifted her hand and moved the hair from Eve's eyes. "I want to sleep with you," she repeated. "And, if it happens again and you need me, I want to be here."

I do need you, Eve thought silently. "All right," she said aloud. "What time do you want me to set it for?"

"Early. I hope you don't mind, but I'm going to do everything I can to stay awake and savor every last minute with you."

Eve wasn't the only one dreading tomorrow. Lainey was apprehensive about going home to Jack. She was so tired of fighting and has been having such a wonderful time with Eve. Tomorrow she would be going back to reality. It didn't help that she knew that reality included Adam and Lainey was not looking forward to his and Eve's reunion. It was selfish of her, she knew, but she just couldn't help it.

When both women were naked, they crawled under the covers and reached for each other. With tomorrow hanging heavy on their hearts, they made love, slowly and tenderly.

Eve traced Lainey's cheekbone with her fingertip. Leaning down, she kissed Lainey tenderly, but passionately. She used her tongue and her teeth to stimulate Lainey, trailing down her neck to her breasts.

Lainey sighed softly. "This is all I wanted, this kind of passion and excitement. Why can't it be like this with Jack?"

If there was anyone Eve did not want to talk about now it was Jack. On the other hand, she had promised Lainey she would help her. "When you are with someone and you want something more than what they are giving you," she said, "tell them. Let them know what you want them to do, what you want to feel."

"I can't do that," Lainey protested. It frustrated her that this woman, whom she'd recently met, knew what she needed and the man she had been married to makes love to her as if it were a chore. Why could she be this open with Eve, but not with her husband? "I feel awkward telling Jack what I want. Besides, I don't know that he cares. He knows what he wants and takes it. And then he goes to sleep. I never get the chance to really express myself, Eve."

Eve kissed her gently. "Tell me what you want now, Lainey." Her voice was just a breath against Lainey's lips. "Tell me what to do to you."

"Kiss me," Lainey murmured, her voice barely audible.

Eve smiled and obeyed, tangling her tongue with Lainey's. Feeling Lainey's body tremble, she deepened the kiss.

"What else?" Eve whispered softly.

"Touch my breast," Lainey whispered back, feeling more daring when she heard Eve moan and felt her touch.

"Mmm. That's it, Lainey. Tell me what else you want."

Eve circled Lainey's taut nipple with her thumb, arousing both of them more.

Lainey hesitated. "What if I can't say it?" she asked shyly.

"Then show me."

Lainey held her breath as she took Eve's hand and skimmed it down her stomach and guided it between her legs. She sighed, her nails raking over Eve's back as Eve touched her. "There's something else I want."

"Tell me."

"It's something I want to do to you."

Eve raised her head from kissing Lainey's breast. "To me?"

"Yes."

"Honey, you're supposed to tell me what you want."

"It is what I want." Lainey's pulse quickened, her mouth was dry. She was unbelievably nervous. She has made love to Eve, knew every part of her body, knew things no one else knew, and yet she was still nervous.

"All right. What do you want to do to me?" Lainey's pulse wasn't the only one that had quickened.

"I want you to lay back."

Eve did as she was told.

"Spread your legs," Lainey instructed.

"Do you have any idea what you're doing to me?" Eve's breath came faster, her body quivered.

"I have an idea of what I want to do to you." Lainey lowered her hand between them and touched Eve, making her moan. She then brought her hand up and tasted Eve off of her fingers.

"Oh my God," Eve moaned. She watched as Lainey licked her fingers, then dip her hand for more. "Lainey," she whispered.

Lainey brought her fingers to her lips again, rolling her tongue over the tip, tormenting Eve. She lowered her head and licked Eve's lips the same way Eve had done to her the first time they kissed.

Eve's body vibrated with need and lust as Lainey kissed her neck, scraping her teeth across Eve's sensitive skin. She took Eve's nipple in her teeth, biting gently while grazing her nails down Eve's sides. Lainey reveled in the way Eve moaned Lainey's name and moved her body with undeniable pleasure.

Lainey moved down more and sank her teeth into the silky skin of Eve's belly, trailing down lower.

"Lainey!" Eve fisted her hands in Lainey's hair. "Are you sure you want to do this?" Lainey didn't answer, just kept her mouth busy. "God," Eve breathed. "Be very sure this is what you want."

Lainey looked up at Eve and smiled, then lowered her mouth to Eve.

"Oh my God!" Eve's body arched, her eyes closed tightly as the sensation of Lainey's mouth and tongue on her filled her with an intense pleasure. "Lainey," she gasped as Lainey's fingers dug into her hips, pulling Eve closer, probing deeper. Eve pulled and grasped at the sheets, trying to hold on to anything as Lainey took her to the edge, threatening to push her over completely.

Lainey moaned. She couldn't believe what she was doing. Even more so, she couldn't believe she was enjoying it so very much. No amount of fantasizing or dreaming could have prepared her for what she was feeling at this moment. She felt Eve's body writhe, heard her moan and cry out in absolute ecstasy and the feeling was overwhelming.

Eve buried her hands in Lainey's hair as the powerful orgasm swept over her. Her body trembled with the thrill she had just experienced. Her legs were watery and weak, her heartbeat rapid, her breath ragged. "Wow!" she whispered, her voice a rasp of desire and satisfaction.

Lainey crawled up to lay next to Eve. She turned on her side, propping her head up with her arm that was bent at the elbow. "How did I do?" She ran a fingertip across Eve's lips and smiled when Eve's lips parted in response. "Be kind, it was my first time."

"Then you're a natural." Eve nipped at Lainey's finger, catching it between her teeth and biting playfully. "Unbelievably amazing."

"You tasted unbelievably amazing." Lainey bit Eve's bottom lip.

"Mmm, Lainey. I do believe you're getting bold." Eve kissed Lainey's mouth once. "And brave," she said kissing her again. "I think I like that." In one swift motion Eve rolled on top of Lainey and smiled down at her. "You're beautiful."

Lainey's heart soared. "You're breath-taking," she responded and saw Eve lower her eyes.

"Beautiful is enough," Eve said quietly.

"Beautiful doesn't describe you, Eve." Eve smiled at Lainey, but it didn't quite reach her eyes. "Why are you so sad?"

Eve looked into Lainey's eyes. "I'm not sad." This time when she smiled, she forced it to reach her eyes.

"Yes, you are. I can see it in your eyes." Lainey lifted her hand and touched Eve's face. "Talk to me."

Eve's mouth moved down her body. It felt so wonderful that she didn't want her to stop, but the sadness in Eve's eyes bothered her. After last night, and the time they just had together now, Lainey was disappointed that Eve still couldn't trust her. Or wouldn't.

"You can open your body to me, but not your heart?" Lainey whispered and felt Eve freeze. Eve lifted her head and stared down into Lainey's eyes. After a moment of silence, Eve rolled away from Lainey and reached for her robe.

"You should go," she said irritably.

"Eve, don't do this."

Eve bent down and picked up Lainey's clothes. "You should go," she said again.

"Eve, please. I'm sorry..."

"You have nothing to apologize for, Lainey." Eve paused and studied Lainey as she lay on Eve's bed. She hated to give Lainey the cold shoulder. She was offering her so much. But it wasn't that simple. And Lainey didn't seem to realize that. "I'm going to go take a shower. You should go back to your room and get some rest. It's been a long day." With one last look at Lainey, Eve turned and walked out of the bedroom and into the bathroom, closing the door behind her.

Turning the jets on full, Eve stepped into the shower hoping the harsh spray of water against her skin would wash away some of the hurt. Her forehead pressed against the cool tile, she let the water pound her, completely closing her mind to every thought that tried to invade it. She flinched when Lainey stepped into the shower behind her and put her hands on her shoulders.

"What are you doing in here, Lainey?" she said softly.

"I didn't mean to hurt you," Lainey told her.

"I don't hurt," Eve lied. "I don't hurt, I'm not sad, I'm not breathtaking. I'm just Eve. Take me as I am." She took Lainey's face in both hands then. "Why did you come in here?"

Lainey answered Eve with a tender kiss. Eve deepened the kiss, slipping her tongue between Lainey's inviting lips. She pushed Lainey up against the shower wall trailing a fingertip down Lainey's neck and chest, and then cupped her breast in her hand.

When Lainey cried out, Eve pressed her body closer and lowered her hand to the soft velvet between Lainey's legs. Lainey's breath caught when Eve touched her and she arched her back to give Eve more. Eve took more, slipping inside Lainey, loving the way she felt in her hands. "Go over for me, Lainey," she whispered, her voice hoarse with arousal.

Eve felt Lainey slip her hand down between her legs and Eve gasped when she touched her. "Go over with me, Eve." They moved together, moaning, bringing each other a pleasure different than either of them had ever felt before. Both of them cried out as they came together.

~ Thirteen ~

"We don't wanna go home, Mommy! We wanna stay here!" Darren had been cranky all morning and Lainey's nerves were wearing thin. She didn't want to go home either, but they had to.

"Darren, we've been through this already." Not wanting to waste her last hours alone with Eve sleeping, Lainey was tired. They had spent the time talking about their wonderful day with the boys, and when they weren't talking, they were making love. The only thing Lainey regretted was that Eve had deliberately steered away from any conversation that involved her or her childhood.

"Yeah, squirt. We have to go back to school tomorrow, remember?" Kevin could tell that his mother was a bit irritable herself, so he tried to help with Darren.

"But, I don't wanna! I wanna stay here with Eve! I don't wanna go to school or go home."

"Darren! That is enough!" Lainey snapped angrily. The whining was just too much for her to handle right now. She heard Darren sniffle and rushed to put her arms around him. "Oh, honey. Mommy's sorry." She kissed him on the top of the head. "You know we have to go home. I'd love to stay here, too, but we can't. You have school, I have a job, and we have to go back to reality." Lainey's voice wavered and she fought to control it. No matter how much she wanted break down and cry with Darren, she couldn't. She had to be strong for him, for both of them.

"But, if we go home, we'll never see Eve again." Darren sniffled again and wiped at his tears.

"Why do you say that, honey? We'll see Eve," Lainey said, even though she understood his fears. Hadn't she also been afraid of things changing and losing what she and Eve have?

"She won't come and see us," Darren said, wiping his nose with a napkin. "And she'll forget about us."

"How could I forget about you?" Eve appeared in the doorway, looking cool and collected in white shorts and tank top.

"I don't know," Darren answered shyly. "We won't get to see you every day, and you'll be busy."

"I'll never be too busy for you," Eve interrupted softly. "Even if we don't get to see each other every day, I'll be thinking about you. You can call me, or come by and visit me anytime you want."

"Really?"

"Really. You and Kevin are very special to me." She glanced over at Kevin and winked. "Your mom is very special to me. You guys are a part of my life now. You're going to see so much of me you're going to get tired of me."

"We'll never get tired of you." Kevin's voice was so quiet that Eve barely heard him. She smiled warmly at him and reached over to kiss him gently on the cheek.

"Thank you," she whispered and turned her attention back to Darren, wiping his cheek. "No more tears. I'm not going anywhere. You're stuck with me, kiddo."

Darren threw his arms around Eve. "Promise?"

"Promise."

"I love you, Eve," Darren said quietly.

Eve froze. She had never said those words to anyone in her life, and the last person who said them to her was Adam. Hearing them from Darren made her heart soar, and at the same time scared the life out of her.

Lainey saw the terror in Eve's eyes and moved in. "Kevin, honey," she said cheerfully. "Why don't you take your brother upstairs and make sure you have everything packed."

"Okay, Mom. Come on, squirt."

Eve let Darren go and watched silently as he hopped down off of the stool and ran after Kevin before she leaned her arms on the counter and bowed her head. "I couldn't say it," she said quietly, ashamed. "I tried, but I couldn't say it."

"It's okay, Eve," Lainey told her. "He knows how you feel."

"How?" Eve demanded. "How could he? I don't even know how I feel."

"Honey, a very smart, very beautiful woman once told me that kids are more perceptive than we'd like to believe. I believed her. So should you."

Eve smiled. "Smart and beautiful?"

"Very." She took Eve's hand. "I can't imagine the pain you went through as a child..."

"Lainey." Eve tried to pull her hand away, but Lainey held on tight.

"I'm not letting you pull away this time. Let me say this." She hesitated, but for only a moment. "I can't imagine what you went through, but, I know that your reluctance to open your heart to anyone is the direct result of what happened to you then. But that's in the past, Eve. Let me in. Let me help you love."

Eve wanted to tell her how much she had helped her. But not here. Not now. "Not now, Lainey," she said. "We should get going."

Lainey didn't want to push Eve. She wished there was something she could say, something that would show Eve just how much she wanted to help her. Whether she believed it or not, Eve had helped her tremendously by bringing out a different side of her. She had made her feel passion and excitement again, and gave her a strength she had never felt before. But, for now, she would back off and wait for Eve to come to her.

When Lainey started past her, Eve reached for her. She glanced up the stairs to make sure they were alone, then brought Lainey into her arms, embracing her tightly. "I want to let you in," she whispered. "I want to, Lainey. Give me a little more time."

Lainey looked into Eve's eyes. "I'll give you whatever you need, Eve."

Eve framed Lainey's face in her hands and kissed her gently. She moved away when she heard the boys coming near. *Thank you*, she mouthed.

All four of them settled into Eve's Jaguar. The flight back had been a somber one since none of them had wanted to return to "reality". Eve had been especially quiet. She didn't know how she was going to be able to drive Lainey and the boys back to the suburbs and leave them. How was she going to go to her apartment and the loneliness she knew was waiting for her there? She hadn't noticed it before. Or perhaps she had and had refused to admit it, just as she had refused to admit so many other things until it was too late.

"All set?" she said, putting the car in gear just as her cell phone rang.

"You're being tailed." The phone went dead.

Eve took down her sunglasses from the visor, slipped them on and glanced behind her in the mirror.

"Something wrong?" Lainey asked her.

"No," Eve lied. She had taken great measures to keep Lainey's home safe from Tony. She wasn't about to just lead him to her now. "I have to make a stop before taking you home. Is that okay?"

"Sure. Where are we going?"

"I have to stop by the gallery." She looked back at the boys. "You guys want to see where your mom works before going home?"

It was a distraction and, as they cheered, Eve found herself praying that neither they nor Lainey would guess that she was taking measures to keep them safe.

The boys fidgeted excitedly on the elevator ride up to the gallery, clearly aware of how important it was that Eve would take them to the place where she and their mother worked. Even if it was a stuffy old art gallery. When the doors opened, Eve immediately spotted the two detectives talking to Mikey. Lainey noticed them, too, and tensed. If the police were here, it couldn't be good news.

"Why don't you take the boys up to your office and show them around," Eve told her.

"Come on, guys," Lainey said. "Let's go see what you can play with in my office."

Both men watched as Eve strolled towards them, her tanned body striking in short white shorts and a tight white tank top. Clearly her beauty distracted them, but only for a few moments before an ominous look crossed Carter's arrogant features.

"Detectives," Eve greeted them unsmiling.

"Where have you been, Ms. Sumptor?" Detective Carter asked.

"Out of town," Eve answered shortly. "Why are you here?"

"Where is Katherine Bushnell, Ms. Sumptor?" Detective Harris finally spoke.

"I don't make a habit of keeping tabs on my employees, Detective."

"You don't find it odd that she didn't show up at work today?" Carter asked.

"I've been out of town," Eve repeated deprecatingly. "I don't know who has shown up for work and who hasn't."

"You don't know, or you don't care?"

"Both. Why should I care that Katherine didn't show up for work? She's been embezzling, she implicated an innocent woman of doing something she didn't do, and she's been slacking. Shall I go on?"

"You're very indifferent, considering people are dying around you because of you and your connections," Carter said accusingly.

"She's missing, Ms. Sumptor," Harris interrupted.

"Missing?" Eve's eyes were blazing. "You consider her missing because she didn't show up for work?"

"Her family filed a missing person's report Saturday when she didn't come home."

"Where is she, Ms. Sumptor? And, where were you this weekend?"

Eve was becoming tired of Carter's suspicions. "Am I under investigation, Detective?" she asked. "Because if I am, arrest me. My lawyers would have a field day with you. No wonder you haven't gotten Tony off the streets. You're barking up the wrong tree."

"Are we?"

"Such hostility," Eve shook her head. She leaned in and put her mouth to Carter's ear. "Tell me Detective, what bothers you more? That you think I'm guilty and have gotten away with murder, or that you want to fuck me but can't have me?" She stepped back. "Arrest me, or get out of my gallery."

"We're not going to arrest you, Eve." Harris stepped between her and Carter, playing the buffer. "We just want to know where Katherine is."

"I don't know where she is, but wherever it is, I'm sure she's safe from Tony." Eve's eyes never faltered. "Stop investigating me and get him off the streets, Detective Harris."

"Or you will?"

"I've been away all weekend and I have things to do," Eve snapped. "Now, if there is nothing else."

"We'll be in touch, Ms. Sumptor." Harris tipped his head and motioned for his partner to follow him.

"I'm sure you will. Hey, Mikey. How did things go this weekend? No problems?"

"Nope. No problems at all. Until – well, until those detectives came in here, asking all kinds of questions about you."

"What kinds of questions?" Eve asked immediately alert.

"Where you were. How long you'd been gone. Whether you'd received any visitors or strange phone calls before you left. I didn't tell them anything. Of course, I didn't know anything, but I wouldn't have told them if I did." He puffed out his chest. "I don't know what they want, but they're not getting it from me."

Eve gave Mikey a charming smile. "Hmm. Holding down the fort and watching my back. Sounds like you deserve a raise."

"I didn't do it for a raise," the young man protested.

"And, that's precisely why you are getting one," Eve interrupted. "You do a great job here, Mikey. I'd like you to join us full time when school is out."

"Are you serious? I have a job?"

"Yes. On one condition."

"Anything."

"Don't call me ma'am. Call me Eve."

"My mother would kill me for being disrespectful." The statement reminded Eve of Jackie. She didn't understand why her family was refusing any kind of help from her. But Eve could only imagine the grief they were going through, so she wouldn't push. She smiled at Mikey. "So we won't tell her." Eve laid her hand on Mikey's shoulder. "Why don't you go and get something to eat. It's quiet here and I'll be here for a while. We'll talk about your raise and everything else a little later. Deal?"

"Yes, ma' - I mean, yes, Eve." He grinned and all but skipped to the elevator.

Eve made her way upstairs to Lainey who was waiting for her in front of the double doors of Eve's office.

"Is everything okay?" Lainey asked her. The presence of the detectives had made Lainey nervous. She didn't know if she could handle more news like that about Jackie's death, and she didn't think Eve could either. She knew that underneath that tough exterior, Eve was just as vulnerable as anyone else. Maybe more so.

"Mmm hmm. Where are the boys?"

"In my office. They found the games on the computer and it's keeping them occupied." Lainey shrugged. "I guess the games are more interesting than art at their age."

"I can't take you home," Eve told her abruptly. She had to make sure that Lainey and the boys were safe, and that meant she couldn't be the one to drive them back to Jack.

"What? Why?" Lainey's heart stopped beating for a split second.

Eve's heart hurt having to say this to Lainey. She looked down at the sell slips in her hand. "I'm sorry, I have a lot of work to do and Mikey just went to lunch," she told her. It wasn't the full truth, but she couldn't tell Lainey the selfish reason.

"Then we'll wait for you." Lainey didn't want to leave Eve yet.

"I don't know how long I'll be. And, it's a lot of tedious paperwork. The boys will be bored to death."

Why was Eve trying to dissuade Lainey from staying with her? There was something here that was not being said. Something important. She was sure of it.

"They'll be fine," Lainey said evenly. "I could help you with the paperwork and they can keep playing games."

"Honey, I can't take you home. I've explained why."

"We can wait," Lainey said stubbornly. "I want to wait."

"Lainey, I can't. I don't want to take you home," she confessed finally. She would be as honest with Lainey as she could be right now. "I'm sorry, but I just can't drive you to the house that you share with Jack and leave you. I can't watch you disappear into that house, knowing he's there waiting for you. I can't drive away, drive back to my apartment, alone, without wanting to be with you and feeling jealous that you're there with him." She reached up and touched Lainey's cheek. "I'm sorry. I just can't."

Lainey was speechless. She had been so worried about how she would feel watching Eve drive away, that she hadn't even considered Eve's feelings. "Eve." Lainey lifted her hand to Eve's, taking it. She walked into Eve's office, pulling Eve in with her and closing the door. "I should have been more sensitive about your feelings. I don't want to leave you either. You must know that." She brought Eve's lips to hers and kissed gently. Lainey watched as Eve's eyes fluttered closed.

"Go home with me," Eve pleaded softly.

"God, Eve. I wish I could. If it were just me, I would."

"I know I'm being unreasonable," Eve told her. "But I had no idea it would hit me this hard. I have someone that can take you and the boys home. Let me just make the call."

"You don't have to do that. We'll take a cab."

"No, you won't. I have a car to take you. Tomorrow, if I can't pick you up, there will be someone waiting to bring you into work."

"I don't need a babysitter," Lainey protested. She knew she had given Eve her word, but this was too much. It made her feel like a child who couldn't take care of herself.

"Lainey, you promised me. Until all of this is taken care of, I don't want you to be alone."

"What is 'all of this'? You tell me that I may be in danger, but you don't tell me why. Don't you think I deserve to know?"

"I will tell you everything, Lainey. Just not now. Let me take care of things, of you." Eve brushed Lainey's hair back from her face. "Until then, all I ask is that you not travel alone."

"No, Eve," Lainey told her, choosing her words carefully. "I'm not going to live my life like a prisoner in my own home. If I need to go to the store, I'm not going to wait for some stranger to take me. I'm not going to be dependent on you or anyone else. That's what I'm trying to get away from. I know you're used to getting what you want, Eve, but I can't do that. If you're not there to pick me up in the morning, then I'll drive myself."

"Then I'll be there to pick you up," Eve promised her. She would make sure that Lainey was safe without impeding her privacy. Eve walked to her desk and picked up the phone. "Tonight, indulge me, and let me call the car for you and the boys."

"Fine, but this time only." Of course, everything that she had said to Eve was true, but Lainey knew that her motive was a little more selfish.

Eve stood in front of Lainey and studied her after making the call. "You think you can fool me, don't you?" she said, pushing the hair from Lainey's neck and bending to brush her lips softly against Lainey's skin. "We all have our motives."

Surprise and arousal battled each other inside Lainey.

"Mommy?"

Eve and Lainey wrenched away from each other at the sound of Darren's voice. Clearing her throat and smoothing her shirt, Lainey went to the door and opened it. "Yes, honey?"

"Kevin won't let me play games on the 'puter. He's hogging it!"

"Am not. You just played."

"Boys, that's enough. Get your stuff ready, we're going to be leaving soon."

"Are we going home now, Mommy?"

"Yes." Lainey hesitated when the phone on Eve's desk rang.

"They're here," Eve said as she hung up.

"Isn't Eve coming, too?" Kevin asked.

"No, honey. She has some work to do, so she won't be able to take us home."

Eve moved to Darren and Kevin. "I'm sorry but I'll see you guys soon. If not during the week, then maybe next weekend. Okay? And remember, if you want to talk to me, all you have to do is call. Your mommy has my number, all right?"

"Okay. Are you going to be lonely without us?" Darren asked, his voice watery with tears.

"Very. Who am I going to play video games with?" Eve gave him a sweet kiss on the cheek and was almost knocked over when he threw his arms around her.

"Don't be lonely, Eve," he said. "If you need to talk to me, you can call me."

Eve's heart melted. "I'll do that." She looked over at Kevin who was standing there awkwardly and gave him a kiss as well. "I'll see you guys soon, okay?"

"All right, guys, go get your stuff and make sure to turn off the computer. I'll be there in a minute." She waited until they left and then turned Eve to her. "You can call me, too," she whispered.

Eve smiled. "You have wonderful sons. They take after their mom."

"I don't want to go, Eve. I want to stay with you."

Eve laid her forehead on Lainey's. "I want you to stay with me, too, baby." More than you'll ever know, Eve thought to herself. She took a deep breath and let it out slowly. "Come on, before I never let you go."

"Kiss me," Lainey whispered.

Eve obeyed and kissed Lainey deeply, passionately. It was all too fleeting, but it still left them both wanting more. "God."

Eve touched a fingertip to her lips and then touched Lainey's. "Dream of me."

"How could I not? Dream of me."

Eve smiled. "How could I not?" She knew she was doing the right thing. They would be safer this way. Tony was after her not Lainey, and the best thing to do right now was to not go with them. She couldn't risk it.

She walked into the dimly lit room and sat in the chair in front of Katherine, who was nervously biting her nails, her pink slacks and matching silk shirt grimy from her surroundings. Slowly, deliberately she crossed her legs, remaining silent as Katherine stared at her.

"I should have known you were behind this," Katherine spat out disgustedly. "You have no right to keep me here. This is illegal!"

"Embezzling hundreds of thousands of dollars is illegal, too, Katherine," Eve said quietly.

"You can't prove that!"

Eve glanced at a figure hidden in the shadows and nodded her head slightly. "*We were supposed to just alter the books.*" On the tape, Katherine's voice sounded harsh. "*Sumptor would lose money and possibly the company and we would get paid.*" Eve watched the horror fill Katherine's face as she heard the recording.

"How did you get that?"

"I have my ways, Katherine. Are you ready to talk?"

"What are you going to do to me?" Katherine was becoming afraid again. "Why are you holding me here? I don't know anything."

Eve laced her fingers together and studied the other woman. "This is the safest place for you to be, Katherine. After you left Meredith's office, she made a call. The same call she made before Jackie was found murdered."

"You're lying." Katherine's mouth was bone dry. "She wouldn't do that."

"She did." Eve nodded to the shadow once again and a glass of water was promptly brought to Katherine. "I could let you go and leave you to fend for yourself, or you can talk to me and I can protect you."

"I'll run." She gulped down the water. Clearly she was frightened and she had every reason to be.

"You couldn't run fast enough."

"I can get out of the country or hide."

"There's nowhere to hide," Eve assured her. "You have no idea who you are dealing with. I do. I know you're scared of me, Katherine. I know you don't trust me. But I'm the only one who can keep you safe now. Tell me who you are working for."

"I don't know. I swear to God, Ms. Sumptor, I don't know." Katherine's hands began to shake. "Meredith talked to him. She never told me anything about him or how she contacted him."

"Are you protecting Meredith?"

"Why would I protect that bitch? She's trying to get me killed! I'm telling you the truth. I don't know."

A man in a dark suit came up behind Eve and whispered in her ear. Eve sighed and leaned up in her chair. "You have a choice, Katherine. Your family has filed a missing persons report. You can call them and tell them you are okay and stay in hiding with my protection, or..." Eve paused. "Or, you can go out there and take your chances at ending up like Jackie. It's up to you."

"Why are you helping me?"

Eve remained silent for a moment. "I don't like what you did, Katherine," she said finally. "You stole from me and you had an innocent woman killed. I don't want any more killings and however I feel about you personally, you are human." Eve rose and smoothed a hand over the gray slacks she had changed into at her office. The crisp, gray button down shirt topped off her outfit giving her an air of authority. "I hope that when this is over, you have learned from your mistakes. I hope you've learned never to cross me again."

"I just needed the money," Katherine protested, pushing an uneasy hand through her hair. "I was tired of living paycheck by paycheck. I wanted to live like you. No one was supposed to get hurt."

"In this world, you earn what you're worth. You don't take it from someone else." Eve paused on her way to the door, her expression somber. "Be careful what you wish for, Katherine. You wanted to live like me. Now you are."

"She's been in there for a while. She has to come out sometime." Carter blew on his coffee before risking a sip of the steaming liquid.

"Be patient," Harris told him, sipping from his own cup.

"I told you she was up to something. She's more involved with this than you want to believe, partner."

Eve slapped her hands down on the opened window of the car door and leaned her head in. "Did you bring enough coffee for me, boys?" She chuckled when both cups overturned. "Ooo. That's gotta hurt." Her smile faded. "What are you doing here?"

"We could ask you the same thing, Ms. Sumptor." Harris responded, blotting at the scorching stain on his lap.

"Why don't we take a look inside the warehouse and see?" Carter said, still wiping at his trousers.

"Do you have a warrant, Detective?"

"We don't need one. This is public property."

"No, it's not. I own this warehouse. So unless you have a warrant, I suggest you leave."

"What are you hiding, Eve?" Harris asked. The news that Eve owned the property surprised him.

Eve gave him a humorless laugh. "Do you think I'm holding Katherine in there? She would certainly be safe from harm if she were here and away from Tony. Not that I have to explain anything to you, but I'm thinking of turning this warehouse into a shelter for homeless people. My lawyer called and asked me to come out to discuss the details."

"This late at night?"

"I'm a busy woman, Detective. When I have an opportunity, I take it."

"You expect us to believe that story?" Carter demanded becoming increasingly irritable as a man wearing a dark suit came around the side of the building. "Who's that?"

"My lawyer," Eve smiled as the two policemen slid out of the car, their hands on their revolvers.

"Do you have ID?"

"Am I doing something wrong? This is a public street and I have every right to be here without being harassed."

"Don't you just love lawyers?" Eve grinned and nodded to the man.

"Happy?" he said, showing them his ID. "Now may I ask why you are following my client?"

"We're not following anyone," Carter snapped back.

"No? First you show up at her gallery and now this? I may file a stalking complaint."

Carter took a step towards him and was stopped by Harris' hand.

"Please, let him follow through," the man suggested pleasantly. "Then I can file a police brutality complaint, as well."

"Why don't you just tell us what you're doing here," Harris said as calmly as he could.

"My client, being the generous woman she is, has decided to turn this warehouse into a shelter. I'm here discussing the details with her."

"Do you have the paperwork for this 'discussion'?"

"You produce the warrant, Detective, and I'll produce the paperwork. Now, since my client has done nothing wrong, I suggest you leave her alone."

Harris looked at Eve and she raised an eyebrow. "I told you, you are investigating the wrong person," she told him. "You wanted me to trust you to take care of this, but how can I when I'm the one you want to accuse?"

"Let's go," he muttered and then, when Carter started to protest, "Let's go. There's nothing to see here. I'm sorry for the inconvenience, Ms. Sumptor." He tipped his head and walked back to his car.

Carter stepped close enough to Eve for her to feel his breath on her face. "I know you're hiding something. I'll be watching you," he said quietly.

Eve closed the gap, her lips almost touching his. "Don't ever get in my face again, Detective," she retorted and shoved him back. "Don't test me."

"That was close," the man with the dark suit said quietly when the detectives were out of earshot. "You're going to have to..."

"I know," Eve interrupted. "I'll take care of it. Just make sure the papers are in order."

"Goddamnit, Harris, she's hiding something. Why did you just give in like that?"

"I've been in this business a lot longer than you, partner. She's hiding something, yes, but she's right. She's not the one we should be investigating." He looked over at his partner with disgust written all over his rugged features. "Are you trying to piss her off? You play too hard, Carter, and she'll play it safer. Back off. Let her make the mistakes, not you."

Harris made a mental note to visit the warehouse again when no one was around. Eve was involved with the disappearance, that he was sure of. But, what she had said about Katherine being safer here than where Tony could get to her was playing on his mind. She was right, but Harris needed to make sure that Katherine was safe.

By the time Eve reached the front door to her apartment, she was exhausted. After Lainey had left with the boys, she had busied herself, doing as much as she could to keep her mind off of being alone. She'd finished paperwork, made calls to clients, visited Christine in the hospital, and even tried contacting Jackie's parents once again to no avail. Then, of course, there were the sessions with Katherine and the detectives.

Eve ran a hand through her hair and sighed wearily as she dug her keys out of her pocket. Behind the door in front of her was a loneliness that Eve had been trying to avoid since she watched Lainey walk out of the gallery.

"Hello, Mrs. Jenkins."

The old woman gave a curt nod and slammed the door shut.

"Well, looks like we're actually getting somewhere," Eve said to herself as she pushed open the door and flipped on the light inside. Empty. Just like her. Locking the door behind her, she threw her keys on the glass-topped table where the maid had left her mail. As she sorted through it, she hit the play button on her answering machine on the way into the living room, and threw herself onto the couch.

"Eve?" The sound of Adam's voice made Eve's pulse jump. "Are you there? It's Saturday afternoon and I'm at the gallery, but you're obviously not here either. I have a couple of things to do, but I'll stop by a little later to see you. I miss you. Talk to you soon."

The message made Eve feel even more miserable than she had felt already. She missed him as well, which confused her even more about what was going on in her life right now. How could two people mean so much to her? And, when or if it came down to it, how was she going to choose which one to hold on to?

"Hello, Ms. Sumptor. This is Dee Cummings with Channel 9 News." Eve frowned. Her phone number was unpublished and it annoyed her that a reporter had somehow obtained it.

"I wanted to talk to you about the recent death of one of your employees. According to the police, foul play was involved and I hope to get your reaction to that. If you could call me back here at the station, I'd appreciate it."

As she left the number and her extension for Eve, thanked her and hung up, Eve made a mental note to find the source feeding this Dee Cummings information, including her phone number. She would play hardball with this woman if she had to, but Dee Cummings would not make Jackie's death into a media circus.

The messages continued. "Eve?"

Eve's eyes closed at the voice. "Lainey," she whispered in her empty apartment.

"I guess you're not home." Lainey's voice carried a hint of accusation and sadness.

"I'm not with him, Lainey," she said to the answering machine.

"I just thought I'd call and see. God! I miss you. I guess I should hang up now. I wish you were there."

Lainey paused for a moment as if she didn't want to hang up, or didn't know what to say. "Don't pick me up tomorrow, Eve," she said finally. "I'll drive myself. I'm sorry."

Eve let her head fall back on the couch. She knew that Lainey thought she was with Adam. Call her, Eve told to herself. Call her and let her know she's wrong. Fuck Jack if he gets upset by the call. Eve reached for the phone, but before she could pick it up and make that call, the next message began.

"Hello, little Eve." Tony's voice chilled Eve to the bone. She could feel the bile racing up her throat and she swallowed hard to keep it down. How had he gotten his hands on her number?

"Didn't think I could find you, did you, little Eve," he drawled on, his voice menacing and arrogant. "I'm one step ahead of you. That's a point for me. Soon, it will be time for a nice family reunion. I've seen how beautiful you've grown to be, little Eve. I'm sure you're definitely more - experienced as well. I've seen how you are with that young man of yours. I'll get a taste myself soon when we're reacquainted. It'll be just like old times. Until then, little Eve."

"You son of a bitch!" Eve cried out. She had grabbed up the phone ready to throw it across the room when the idea hit her like a lead pipe.

"Let's see who's one step ahead," she said, smiling sardonically. "Let's see who wins this time, Daddy."

Tony sat at his desk, grinning, still in the good mood he had been in ever since he acquired Eve's phone number. It was going to be much harder than he expected it to be to get into her building, but that was only a matter of time. The best security in the world wouldn't be able to keep him from his little girl. Tony let out a quiet laugh as he sat back in his chair and played his messages.

"One step forward, two steps back, Tony." The voice was Eve's. "Can't really blame you, I suppose. You've been away for a long time, and you've lost your - edge." Her voice dropped to an icy whisper. "I'm not a little girl anymore. I'll be waiting for you, *Daddy*. This time, I'll be the one who wins."

Tony picked up the first thing he could find and threw it across the room. The letter opener stuck in the door with a vengeance that he wanted to use on Eve herself. One of his men tentatively opened the door.

"Is everything okay, sir?" he asked.

"No. Everything is not okay," Tony growled. "Get in here!" Eve was not going to get away with this. It was time for him to teach her a lesson, and he knew just how he was going to do it. Because, better than anyone else on earth, he knew exactly how to bring Eve to her knees.

The object of Tony's obsession stepped out of the elevator and into her gallery. Eve's night had been extremely restless and she was feeling the effects of it now. Already on her second cup of coffee, she greeted Mikey who told her that there had already been a call for her.

"A Miss Cummings," he said.

"What did you tell her?" Eve interrupted. Her voice was terse.

"Nothing, ma'am." He looked at her curiously. "I told her that you were not in."

"I'm sorry," Eve told him. "I didn't mean to snap at you. If she calls again, please tell her that I'm not interested in talking with her. Now, I need you to do something for me."

"Yes, ma'am." He was still a little cautious of Eve's mood.

"There are a couple of deliveries that have to be made today and I would like you to go along and see that everything goes smoothly." She took a set of keys out of her pocket. "Our first priority here at Sumptor Gallery is customer satisfaction. See that all of our clients are handled with care and courtesy."

"Yes, ma'am."

"Mikey, call me Eve," she said, giving him the keys. "I apologize for snapping at you earlier. I've had a long night, but that's not an excuse. Two deliverymen will be here in about ten minutes. The list of the client's addresses and their purchases are in the computer, so you'll have to print them out. Make sure they take special care of the merchandise when they are loading and unloading. You know where the van is parked. If you have any questions don't hesitate to call me, okay? I should be in my office all morning."

"Okay. I shouldn't have any problems. Piece of cake."

When Lainey heard the light knock on the door, her heart began to pound almost painfully in her chest. She wanted so much to hear Eve's voice, to touch her, but she was so afraid of what she would see in Eve's face. How was she going to handle knowing Eve had been with Adam? How much would it hurt?

"Come in," she said, starting toward the door, her palms dampening. Her new navy skirt and cheerful, floral blouse did nothing to help lighten her mood.

Eve was also wary about seeing Lainey. Had she made love to Jack last night? If Lainey had thought that Eve was with Adam, would she have been with Jack in retaliation? God, she hoped not. She didn't know if she could handle that right now. Taking a deep breath, she walked into the office and almost melted with relief.

She hadn't, Lainey thought with immense relief. And then, determined to be direct, "I was afraid that you were with Adam last night. And I knew that if you were, I'd see it in your face this morning."

"I know. I wasn't with him, Lainey," Eve said quietly. "I'm so sorry I missed your call, but I was alone last night." She opened her arms and Lainey walked into them, holding on to Eve tightly.

"I wanted to hear your voice." Lainey leaned back enough to kiss Eve gently on the lips. "I missed you so much last night."

Eve ran her fingers through Lainey's hair. "I missed you, too. I didn't sleep at all. Every time I closed my eyes, I could see you with him."

"I wasn't..."

"I know. I knew the moment I saw you." She brought Lainey's lips to hers and gave her a long, slow, deep kiss, the one she had been dreaming of giving her all night. Eve cleared her throat and took a step back. "Maybe we shouldn't do this right now."

"You're probably right." Lainey's lips still tingled. "Mikey's downstairs."

"Actually, he's on his way out to make some deliveries. He'll be gone most of the morning." She saw Lainey's eyes darken with desire as she stepped closer to her.

"Really? We'll be all alone?"

Eve smiled. "Yes."

"All alone. Whatever shall we do?"

"Hmm, unfortunately, the gallery is still open." Eve pulled Lainey to her, their bodies meshed together. "But, tell me what you had in mind and when Mikey comes back, we'll take a long lunch."

Lainey laughed and whispered exactly what she had in mind in Eve's ear.

"Mmm. A very long lunch," Eve reiterated, her voice full of desire. "What are you working on?" She needed to change the subject and fast or she's not going to care if anyone walks in while she and Lainey did what Lainey had just described.

Knowing exactly how Eve felt, Lainey walked back around her desk and sat. "Just a little bookkeeping and inventory. Picasso is very hot. So is Dali." She looked up at Eve. "What do you do when you run out of them?"

"Go shopping for more." Eve smiled. "There's an auction that I'm going to in a couple of days. They're going to have some beautiful pieces. I should come back with an armful of wonderful items."

"An auction? That sounds fun."

"It can be. Would you like to go with me?"

Lainey's smile broadened. "I'd love to. Is that how you get most of your items? From auctions?"

"Mostly. I go all over the world to find the best pieces. It's a dream for the true art lover." She studied Lainey for a moment.

"There's another auction that I have to go to," Eve paused and flipped through her mental schedule. "Next week sometime," she said a little unsure. "I have it marked down. I'll be gone for a few days."

Lainey frowned. "A few days? Where are you going?"

"Paris."

"Paris? France?"

Eve chuckled at Lainey's surprise. "Yes, Paris, France." She had made the arrangements months ago and had been looking forward to it. But, just now, looking at Lainey, and thinking of being away from her, turned that excitement into a bit of dread.

"Go with me," she said. The words were out of her mouth before she even had a chance to stop them.

"What?" Lainey couldn't believe what Eve just asked her.

"Go with me. Wait." Eve held up a finger before Lainey could speak. "Don't answer yet. Just think about it, okay? A few days, three, maybe four tops." Now that it was out, Eve knew that that was precisely what she wanted. What she needed. Time alone with Lainey so that they could work out what exactly was going on between them.

"What about Kevin and Darren? What about Ja..."

"Jack can take care of Kevin and Darren. He's their father. I'm sure the boys will understand if you have to go away for work for a few days. Please, Lainey. Think about it. Go with me. Be with me."

Everything inside Lainey screamed for her to say yes. To be with Eve, alone. To work out what was going on between them. Jack had been surprisingly warm when she and the boys had returned, as though he were relieved that she had come back to him. But she was still confused as to what she wanted now.

"What about Adam?" Lainey hadn't wanted to ask. Didn't know why she did, but there it was.

"What about him?" Eve eased her hip on Lainey's desk. She was wearing all white today. Skin tight pants with a sleeveless shirt that was just as tight, the kind of outfit that drove Lainey crazy.

"Lainey, I'm as confused about my relationship with Adam as I am with ours." Eve paused and lowered her eyes so that Lainey couldn't read what was in them. "Besides, I'm not what he needs." She gave Lainey a small smile.

"Why do you say that?"

"Because it's true. You don't want to talk about Adam, Lainey," she continued when Lainey opened her mouth to speak. "Let's just leave it at that."

"Wait, Eve," Lainey said warmly, placing a hand on Eve's knee. "I want you to be able to talk to me about everything. That includes Adam. I really have no right to be jealous."

"You have a right. Just as I do to be jealous of Jack." Eve leaned forward and touched Lainey's cheek. "We just have to find a way to deal with it. I don't think you have anything to worry about anymore."

Eve sighed and got up to pace.

"Why? Did you and Adam..."

"I don't know." Eve laughed. "Isn't that funny? I have no idea what's going on between us. I haven't spoken to him since Sunday morning."

Lainey frowned. "Sunday morning? When? I was with you all..." She stopped. She hadn't been with Eve all morning. There had been that hour when Lainey thought Eve had been resting.

"I didn't do it to go behind your back or to keep anything from you, Lainey." Such an open book, Eve thought. "I felt bad about what happened between us, so I called him to apologize. Not that it did any good. It seemed like he didn't even want to talk to me. And, I can't blame him."

"Well, if he can't get over whatever it is you two are fighting about, then he doesn't deserve you."

Eve chuckled. "You're such a good and loyal friend. Much, much more than a friend. But it's not his fault. It's mine."

She sat back down on Lainey's desk and massaged her neck absently as a dull ache began.

"Saturday was two years for us and I forgot," she said. "I left without telling him and I was a bitch to him when he called. Now, can you blame him if he never wants to see me again?"

"Two years." Lainey thought that she was beginning to understand the kind of person that Eve really was. Any relationship that had lasted two years had to mean that it was very important to Eve. "Was it my fault?" Lainey asked quietly.

Eve frowned. "Was what your fault?"

"Everything. Did you fight with him because of me, because I was with you? Did you forget that it had been two years because of me?"

"Nothing is your fault, Lainey. It's me. It's always been me." Eve paused and took a deep breath. "He knows that, I know that. Adam needs someone that can be the kind of woman he deserves. I don't want to lose him, but it would be selfish of me to hang on to him when I'm so cold and dead inside."

She went to the window and stared down at the sea of people on the sidewalk below. New York was so alive, bustling with individuals of all shapes and sizes. Although life was going on around her, she really didn't feel a part of it. She didn't know what it felt like to be truly happy.

"Honey." Lainey came up behind Eve and laid her hand on Eve's shoulder. "You are not cold and dead inside. No one who makes love the way you do could be anything but vibrant and alive inside."

"I don't do self-pity very well," she admitted, turning and pulling Lainey to her. "There are things you don't know about me, Lainey."

"Then tell me. Let me be there for you."

"And risk you running away from me?"

"Don't joke about that, Eve," Lainey said quietly. "Nothing could change the way I feel about you." She couldn't imagine anything being so bad in Eve's past that it would make her run. This woman in front of her had a firm hold on her heart. "I feel that there is so much that you want to say, that you need to say, but you keep closing yourself to me. Why are you so afraid?"

Eve just stared at Lainey. Afraid. Is that what she was? Was being afraid what was keeping Eve from feeling? All of those emotions that she craved, that she had dreamt of feeling for so long now, were they always out of reach for her because she was afraid? It seemed so weak that it should have pissed Eve off, but instead it made her think. "Will you have dinner with me tonight?"

"Yes." Lainey didn't hesitate. Eve needed to talk, she could feel that deep inside, and she was determined to be there for her.

Eve smiled. "Good. I'll cook something special for you."

"I'd love that." Lainey leaned in and kissed Eve on the cheek. "I should get to work," she whispered in Eve's ear. "I don't want the boss to think I'm slacking."

Laughing, Eve tapped Lainey on the rear. "That's probably a good idea. I hear she can be such a bitch."

"Hmm, yes, but, a very sexy bitch."

Eve took Lainey's chin in her fingers. "You're the only one who could get away with that," she said grinning. "And, that's only because I like it when you call me sexy." Eve gave Lainey a quick kiss. "I'll be in my office if you need me."

"Mmm, I do need you. So why don't you stay here in my office."

"Hmm, Lainey. You really are getting bold. I'm definitely liking the new you. That's why I'm going to drag myself out of this office before I attack you."

"I may like that."

Eve groaned. "I'm leaving, Lainey."

Lainey laughed. "Okay, I'll stop. Oh! I have something for you." She walked around her desk to pick up her purse.

"You have something for me?" Eve smiled. She was used to being the one giving not receiving. It was what she was more comfortable with, but she found that the thought of getting a gift from Lainey thrilled her.

"Yes. It's not much, but I thought you would enjoy it."

It was a photo of Eve, Lainey, Kevin and Darren at Disney World. The photo was framed, in true Disney fashion, in a silver frame with the famous mouse himself cut-out in the border. The four of them looked so happy, as though none of them had a care in the world.

Lainey waited apprehensively for Eve to say something, anything, but for a long moment she didn't said a word.

"I bought the frame while you were keeping the boys busy," Lainey told her. "I know it's not your style and you can change it if you like."

"It's perfect," Eve said quietly. It was Eve's first family photo. That was exactly how she thought of Lainey and her sons, as family. She knew that she would cherish the photo far more than any of the priceless art she carried in the gallery. "Thank you," she whispered, not masking any of the emotions she felt inside. "Thank you," she said again, kissing Lainey gently on the lips.

Knowing that both of them wanted more than what they could have at the moment, Lainey stepped away from Eve. "I'll be downstairs. Call me if you need me."

"I do need you," Eve whispered as Lainey disappeared. "God, help me, I do."

Eve's phone was ringing when she entered her office.

"Sumptor Gallery," she said, placing the framed photograph on her desk. "This is Eve."

"It's me. We have a problem. You pissed him off this morning when he received your message."

"Good. He pissed me off when I received his."

"Eve. He's going to go after Mrs. Stanton."

Eve's stomach churned with a dread and sickness she had never experienced before, emotions so intense that she had to fight to stay in control. Her grip tightened on the receiver until her knuckles were white.

"No!" she said, her voice tight with terror.

"I'm sorry but I thought you must know."

"I don't care what you have to do," Eve told him heatedly. "But you keep him away from her!"

"What can I do, Eve? He's made up his mind. You know how he is."

"And you know me. I'll kill him before he can get to her."

"You can't do that. The cops are watching you."

"I don't care about the fucking cops!" Eve took a deep breath. She had to stay in control. "Do you really think I care what happens to me?" she demanded. "I'll do anything I have to do to keep Lainey safe. Do you understand me? Anything. You tell Tony whatever you have to in order to get him to back off. If he doesn't, he's dead."

"I'll do everything that I can, Eve. Do you want us to put more people on Mrs. Stanton?"

"I'll take care of her. You just take care of Tony. Or, I will. I also want to know everything he knows about Lainey. Why is he going after her?"

"He's been making inquiries about her since Meredith had mentioned that she might be a problem. He knows that she was the one who accompanied you on your trip over the weekend. Tony also knows that you have taken great measures to keep Mrs. Stanton safe, so he's presumed that she means a great deal to you. He thinks that getting to her maybe the easiest way to bring you down."

Eve was confused. Tony knows about Adam, too. He had mentioned him in the message he had left Eve. So why had he chosen Lainey? Eve wanted to know exactly how much Tony knew about her. She was also going to pay Meredith a visit and do a little rethinking about helping her.

"I want more details about what Tony knows or thinks he know," she said. "If he leaves his little hole, I want to know where he's going."

"Yes, ma'am."

"One more thing. I want you to make sure Adam is safe."

"I don't think..."

"Just do it. Have him watched, and don't let anyone in Tony's camp near him. I will not let anything happen to him either. Understood?"

"Yes, ma'am."

"Keep me informed on what's going on. I'm counting on you to do anything you can to change Tony's mind. You have to get him to understand that it is not a good idea for him to mess with either Adam or Mrs. Stanton. If you can't do that I'm taking him out of the game. For good."

Eve hung up and dropped her head in her hands. What has she gotten Lainey in to? She picked up the photo Lainey had given her and touched a finger to Lainey's image.

"Eve." Lainey poked her head around the door. "There's someone here to see you. God, honey! What's wrong? You look terrible."

"Nothing," Eve lied, replacing the photograph. "There's nothing wrong. Who wants to see me?"

"Dee Cummings," Lainey told her, noticing the change in Eve's eyes when the name was mentioned. "Who is she?"

"She's a reporter," Eve told her grimly.

"I thought I recognized her. Does she want to do a piece on the gallery?" Lainey didn't understand why Eve didn't want to speak to the press. It could only help the gallery.

"No. She's here about Jackie."

Lainey stepped closer to Eve's desk. "Why?"

"I don't know." But, she would find out. She would also find out who was feeding her information. "Send her up, please."

"You're going to talk to her?" Now that Lainey knew why the reporter was here, she understood why Eve's mood had changed.

"Yes. It's the best way to find out what she knows."

"Are you sure you want to do this?"

"Looking out for me?" Eve grinned. "Yes, I'm sure."

"I'll send her up then. Don't let them say anything bad about Jackie, Eve. That poor woman's family has been through enough."

"They won't, Lainey. I promise."

Eve waited until Lainey closed the door behind her and then picked up the phone.

"I want Lainey watched closely at all times," Eve said. "She is not to be alone at any time, is that understood. The stakes have been raised."

"Yes, ma'am. She will be safe."

"Make sure that she is." Hearing a sound outside her door, Eve lowered her voice. "If anything happens to her, I'm holding you responsible. If you see him or any of his group, I want to know immediately."

Striding to the door, Eve threw it open. "Do you make it a habit of listening in on other's conversations, Ms. Cummings?" she demanded.

Dee Cummings was taller than Eve by a couple of inches, beautiful and slim with great legs, a great combination for a TV personality. Her light, coffee colored skin was as smooth as that of a much younger woman. She was dressed immaculately in a lavender skirt and matching jacket.

"I was not eavesdropping, Ms. Sumptor," she said, clearly offended. Her voice was silky and soothing and held a hint of a southern accent, a voice that worked well with charming the viewers or keeping them calm as she told them about whatever violence was going on in the world. "But I am sorry for just dropping in like this."

"No you're not." Eve gestured to the chair in front of her desk as she sat back and crossed her legs. "You assumed that if you just showed up I would have no choice but to speak with you."

"It seems I assumed correctly then."

"Not necessarily." Eve's eyes were amused. She was used to playing these games with the media and she always won. "What can I do for you, Ms. Cummings?"

"Well, Ms. Sumptor. I would like to talk to you about Jackie Sawyer."

"What about Jackie?"

Dee took out a note pad and poised her pen over it. "How do you feel about being a suspect in Miss Sawyer's murder?"

, Eve lifted a brow. "A suspect? I'm not a suspect, Ms. Cummings. Who told you that?"

"I have a very reliable source, Ms. Sumptor. And, yes, your name has been mentioned as a suspect in this case."

"Strike one, Ms. Cummings," Eve said coolly. "I have no reason to think I'm a suspect. If I am, no one has told me. What else has your source told you?"

"I've been informed that you were also a suspect in the disappearance of another employee, Katherine Bushnell."

"Were? Does that mean I'm not a suspect anymore?"

"She, by the grace of God, called her family last night. Apparently she had gone on vacation without telling anyone and is fine."

"Hmm. That was awfully thoughtless of her, wasn't it?" Eve laced her fingers together on top of her desk. "Strike two, Ms. Cummings."

Dee Cummings frowned. "Can you tell me how you felt about Miss Sawyer embezzling from your company?" she continued. "I have the documentation right here in my briefcase."

"I don't care what you think you have," Eve said icily. "Jackie embezzled nothing. I hope you do your homework very thoroughly before you go on air with this - story, Ms. Cummings."

"I always do my homework, Ms. Sumptor. I have the papers right here." She held them out to Eve, and frowned when Eve didn't take them. "Don't you want to see them?"

"I've seen them already, Ms. Cummings. Strike three."

"What do you mean? It's all here in black and white."

"You of all people should know not to believe everything you read, Ms. Cummings." Eve turned up the heat in her eyes. "I'm warning you, don't drag Jackie's name in the mud. She was a wonderful young woman, an excellent employee and she never did anything wrong. Let her family grieve for her without having to put up with listening to lies about her."

"I would never do anything to upset her family any further, Ms. Sumptor, but if the evidence suggests..."

"The evidence, as you call it, is fake. I have never had a problem with Jackie, and for someone to do this to her is inexcusable. I'm asking you to believe me on that, Ms. Cummings. Don't use these papers for whatever story you intend to cook up and call news."

"It is news, Ms. Sumptor." Dee sat back in her chair and crossed her legs. "Tell me something. Why are you protecting a family that wants to file a lawsuit against you?"

It was Eve's turn to frown. "A lawsuit? Against me? I'm sorry, Ms. Cummings, I'm afraid you're going to have to explain this one to me, too."

"You don't know? The Sawyer's believe that you are responsible for their daughter's death. Don't tell me you didn't know."

"They think I did it?" Eve asked quietly, flooded by a sense of horror. It wasn't possible that this could be true. All of a sudden it made sense that they didn't take her calls and why she was told that the funeral was closed to family members only.

"I'm sorry. My source has told them everything he's told me. He even told them about your mother."

"What about my mother?" Eve demanded. She was fighting to stay in control, but it was getting harder every second. The pain deepened as her past began merging with her present.

"Jackie and your mother died in much the same way, Ms. Sumptor. I understand that the authorities feel that the similarity is too great to ignore."

"I was fourteen when my mother died," Eve whispered. "Do they think I had something to do with her death as well?"

"My source told them about your record..."

"What record?" Eve couldn't believe what she was hearing.

"Your juvenile record."

"I don't have a record. I've never been in trouble with the law." She watched incredulously as Dee took more papers out of her briefcase.

"These are copies of what he showed the Sawyers."

Below the word **SEALED**, the paper was titled **The Juvenile Records of Eve Marie Sumptor**. Son of a bitch, Eve thought. She could feel the heat of her rage creep through her carefully maintained control.

The son of a bitch! Whoever the hell he was, he was setting her up. She didn't think Tony was behind this, it wasn't his style. So, who the hell was it?

"Someone is playing you and the Sawyers, Ms. Cummings," she said evenly. "As I've said before, I don't have a record."

"Ms. Sumptor, these are legal documents..."

"My middle name is not Marie, Ms. Cummings. At least, it wasn't when I was fourteen."

"I don't understand."

"My parents didn't give me a middle name when I was born. Check my birth certificate if you must, but that's the truth. I added Marie when I was in my early twenties. It was my mother's name. You've been given forged material."

"But who would try to ruin you like this, Ms. Sumptor?"

"You tell me. Who's your source, Dee?" To be familiar, she told herself, would do no harm. Certainly she would gain nothing from continuing to be abrasive.

"I'm a reporter, Eve. I can't just give you my source. That's practically reporter suicide."

They each had something the other wanted and Eve knew that this woman was prepared to see how far Eve would go to get hers.

"Would you like to make a statement on everything you've told me?" Dee continued. "I have a camera crew downstairs and we can do it here and now if you like."

"How important is this interview to you?" Eve demanded, leaning across the desk, eyes narrowed. "What will you do for me, Dee, if I get in front of that camera and give you a story?" It was clear to Eve that this was an extremely important story as far as she was concerned.

From a journalist's point of view, Eve's beauty would draw an audience but no doubt conspiracy and murder had the makings of a newscaster's dream.

"Do you have a restroom I can borrow?" Dee asked suddenly. The unexpected request had Eve stunned for a moment but when Dee was gone, she saw that the reporter had left her notebook full of notes, names, numbers and dates, on the edge of her desk. Eve's eyes glanced down at the pad of paper, then with a small laugh, picked it up. Dee had decided to help her after all, she thought as she flipped back a couple of pages and read the neat handwriting. Initials, not a name. She grabbed a pen and a piece of paper. D.C., she wrote and then the phone number that was next to it. Underneath the initials were notes about her. Suspect. Murder. Cover-up? She read on, until she heard Dee in the hallway, then put the notebook back in its place and slipped the piece of paper she had written on under her keyboard.

"Did you find everything okay?" she asked Dee when she was seated again.

"Yes," she said and looked at Eve with sober eyes. "Did you?"

Eve smiled. "I can't give the interview right now. But," she continued when Dee opened her mouth to protest, "you'll be the first person I come to for an exclusive. After what you've told me today, there are things I need to check on first. And, apparently I need to speak to my lawyer about this business of my being a suspect." Eve sighed. "The person that is after me, who wants to hurt me, that's who everyone should be looking at. Not me."

"Who is that person, Eve?"

"I don't know, Dee. You're the reporter, you figure it out. Evidently the police are not trying too hard if you've gotten the idea that I'm a suspect. Have you spoken to Detective Harris or -"

Detective Carter.

"Son of a bitch. I'm sorry, I have things I need to do now. If you talk to the Sawyers again," Eve said as she walked the reporter to the door, "please tell them that I had nothing to do with this."

"What are you going to do about the lawsuit?"

"I don't give a damn about the lawsuit. If they want money, all they had to do was ask me. I've already set up a foundation at Sumptor, Inc. in Jackie's name. I told the detectives to please tell the family if they ever needed anything I would do everything I could for them."

Detective Carter, Eve thought with disgust. The same damn detective that was trying to fuck her over.

"It's not the money I'm worried about," she added. "I just need them to know that I didn't hurt their little girl."

"I'll tell them everything you've said, Eve." Dee held out her hand. "Call me when you are ready for that interview."

Walking to the wall overlooking the gallery, she spotted Lainey.

Something was wrong, Lainey thought, when she saw Eve's face. She wanted to go up to Eve, to make sure she was okay but she had customers to tend to. So instead, she made a mental note to ask Eve about her conversation with Dee, and do anything she could to take that haunted look out of Eve's eyes.

Eve sat at her desk and buried her head in her hands. Things were getting out of control. She knew what she should do. She knew that she was being selfish keeping Lainey close to her, keeping anyone close to her, but she couldn't help it. For the first time in her life, she needed someone. And, now, she would do whatever it took to keep those she needed, safe. Eve reached for the phone.

"Federal Bureau of Investigations. How may I direct your call?"

"Agent Donovan, please."

"May I say whose calling?"

"Eve Sumptor."

"One moment, please."

Eve took a deep breath as she waited. She was taking a step back into her past, a past that she would rather keep hidden and tucked away. But, it seemed that no matter how hard she tried to keep it hidden, someone out there was trying to bring it forward. But instead of letting the past take her down, she would use it to her advantage, an advantage no one was expecting.

"Eve?"

"Hi, Billy."

His eyes closed at the sound of her voice. It had grown deeper, sultrier over the years. Although it still held that breathy seductive sound of her youth, it had definitely matured beautifully. With his eyes closed he could see her face, the gray, striking eyes, those luscious lips. He wondered if her body and appearance had developed as much as the voice had.

"No one has called me that for years," he said. "How are you, Eve?"

She wasn't going to lead him on. She respected him too much, and has grown too much to do that to him. "I'm well, thank you. How have you been?"

"I'm better now. It's been a tough day. Hearing you has definitely brightened things up. To what do I owe this pleasure?"

"I'm in trouble, Billy. I need your help."

He frowned. Eve would never ask for help unless it was life or death. "What is it, Eve? What do you need?"

"I can't go into it now. Not on the phone. Will you meet me?"

"Of course. Dinner? Tonight?"

Eve looked over at the photo Lainey had given her and remembered that she was having dinner with Lainey. "I can't tonight. Lunch, tomorrow? I can have a plane there to pick you up in the morning..."

"That's okay. I'll find my way there. Where would you like to meet?"

"The Garden of Eve, two o'clock. Is that all right?"

"I'll be there."

"Billy," she stopped him before he could hang up. "Thank you."

"Don't thank me, yet. Let's see if I can help you first. Tomorrow, Eve."

Agent Donovan stretched his broad shoulders and ran a hand through his wheat colored hair. His alert, hazel eyes held concern as he sat back in his chair and thought about Eve. The prospect of seeing her again was exhilarating for him. Their encounter with each other had been brief all those years ago, but he had come away from it knowing what it was to be in love. He also found out how much being in love with the wrong person could hurt. He knew Eve hadn't felt the same way about him, but he would see how the distance and years had changed her. He turned to his computer and started making the arrangements to fly into New York City and see the woman who had invaded his dreams for the last ten years.

The headache was getting worse. Eve tried to relieve the pressure by massaging her temples but it wasn't working. She knew plain aspirin wouldn't work on this kind of pain, but she didn't want to take anything else. She had been doing fine without the stronger medication and she wanted to keep it that way. She wasn't going to let Tony get to her this way. She closed her eyes, her head in her hands and willed herself to relax.

Lainey silently came up behind Eve and began massaging. When Eve felt Lainey's cool fingers on the back of her neck, she felt a deep sense of relief.

"Hi. I didn't hear you come in."

"I know. Do you want me to get you something for your head?" Lainey buried her fingers in Eve's hair and massaged her head.

"Mmm. No, you're doing a great job. You have magical fingers," Eve told her with a sly grin.

"Mikey's back," Lainey whispered in her ear. "Want to go to lunch?"

"Yes." Eve lifted her hand to Lainey's face and pulled her closer to give her a kiss. "I'm starving," she said quietly.

"We could talk about what that reporter wanted and why you were so upset when she left," Lainey said in a low voice. It was odd to see Eve so vulnerable.

The headache that had been fading came back with full force.

"I'm sorry," Lainey apologized. "You're tense again."

The woman saw way too much, Eve thought. "You didn't. I just need to eat. Would you like to go to the restaurant?"

"Sure." Way to go, Lainey, she scolded herself.

"Lainey. I don't want to talk about reporters. Not now, please? I'll talk to you about it, just not now. Okay?"

"Okay." She could see that Eve was in more pain than she led on, so Lainey wouldn't push her to talk. She noticed the photo on Eve's desk. "You don't have to keep that there if you don't want to."

"I like it there."

"You could take it home," she whispered.

Eve kissed her gently. "How about I leave this one here and you can pose for a different kind of picture. Just for me." Eve wanted to paint Lainey, in a particularly stimulating pose. She hadn't known how to bring it up or how Lainey would feel about it, but this seemed to be the perfect time.

"You want me to pose for you?" Lainey chuckled.

"Yes. I want you to pose for me." Eve traced a fingertip down Lainey's chest. "In so many different ways." She kissed Lainey gently on the forehead. "Come on. Let's go to lunch."

~ Fourteen ~

As soon as Lainey and Eve entered the restaurant together, they felt the stares. It still amazed Lainey that Eve was totally unaffected by how people looked at her.

"Everyone is staring at you," Lainey whispered close to Eve's ear.

"They're staring at you," Eve told her. "Good afternoon, Elliot."

"Good afternoon, Ms. Sumptor. Your regular table?"

"No. My companion and I have business to discuss, so if you could put us as far away from everyone as possible, that would be wonderful."

Once they were seated in a secluded area behind a wall decorated with exotic flowers and left alone, Lainey smiled at Eve.

"Your companion? I like that. And, they were staring at you. Who could possibly see me when you're around?"

"Stop it." Eve paused as the waiter came up to them and set a glass of water in front of them both. Each of them ordered iced tea and a salad, and when the waiter left, Eve looked at Lainey intently. "You have no idea how beautiful you are, do you?"

Lainey blushed slightly and lowered her head. "Eve, I'm not..."

"Yes, you are." She wanted to reach out to Lainey and take her hand, but couldn't. So, instead, she held Lainey's eyes with hers. "Everything about you is beautiful. I wish you would start believing it."

Lainey shrugged. The way Eve was looking at her stirred her more than she could say. "How do you deal with it? People staring at you, obviously wanting to get to know you a little better? It must make you feel good."

"It annoys me." Eve said simply.

Lainey frowned. "It annoys you? Why?"

"Lainey, honey, I don't want to talk about me. We're always talking about me. I want to know more about you." Eve sipped her water and peered at Lainey over the rim. "I didn't ask you earlier, perhaps out of selfishness, but how did things go with Jack last night?"

Lainey groaned. "You don't really want to talk about Jack, do you?"

"This morning you told me that you wanted me to be able to talk to you about anything. Including Adam. Now, I'm telling you the same thing. I want you to be able to talk to me about Jack, about Kevin and Darren, about whatever is on your mind." She smiled at the waiter as he set the iced tea in front of them and hurried off. "So, tell me what happened when you went home last night."

Lainey sighed a little and studied Eve. She wanted to be open and honest with her, and she wanted Eve to be the same. This was the first time she had had someone that she could really talk to, to really be herself with.

"Jack was happy to see the boys," she began. "Hugged them. Told them he loved them and missed them. Then he asked what they did over the weekend. He was, of course, a bit angry that I had taken them out of the state without telling him."

"I'm sorry," Eve said quietly. When she had made the decision to take them to Disney, she hadn't even given a thought to how Jack would feel. She was always used to doing things her way, how and when she wanted to do them.

"It's okay. I was expecting a fight," Lainey looked out the window at an elderly man who was feeding the pigeons across the street and thought about the night before. "But, he just let it go. He came up to me and kissed me, telling me how much he missed me."

Her voice trailed off. Jack's actions had surprised her so much that she hadn't known how to respond to him.

Eve was trying not to imagine the scene. She didn't want to think about Jack touching Lainey, or kissing her. She knew how selfish she was being, but couldn't seem to help the way she felt.

"I don't know what got into him," Lainey continued. "One minute I'm preparing myself for the yelling and accusations, the next I'm in his arms and he's leading me to the bedroom." Lainey saw Eve lower her eyes and didn't know if Eve would want her to go on. "We don't have to talk about this, Eve."

"It's okay," Eve touched Lainey's hand briefly. "Go on."

Lainey blew out a breath. "It was everything that I had wanted. He was being attentive, loving, passionate - but I just couldn't do it. I couldn't be with him."

"Why?"

Lainey looked Eve in the eye. "Because of you."

Eve eyebrows furrowed. "Because of me?"

"Eve. I couldn't be with Jack right after leaving you. I felt guilty about everything. Guilty that it would hurt you. Guilty that I couldn't be with my husband, even though he was trying so hard to show me he'd missed me. And, I didn't know if he was doing it because he's just as tired of fighting as I am, or if he really meant it. I've never been so confused in my life, Eve. And I don't know what to do about it."

Eve remembered that this had all begun when she had told Lainey that she would help her with her marriage. Of course, she had no way of knowing that, between them, they would set off fireworks. She never anticipated the relationship that had developed between them, but she would keep her word whatever the cost to her happiness may be.

"Maybe Jack realized that you were serious about needing change," she said. "He's afraid of losing you." And I understand exactly how he feels, she added silently.

"Somehow I'm not as sure about that as you are." Picking at the salad with her fork, she realized suddenly that she had lost her appetite.

Eve watched her closely. "Lainey," she said softly. "You know Jack loves you. There are things happening in your life right now that understandably have you confused. But, ultimately you're in love with Jack."

"I'm not so sure of that either, anymore," Lainey interrupted quietly. "If I am, why couldn't I be with him? Why did I spend my night in the guest room thinking about you? Wanting to be with you."

"Then leave him," Eve said abruptly.

The words shocked Lainey enough to have her head whipping up in surprise. "What?"

"You heard me. Leave him. Move in with me. Be with me. Divorce Jack and be with me, Lainey."

Lainey couldn't believe what she was hearing. Part of her was overjoyed. These were the words she had dreamt of hearing. The other part of her knew it could never be.

"I have room for Kevin and Darren," Eve continued eagerly. "Or, we could buy a house in the suburbs. I care about your boys, Lainey. You must know that."

Just the thought of the boys made reality set in. Lainey knew that she could never take them away from Jack. Sure he and she had problems, but they could work them out. She just needed a little more time to sort out everything she was feeling, but she was suddenly certain of one thing. She knew she didn't want to leave Jack, not only because of the boys, but for her own sake as well. Jack had been a huge part of her life for so long. They both had invested so much time in each other. Whatever happened, she wasn't ready to give up on that.

"Eve, I can't. I'm..."

"In love with Jack," Eve finished the sentence for her. "I know. But I thought you needed to be reminded of that."

Lainey frowned. The joy at hearing those words from Eve turned to disappointment and annoyance. "You didn't mean it."

"Yes, I did, Lainey. I meant every word." Eve took a drink. It had been harder for her to admit that than she had imagined. When she had first asked Lainey to leave Jack, she had only been trying to make her face the fact that she was still in love with him. Or so Eve had thought. But now she realized that making Lainey a permanent part of her life was something that she truly wanted. And that frightened her because never before had she dared to risk so much of herself. Never before had she taken the chance of putting her happiness in someone else's hands.

"I don't understand." Lainey's heart continued to pound in her chest.

"I meant it," Eve said again quietly. "I knew what you were going to say."

Eve looked out the window. She watched the people walking by. Business men and women hurrying from one place to another. Tourists taking in the sites only New York could offer them. Lovers holding hands, looking at one another as though no one else existed as the world turned around them. All of them looked to Eve like they had a clear destination. At the end of the day, how many of them would go home to a loved one? And, how many of them would go home alone? Like Eve.

"If you knew, why did you ask?"

"You were right, you know," Eve interrupted. "I'm afraid." Eve let out a small laugh. "Not even two weeks ago, if someone had told me I was weak and a coward, I would have destroyed them. Just to show them I could. And then you come into my life and turn it upside down. You've opened doors that I didn't want opened. Doors that I've fought so hard to keep closed. And, you did it so easily. As though you'd had the key all along. I'm not sure how I feel about that, Lainey."

"You can't begin to know how much I've wanted you to open up to me this way," Lainey began.

Eve held up a hand and cut Lainey off. "I said those things to you because I knew what you would say. I can let you spend the night with me because I know that in the end, you'll go back to your husband. You're safe for me. I'm too much of a coward to open my heart enough to let someone in."

"You're not a coward, Eve."

Suddenly Eve frowned and Lainey saw hurt and astonishment in her eyes as she looked across the room to where Adam was just leaving with a stunning, young, brunette on his arm that wasn't his sister or her friend.

"Oh, Eve," Lainey exclaimed. "I'm sorry. You don't deserve that. The bastard!"

"It's not his fault, Lainey," Eve said as Adam walked out of the restaurant with his arm around the woman. "I deserve to see that, and he deserves to be with someone who can give him what he needs. For two years, I've kept Adam at arm's length. I pushed him away when he tried to get too close. Never once did I let him stay the night with me. Do you know how hard it is to explain why I can't let him sleep with me? Why I can't wake up with him in the morning? Especially when I didn't know why myself." She gave a humorless laugh. She reminded herself over and over that this was what was best for him, but it was killing her inside. "I didn't even cook for him. Isn't that funny? I didn't cook for him because it was too intimate." Eve turned to look out the window just in time to see Adam pass by. He was laughing, his hand on the small of the brunette's back in the way that was so familiar to Eve. It hurt so much. All of that work and effort to keep her heart out of it so that she wouldn't get hurt and for what? She had been a fool to think that she could involve herself with someone like Adam and keep her heart out of it. "Excuse me."

Eve made her way to the restroom. When she was sure she was alone, she leaned on the sink and lowered her head. Tears threatened, but she knew they would never come. Someone as dead inside as she was could never cry.

Lainey waited impatiently for Eve to return. Seeing the way Adam had hurt Eve angered her. She had heard Eve's explanation absolving him of blame, but Lainey couldn't understand how he could just give up on Eve like that. Couldn't he see that there was so much there underneath the controlled façade that she showed people? Couldn't he see how hurt and vulnerable she was? If he couldn't, then Eve was right. He didn't deserve her. Not because she wasn't enough for him, but because he wasn't enough for her. Lainey saw heads turning and knew Eve was coming back.

"Sorry about that," Eve said. "Look, I know that I asked you to have dinner with me tonight, but..."

"No. Don't do that," Lainey interrupted. "I'm not going to let you push me away. I'm coming over for dinner whether you like it or not."

Eve raised an eyebrow. "And if I burn the food on purpose?"

"Then I'll eat it anyway."

"You should be with your husband. Try to work things out with him."

"Eve, I want things to work out between me and Jack, I do. But, I have to figure out who I am first. It's not just about the fighting or the boredom anymore. It's about me and what I want." She was trying so hard to make Eve understand. And it was all so complicated that she was not certain that she understood it herself. "Besides," she added. "I have to know if I'm really falling in love with you."

Eve's heart stopped. She had thought when she had first met Lainey and first felt that strong physical attraction that she knew the sort of woman she was. Beautiful. Frustrated. Unfulfilled. And there had been a challenge there. She might as well admit that. She had wanted to awaken her. And, even though more had happened than she had ever planned, even though her own life was being affected in ways she never could have guessed, she had still thought that she could predict what Lainey might do and say. And now this! She was stunned.

As they left the restaurant together, Eve wondered how she was going to deal with everything that was going on. More than ever before in her life, she needed to focus on what was happening to her. Without it she could very well lose everything. And she was determined not to let that happen – no matter what she had to do.

They drove back to the gallery in silence. Eve's head was still spinning from what Lainey had told her over lunch. She wanted to say something, to reassure Lainey that everything between them was still okay, but she didn't know what to say. How do you explain to someone that hearing them tell you they may be falling in love with you had not only confused you and scared you to death, but also brought you more joy than you had ever felt in your life?

I shouldn't have said that, Lainey thought to herself. What on earth had she been thinking? She knew that a declaration of that sort might have made Eve shut down completely. She knew that if Eve felt emotionally threatened enough, what they had between them would be over. And Lainey didn't know if she could bear that. She wanted to say something to Eve, needed to make sure that she hadn't lost the best thing that had ever happened to her. But, what could she possibly say?

As they approached the gallery, Eve gave Lainey's hand a squeeze and her pulse jumped. Maybe everything was going to be all right after all.

Eve turned into the garage and noticed that Pauly wasn't there. In his place was a very tall, very big man with dark hair and dark eyes. Instantly suspicious, Eve frowned and slowed to a stop.

"Good afternoon, ma'am." His accent was pure New York. From the Bronx, Eve guessed.

"Where is Pauly?" she asked.

"Don't know ma'am. All's I know is that the company called and asked me to come in and fill in for some guy that didn't show. You want I should call and ask?"

Behind her dark sunglasses, Eve studied him. Something about him was not right. "What's your name?"

"Jackson, ma'am, but people call me Sonny."

"Is everything all right, Eve?" Lainey asked after they had parked and were taking the elevator up to the gallery. "You're awfully quiet. Is it because of Adam?"

Eve ran a hand over Lainey's hair. "I have things I need to think about," she told her. "But I don't want you to think things are strained between us. Because they're not." Eve dropped her hand as the elevator doors slid open. "The Parkers are here," she told Lainey and inclined her head towards the couple browsing the gallery. "They have a lot of money and are extremely happy to spend it, a lot of it. And I'm more than happy to help them with that. Go to them. I'd like you to show them some wonderful Degas or Cassatt pieces. Something that will look perfect in their house at the Hamptons. I've been there and they could use a little more help in the decorating department." She shrugged. "They have money, but its new money and they're just starting to learn how and what to spend it on. Their friends have told them that art was the best way to show your wealth and taste."

"They believed that?" Lainey looked over at the Parkers. They didn't look gullible, but these days you could never tell.

Eve smiled. "I should hope so. I do own this gallery and I depend on people like the Parkers to come in and buy this beautiful art. It helps to get to know them a little, their personalities, their opinions. Then show them the perfect piece of art that compliments them for their home here in the city."

"But, I've never seen their home."

"It's okay. Once you get to know them, you'll know exactly what will fit. I have a few things I have to take care of, so if you need me I'll be in my office."

Lainey frowned. She didn't want to think that Eve was avoiding her, or keeping her busy so that she wouldn't have to spend time with her.

But, she just wasn't confident that what she had said over lunch hadn't spooked her.

"I don't have to come over for dinner tonight if you're not up for it," she said.

Eve gave Lainey a crooked grin. "I thought you were coming over whether I liked it or not."

Lainey chuckled. "That's right. Disregard what I just said then."

"I'm not trying to avoid you, Lainey," Eve told her. She had so much to think about. She felt as though her entire world had been turned upside down. It wasn't a feeling she was used to at this point in her life. "I told you that everything was fine between us. I really do have things to take care of."

"Are you going to call Adam?" The question was out before Lainey could stop herself. She saw Eve's eyes cloud over and laid a hand on Eve's arm. "I'm sorry. I didn't mean to interfere."

"It's okay." Eve's voice was quiet. "No, I'm not going to call. What would be the point?"

"The point would be that he needs to know what he did hurt you. He needs to know that it was in bad taste to bring that slut to your restaurant. You need to know what is going on between the two of you."

Eve had been trying to forget about Adam, and she had been doing a good job at it by thinking of Lainey or talking about the Parkers. At least, that's what she had told herself. But it did hurt. More than she ever knew possible. And knowing that Lainey saw the hurt made it even worse. Was she losing that cool detachment that she worked on for years? She couldn't let that happen. She would be damned if Adam knew that he had hurt her. She wouldn't give him that satisfaction.

"Seeing him did hurt, Lainey," she confessed. "But he has every right to date someone else. As for bringing the woman to the restaurant, well, it is a public place and he has every right to be there, whether it was in poor taste or not." And it was in poor taste as far as she was concerned. He brought that woman to her territory and he had to know she would find out. "And, I do know what is going on between the two of us. I've known for a while that I'd drive him away. I'm not the one for him. I wish I could be, but I'm not."

She glanced over at the Parkers. "Now that we have all of that cleared up, please, go and help the Parkers."

Lainey's heart ached for Eve as she watched her disappear upstairs. Why didn't she let her emotions out? Why wasn't she showing the pain and anger she must be feeling?

The dull ache behind Eve's eyes was fast becoming a full-blown migraine. She tried willing it away, but the events of the day, the problems that she was having with Tony and everything else that was going on in her life wouldn't leave her mind. They were there from the time she woke in the morning - if she were lucky enough to fall asleep - until the time she lay her head back down at night.

Things would be so much easier for her if it were as simple as just having Tony killed and get it over with. Then the people she cared about would be safe and she could focus more on her gallery and cleaning up her personal life. But nothing is ever that simple, and Tony is much too clever. Maybe he was the reason her defenses were slipping. Too much was happening and she was struggling to keep up and stay in control. Eve wouldn't let anyone else know that she was struggling, but she couldn't hide it from herself. She slowly lifted her head and picked up the phone.

"It's me," she said when the person on the other end answered. "We might have a situation."

"What's going on?"

"I need you to check on my garage attendant, Pauly. He went to lunch and apparently never made it back. There's another man here. He says his name is Jackson, but people call him Sonny. Ring a bell?"

The man on the other end paused to think. "No, ma'am. Maybe this Pauly just got sick and Sonny's his replacement."

"I would like nothing more than for that to be the truth," Eve said honestly. "But there are just a few things wrong with that scenario. Number one, Pauly never takes off. He's always here no matter what. Number two, no one is hired or brought in as a 'replacement' without my knowledge or authorization. After what happened before with the gallery, it's a requirement. And, finally, I don't think a garage attendant can afford to wear Italian leather shoes."

"Damn! I think you're right. We'll check it out."

"Pauly has a wife and kids," Eve said, almost to herself. "I hope to God he's alright."

She rubbed her throbbing head. "Check Lainey's car. Make sure everything is okay. Mine is down there now, too, so check it as well."

Eve was tiring of this whole game and wanted it to end now. She was going to try one more time with Meredith and then if that didn't work, she'd take matters into her own hands. She knew she was taking a chance, especially with the cops watching her, but she didn't care anymore.

"Set up a meeting with Meredith," she said grimly.

"Meredith is missing, Ms. Sumptor," the man said hesitantly.

"What?" God, the pounding wouldn't stop. Eve's vision began to blur from the pain. "What do you mean she's missing?"

"She's not at her home. She hasn't shown up at Sumptor, Inc. We can't find her ma'am."

"You were supposed to be watching her," Eve whispered. Her voice was laced with ice cold rage. "How could you lose her?"

"There's no excuse ma'am. I had a couple of men watching her. She left her house on her own and hasn't returned. Neither have my men. I take full responsibility for this."

"I don't give a fuck whose fault it is! I want her found! She's the only one who can give me Tony. Find her, or I will take him down myself. You have seventy-two hours. After that, I'll do what I have to do. Don't cross me. If I find out that you are involved with any of this..."

"I'm not. I swear to God, Eve, I'm not. I'm risking my life to help you. Please believe that."

"Seventy-two hours."

Through the pain, Eve remembered another detail. "He knows where I live. You have the list of every one of my employees, including the doormen at my apartment building. Make sure all of them are safe. Especially Henry. Don't mess up this time. I don't want Tony to be able to invade my home. Is that understood?"

Eve replaced the receiver and leaned back in her chair. Son of a bitch, she thought. You clever, clever boy. She knew that Tony had taken her attention off of Meredith by threatening Lainey. She knew that somehow Tony would know that the threat would get back to her and she would protect Lainey. Was his plan to then get Eve's focus off of Lainey by taking Meredith? It's not going to happen, Daddy, Eve promised. I won't let anything happen to her.

Eve's computer sounded as a message came through. She knew exactly who it was from when she saw the chessboard appear with the word CHECK.

"You never were very good at chess were you, Daddy," she said sardonically as she made her own move to protect her queen. It had seemed to add to the excitement when it had all begun, this chess game that they still continued, but now it was becoming too dangerous. She wasn't worried about herself, but those around her that she had started to care about so much. Eve laid her throbbing head back on the chair and closed her eyes. Why wouldn't the headache just go away? Unable to take it anymore, Eve opened her desk drawer and took out the prescription bottle, hating herself for being so weak.

"Damn it!" she hissed as she opened the bottle reluctantly, dumping two pills into her open palm.

"Eve," Lainey stopped abruptly when she saw the pills in Eve's hand. "I'm sorry," she said quietly, retreating.

"Lainey. Wait," Eve said replacing the pills. Lainey had unsettled her by walking in on her most vulnerable moment.

"I didn't mean to just barge in here."

"It's okay." Eve gave Lainey the bottle. "Take them away. I don't want them where I can get to them."

"But, if you need them..."

"I don't. And, I don't want to need them. They're an easy way out for me and I don't want to have to depend on them."

"Then why do you keep them?" Lainey took the pills and put them in the pocket of her jacket.

"For the same reason I keep cigarettes around. To remind myself that I don't want to go back to that kind of life, if that's what you could call it."

"You look like you're in pain," Lainey said, studying Eve. She looked so pale. There was more going on than what Eve was telling her, and she could see the toll it was taking. "Are you sure you don't need anything?"

Eve pulled Lainey close. "I need you," she said, shocking them both into silence.

Lainey thought Eve looked so incredibly vulnerable at that moment. And, so incredibly beautiful.

"God," Eve whispered, moaning when Lainey began massaging her temples and started to unwind. "That feels amazing. I'm sorry, hun, you were telling me why you came up here?"

"I just came up here to see if you are all right," Lainey said. She could practically feel the tension draining away and found herself wondering what had upset Eve so much. Even though the tension was dissolving, and no matter how hard Eve tried to hide it, Lainey could still see that she was exhausted. And yet she didn't know why. Just two days before, Eve had been relaxed and happy. But since they had come back to New York there had been a change. She knew that Jackie's death was troubling her. And, of course, there had been the fact that she had seen Adam with another woman. But still, the feeling that there was so much more lingered.

"I want to come over tonight," Lainey said. "But if you're not feeling up to it I don't have to."

"Come around here and let me see you," Eve said gently. "I want you to come over. Okay?"

"Okay." Lainey smiled, relieved. "But, you don't have to cook. We could just order in if you like."

"No, actually cooking relaxes me." Eve ran a fingertip down Lainey's cheek. "Damn! I forgot. I have to go to the grocery store. Now that's something I haven't done for a long time. I picked a fine time to give Maria the day off."

"I can go with you." The vision of Eve grocery shopping tickled her. "Oh, and by the way. You were completely right about the Parkers! I sold them both the Degas and Cassatt."

"Well done. People are so predictable," Eve told her as she removed a key from her key ring. "Here. It's to my apartment. Believe me, I'm just as surprised as you are. Take it."

Lainey took the key in her hand and closed her fingers around it, cherishing it. Eve didn't have to tell her that she had never given anyone else a key to her sanctuary. "Why?"

"Because I know I can. I trust you, Lainey."

The words were spoken softly, but Lainey heard them loud and clear and treasured them.

"Why don't you go and do what you need to do with those," Eve said, indicating the pay slips Lainey had brought with her. "I have a quick call to make and then I'll head out to the grocery store. Meet me at my apartment?"

Lainey felt as giddy as a little girl.

"If you get there before I do, just let yourself in and make yourself at home," Eve told her, remembering how Lainey had looked so at home in her kitchen after their first night together.

"Would you like me to pour some wine for when you get home?"

"Mmm. That would be lovely."

"Anything in particular?"

"Surprise me." Eve winked.

Lainey smiled and stood up. "Okay. How is your head? Do you feel better?"

"The headache has almost disappeared, thank you."

"Hmm. Let's try one more thing. If that doesn't work, you'll have to wait until we're completely alone to try the others." Lainey bent and kissed Eve's temple gently.

Eve sighed. "Well, I'd say that that made it all better. But, I'm too intrigued by the other 'remedies' you've offered." It was incredible how Lainey could shift her focus, Eve thought. She had so much real trouble – even danger – on her plate, and yet the thought of being alone with Lainey, even for a few hours, could make her forget that her world could be about to crash down around her. "Go on. Hurry with those things. I'm almost eager to know what it feels like to come home to someone."

Lainey's smile brightened and she walked to the door. Before opening it, she turned back. "Eve." She waited until their eyes locked. "Not all people are predictable."

Lainey was right, Eve thought as the door closed behind her. Not all people were predictable. Even Eve couldn't have predicted what she herself just did. But, something about giving Lainey the key to her apartment felt right. Something about Lainey seemed right to her and that scared her more than anything. She could feel her heart opening, and no matter what she did, she couldn't stop it. She found herself wanting to open up to Lainey.

She also knew that she would do anything to keep Lainey safe from her past and future. No matter what it took, Eve promised, she would protect Lainey. She picked up the phone and dialed.

"Hello?"

"What's the situation?" Eve demanded.

"Clean. Everything's clean. We found a tracking device on Mrs. Stanton's car, but it has been removed. Your car is clean. I don't think Sonny had the chance to finish his job."

"Where is he now?"

"Being held. Whenever you're ready to question him, he'll be ready."

"See what you can get out of him first. I have plans for tonight and unless something urgent happens, I don't want to be disturbed."

"Yes, ma'am."

"Any word on Pauly or Meredith?"

"Nothing yet, ma'am, but I'm working on it personally."

Eve hung up, knowing that he would. She only hired the best. And they were loyal. More than that, they knew it was their job to keep her happy. But tonight she didn't need them. Tonight happiness would come of its own accord.

Lainey hesitated before unlocking Eve's door. She was nervous. She couldn't believe it was true, but she was nervous. This was a huge step for

Eve, and in return a huge step for their relationship. Sure, it confused her even more than before, but, at least it was a step toward finding out what was really going on between them. She heard a creak and smiled at Mrs. Jenkins who was peering out at her suspiciously.

Once inside, Lainey stood by the door and just took in everything. Here she was, standing in Eve Sumptor's apartment, an apartment to which she had a key, alone. She set her pocket book down and resisted sifting through Eve's mail. She wouldn't mess this up by meddling into Eve's personal things. Eve trusted her, and Lainey wanted to keep it that way. She decided to make her call to Jack from the kitchen before selecting the wine.

"Hello?"

Lainey smiled at the sound of Darren's voice. "Hi, honey. It's Mommy."

"Hi, Mommy! Are you on your way home?"

She felt a tug of guilt. "No, honey. I'm at Eve's house. I have a few things to do so I won't be home for awhile."

"Oh. Okay! Will you tell Eve I said 'hi'? And, that I miss her?"

"I sure will. She misses you, too. Maybe we'll all get together and do something this weekend, so you'll be able to see her. Would you like that?"

"Yeah!"

"Good. Is your daddy around, honey? I need to speak with him."

"I'll get him. I love you, Mommy!"

"I love you, too, sweetie." She leaned against the wall as she waited for Jack to get on the phone. Speaking to Darren was easy, and wonderful. He never complained, never questioned her on why she had to do things. Jack was a whole different story. This was the conversation she had been dreading since Eve had asked her to have dinner with her. She hated the fact that talking to her husband should make her apprehensive and defensive when it should be as easy as talking to her son. But, she knew that that was as much her fault as it was his.

"I'm going to be late coming home tonight," she said when he answered.

Jack was silent for a long moment. "Where are you?" he asked finally.

"I'm at Eve's. She needs my help on a project that she's doing," she lied, feeling terrible. "So, I'll be here for a while."

"She can't do it herself?" Jack had told himself that he would be more supportive of Lainey. He knew now that they had problems to work out. But, how could they work them out if Lainey was never home?

"Please don't," Lainey said quietly.

"Fine. Should I wait up?"

"I really don't know when I'll be home. I'm sorry, Jack."

"It's your job, right? I have to respect that. I trust Eve will feed you dinner."

"Yes. I'll be fine, don't worry about me."

"Very well. Be careful." He hesitated. He was annoyed that she wasn't coming home, but he needed to show her that he was at least trying to make the effort to be understanding. "I - I love you."

Lainey shut her eyes. The words that she had been aching to hear for so long now made her hurt. She felt an unreasonable anger at his timing, and guilt because she couldn't say the words back.

"Me, too," she said. "I have to go, Jack. I'll talk to you later."

Lainey hung up quickly before she lost control of her emotions. How could she stand here in Eve's home, wanting Eve so much and tell the man she was cheating on that she loved him? Even if she knew she did. But, how much? Had her feelings for her husband, the man she had vowed to love and cherish till death did them part, changed? She didn't know. The only thing she was certain of was that she had changed. Everything else, Jack, her feelings for Eve, was a source of total confusion. Instead of dwelling on it, she examined the wine rack. She wouldn't think about anything tonight except her and Eve. After that, after one incredible night with Eve, she would make decisions. Or at least attempt to.

Eve hefted the bag of groceries onto her hip as she fished for her keys. "Hello, Mrs. Jenkins." Eve smiled. She sensed the woman watching her carefully, and wondered if it was because of Lainey. My own personal watch dog, Eve mused as she let herself into her apartment to find Lainey waiting for her holding two glasses of wine with a beautiful smile on her face. Eve's heart began to race. "Hey," she said.

"Hey, yourself." Lainey handed the glass to Eve and watched her take a sip.

Eve could definitely get used to coming home to someone. No, not someone, she thought. Lainey. She caught a glimpse of the answering machine blinking, but wasn't in the mood to check it. "Come on," she said happily. "Let's take this stuff into the kitchen."

Eve walked into the kitchen and set the bag down on the island. "Garlic bread." Eve pulled the bread from the bag and tossed it to Lainey. "What do you say to a nice Fettuccini Alfredo with broccoli and chicken? And, a great tossed salad with an oil and vinegar dressing. All complimented with a beautiful vintage white wine?"

"Sounds spectacular," Lainey told her. And it did. Eve's talents seemed to be limitless. She was, in a word, perfect.

Eve smiled warmly. "Good. Let me get things started and then we'll go and change."

"We?"

"Of course. I'm sure I have something that you would be more comfortable in," she said with a mischievous twinkle in her eye.

Tonight they would put their troubles behind them for a few precious hours, Eve thought as they went upstairs, arm in arm. It was their time now, and she didn't know how much longer she would have these special moments with Lainey. She'd make the best of their borrowed time.

~ Fifteen ~

They sat on the floor of Eve's living room, vinyl records surrounding them, as the sounds of songs from generations past filled the air. Lainey sipped her third glass of wine slowly as she sifted through Eve's extensive collection of 50's and 60's classics. Dinner had been wonderful, just as Lainey had expected, a study in elegant simplicity, just one more thing to endear Eve to her. And, now, there was Eve's music collection.

"I can't believe this collection!" Lainey told her. "I love this stuff! I never get to hear this kind of music anymore. Jack hates it."

She winced a little at mentioning Jack's name, but a quick glance at Eve showed her that it was all right.

"I love this song!" She looked at Eve with a grin. "May I?"

"Of course." Eve sat back against the ottoman of the oversized chair and followed Lainey with her eyes as she got up to change the record. Her thoughts wandered to the last time she had been on this chair, making love to Adam, and her chest tightened with regret and another feeling she wasn't used to. What was it? Sorrow? Pity?

Get over it, she told herself. Though she hated to, she had to face the fact that what she had with Adam was over and there was nothing she could do about it. Because, there was something he needed that she couldn't give him. As the strains of Leslie Gore's 'You Don't Own Me' flooded the room, she remembered that, when she was younger she had worn out her first two copies, pretending that it was her singing, telling the whole world that they didn't own her and that she could do what she wanted.

Lainey came back and sat in front of Eve. She saw the defiant smile and understood that it was a song that Eve took to heart. But, even with the smile, Lainey could see the sadness that was always shadowed in Eve's eyes. "Eve?"

"Hmm?"

"I still have two questions that you promised to answer. Can I ask them now?"

Eve hesitated, swirling her wine around in her glass. She had expected this, but didn't know if she would actually be able to go through with opening up. Revealing herself, her past, could mean losing Lainey forever, and she certainly wasn't ready for that.

Wary about the questions Lainey would ask, Eve stood and walked to the bar in the living room. She was definitely going to need something stronger than wine to make it through this.

Lainey read the expression in Eve's eyes and it surprised her. Fear wasn't a word that she had ever associated with Eve Sumptor. She watched Eve pour the brandy in a snifter and frowned. Did Eve need the jolt of something more powerful than wine to open up to her? Didn't Eve feel safe with her? Didn't she know that she could tell her anything?

Eve sat back down on the floor, crossing her legs in front of her. They were both wearing cotton shorts and t-shirts and she found herself wishing that they were, in fact, girls again with nothing more serious on their minds than homework or who's going to take them to the school dance. She was trying to act nonchalant about everything, like nothing was wrong, but the concern on Lainey's face told her she wasn't pulling it off.

"What do you want to know?" she asked, almost reluctantly.

"Everything," Lainey said simply. She got to her knees and moved close to Eve. "I want to know who you are. I want to know why you have this sadness inside you. I want to know what I can do to take away the loneliness and emptiness that I see in you." She framed Eve's frowning face in her hands. "I want to know why you feel as though you're not right for Adam. For anyone." Lainey lowered her voice to a whisper. "Why do you feel you're not good enough, Eve? Tell me. Talk to me. Let me be there for you."

Eve searched Lainey's face. There was nothing more she wanted than to be able to give her what she wanted. "I can't."

The words were out before she had a chance to think about saying anything else. It was a defense mechanism for her, she thought.

"Why? I thought you trusted me, Eve."

"I do! Oh, Lainey, I do. Please, believe that." Eve stared into her brandy as though she could see the horrors of her past in it. "I'm scared," she whispered and found that the admission rocked her as much as it clearly did Lainey.

"You're scared? Of me?" Lainey lifted Eve's chin. "Baby, you have nothing to be scared of."

"There are things in my past, Lainey. Things that I had no control over. Things that have made me such a control freak now." She held Lainey's eyes with hers. "If I tell you, you'll feel different about me."

"No, I won't."

Eve laughed a little. "You will. You won't look at me the same way. You'll see things that I never wanted anyone to see. I don't want that, Lainey. I can handle just about anything that comes my way, but I don't know if I could handle losing you. Because that would be what would happen. I'm certain of it."

"You're not going to lose me," Lainey said firmly. "Nothing will ever change the way I feel about you. No. Listen to me. I told you earlier today that I was confused about how I feel about you. I've thought about this so much. I've lain in bed, awake at night trying to figure out everything that I'm feeling, but I know that I love you."

Eve made no effort to hide the shock she felt. She had never imagined Lainey saying this to her.

"There are different kinds of love, honey," Lainey explained. "There's the love a mother feels for her children. The love one feels for a wonderful friend. Being in love with a lover. You're not my child, and I'm trying to figure out the lover part because that is what is confusing me the most."

Lainey paused and took a breath. All she could pray for was that what she was saying wouldn't end up driving Eve away.

"I don't know yet if I'm in love with you," she went on, "but, one thing I am certain of is that I do love you. You are the best friend I have ever had, and I want to be able to help you." She tucked Eve's hair behind her ear. "When I first met you, do you know what I saw?"

Eve shook her head. She was speechless, trying to comprehend everything that Lainey was saying to her.

"I saw an incredibly beautiful, successful woman, intelligent, with an amazingly sexy voice. Then I got to know you, and I saw more. Behind that generosity, behind that control and tough exterior is a woman who is being haunted by things no one else knows about. I see it, Eve. In your eyes. I see the pain. I see the hurt you're hiding from everyone in your life."

Eve frowned. "Apparently I'm not doing a very good job of it."

"You are, honey. A very good job."

Eve looked at Lainey, her eyes narrowed. "I always knew you see too much."

How was she going to do this? How could she possibly tell Lainey everything? She would lose her. It didn't matter what Lainey said, Eve knew things would change once Lainey found out about her past. She lowered her head and swished the brandy around in the glass. Of all of the things she has had to overcome in her life, this was fast becoming the hardest.

"I don't know where to begin," she said quietly.

Lainey sat back on the floor, giving Eve space. She had wanted Eve to open up to her. So why was she so nervous now? Lainey knew without a doubt that her feelings for Eve would not change, but what if there was nothing she could do for Eve? What if she failed to help her? You'll do everything you can to help her, Lainey told herself. Listen, care, and be there, she thought. Maybe that's all Eve needs.

"Just start," she told Eve. "Whatever it is that's hurting you inside, let it out. I'm here." She saw a hint of a sad smile curve Eve's lips. She doesn't believe me, Lainey thought with a sadness of her own. I'll prove you wrong, Lainey promised silently.

Eve took her first sip of brandy and winced when the sting of it hit the back of her throat. "Now I remember why I don't drink this stuff anymore," she said, stalling for time. And yet why shouldn't she just get it over with, she asked herself. The faster it was done, the faster she could overcome losing Lainey. The only problem with her theory was that she didn't think she would be able to overcome that loss.

"I was fourteen when my mother died."

~ Sixteen ~

It had been the worst day of her life and she remembered every detail vividly. That day at school she had felt ill. Something had told her that she needed to get home and so she had run the four miles from school as fast as she could.

When she reached the house, she had called for her mother, needing to see her, needing her to tell her that everything was all right. But there was no answer. Exhausted, Eve went up to her bedroom. She wanted to just lie down, to rest. And there her mother was, lying on the floor, just inches from Eve's bed. It was the one place she went where she could feel safe. When Eve's father would get violent, Marie would lock them both in Eve's room. Partly to keep Eve safe from him, but also to keep herself safe. They would move the dresser in front of the door and sit on the bed hugging each other tightly until he stopped banging on the door, and then fall asleep protected in each other's arms.

Eve had known immediately that her father was responsible for what happened to her mother. She never would've left her like that, never would have left her daughter alone with that man. Certainly, she wouldn't have wanted Eve to find her like that. There had been a note, of course. 'I can't take anymore.' Marie had apparently 'overdosed' on Pentobarbital. But Eve had known even then that it wasn't from her mother.

She had gone to the police and told them what she suspected, but being only fourteen, it had been a difficult task getting them to believe her. She had to get them to at least suspect foul play so they would investigate and find things out about her father that he wanted to keep hidden from the police. She had been invisible to Tony most of the time, unless he was drunk, which suited her just fine. But still she had heard things he hadn't intended her to hear. Seen things she never should have seen. And she took everything that she knew, took documents that she didn't understand then, to the police. It had been enough to start an investigation and find reason to suspect her father in her mother's death.

Eve's father had never been a very smart man. He had made mistakes that brought him down. Further into the investigation, they found Tony's fingerprints on the bottle of pills that killed her mother. Marie's were never found on the bottle. Then Eve had found out that he killed her for money.

About a month before her death, he had taken out a life insurance policy on Marie for one million dollars. He had needed it to pay off his gambling debts. After he was arrested, they had learned that Marie had had a hell of a lot more than that. She had millions. Neither Eve nor her father had ever expected that. Nor did they expect that every bit of it would be left to Eve. It had been like she knew what was going to happen to her and she wanted Eve to be taken care of.

If her father hadn't hated Eve before, he sure as hell did then. He was convicted of Marie's murder, which meant that he didn't get the million he had killed her for. Then, knowing Eve inherited everything pissed him off even more, and he threatened her. He told her that it didn't matter how long he was in prison for, she would pay for what she had done to him. He let her know, in no uncertain terms, that he being in prison wouldn't save her, because he could find someone to do the job for him. The authorities had brought in the FBI to keep Eve 'safe' from her father. They were going to put her in the witness protection program where she would have to change her name and stay with some foster family and never again be able to speak of her mother. It wasn't what she wanted. They didn't know her father the way she did. They didn't know what kind of contacts he had. He would find her.

The bureau assigned an agent to Eve to take her home and get a few things that they approved of, and then transport her somewhere 'far away' from danger. Unfortunately for them, they had assigned a rookie to Eve, never thinking that a fourteen year old would run from the FBI. They didn't know just how good of a liar Eve was. She had told the agent to wait in the car while she ran in really quick. While inside, she had found her passport, and a stash of money she had been saving herself, and ran.

Eve hadn't had a plan. She just knew she had to get out of there. She had been scared that the ticket agents wouldn't let her on a plane, scared that the authorities would find her before she could get out, so she paid a cab driver to go inside the airport and buy her a ticket. Not knowing why then, she chose Paris as her destination.

It hadn't been her first time to Paris. She remembered when Tony had taken them once when he was on a gambling high. They had stayed with a woman named Madame Bussiere who was hosting a high stakes game he had wanted in on. Bussiere had hated Eve's father almost as much as Eve did. She also did illegal business at her cafe, so it was the safest place she could think of to go to without anyone going to the authorities.

Eve had shown up on Bussiere's doorstep with nothing but the clothes on her back and three thousand dollars in her pocket. And the money was the first thing Bussiere took from her. The old woman had told her that if she wanted to be kept away from the authorities and her father, then she would do as she was told. Eve was to do chores, serve Bussiere, and in return she would get room and board and a hiding place. Not knowing what else to do, Eve had agreed. She would finish the things Bussiere had her do, and then go up to her tiny room and escape from it all.

Fortunate enough to have a balcony outside her window, Eve would take paper and a pencil out there each night and draw. It was the only thing that kept her sane. Paris had been so beautiful at night, and she would draw everything in sight. The people, the trees, the cars. Eve remembered that she had wanted paints so badly to be able to catch the colors and character of everything that surrounded her. Something a pencil couldn't do, but she had no money to buy the things she needed, so she settled.

Until one day, when Madame Bussiere came into her room – as she regularly did to make sure Eve hadn't stolen anything from her – and she found the drawings Eve had done. Eve recalled Madam Bussiere not believing that Eve had drawn them at first, and demanding that she draw her. Seeing it as an opportunity to get the supplies she needed, Eve told her that if she had paints and a canvas, she could paint her portrait. The next thing Eve knew, Bussiere had bought one canvas and the cheapest paints she could find.

She sat for Eve, and all Eve could think at the time was the woman had been the worst subject she had ever had to paint. Not only because she was overweight, missing most of her teeth and hardly showered. But she was also a horrible, horrible person. Eve painted her nonetheless and did her best, thinking that maybe she would keep getting paints if she pleased her. It had been one of Eve's biggest mistakes. Bussiere had found a way for Eve to make her money. She started advertising Eve to her patrons and they would pay her five hundred francs to go up to Eve's room and have her paint for them. At first, it hadn't bothered Eve, because she got to do something that she loved to do. Of course, she never saw a cent, but the paints got better and she got all of the canvases she needed. As far as the patrons went, some would want straightforward portraits, some portraits of their families or pets, and some wanted Eve to paint them in the nude.

She did whatever she was asked to do, until she started to get tired. She would be doing four, five or six paintings a night without a break, but if she dared complain or refuse to do a painting, Madame would hit her until she changed her mind. Although she didn't hit as hard as Eve's father, Eve learned not to refuse her.

It was when Eve was sixteen that everything changed. Her body started to change no matter how hard she tried to stop it from doing the things it was doing. She hadn't wanted her breasts to grow, hadn't wanted to be attractive and have people look at her differently. The way they had her mother. She had known what sex was, and she didn't want it. She wouldn't wear make-up, wore her hair up in a ponytail all the time, but no matter what she did, her body betrayed her. When her body changed, so did the clientele. They came in now, not to see the young artist, but to see the young woman. Then one of her regulars had come in, after already having four portraits done. She remembered thinking it was odd that he would come in so many times, but Eve was naïve enough at the time to think it was because of her work, not her. But then she had heard him talking to Madame one day.

"Si doué." 'So talented', he would say. "Elle est ahurissante." 'She is breathtaking'." "Regardez ce beau jeune corps." 'Look at that beautiful, young body.' She didn't realize that what she heard in the man's voice was a craving for the young girl.

She never knew how much he offered Madame that day. All she knew was that he didn't pay her for a painting this time. This time he paid to fuck Eve.

She hadn't known what to do. She'd begged Madame not to make her do it, but the older woman threatened her, telling her that if she didn't give the man what he wanted, she would tell the authorities where Eve was. Or, maybe she would just tell her father, and see how much he was willing to pay to get rid of Eve and maybe she would do it herself. Eve remembered actually contemplating her choices. She honestly couldn't decide which she would be better off choosing. Death or giving herself to this man.

She had made her decision. She hadn't known what else to do, had nowhere to go. Eve thought that if she just got it over with, everything would go back to being the way it was. So, she just laid there as he did whatever he wanted to her. What he'd paid for. He was in his forties, married with children, and she couldn't believe he was doing this to her. But he wasn't the only one. There were others that paid to have Eve, and each night she had to endure what these men did to her.

There had been nights that Madame would give Eve time to be alone. But they were very few and far between. When Eve was to have her seventeenth birthday off, she had been grateful. She had planned to use that time to make plans on how she would get out of this miserable life she was living. Eve would sit out on the balcony, even if it were freezing out there, because she couldn't bring herself to sleep in that bed. She couldn't sleep anymore anyway since every time she closed her eyes she would see those men hurting her. She had to get out, but she just didn't know how without any money. She would leave no matter what she had to do and she would take her night off to figure out how.

But she didn't get the night off. Perhaps what Eve would always remember most was the night a very prominent, very influential man had come in demanding that she service him – that was what they called it - right away. It turned out that he had learned about her from the streets and wanted to sample the goods for himself. He paid Madame a very large sum to forget that she had ever seen him and to be deaf to anything that went on upstairs and she agreed.

"Then," Eve said quietly. "He and a few of his friends, decided to take turns with me..."

~ Seventeen ~

"Stop!" Lainey couldn't listen anymore. Weeping openly, she stood to pace the floor. She felt sick to her stomach. "I can't...I don't want to hear anymore."

Eve's heart shattered. She should have been prepared for this. She should have known that Lainey wouldn't be able to bear to hear the truth about her. And, as much as she tried to fight the anger, the hurt, to try to understand, she couldn't.

"No!" she said severely. "You wanted to hear this, Lainey! You're going to hear all of it! Do you have any idea what they did to me? Do you?"

"Please, Eve! I can't!"

"They tore me apart, Lainey!" Eve said roughly, ignoring Lainey's plea. "Every bit of hope, every bit of emotion that I had inside me, died that night!" She rose and turned Lainey to face her. "You wanted to know why I'm not good enough for you or for Adam. That's why! You never expected to hear that I was a whore did you?"

"Stop it!" Lainey tried to free her arms from Eve's grip, but found she couldn't budge.

"Stop what? Isn't this what you wanted? To know everything about me? Well, now you know. I'm a whore! Everything that you thought you saw in me was a lie!"

"You're not a whore, Eve! Stop saying that!" Lainey cried. She took a breath to calm herself. "What happened to you was not your fault. Please, you're hurting me."

"I'm sorry." Eve sank to her knees there in front of Lainey and buried her face in her hands. "I never should have told you. Your illusion of me was far better than my reality. I should have let you keep believing I'm who you thought I was."

"Eve." Lainey got down on her knees with Eve. "Please, look at me."

"I can't."

"Do you think I'm ashamed of you? Do you think I could judge you for what those bastards did to you? My God, Eve, do you honestly think I would blame you for what happened to you?"

"I'm a whore."

"No, baby, you're not." Lainey wrapped her arms around Eve tenderly.

"You didn't want to hear..."

"I didn't want to hear because I couldn't stand hearing how those bastards hurt you," Lainey interrupted. "You're right, I never expected this. I never expected that you would have gone through so much, been hurt so badly and yet still turn out to be the wonderful woman you are today. I never expected to hate this much. Not you, baby. Them. Everyone that ever hurt you. I've never been a violent person. But, I would give anything to see them burn in hell for what they did to you, and I would give anything to be the one to put them there."

Eve still saw in Lainey the trust and affection she thought she would surely lose. The tears that fell from Lainey's eyes were for her. No one had ever cried for Eve. She touched her fingertip to one of the falling tears. "Why can't I do that?" she asked softly. "Why can't I cry?"

"You've closed yourself up for so long, Eve," Lainey told her, wiping her eyes with the back of her hand. "You're afraid to have emotions, because you're afraid of being hurt again. But I won't hurt you. I swear."

It was Eve who deepened the kiss when Lainey touched her lips to hers. She had needed it. Needed to know that nothing had changed for Lainey. But, Eve felt in the kiss that things had changed. For both of them. Her heart pounded almost painfully at the realization. "There's more," she whispered reluctantly.

"We have all the time in the world for you to tell me everything, Eve," Lainey said and brushed her lips to Eve's. "But, let's leave the rest for later. I think you've been through enough tonight." She knew Eve had a headache, saw the fatigue in her eyes. "I'm sorry. It's my fault that all of these horrible memories are in your mind now."

Eve shook her head. "It's not your fault. I live with this every day of my life. It doesn't matter how hard I try to forget it and move on. It will forever be there."

She felt the sting of tears in her eyes, willed them to fall. Just once she wanted to cry. She wanted to release this pain that was trapped inside her.

"I have to finish, Lainey," she said insistently. "I don't know if I could ever do this again, so I need to do it now while I can." She studied Lainey for a moment. "Are you okay?"

The question was so absurd that Lainey laughed. "I'm sorry," she said. "There's nothing funny about any of this. It's just that I should be the one asking you that. How about we get comfortable? I'll make us some tea and you can finish."

When they were standing, Lainey pulled her close. "Look at me, Eve," she said. "Look me in the eye. Things have changed for me. I thought that no matter what you said, my feelings for you wouldn't change. But, they did."

Eve nodded. She had expected things to change, but not in the way they had. Her heart was racing, her palms were sweating and all she wanted to do was sit down and weep.

"I didn't believe it was possible for me to respect you any more than I did," Lainey told her. "I didn't realize just how strong you really were. Now I do. I know you were expecting me to run away from you or make judgments about you because of these awful things that have happened to you. Well, I hope this doesn't disappoint you, but I'm not going anywhere. I love you."

Eve sat at the island in the kitchen, silently watching Lainey move about the kitchen, preparing tea for them both. She was trying to gather her senses and wrap her mind around everything that Lainey had said to her. She had heard the words 'I love you' many times in her life, mostly spoken by men who knew nothing about her and 'loved' her body. Her mother had told her that she had loved her of course, but in the years that had passed since the words had lost their meaning for Eve. Then, Adam had told her that he loved her and she had believed him, seen in his eyes that he meant what he was saying. But, he didn't know her either. Not the real Eve but her image and she had never dared having him see her as she really was.

She reminded herself that she had thought the same thing about Lainey, certain that when she came clean about her past, Lainey would run. But, she hadn't. She was standing here in Eve's kitchen, making Eve tea, telling Eve that she loved her. Now that she knew everything – or nearly everything - she was still here.

The object of Eve's innermost thoughts turned to her then, as if she could hear Eve thinking. Lainey poured the tea into two porcelain cups. "Can I ask you something?" she said. "You said that your mother had left you an inheritance." She hesitated for a moment, not wanting to upset Eve. "Why didn't you..."

Eve grinned. "If you want to know everything about me, Lainey, you're going to have to be bolder than that. Don't be afraid to ask me questions. You want to know why I didn't use the money to live off of instead of going to Paris. Honey, it's okay. I understand that you're going to have questions and I'm prepared for them. The money was in a trust fund that I couldn't get to until I was twenty-one. If something were to happen to my mother before I turned twenty-one, it was stipulated in her will that I was to get an allowance each month for living expenses. My college tuition would be paid for, along with an apartment off campus if that's what I preferred. But, when I ran, the funds were frozen. I suppose they thought I'd be desperate enough to come back if I didn't have access to any money."

Lainey sipped her tea and studied Eve over the rim. "Do you ever think that you made the wrong decision by running?"

Eve considered Lainey's question. "Yes. Every day of my life. But, we all make our decisions, and we have to learn from them. We have to live with them. When I turned myself in..."

"When did you do that?" Lainey demanded although she thought she knew when Eve had finally escaped from the hell she was living in.

"That night," Eve said insistently. "I couldn't take it anymore. I was so tired, in so much pain." She hesitated for a moment, remembering everything. "I knew that I had to get out of there or I would end up dead. I had gone there to stay alive, but I couldn't live like that anymore, so I turned myself in. I ran away, called the authorities from some shop a few miles away. I was too scared to stay in the area, afraid that one of Madame's 'patrons' would tell her where I was."

She followed Lainey back into the living room with their tea. "You know, when I asked you to dinner tonight, I don't think I expected this," Eve said softly when they were sitting together on the couch. "I knew I wanted to talk to you, but not about all this. I'd explain that I lost my mother when I was very young. Perhaps add a few details about my father. Just enough to satisfy you. And then we'd end up in bed together and we would make love instead of wasting our time together talking."

"I don't feel like this is a waste of time, Eve." Lainey rested her hand on Eve's leg. "We are being intimate, just not physically. Yet."

Eve smiled. "I don't feel like it's a waste of time either. I feel like a boulder has been lifted off my chest. Don't worry I'm over the nastiest part of my past. It was difficult, but I made it through. Thanks to you." Lazily, she wrapped a strand of Lainey's hair around her finger. "Hmm. I should finish this before I say to hell with it and take you upstairs."

Lainey's heart skipped. She was tempted to tell Eve to do just that. She wanted to be with her so badly, wanted to show her that she was more attracted to her now than ever. Eve's strength amazed her. Her character, generosity and kindness meant more to Lainey now that she knew how complicated Eve's life had been. Eve could easily have become quite a different person considering the challenges she's had to endure.

While they sat there, close to each other on the couch, Eve went on then to tell Lainey that, thanks to the help of Agent Donovan, the rookie she had run from 3 years before, she had been taken in by a couple who had been his long time friends. Then there had been the part time jobs, the one room apartment when she turned eighteen, and the stabs at taking the few college courses with the help of the inheritance.

"I was alone and the only things I had to keep me company were my memories," Eve said distantly. "That's when I started smoking, drinking heavily and taking my frustrations out on unsuspecting men."

Lainey frowned. "What do you mean by that?"

"I made it my mission to ruin the lives of men who reminded me of the ones who had hurt me before." Eve shrugged. "I guess it was a way for me to feel in control of my life again. A way to punish them for what they did to me. I didn't care who they were, or who they had in their lives that would be hurt by what I was doing."

"Eve, you didn't..."

"Fuck them?" Eve was ready for the question, and didn't blame Lainey for thinking it. "No. I used them in other ways. Men are easy to manipulate when you're a 'beautiful' woman who pretends to pay attention to them. They would buy me things, give me money, give me whatever I wanted. And, in return, I would set them up. I would call their wives, tell them that if they wanted to know what their husbands were up to, they would be at the place I told them, at a certain time. Then, I would make sure their husbands were caught in a compromising position with me. But, I never slept with them."

"Did it make you feel better?"

It wasn't disapproval that Eve heard in Lainey's question, but understanding, and that surprised Eve. "No. Temporary power, maybe, but it didn't make me feel better."

"What would you have done if the wives hadn't shown up? Or, if they had, but had wanted to hurt you?" Lainey understood why Eve had done what she had. It was a wonder to her, knowing as she did now how she had been abused, that she hadn't been worse.

Eve lifted a careless shoulder. "I took the chance. If something had gone wrong, I would have dealt with it. But, I researched my 'victims' beforehand. I never went into anything blindly. Most of their wives were having affairs of their own, and what they really needed to get out of the marriage and keep the money, was to catch their husbands having an affair."

"I see. So, you ruined the men, helped the women and got revenge at the same time." Eve might try to sound nonchalant but, Lainey could still see how unhappy those times made her. "What changed you, Eve?" she asked. "Because that's not the woman you are now."

"My mother," Eve answered after a moment of silence. She smiled at Lainey's confusion, and explained. "When I turned twenty-one, a whole new world opened up for me. A trust fund was handed to me. Something else was handed to me that day as well. Something that was more valuable than any amount of money in the world. A key."

"A key?"

"Yes. It was to a safety deposit box that belonged to her. No one knew what was inside that box until I opened it that day. God, I've never told this to anyone." What is it about you, Lainey? Why am I telling you things I never wanted anyone to know? "There were three things in that box. Three things that mean more to me than anything I'll ever own. There was a locket with a photo of my mother on one side and me as a baby on the other. It was engraved." She paused for a moment, thinking of those words that would forever be imprinted in her mind. "On the front it said, 'Two bodies, One soul', and on the back it said, 'I give you my strength'."

"That's beautiful." Lainey tried to swallow the lump in her throat, not wanting to lose it now. She wanted to be strong for Eve, to help her get through all of this.

"Yes. It was. Is. There was also a letter and a journal with only a few pages filled. Her last entry was made the day she died. It was as though she knew. Her last words were; 'This is where I end, and you begin'."

Lainey could see the pain in Eve's eyes when she spoke of her mother. But there was something else there, too. It was clear to Lainey that, as Eve spoke, all of the love she had left for her mother was overwhelming her.

"My mother also left a letter," Eve said and now the words were pouring out of her. "I've read that letter hundreds of times. I can recall every word. She told me that there would be people in my life who would try to break me. 'Don't let them get you, baby girl'. 'Don't ever let them take anything away from you.' She said that love does exist, and that I should never let anyone take that away from me. It was the one thing she insisted on. 'Find love, baby girl. It's waiting for you.' Of course, she wanted me to be successful in life, to make sure no one could take away my hopes and dreams. But, it was love she wanted for me the most. 'If I could give you anything in the world, baby girl, it would be these three things.'" Eve paused, but only for a moment. Her face was slightly flushed and there was a far-away look in her eyes. "She wrote 'I give you my strength to triumph through times of adversity and become the woman I know you were meant to be. I give you my courage to walk away from those who hurt you, with your head held high. Something I never could do. I give you my heart, full of love, to add to yours so that you can pass it on to the world.'"

Now Lainey knew where Eve had gotten her generosity and amazing inner beauty. All Eve needed, was to know how to set her heart free. She knew the love inside Eve was enormous, and amazingly true.

"I did everything she asked of me," Eve continued, cutting through Lainey's thoughts. "I became a successful business woman. Went to school around the world to 'broaden my horizons'. I gave up on revenge. It did nothing but make me feel miserable anyway. I focused on giving, instead of taking. I had the strength and courage to walk with my head held high and triumph over everything that happened to me. And, yet, I was still empty inside." She drew up her knees to her chest, wrapping her arms around them. A movement of uncharacteristic insecurity. Eve looked very young just then. Unsure of everything.

"I began to think that maybe Mama was right about love," she went on. "Maybe that was what I was missing in my life and why I felt so alone. So...I started dating."

Something that was a cross between amusement and annoyance lit Eve's eyes. "I hated every minute of it. If the men weren't completely boring and self-absorbed, they were complete assholes. None of them wanted to know me. I was an ornament for them, a beautiful woman to hang on their arm. To have sex with afterward. At least that's what they wanted. But it was something they never got. I stopped dating because it was just aggravating me and focused my energy on making my galleries the most prestigious in the country. And then I met Adam."

It was a relief to be back in the here and now, Eve thought, suddenly aware that she was emotionally exhausted.

"And what about Adam," Lainey asked. "Are you in love with him, Eve?"

Eve frowned. For a split second, she thought she was going to say yes. "I don't know how to love, Lainey. If I were in love with him, wouldn't he be here right now instead of you?" She closed her eyes and swore softly. "That didn't come out right."

"It's okay. I understand." It stung, but she honestly did understand.

"No, it's not okay. I didn't mean to say that. It's just that I'm as confused about what's going on between us as you are. I have feelings for you, Lainey. Very strong feelings. But, I also have very strong feelings for Adam. Not that it matters anymore. He's moved on, and it was the best thing for him to do. I've spent my energy trying to protect him from my past so that I wouldn't lose him. I just couldn't give him enough of me, or maybe I couldn't give him the part of me he really wanted. He would ask me about my past. Wanted so much to know what happened, to make it better. He was the first man to be sensitive enough to know I'd been hurt. And he wanted to know who had done it. He was ready to fight the ghosts of my past for me. I looked into his eyes...oh, Lainey, he was so sincere. And, for a moment, I wanted to tell him."

"Why didn't you, Eve? Why don't you? He loves you. I see it in the way he looks at you. He'll understand."

"I can't. Lainey, he gets upset when another man talks to me. He would tell me, 'They want to sleep with you, Eve. Can't you see that?' How can I tell him what I did? Do you really think he'll just look over the fact that I was a whore?"

"Stop it! Damn it, Eve, stop saying that about yourself."

Eve reached for Lainey's hand. "Honey. No matter how rose colored your glasses are when you look at me, that's what I was. I slept with men for money. I didn't want to do it, and I never saw the money, but the fact still remains."

"I don't like that word, and that's not you."

"There are no pretty words for what I did. Prostitute, hooker...call girl. Whatever you want to call it, I couldn't tell Adam, and if I have any chance of getting him back, it has to stay locked away."

"I think you're wrong," Lainey said simply. She truly believed that Adam would be there for Eve, that he wouldn't turn away from her. And, if he did turn away from her, he wasn't the man Lainey had thought he was. He certainly wasn't the man for Eve if he couldn't stand beside her no matter what.

"He was the first man I ever made love to," she said in a low voice. "He was the first man to ever touch me so tenderly, the first to look at me as though I were the only woman in the world. He was the first and only man I've ever kissed."

"So, Adam was your first." Lainey was still trying to grasp the idea of that. "That's wonderful."

"Are you sure you wanted to hear this?" Eve asked her.

"Yes. Eve, I'm sure," Lainey told her. "This is what best friends are for, honey."

"I've never had one," Eve said quietly. "And I certainly never imagined that my first best friend would also turn out to be my lover." She smiled when Lainey blushed.

Eve had never felt so completely content as she did at this moment finally letting out everything she had kept locked inside for so long.

"I don't want to talk anymore," Eve said, exhausted. "I've told you everything. I've bared my soul to you."

"We can stop, okay?" Lainey said and kissed her.

Eve sank into the kiss. "Would you do me a favor?" Eve whispered. "Will you go upstairs with me? I want to lay with you, have you just, just hold me before you have to leave."

"Come on," Lainey said softly. And hand in hand they walked up the stairs.

~ Eighteen ~

Eve was asleep, breathing softly, one arm and leg wrapped across Lainey. The horrors she had heard would have kept Lainey awake even if she hadn't had to go. The clock read eleven o five. She would give herself a few more minutes with Eve, then she had to go home. But, the thought of leaving upset her.

She turned her head back towards Eve and drew in her scent, as though it were the breath of life. You have to figure this out, Lainey, she scolded herself. What are you doing - or more importantly, what are you going to do?

"So beautiful," Lainey whispered, touching Eve's lips gently with her own. Eve's response, which was to open her mouth to the kiss, left Lainey breathless.

"Hi." Eve yawned and stretched lazily.

"Hi." Lainey couldn't help but smile. The feel of Eve's body against hers, was incredible, even with both of them being clothed in the shorts and t-shirts they had changed into before dinner.

"I'm sorry. I didn't mean to fall asleep."

"It's alright. You needed to rest." Lainey tightened her arm around Eve as she snuggled closer. She had been dreading this moment all evening. The moment she had to say goodnight to Eve. "Eve?"

"Hmm?"

"I have to go," Lainey told her. It was hard to say the words.

"I know," Eve murmured. Though her heart ached, Eve wouldn't argue.

"You could at least act like you want me to stay," Lainey told her. What in the hell was she doing? Why was she so upset that Eve understood?

Eve looked at Lainey intently. "Stay," she whispered. "I want you to stay." Eve closed the gap between them and kissed Lainey with a heated passion.

Lainey broke away, gasping for air. "God. You had to say it that way?" Rolling over, she picked up the phone.

"What are you doing?" Eve asked her.

"Jack. It's me," Lainey said, pressing a finger to Eve's lips. "I'm sorry. This project is taking a lot longer than I expected and it's getting late."

"What are you saying, Lainey?" Jack asked, even though he knew the answer already.

"I'm saying that I'm too tired to drive home, so I'm just going to stay here tonight." She caught Eve's look of surprise and disapproval. But that couldn't be. Eve couldn't be disappointed that Lainey had made the decision to stay.

"Are you mad at me for some reason?" Jack asked her. "Is that why you're not coming home?"

"No, Jack. I'm not mad at you," Lainey said quietly. "I just told you that I'm tired. I have more to do here and I don't want to drive all the way home. I'll be home tomorrow."

"All right," Jack said after a long pause. "I'll tell the boys in the morning that you stayed with Eve. They like Eve, so they'll understand. I – I love you, Lainey."

Lainey's heart skipped. Instantly, involuntarily, she wished they had come from Eve instead, and felt horribly guilty for that. "I...love you, too," she murmured and felt Eve move away from her.

"Why did you do that?" Eve asked when she heard Lainey hang up the phone.

"You told me you wanted me to stay," Lainey protested.

"You told me to tell you to stay." Eve felt Lainey go rigid beside her and swore under her breath. Rolling over, she pinned Lainey beneath her before she could get up. "I do want you to stay, Lainey. I always want you to stay. But, I also understand that you have a family that you need to be home with. I promised you that I would help you with your marriage, and all it seems like I'm doing is hurting it."

"It was my decision to change my life and go back to work. It was my decision to become your assistant, even though I knew I felt something for you from the moment I met you. It was my decision to become your lover, something I'll never regret. And, it was my decision to stay tonight, Eve. Don't feel that this is your fault. My marriage was in trouble before I even met you."

"Yes, but, I was supposed to help you fix it, not break it even more." Eve remembered Lainey saying that she would never regret becoming Eve's lover. She hoped and prayed that would remain the truth.

"Eve, you're not doing anything except being there for me. I was lying here, listening to you breathing as you slept, dreading the moment I had to get up and leave you. After everything that you told me tonight, I didn't want to just go."

"Is that why you're staying?" Eve interrupted, heatedly. "Because you feel obligated?" The intensity of her anger took her by surprise. "I'm not vulnerable, Lainey! I'm not a child!"

"Don't you dare pull away from me!" Lainey cried. "And don't you dare talk to me that way! I just lied to my husband! I'm not going home to my sons! Do you think I would do that just because I feel obligated to stay here with you? I am so fucking confused about what's going on in my life right now, Eve, but I know that I have never felt obligated to be with you! I wanted to stay!"

"I'm sorry. Baby, I'm sorry," Eve said as Lainey released her. She didn't know what else to say. She had been completely wrong about Lainey, and it wasn't the first time. Why couldn't she learn that Lainey was different from everyone else? "I'm always screwing up," she murmured. "I don't know how these things work, Lainey. Relationships. I know how you feel about me, or I know how you say you feel about me. I have a hard time believing anything that wonderful. I've always had trouble believing the good things. And, I've always tried to control everything."

"Don't you ever want to give up that control, Eve?" Lainey interjected. "Just for a little while, let someone else take control?"

"Yes," Eve whispered. "Yes, I do want that. But, I'm afraid. What if I can't get it back? What if I fall?"

Lainey brushed a fingertip over Eve's cheek. "I won't let you fall. Lie back."

"What?"

"Lie back. Let me be in control for you." She watched, satisfied, as Eve did as she was told, then rolled over until it was Eve that was pinned beneath her. "Let go for me, Eve," she whispered.

Her hand caressed Eve's breast through her t-shirt but when Eve's hands began their own exploration of Lainey's body, Lainey stopped her.

"No." Lainey put Eve's hands above her head, and the look in her eyes told Eve to keep them there. "This is for you." She let her hands roam over Eve's beautiful body again; the soft curves paired with toned muscles, excited her. Hearing Eve's breathing coming quicker, her small moans of pleasure as Lainey touched her was intoxicating. When she slipped her hand inside Eve's shorts, she heard the sharp intake of Eve's breath as Lainey touched her. Lainey's own heart was beating faster, and twinges of pleasure shot through her when Eve started to move. "I love you."

The words were a breath in her ear, but she heard them clearly. Eve's body quivered in response and her closed eyes flew open. Lainey had said the words to her before, but never like that. Never like this. She opened her mouth, but, as always, the words didn't come even though there was nothing she wanted more than to tell Lainey that she loved her, too.

"You don't have to say anything," Lainey said softly. "Just let go. Please." Lainey's voice was ragged and raspy with desire.

Eve writhed beneath Lainey and she knew that Eve was close. Suddenly she felt Eve shudder and held her close as she cried out in pure ecstasy.

A single tear slid down Eve's cheek. Eve was crying. It wasn't the bucket of tears Lainey knew Eve needed, but it was a start and Lainey was grateful for that. She bent her head and kissed the tear from Eve's cheek, then cried tears of her own as Eve held her tightly.

The moonlight filtered into the room, casting a faint glow across Eve's face as she stared out the window. She couldn't close her eyes, because if she did, she would see too many images from her past. Talking about it had brought it to the surface and now, in the quiet of the room, it came back, making her afraid to fall asleep again. What if she had the nightmares that plagued her most nights and lost it? Yes, Lainey had seen her lose control before, but that didn't mean that Eve wanted her to see it all over.

For her entire life, Eve had struggled to be perfect. For her mother, who saw Eve as perfect no matter what she did. For her father, who thought she was nothing but nuisance or play toy. For everyone else that passed through her life, including Adam and Lainey. But, now, Lainey knew everything. There was no pretending with her anymore, and Eve knew that Lainey had wanted it that way. She didn't want Eve to be perfect, just herself. Why couldn't Eve be sure that Adam would feel the same way?

"Eve?" Lainey's quiet voice sent a shiver through Eve's body.

"Why aren't you sleeping?"

"Why aren't you?" Lainey countered. "I guess I'm a bit restless."

Eve studied Lainey. "You keep thinking about it, don't you?" She could see it in Lainey's eyes. Eve sighed. "I shouldn't have told you."

"Don't say that. I'm glad you told me, Eve." Lainey sat up and pulled the covers up around her breasts. "It upsets me that something like this happened to you, but it makes me happy that you can trust me enough to open up to me."

"Come on." Eve tossed the covers to the side and slipped out of bed.

Lainey was fascinated by the way the moonlight washed over Eve's tanned, naked body. "Where are we going?" She couldn't take her eyes off of Eve as she walked to the dresser.

Eve flashed Lainey a grin over her shoulder. It felt good to have Lainey looking at her like that. She took two nightshirts out of the dresser and threw one to Lainey. "Put this on." She watched as Lainey dropped the sheet and stood up, enjoying the vision of Lainey putting on her shirt as she slipped on her own.

Walking to Lainey, she took over buttoning the shirt, stopping at the third from the top. Eve feathered a finger down Lainey's cleavage, then took her hand and led her to the sitting room towards the piano.

"The first time you were here, you asked me if I would play the piano for you," she said, sitting down on the bench. "When I can't sleep, I do one of two things. I paint. I'd still love to paint you, you know."

"Like you did Adam?"

"Right. But as easy as it would be for me to paint every inch of your body from memory, I'd rather you pose for me. It's more...intimate." Eve grinned wickedly.

Lainey flushed, letting the pleasure of Eve's words wash over her. "This is the other thing you do? Play the piano?"

Eve smiled. She had noticed the flush on Lainey's cheeks, and found it endearing. "Yes." She began playing softly. "I taught myself as sort of a defense mechanism. Or, maybe just a way to get away from all of the pain. It relaxes me, takes me to a whole other place where I don't have to think about the things that are going on in my life."

The beautiful strains of a sonata by Chopin captured Lainey. It was clear from the expression on Eve's face that she was feeling every note she played.

Unable to help herself, Lainey walked around until she was standing behind Eve, and kissed her neck. Startled, Eve paused.

"Don't stop," Lainey whispered in her ear. "It's beautiful." Lainey slipped her hands inside Eve's shirt and caressed her, loving the way Eve's nipples grew taut with her touch and how Eve's breath quickened and heart beat faster as Lainey trailed her hands further down.

Eve moaned quietly as Lainey touched her, her playing becoming more passionate as she neared the peak. The music, Lainey's touch, it was almost too much for her. She climaxed quickly, intensely, no longer able to play as her body quaked with pleasure.

"God!" Eve leaned back against Lainey. "I can honestly say that's never happened before." She turned on the bench until she was facing Lainey. "Come here." Pulling Lainey to her lap, she held her tightly against her. "Wrap your legs around me," Eve whispered, closing her eyes and smiling as Lainey did as she asked. Eve took Lainey there on the bench, her fingers moving as expertly on Lainey's body as they did on the piano.

They never made it back to the bed that night, falling asleep instead on the oversized couch in the sitting room. Lainey awoke to Eve's soft body underneath her, and her arms wrapped around her. It wasn't a bad way to wake up, Lainey thought. The shower that they took together was even better. These were the thoughts that ran through Lainey's head as she dressed for the day. Borrowing some of Eve's clothes, Lainey dressed slowly, not looking forward to the rest of the day and having to share Eve with others. Then, she had to think about going home and not being with Eve tonight. It saddened her, and made her feel guilty at the same time. She truly did love Jack, and knew that she couldn't imagine her life without him or her children. But, at the same time, she couldn't imagine her life anymore without Eve.

Lainey sat on the bed and watched Eve through the open bathroom door. She wore nothing but a towel around her damp body, and was doing nothing but combing her fingers through her wet hair. Lainey thought then that Eve was easily the sexiest, most beautiful person she had ever seen. When the phone rang, it startled Lainey enough to make her jump.

"Could you get that for me please, honey?" Eve called to Lainey. Eve smiled knowingly to herself in the mirror. She had felt Lainey's eyes on her and had enjoyed the way it made her body react. She was glad now that she had confessed so much to Lainey the night before. This morning she felt lighter, emotionally, for the first time since she could remember. When they had finally fell asleep together, Eve hadn't dreamt. It had been the most peaceful night of sleep she had ever had.

"It's someone called Billy," Lainey said uneasily.

Eve took the phone from Lainey and placed her hand over the mouthpiece. "It's not what you think," she whispered. "I'll explain everything to you later." When Lainey started to leave, Eve caught her arm keeping her in place. There would be no secrets between them anymore. Lainey needed to know everything, especially about Tony. She deserved that much.

When Eve finished confirming plans to meet Billy, she leaned against the sink and pulled Lainey to her. "It's time I told you what is going on," she said. "I don't particularly want to. All I want to do is protect you." She leaned forward and kissed the tip of Lainey's nose. "Let's go make some breakfast. I think better on a full stomach. Last one to the kitchen owes the other a full body massage."

The playful mood between them hadn't lasted after Eve told Lainey everything. Lainey had, she said, the right to know that her life was in danger. Even the drive to the gallery had been silent and somber. The more she thought about it, the angrier Lainey became. When Eve pulled up to the curb in front of the gallery, Lainey turned on her.

"How could you keep this from me?" she demanded.

"I was trying to protect you," Eve interrupted. "I didn't want to scare you. I didn't want you to be upset over this. I'll take care of it. I'll protect you from him, Lainey. Please believe me."

"Like you did Jackie?" She regretted the words as soon as they were spoken. The pain that filled Eve's eyes made Lainey want to cry. "Damn it! I'm so sorry."

"Why? You're right. I couldn't protect Jackie." Eve deliberately shielded the hurt inside. "She had nothing to do with this and he came out of nowhere. But I'm ready for him now."

"Are my children in danger, Eve?"

Their eyes locked. "I won't let him get to Kevin and Darren. Or Jack. That I promise you. I won't let him get to you. It's me he wants, Lainey, but he may try to get to me through you and I won't let that happen. He has to kill me first if he wants to get to you."

"Do you think that makes me feel any better? You know how I feel about you. I can't lose you either." Lainey ran a hand through her hair. "You should have told me. You've had people following me, following my children. I should have known."

"I know. And, I know that me telling you now doesn't make up for it, but, Lainey, you have to understand that all I wanted to do was protect you. I've done everything in my power to keep you and your family safe, and I'll continue to do that. I didn't want you to have to worry about it."

Lainey remained silent and Eve sighed silently.

"I have to go to Sumptor, Inc. and take care of a few things before I meet with Billy," she said.

"Do you want me to go with you?"

"Of course I do," she said quietly. "But, you should stay here and help Mikey until the others come in. Do you want me to pick you up to go to the auction, or do you want to meet me there?"

In fact, Lainey welcomed having some time alone so that she could think about everything Eve had told her. Things were more complicated now that there was a possibility of her sons being involved or in danger. She had to seriously consider her actions and their consequences from now on.

"I'll meet you there," she said. "Listen, Eve, be careful. I'm not mad at you, honey. You just have to give me some time to adjust to all of this. I know that I sound ungrateful for what you've done for me, and I'm sorry for that. I'm scared...for my children, for you. When I look at you, I can see that you mean what you say. I know you'll protect me, but at what cost, Eve?"

Eve risked touching Lainey's hand briefly. "I couldn't help my mother, I was too young. I couldn't help Jackie because I wasn't prepared. But I swear to you, I'm prepared now and nothing is going to happen to you or your family." She wanted to tell Lainey that she loved her but the words still wouldn't come. She could only hope that Lainey could see love in her eyes. "I have to go," she whispered.

'I love you, too.' Lainey mouthed as Eve drove away.

Eve dialed as she drove towards Sumptor, Inc. "It's me," she said when the other party answered. "I'm on my way to Sumptor, Inc. now. Any word about Meredith?"

"No, ma'am. We're trying to get information from inside, but no one is talking. If Tony has her, he's not telling us."

"Do you think he suspects you?"

"No. I think we would be dead if he did."

A pang of guilt passed through Eve. "If you want to get out of this while you can, I understand."

"Frankly, Ms. Sumptor, we're glad to be on your side. I think we could handle Tony if it came down to it. We like to be on the winning team, and I believe we are."

Eve wished she was so sure about that. "Thank you. Any word on Pauly?"

"It's not good, ma'am, but he's alive."

Goddamnit! "Where is he?"

"Same hospital as Christine. He was pretty roughed up, but it looks as though he held his own. Doctors say they need to wait for the swelling to go down before they can determine whether the paralysis is permanent."

"Son of a bitch!" Eve whispered vehemently. "He's gone too fucking far this time. This is going to end very soon. I trust that Pauly is safe now?"

"Yes. He and his family are now under protection."

"Good." She looked up at her rearview mirror. "I seem to have company."

"Do you want us to get rid of them for you?"

"I have a meeting after this stop, and they're not invited. Make sure they get lost so they can't crash the party."

"Yes ma'am. Consider it done."

"Thank you. I'll be in touch." She ended the call and checked her rearview mirror again. "Enjoy it while you can, Detective," she said under her breath. "I'm taking you down along with Tony. I promise you that."

Her visit to Sumptor, Inc. had left Eve with a headache. She had had to do a lot of fast talking and make a lot of promises to keep everyone from quitting on her. The cops had been by to talk to the employees, and, as a result, morale wasn't exactly high. They had been told, in so many words, that their boss was under investigation for two disappearances and one known murder.

It was a good thing for Eve that her employees had a little more faith in her than the cops did. Most have been with her since the beginning and helped convince the new hires that Eve Sumptor could never do what the cops were accusing her of. In any case, Eve knew her time was limited and she was going to have to finish this game with Tony quickly or not at all.

At precisely two o'clock, she stepped into The Garden of Eve. As usual, she was met with stares and suggestive smiles, but she held her anger in check, which was quite a difficult task at the moment.

"Good afternoon, Ms. Sumptor." Elliot greeted Eve with a genuine smile. "Your guest is waiting."

"Thank you. It's okay," she smiled at him sweetly, "I'll find him."

She knew that Billy would be sitting at one of her regular tables in the back, and sure enough, there he was, dressed in a black, crisply pressed suit with his light hair neatly parted on the side.

He'd been waiting for her, sure that everything he had felt for her all those years ago had passed. He had moved on, of course, so why was he so nervous? But when he saw her walking towards him, his heart dropped to his feet. "Christ," he whispered as he rose to greet her, instantly aroused, praying his body would not betray him.

"Billy." She closed the gap between them and kissed him softly on the cheek.

The scent of Eve was intoxicating, and Billy realized then that all of those feelings he had for her were still there. "You..." He was having trouble forming words. Clearing his throat, he started over. "You look amazing."

"You don't look so bad yourself," she said, flashing him a grin that had him melting inside. They remained silent as the waiter brought Eve a glass of iced tea and set it in front of her. "Perk of owning the restaurant," she said, seeing that he was impressed. "They always know what I want."

My God, why does she have to be so beautiful? Billy shook himself, picking up a breadstick from the basket in front of him. He would focus on that instead of her, then maybe he would be able to think of something intelligent to say to her. Much to his dismay, the breadstick wasn't helping. He was still thinking of her and nothing else.

"Billy? Are you all right?"

He forced himself to look at her, blanking the emotion from his eyes. "Yes, I'm fine. I guess I'm suffering from a little jetlag." Jetlag? What are you stupid? I can't believe you just said that to her. Jetlag. From Washington, D.C. to New York?

Eve chuckled. "Well, I'll try not to keep you long."

"I don't mind the company. After all, you are why I came here."

Eve's smile faded. It had to be done; she had to talk about it. Might as well get it over with, she thought. "You know I wouldn't have gotten you involved in this if I didn't have to," she began.

"I know." Taking his cue to get down to business, Billy opened his briefcase and handed two files to Eve.

"What's this?" Eve flipped open the first and frowned when she saw her name in big, black letters.

"Your files," Billy explained. He had taken the liberty of pulling them for this meeting. Finding the one that had been altered had been a shocking bonus. "The one you're reading now is the real file the FBI has on you. The other has been altered."

He watched as Eve sifted through the file that he had read so many times. Over the years, he would bring out that same file, minus the photos – it was just too hard to look at her – to make sure she was doing well.

Eve's whole life was outlined in these pages, from school, to the gallery, to almost everything else she has done. Even her relationship with Adam was chronicled here, including photos of the two of them on various occasions. "Well, well. Big brother *is* watching," she mumbled, frowning.

"It was all done for your protection, Eve." And, so I could keep tabs on you, he added silently.

"Right. What does my relationship with Adam have to do with my protection?" She didn't expect an answer, nor did she get one. Eve pushed her 'real' file to the side and opened the other.

As soon as she opened it, she knew it had been written by someone who didn't know a lot about her.

Billy saw her glance move across her name in the file. "He doesn't know you," he said, echoing her thoughts. "When you look up your birth certificate, it gives you the modified copy – unless you specifically ask for the original. This person apparently didn't know that you added your mother's name as your middle name in your twenties. I think we can rule Tony out on this."

"Unless he's the one who hired the moron," she countered. "Besides, I doubt he would even remember that they had chosen not to give me a middle name. Tony has to keep his hands clean of any involvement in this, so he wouldn't have direct contact with him on this."

There was something in the way she said it that made Billy think she knew more about this. "Do you know who it is, Eve?"

"I don't have evidence," Eve said carefully. "But, I have a feeling."

"Fill me in. I need everything I can get in order to help you." He took a notepad and pen, standard for all FBI agents Eve suspected, from his standard black jacket.

"Detective Maurice Carter," Eve said tersely.

Billy paused, pen in air. "A detective? You believe a cop is involved with this?"

"Surely, you're not that naïve, Billy. Agents from your own bureau have tried to have me killed. Why not a cop?"

She was right, of course, but he still didn't want to believe that someone who was sworn to uphold the law, would break it.

"I'm going to need more than a hunch to bring him down, Eve. If we can get him, maybe he'll give Tony up."

"Would a taped confession be enough?"

"It would be more than enough, but how do you plan on getting him to confess?"

"I've seen the way he looks at me."

"No! Absolutely not. You're not to get any more involved in this than you already are."

Eve's eyebrow came up. "I asked you here for your help," she told him. "Not so you could tell me what I can or cannot do, Agent Donovan."

Now he understood why she was so successful in business. That look was enough to make any grown man sweat. "I'm trying to help you, Eve. I can't just let you go into a potentially dangerous situation."

"I'm already in a 'potentially dangerous situation'," she told him irritably. "I can't sit back and wait for someone else to get hurt, Billy. Too many people have suffered because of the game I've had to play with Tony and it hurts too much. I'll do anything and everything that I have to do to keep those that I care about safe. And if that means putting my own life on the line, then so be it."

He had never heard her be so open with her feelings and it floored him. To his surprise, and shame, he also envied the people in her life whom she had confessed to caring about.

"Very well," he agreed unwillingly. "But, you have to work with me on this, Eve. I need to know that you will do as I ask. You may not want anyone else to get hurt, but I don't want anything to happen to you in the process."

Billy pointed to the file.

"Whoever is doing this to you has no conscious and will do everything they can to hurt you. And, not just physically, Eve, judging by what's in that file."

"I'm not surprised by that. I'm being framed for my mother's death, for Jackie's death and Lord knows what else."

"There are lies, disguised as sealed records, lies about your being a prostitute in Paris." Flipping through the pages of the file, Billy didn't notice when her face went completely white. "If someone wants to dig enough, they'll find this information."

Eve struggled with every ounce of strength inside her to stay calm. How had Tony found out? Madame Bussiere must have gotten in touch with him. Still she couldn't prove that Eve had sold herself. Could she? Surely none of Eve's 'customers' would have wanted to come forward.

"He's going to ruin me," Eve told herself.

"Eve?" Billy took her hand. It was as cold as ice. "They're just lies and we'll get rid of it before anyone can find it."

"You don't understand." Eve pulled her hand back. "My galleries, their prestige – it will all be over if this gets out there. My image, my name will mean nothing. No. Worse than that. I'll be a disgrace."

"People will know they are fake records, Eve. I promise. Look, after I get done here, I'm going to visit the Sawyers. They need to know that everything they have been told is lies and I'll get information from them about who is feeding them this false information. It can only help us."

"Don't press them, Billy. They've been through enough already. Talk to Dee Cummings with Channel 9 News. She should be able to help with that. All I want the Sawyers to know is that I had nothing to do with the death of their daughter. Please, make sure they know that."

The plea was so desperate that Billy would have agreed to do anything for her. In spite of everything she was going through - the pending lawsuits, the accusations - she still thought of the comfort and happiness of others instead of her own. Was it any wonder he felt the way he did about her? He sat back in his chair and rubbed his chin with his left hand.

"You're married!" she exclaimed, seeing the broad gold band. "How long?"

"Six years," he told her and watched as her eyebrow lifted once again. It was a quirk he had come to enjoy immensely, one he had thought of many times over the years, but it also meant that she had seen more than he wanted her to.

"Do you have children?" Eve knew she probably shouldn't ask, especially since marriage seemed to be a sore subject for him, but she couldn't help herself.

At the mention of children, Billy brightened. "Yes. Two." Billy reached into his inside coat pocket and pulled out his wallet. "Ashley and Billy." He shrugged sheepishly. "You're the only person who ever calls me Billy." Handing the wallet over to Eve, Billy held his breath. He didn't know why, but Eve's opinion mattered to him greatly.

Eve took the wallet and studied the photos of Billy's children. "They're beautiful," she told him sincerely. "How old are they?"

"Two and four and a half. I love them very much."

"And their mother?"

Eve certainly wasn't the kind of woman to hold back, he thought. She had noticed his uneasiness, and he should have expected these kinds of questions. "She's a good wife," he said. "A good mother. A wonderful woman."

He hadn't answered her question, Eve observed. "Are you happy?"

Billy was quiet for a moment as he thought about his answer. "Content," he said finally. How could he tell her that she was the reason he couldn't give his heart to his wife? How could he confess that all of these years, he had held on to the hope that Eve would contact him and tell him she was in love with him? It was a fantasy, he knew, but now here she was, sitting in front of him.

Eve read everything he was thinking on his face. "I have to go," she said quietly. She was grateful to him. But he belonged to the past. A past she wanted desperately to forget.

"But you just got here." Did she know? "At least have lunch with me."

"I can't, I'm sorry. I have an auction to go to." She lifted a shoulder. "Might as well get everything I need while I still have my good name."

"But it's been so long, Eve. We have a lot to talk about."

She held up a hand to stop him. "Don't get up. You know how to get in touch with me, I assume. I'll wait for you to set up something with Detective Carter. Just don't take long; I want this over with soon. Thank you, Billy. For everything." She paused before leaving. "Forget about me."

"What?"

"Let me go. I'm grateful to you for coming to help me, but you have to let go of these feelings you have for me. You're a wonderful man, and you deserve all the happiness in the world. So, let your wife give that to you. I don't love you, Billy. I'm sorry but I never will," she said softly. She didn't say it to hurt him, but for closure, and he knew it.

~ Nineteen ~

"Good afternoon, Ms. Sumptor," Eve was greeted as she walked into the auction house. "It's very nice to see you again."

The woman behind the counter looked Eve over as discreetly as she could. Eve had always been a topic of discussion around here. For the men, she was a fantasy. For the women, she was either what they strived to be, or if they were jealous, what they hated most. The young woman behind the counter was one for whom Eve was the embodiment of the perfect woman: strong, independent, beautiful. "Your assistant has arrived already and is waiting for you in the second row," she said, handing Eve a numbered paddle and a program.

As soon as she entered the long, narrow room, filled with chairs and chattering people she felt his presence. The sick feeling that gripped her whenever Tony was near washed over her, and she fought the urge to turn and look for him. Spotting Lainey in the second row, Eve strode towards her, deliberately keeping every movement casual, unwilling to give him the advantage of knowing that she had realized he was there.

Lainey's pulse jumped when Eve slipped into the seat next to her. Out of the corner of her eye, she saw Eve gracefully cross her legs and Lainey's fingers itched to touch them.

"Hi." Eve's voice was breathy and held a hint of desire. Leaning closer, she put her mouth close to Lainey's ear. "I love the reaction my body has when I'm near you."

The sound of Eve's voice, her nearness, had as much of an effect on Lainey as the words Eve spoke. She had spent the entire day thinking of everything that Eve had revealed to her this morning. She should have been scared. For her, for her children. But, oddly enough, she wasn't. She believed Eve when Eve told her that she would never let anything happen to her or her family.

Of course, she was still concerned, but she only had to look at Eve to forget danger as she recalled every touch, every look, every kiss. Using her numbered paddle, Lainey fanned her warm cheeks.

"Have you ever been to an auction before?" Eve asked, relieved that Lainey no longer seemed upset with her. "Because if you haven't, I want to warn you not to make any sudden movements. Bids are made very discreetly by most of the members here, so a scratch, a raise of an eyebrow, anything can be considered a bid."

"What are the numbers for?"

"You can use them to make your bid if you're not interested in being discreet. They use the number to record who the highest bidder is for each auction."

"I've been looking over the program while waiting for you," Lainey told her. "There are some really great pieces. This one in particular is fabulous."

Lainey pointed out a jade statue of Buddha with rubies and diamonds encrusted in the necklace around the neck of the portly figurine.

"Beautiful."

It was the way Eve said it that had Lainey questioning if she meant the statue or Lainey herself.

"They're starting the bid way below what he's worth," she said. "Why don't you bid on it?"

The question nearly made Lainey laugh out loud. "It's starting at $10,000, Eve. I could never afford that. Even if I could, Jack would kill me if I bought it."

"It's a beautiful piece, Lainey, and well worth it. This is your first auction. Have fun with it." She was trying hard to concentrate on the fact that this was a new experience for Lainey, and exciting happening. But Tony remained in the back of her mind.

'Having fun with it' was easy for someone like Eve to say. She had more money than she cared to admit and had room to play with it. However, bidding did sound intriguing. Maybe she would, at least once, just for the hell of it. She was certain she wouldn't win anyway, so why not do as Eve suggested and have fun with it? But then, she noticed that Eve, the woman who seemed to have no nerves at all, was tearing the edges of her program. "Is something wrong?" she asked. "You seem upset. Did something happen during your meeting with Agent Donovan?"

Eve heard the bite in Lainey's voice, and found herself wishing they were alone so she could explain that Billy wasn't the one that upset her. "They're about to start. I'll tell you everything later, okay?"

Lainey agreed grudgingly and settled in to enjoy her first auction. At least she hoped she could enjoy it. It was those times when she caught Eve unguarded that upset her the most because she could see then just how vulnerable Eve really was.

The silent competition between bidders intrigued Lainey. She was astonished at how high the bids became, and wondered just how much money these people had to just spend it so freely.

As for Eve, she took pleasure in watching Lainey's expression which ranged from excitement to awe to total confusion. Between bids, Lainey would lean over to Eve and whisper something like, "*Why would they pay that much money for something so hideous?*" The only thing marring the moment for Eve was Tony. She could feel his eyes on her the whole time, but she wouldn't risk Lainey knowing he was there.

When the jade Buddha came on the block, Eve noticed how Lainey had straightened slightly in her chair as though poised for a fight. Clearly she was relishing the rush of just being in the game. Lainey's eyes lit up as the Buddha was brought on stage, and placed on a stand beside the auctioneer's podium. Discreetly, Eve positioned herself where she could easily and unnoticeably make bids if necessary.

The auctioneer gave a brief description of the item and started the bidding. "Ten thousand is the first bid," he said. "Do I have ten-five?"

Hesitantly, Lainey lifted her hand.

"Ten-five," the auctioneer announced, pointing towards Lainey.

It was a rush, she thought cheerfully. But she must be careful not to go too far.

"Do I hear eleven? Eleven." He pointed towards the opposite end of the room and looked back at Lainey briefly, questioningly, before continuing. "Eleven-five?" Lainey raised her hand. "Eleven-five." The man smiled at Lainey. "Twelve?"

Before Lainey had a chance to get back into the action, the bid was up to twenty-five thousand. Deflated, she sat back and watched the little Buddha she had wanted slip through her fingers. She had known that she couldn't have it anyway, but that didn't stop the disappointment.

Eve caught the auctioneer's eye and nodded ever-so-slightly. He had been the auctioneer at many of the auctions she had attended, and they had an understanding with each other. He knew when she wanted to be unnoticeable and this was one of those times. Bidding climbed steadily, with Eve not backing down. She was going to possess this little green statue no matter what the cost.

"Bidding is at sixty thousand. Do I hear sixty-five?" He paused and scanned the room and sea of faces for any sign. "Sixty, going once. Going twice." Pause. "Sold for sixty thousand to number," with a quick glance at Eve's paddle, he smiled. "Seven-four-one-three."

"My goodness!" Lainey exclaimed. "Sixty thousand for that little, green pot-bellied man? I almost wish I had it to spend."

"Look," Eve said. "This is what we came here for."

Lainey's breath caught. "It's beautiful. How much is it worth?" She kept her voice low, and leaned close to Eve. Lainey told herself that it was because the atmosphere was quiet, but she knew deep down it was because she loved being this close to Eve. Loved the smell of her, the feel of their bodies lightly touching.

"It's priceless, really," Eve told her as two men placed the painting of a nude with blue eyes and flesh reflected in lilac tones on the easel. "The frame is original and it has never been retouched. It's even signed twice."

Eve's eyes became an almost translucent gray as she waited for the bidding to begin. She had already promised herself that no amount was too much for this magnificent piece of art.

"We'll start the bidding off at one million." Eve heard the auctioneer say and immediately made sure he knew she was interested. Catching his eye, Eve nodded.

"We have one million, do I hear one point five?"

"So she thinks she can just spend one million of my money, does she?" Tony could barely contain himself as he watched the bidding go higher. He saw Eve nod again and on impulse born of fury raised his hand to make his own bid.

"Sir, what are you doing?" Tony's companion whispered. "You're not registered to make bids."

"I know. That's why I'm bidding, you moron. She'll eventually give up and I won't have to buy it once they find out that I've been disqualified. But, she won't get it either."

Tony's companion said nothing. He knew Eve, better than Tony, and he knew she would fight for this piece. He'd spent enough time watching over Eve to know that.

"I have three point five from the back," the auctioneer called out. "Do I hear four million?"

Eve frowned. She glanced back at Tony who had an arrogant smile as he brought the price up. Why was he bidding?

Nodding, she brought the painting up to four million.

"Four million. Do I hear four point five?" The war was now between Eve and Tony, and it was more than just a bidding war. She knew what he was trying to do now, so she would play his game. And, she would win.

"Now five. Five million?" The auctioneer looked at Eve for confirmation. When he received it, he looked back at Tony. "Five point five?"

Furious, Tony brought the painting up to five point five million. The bitch was not going to spend his money on this overrated piece of canvas with paint strewn everywhere.

"Thank you. Five point five. Do I hear six million?"

Eve raised an eyebrow. Tony was underestimating her if he didn't think she knew what he was doing. She nodded again and brought the painting up to six million.

"Six million." Murmurs filled the room. *Can you believe it's getting that high? Eve Sumptor really wants that painting. Who's bidding against her?* "Do I have six point five?" the auctioneer demanded.

"Bitch," Tony muttered, and bid six point five million.

"We're at six point five. Will we go to seven? Seven million?"

The auctioneer glanced at Eve. He couldn't say why, but he could have sworn he saw her smile before shaking her head. He was surprised, and a bit disappointed that Eve bowed out of the bidding.

"Six point five going once. Going twice. Sold to...your number sir? Sir, I need your number."

Tony just waved off the question without concern. He would stay until he was sure Eve wouldn't bid on anything else, then he would leave. It would be easy. Revenge and rage blinded him to the fact that this was a flawed plan.

"Sir, if you do not have a number, you cannot bid. Do you have a number?" The auctioneer, becoming more annoyed by the minute, made eye contact with security. "You'll have to leave if you are not registered, sir, and your bids will become void. Ms. Sumptor? Before this man's bid of three point five million, you had the highest bid at three million. Would you still like this piece?"

Eve smiled and nodded. It was a small victory, but a victory nonetheless.

"Very good. Lot number nine-six-two, sold for three million to number seven-four-one-three."

Eve turned and locked eyes with Tony, who was in the process of being escorted out. She could see that her smile and mocking wink incensed him as he stormed out.

Seven-four-one-three. It took a moment for the numbers to register in Lainey's mind. "Oh my God!" she exclaimed. "It was you who bid on the Buddha!"

"Shh," Eve whispered. There would be time to talk about the Buddha later.

Later, as they walked side by side out to the reception area, Eve could feel the tension as tight as a guitar string in Lainey. Throughout the rest of the auctions, Lainey had fidgeted in her seat, torn at the edges of her program and kept looking over at Eve with a look that was a cross between being infuriated and incredulous. It had taken all of Eve's control just to stay composed.

Her triumph over Tony was only the frosting on the cake. Pleasing Lainey was, she found, far more important.

"Did you enjoy yourself, Ms. Sumptor?" the receptionist asked as she took Eve's number.

"Absolutely."

"Do you want all of your acquisitions to be delivered to your gallery?"

"Yes, please. Except the Buddha. I'll take that with me."

"Yes, ma'am." The woman picked up her two way radio and called back to have Eve's little statue brought to the front.

"Ms. Sumptor."

Eve turned and smiled at the man. "Hello, Don. Wonderful auction today."

"I'm always glad to see you at one of our auctions. You make them, shall I say, very interesting."

"You just like how much I spend here," Eve teased. She turned to Lainey. "Lainey, this is Don Ferrill, auctioneer extraordinaire. Don, this is Lainey Stanton."

"Ahh, yes. Ms. Stanton, it's very nice to meet you. I admired your display at the gallery on opening night. It was quite beautiful."

"Thank you so much, Mr. Ferrill. You've made my first auction a wonderful experience."

"I'm glad you enjoyed it. I think the man in the back was trying to get your attention," he said to Eve with a grin.

"I think he got more attention than he wanted," Eve answered. "But, it worked out well for me."

Spending this time with Lainey had been bittersweet for her. She had gotten what she had come for, and acquired something special for Lainey in the process. But she knew that she had not heard the last from Tony.

"Why did you do that?" Lainey couldn't hold the question in a minute longer. They were standing on the sidewalk waiting for valet to bring Eve's car around, and Lainey just couldn't stay quiet anymore. "Why did you get this for me?"

"Because you wanted it," Eve said simply.

"Eve, it cost sixty-thousand dollars! You can't just buy me something that costs sixty-thousand dollars!"

"Why not?"

"Why not?" Lainey threw her hands in the air. "What do you mean, why not? That is too much money..."

"You wanted it. I bought. It's yours now. It's a simple as that."

Eve's matter-of-fact, blasé attitude only served to infuriate Lainey more. "It's not as simple as that. I can't accept that. I can't take that home with me."

"Why not?"

"You're not listening to me!"

"Honey, I am listening to you," Eve interrupted. Lainey's display of anger was amusing, but soon they would be creating a scene and that's not what Eve wanted. "I just don't agree with you. You can accept it. It is my gift to you. Take it home. Put it on your desk at the gallery. Do whatever you want to do with it. It's yours."

A block from the auction house, Eve brought the car to an abrupt stop.

"You don't want to take the damn thing because it cost sixty-thousand," she told Lainey, her own temper was rising. "Money doesn't mean anything to me. Don't you understand that? I have a lot of it, I spend it. What the hell else am I supposed to do with it? Why can't you take it home? Because of Jack? No offense, honey, but I don't think he'd have a damn clue what something like that is worth."

"And if he asks?"

"Lie! That shouldn't be that hard for you." Eve closed her eyes and swore. Had she really said that? "I'm sorry. I didn't mean to say that."

"Yes. You did." Lainey took off her seatbelt and reached for the door handle. "I think I'll walk back to the gallery."

"No," Eve said softly, gently placing her hand over Lainey's. "Please, don't. I am sorry, and I didn't mean to say that. Look at me. Please." She took Lainey's chin in her fingers and turned her face towards her. "I wanted to get it for you because I..." Why couldn't she say the words? It should be so simple and yet she couldn't force herself to do it. "You've done so much for me," she said softly. "You've given me more than any amount of money could buy, and I wanted to do this as some small way to tell you 'thank you'. Is it so wrong of me to want to do something for you?"

She touched Lainey briefly, knowing she wanted so much more right now. "I'm sorry if this makes you uncomfortable, that's not what I wanted. I just want to make you happy."

Lainey did know what Eve was trying to say to her and it touched her more than any jade statue ever could. "You do make me happy. I don't need gifts for that. I only need you."

Eve wanted to kiss Lainey. The urge to do so was very strong, but she resisted. "Take it home with you tonight," Eve said softly. "I doubt Jack will ask you about it and if he does, just tell him that I gave it to you as a thank you for all of the hard work you've done at the gallery. That's not a lie. Not the whole truth, but not a lie. I want you to put it on the nightstand next to your bed. Think of me while you're lying there."

"Eve..."

"Lainey. Jack gets you. Let me have this. Please?"

"I'll take it home with me," Lainey told her. "But I don't need it to think about you, because you're in my head, my heart, every second. I'll take it with me because you want me to."

Eve knew it was because of her that Lainey felt guilt and unhappiness at lying to her family every day. How long was she going to continue to be selfish?

The rest of the day went by quickly for Eve, and time with Lainey had been minimal. Either Eve was busy with paperwork, having just spent millions of dollars on new art, or Lainey was busy with clients. When they walked past each other, they would touch. Whether it was involuntarily, or if they both were conscious of doing it, Eve didn't know. What she did know is that it was driving her insane. Lainey wouldn't be going home with her tonight, and Eve didn't know when or if they would be together again.

It has to end sooner or later. The thought was in Eve's head constantly, no matter how hard she tried to ignore it. You'd better prepare for it now, Eve, she told herself, picking up the photo taken in Florida. And yet, looking at Lainey and the boys, she didn't know if she would ever be able to prepare herself for that.

The phone beside her shrilled and Eve jumped. Nerves, she thought disgustedly. That was one thing she had to get over, now. It certainly wouldn't do for her to lose it now when there was so much at stake. "Sumptor Gallery. This is Eve."

"You keep pissing him off."

"What the hell was he doing there? How did he know I'd be there?"

"A woman, posing as a society reporter, went to the gallery and asked Mikey to speak to you. He told her where you were."

"Is this woman someone we need to worry about?"

"No, ma'am. She was just someone off the street that he paid for a favor. She's not an issue. But, ma'am, he's more determined than ever to destroy you after today. He's pissed that you keep spending his money. His words, not mine, ma'am."

"Aww, my heart breaks for him," Eve answered with dripping sarcasm.

"I don't think you understand..."

"I understand perfectly. He's called a meeting hasn't he?"

"How did you know that?" It was exactly what he had called her about. For her to know about it already, spooked him. The woman knew more, saw more than anyone he had come across. The thought was almost frightening.

"He's my father, God help me. He's predictable, angry and out for revenge. People like that tend to make more mistakes. He wants to do this now, doesn't he?"

"Yes. He's making arrangements to win this game very soon."

"Did you tell him that going after Lainey would be a mistake?" Because it would, Eve continued silently. Try to hurt her, Daddy, and I swear to God you'll wish you were back in prison.

"I did my best. I don't know if I did any good, but at the moment, he's focused on you and you alone."

"Well, as much as I'd love to end this silly game, he'll have to wait. I'm going out of town for a couple of days."

"He's really not going to like that, ma'am."

Eve heard the humor in the man's voice and smiled. No. Tony wasn't going to like it, and it put her at even more of an advantage. The more rage he has, the more errors he'll make.

"What a shame. I take it there's no word on Meredith."

"There may be. But, it's not good." He took a breath. "He has someone on the outside, someone not in the organization working for him. I don't know who it is, yet, but I'm trying to find out. From the one-sided conversations I've heard, I have reason to suspect that Meredith has been 'taken care of.'"

"Damn it! You don't know this for sure?"

"He never mentioned her name, so no, I don't know that it's Meredith for sure. But, ma'am, there's really no one else he could be speaking about."

"Do what you can to find out more information on your end. About Meredith and this other person he has working for him. We can't afford any surprises in this stage of the game."

Eve had a very good idea who this 'other person' was, but she needed the proof. However confident she was with Billy, she was unquestionably not looking forward to having a wired session with Detective Carter. The thought of pretending to be interested in him was enough to make her nauseous.

"As I said before, I will be out of town for the next couple of days. You know how to get a hold of me. Is there anything else?"

"No, ma'am. I'll get working on finding out more information for you."

"Be careful. There have been too many deaths already. I'll be in touch."

Eve replaced the receiver and sat back in her chair. "There's only one other death to come out of this game," she said to herself. "And that's yours, Daddy. That's yours."

Lainey was trying her best to concentrate on the client in front of her, but it was becoming increasingly difficult. Her mind, involuntarily, kept wandering back to Eve. The talk they had the night before, their love making, the feelings between them, everything that was happening with Eve's father, and now the statue. Everything came to Lainey all at one time and overwhelmed her. *You have to figure this out, Lainey, before you go insane.* She smiled and nodded as the woman in front of her kept talking and talking. *Why won't she just shut up,* Lainey thought, annoyed at herself and the customer at the same time. This was part of her job, she should be able to listen to anyone and be pleasant and polite. Just when she thought she couldn't stand anymore, she felt a tap on her shoulder.

"Yes?" Lainey turned as she spoke, then nearly froze when she saw Adam standing there. "Adam. Hi."

"I don't mean to interrupt. Are you all right?"

"I'm sorry." *For thinking about the woman you love. For loving the woman you're in love with.* "Will you excuse me please?" Lainey told the customer. "I'll be right back. Why don't you go and look at the black and white photography on the back wall. I think you'll find something that will compliment the modern look you desire for your apartment perfectly." *Well, hot damn, I was listening.* Lainey turned back to Adam, anger rising inside of her. *How dare he come into Eve's gallery after taking some bimbo to Eve's restaurant?* "What can I do for you, Adam?" She kept her voice level and calm. It wasn't her place to tell Adam to go to hell for Eve. Eve should do that for herself.

"Is Eve in? I need to speak with her." *Was that disdain he heard in Lainey's voice? It couldn't be, he thought. He must be imagining things.*

"Eve is busy at the moment. You can leave a message with me, and I'll be sure she gets it." Maybe, she added silently. It was a petty thing to think, but sadly, or perhaps selfishly, she didn't care.

"Have I done something to upset you, Lainey? Have I said something? Or, is what's happening between me and Eve the reason for this hostility? Because honestly, I don't know myself what is going on."

The look he gave her, the fatigue she saw in his eyes, softened her. Clearly he was unhappy, uncertain, lost. "Eve is my friend, Adam. My best friend. I'm sorry if I'm a little partial." Lainey hesitated for a moment and glanced up the stairs towards Eve's office, remembering how miserable Eve had been when she had spoke of losing Adam the night before. "Open your eyes, Adam," Lainey whispered. "See what she doesn't want you to see."

He had to strain to hear her, but the words deeply affected him for reasons he couldn't explain. His eyes closed, his heart pounded inside his chest, his breathing quickened. Eve was near. He could feel her inside his soul.

Confused by Adam's reaction, Lainey looked up just in time to catch Eve at the top of the stairs. She saw the intake of breath, the look of joy and sorrow combined.

Eve's hand fluttered to her heart, dropping it instantly when she caught Lainey's eye. She struggled to stay calm as she neared him. "Adam?"

He turned to her, using all of his will power not to take her in his arms and just hold her. He had thought he could forget her and move on. But, every night he dreamt of her, ached for her.

"Hi." He dug his hands into his pockets to keep from touching her.

"Why are you here?"

Lainey took a step away from the couple. She didn't know if she could stand there and watch the way they looked at each other, or listen to what they had to say to each other. "I'll just go."

"No, Lainey." Eve stepped to Lainey's side and laid a hand on her arm. "Please, stay."

Lainey heard the silent desperate plea, and stayed.

329

"I need to speak with you, Eve," Adam said, his heart sinking. She didn't even want to be alone with him. "I was hoping we could do it privately."

"I'm sorry, Adam, I simply don't have the time today."

"Tomorrow then?"

"I'm going out of town tomorrow, and I'll be gone for a few days." Eve felt Lainey tense beside her. This wasn't the way she had intended to tell Lainey, but then she hadn't expected to see Adam. "Shall I walk you to the elevator, Adam?"

"So that's it?" He asked her when Lainey was out of earshot. "This is how it ends? You won't even talk to me."

"I told you, I'm busy," Eve said. She wanted so much for him to take her in his arms and make everything right. But she knew he couldn't. "You just caught me at a really bad time."

"Is there a good time to talk about our relationship with you?"

"That's not fair. You don't call, you act as if you didn't want to talk to me when I called you..."

"I was upset, Eve. Can you really blame me for that? Hell, you didn't even remember what day it was."

"I apologized for that," Eve said softly. "There's nothing more I can say. I can't change what happened."

"It showed me just where I stand in your life, Eve."

Eve was silent until the elevator doors opened and Adam stepped in. "You see nothing, Adam," she said quietly as the doors slid shut.

"Are you okay?" Lainey laid a hand on Eve's shoulder. Eve hadn't moved from in front of the elevator since Adam had left a few minutes earlier.

"Fine." After another minute of silence and sadness, she took a breath and turned to Lainey with a smile. "I'm fine."

"Eve, I know this is hurting you. Talk to me."

Eve sighed. "Lainey, I can't think about this right now. Adam is better off this way." She held up her hand to stop Lainey from commenting. "Before you say anything, let me just say, I know how you feel about me, and you're a bit biased. Look, I have to clean up the mess that my life is in right now before I can worry about my relationship with Adam."

"Does that mess include me?"

"Of course not! You're not a part of my problems."

Lainey let out the breath that she was holding and relaxed. "So, to keep Adam away, you told him you were going out of town?"

"I am going out of town. I'm going to Paris tomorrow."

"I thought that was next week." Confused, Lainey thought back to her conversation with Eve about the auction in Paris. She was positive that it was next week.

"It was, but certain matters have come to my attention, matters I have to attend to."

"Then I'm going with you," Lainey said. After all Eve had told her, how could she really think Lainey would let her face her world on her own?

"No, Lainey. What I have to do there, I have to do alone."

"Why? Why must you do everything alone? Is it that you don't want me to go with you?"

"I do. That's why you need to stay here. Lainey," Eve saw the hurt in Lainey's eyes and wished she hadn't put it there. "Please don't be upset. I can't keep asking you to disrupt your life for me."

"You're not asking. I want to be with you, and I won't let you keep pushing me away." Lainey lowered her voice. "I love you, Eve."

Eve raised a perfectly shaped eyebrow and glanced around at the people in the gallery.

"Afraid someone might hear me?" Lainey asked. Oddly enough, she wasn't afraid or ashamed.

"Do you think I care who hears?" Eve asked with an almost proud smile. "It's not me I'm worried about." She gestured towards the stairs. "Come on. Let's go to my office for some privacy."

Eve waited for Lainey to enter the office and closed the door behind her. "I have to do this alone, Lainey," she said.

"You're not alone anymore, Eve," Lainey insisted. "You've been through so much in your life, with no one else to help you. But now I'm here."

The sentiment alone touched Eve. She smiled at Lainey. "I've been back to Paris since then, honey."

"Not there," Lainey said simply. Somehow, she knew where Eve was going and knew how hard it would be for her. "You're scared."

Eve locked eyes with Lainey. When she spoke, her voice was low and quiet. "How do you do that? How do you see what's inside me?"

"I told you, honey. I love you."

Eve began to pace. "Whether I'm scared or not, I have to do this by myself," she said. "I can't keep taking you away from your family, Lainey. Jack, Kevin and Darren need you here, and I have to stop being selfish." She came to a stop in front of Lainey. "This is my problem, and what I have to do to fix it, I can't involve you."

"What do you mean by that?"

"I mean just that. I can't say much more than I've already told you. I'm not going to let you be implicated in anything – distasteful that I might have to do."

"You're starting to scare me. What are you going to do, Eve?"

"Only what has to be done," Eve answered simply. "He knows, Lainey."

"Knows what?"

"What I did in Paris. He knows. They're trying to destroy me, and if I don't take care of this now, they will."

"Oh my God. How?"

"That's what I need to find out. By any means possible. There's a file on me, a file that the authorities have. Billy showed it to me."

"Billy knows, too?" How had Eve handled it all? How had she made it through each day with all of this going on around her?

"He doesn't believe it. He thinks they planted it as another way to bring me down. If I don't do something about this, they'll succeed."

"Who are they, Eve?"

"There's someone else, and I don't know how involved he is in this with my father. Don't ask me who," Eve said quickly, when she saw the question form in Lainey's eyes. "I'm not going to tell you, not yet. I don't have any proof." She hesitated, debating on how much to say to Lainey, then took a breath. "Just trust me, baby, when I tell you that the less you know, the better. They're not playing by the rules, Lainey. There's only one way this game between me and Tony is going to end. One of us will die."

"Don't! Don't say that, Eve." Lainey's heart pounded painfully in her chest, and she started to feel light headed. Losing Eve was something that Lainey couldn't think about. She had just found her and there was no way now that she could live without her. She dropped onto a chair and Eve fell to her knees in front of her.

"I don't intend to lose, Lainey," she said in a low voice.

"But what are you going to do, Eve?" Lainey demanded. "You aren't going to kill your father, are you?"

Eve found that she was unable to look Lainey in the eye.

"Eve, you can't!"

"What am I supposed to do, Lainey? I've lived looking over my shoulder my whole life, wondering who he's hired to kill me, or destroy me. I can't live like that anymore. If any of this gets out - what they know about Paris - I'm finished. All of this," Eve gestured widely with her arms. "All of it will be over. My galleries, everything that I care about will be gone."

She knew Lainey understood that she meant Adam as well.

"Then have him put back in jail, Eve. You can't...kill him."

"Jail doesn't solve my problem, Lainey. He can still hire people, I'll still be looking over my shoulder. I'll spend every day worried that he'll come after those I care about. I won't do that to you or your family. I won't let you live with that fear. Maybe it's a curse to be loved by me."

"Do you?" She whispered, stunned by Eve's words. "Do you love me, Eve?"

Eve looked at Lainey in silence for a long moment. Had she really said that? And then, just as she began to speak, an angry knock sounded at the door. "Just a minute," she called out.

"Lainey, I..."

The impatient knocking continued.

"Damn it!" She stalked to the door, wrenching it open. "What?"

Dee Cummings pushed her way through the door. Turning on her heel, she faced Eve with her hands on her hips. "I trusted you!" she said in a shrill voice.

Eve raised a brow, too confused to be furious. "Dee," she said evenly. "What brings you here?"

"What brings me here? You sending the Feds after me is what brings me here. I trusted you, gave you information and you pay me back by sending the FBI knocking at my door?"

"Calm down. I didn't send the FBI. Agent Donovan is a friend of mine, Dee. He's doing me a favor, and I need you to cooperate with him."

"Cooperate? You mean give him my sources? In this case, Eve, that means more than just journalism suicide. Do you know what these people could do to me?"

Eve glanced over at Lainey, who was listening intently to every word. "Yes. I know very well what they could do. What they will do, regardless if you give up your source or not. I can protect you, Dee."

Dee looked at Eve. She had no doubt that Eve would do as she said. "You should have warned me."

"I know, I'm sorry. I spoke to him today, and I didn't have a chance to call you. He's working fast. Please, Dee. I need you to tell Agent Donovan what you know."

"Why do you need me to do this? You have all of the information I have, why can't you tell him?"

Eve looked at Dee. "I don't have all of the information. Do I? I'm sure there are things that have been said that you didn't write down. Besides, it's my word against his. I'll need you to corroborate what I've told Agent Donovan as the truth. Please." Eve laid a hand on Dee's arm. "I'm asking you to help me."

The anger in Dee gave way to weariness. "Give me the interview you promised and I'll tell him everything I know."

"I will, but it can't be now."

"I need something, Eve. I'm putting my career, hell, my life on the line for you. I need something in return."

Sighing, Eve walked to her desk and rested a hip on it. "Fine. I'll answer one question for you now. Off the record." She held up a hand when Dee started to protest. "That's the way it has to be, Dee. I will tell you what you want to know, but you have to keep it between us until this is over."

"I need a story, Eve."

"And, you will get one. That's the deal, Dee. I can't go public with any of this yet. Too many people are watching me, waiting for me to make a mistake."

Eve glanced over at Lainey again. There was too much for her to lose.

"I won't make a mistake. Ask me what you want to know, and keep it to yourself until I tell you otherwise."

Curiosity won over and Dee reluctantly agreed. There was something she wanted to know, and if these were the terms, she'd abide by them. "Very well. Do you know where Katherine Bushnell is, Eve?"

Eve's eyes darted to Lainey, then back at Dee. "Yes." She heard Lainey's soft, surprised intake of breath. "She's safe. That's all I can tell you."

Dee considered pressing more on the issue, but decided against it. For now. Instead, she was going to try her luck with one more question, even though Eve had only agreed to one.

"And Meredith Lansky?" She watched as Eve's eyes clouded over and became unreadable.

"I said one question."

"I'm a reporter, Eve, you had to expect that I would press you for more information. I think I deserve at least this much. I can start building my story. Do you know where Meredith is, as well?"

Eve glanced at Lainey who stood beside her now. She didn't want to say this in front of her, but at the same time, she deserved to know the whole story. "No," Eve said quietly. "I don't know where she is."

The part of her that was trained to read people told Dee that Eve knew more than what she was revealing. The regret in Eve's voice put Dee on alert. "Do you think she's dead?"

"I don't know."

"If you had to guess, knowing what you know, do you think she's dead?"

Damn it! The woman was persistent, and Eve couldn't ignore the question or her instinct. "Yes."

"Oh my God," Lainey gasped.

"Meredith refused to work with me," Eve said softly. "She thought she was more important in this game than the main players did. She wasn't. I tried to help her, but she wouldn't let me."

Eve might feel responsible for what had happened to Meredith but it was clear to Dee that she was sorry for the woman.

"It's not your fault."

"That's it," Eve said crisply. "No more questions. Now, keep your end of the deal and tell Agent Donovan what you know. After that, I suggest you take a vacation."

"I'm not running, Eve." She snorted which surprisingly only added to the woman's charm. "I'm a reporter, remember? We get more death threats daily than anyone else I know of."

"Not from someone like this." The urgency in Eve's voice caught Dee's attention as she meant it to. "I don't know the fate of one person who refused my help; don't make me worry about another. Take a vacation."

"I am due for one." Dee bit her lip and then capitulated. "I'll put in for one tomorrow."

"Thank you. I'll make the arrangements," Eve told her. "Someone will be at your home to pick you up tomorrow evening."

Dee was starting to understand why Eve was so successful. Who could argue with her? "Fine," she said. "Let me write down my address for you."

"I know where you live," Eve interrupted, and smiled at Dee's surprise. "You're not the only one that can do research, Ms. Cummings. Watch yourself."

When Dee was gone, Lainey took charge, locking the office door and leading Eve to the couch. This time, it was Lainey who got down on her knees in front of Eve. "I don't know how you live with this every day. No." She placed a finger on Eve's lips to stop her from speaking. "I don't want you to think about it right now. I'll stay here while you fight your demons in Paris, even though I wish you would let me go with you. I'm going to miss you."

"I'll call you." Eve's heart beat faster and she itched to take Lainey in her arms.

"You better. When you wake up, before you go to bed and any time in between when you have a chance. For now, we're going to make up for a little bit of the time we're going to lose together." Lainey feathered her fingers over Eve's bare thighs, pushing them apart, placing herself in between them.

"Lainey?"

"Shh. No thinking, no talking. Just feel me." Lainey got to the hem of Eve's skirt and paused. With a sly smile, Lainey bent her head and ran her tongue just underneath that hem. She heard Eve moan, and her smile broadened.

Lainey made love to Eve there in her office, making it last as long as she possibly could. Eve would think of her every minute they were apart. Lainey made sure of that.

~ Twenty ~

Eve stepped out of her car onto the sidewalk in front of her apartment building. As always, Henry was there to greet her.

"Good evening, Miss Eve. Long day today?" Henry smiled warmly at Eve, but behind the smile was concern. She looked tired and on edge.

"Does it show?" Eve smiled and patted Henry on the arm. "Nothing a good night's sleep won't help." An idea came to her as she started through the door that Henry held open for her.

"Henry," she said. "When was the last time you, Trudy and Stevie had a vacation?"

"Um, well, ma'am, funds have been kind of tight."

"I'm sorry, I wasn't trying to pry," Eve apologized when she heard Henry's discomfort. "I'm going out of town for the next couple of days, and it had me thinking. What if I could arrange for you and your family..."

"Ma'am, you've done way too much for us already. I can't be accepting a vacation from you. The missus would kill me."

"Please, Henry. I was supposed to go to Jamaica with a couple of friends," she lied. "But unfortunately this business deal came up and I have to make that trip instead. So, I thought that you and your family could go instead and have a real vacation."

Tears came to Henry's eyes. "That's very generous of you, Miss Eve, but what about your friends? Aren't they still going to go?"

"No. We've all decided to postpone it until later. The hotel is paid for. Everything is paid for. Why let it all go to waste? Say you'll go, Henry. Go home tonight and surprise your wife with an all expense paid trip to Jamaica."

"She's always wanted to go there," Henry said thoughtfully. "I would never know how to repay you."

"Just have fun," Eve said with a smile. "You'll leave tomorrow."

"Tomorrow? But, I have to arrange for time off."

"I'll arrange it. All you need to worry about is going home and telling your wife that you're off for a wonderful vacation tomorrow. I'll have a car to pick you up tomorrow morning and everything will be set. Don't forget to pack a bathing suit."

"I don't know what to say. You are truly an amazing young woman."

Eve looked away. If only he knew the truth of why she wanted him to leave, he would feel differently.

"You deserve the best, Henry," she said briskly. "Have a good time for me, okay?"

Standing on her tip toes, she kissed him gently on the cheek. "Good night," she whispered and disappeared through the doors.

She was so unbelievably tired. After her beautiful time with Lainey that afternoon, Eve's evening had gone straight downhill. She had spoken to Billy again, gathering more information from him. Thankfully, Dee had kept her word and told Billy everything she knew. Then Eve had had a meeting with those working with her against Tony, and the news was not good. Those people closest to her were in more danger than she suspected, and it was her responsibility to keep them safe. Adam had also been mentioned in this meeting. Apparently Tony didn't like the fact that his daughter was sleeping with the man, and wanted him taken out of the picture. Eve would die before she let anything happen to Adam, and she made it very clear that if any harm were to come to him, she would deal with all of them personally. But, Eve knew that she had to do her part to keep Adam safe, as well. If that meant losing him forever, then it was a sacrifice she would have to make.

Eve had convinced Lainey to stay home, and not go into work, while she was in Paris, a task which had proven to be extremely difficult and had involved making Lainey countless promises, one of which included taking Lainey to Paris when this was all over. Eve intended to keep all of her promises. She simply could not lose this game.

Weary, she drug a hand through her hair and was grateful when the elevator doors slid open on her floor. Just a few more steps and she would be inside her apartment and could lock the world away. She stopped cold in her tracks when she saw Adam standing at her door. He was wearing Levis and an old New York Yankees t-shirt, and his hair was disheveled as though he had run his hands through it repeatedly. Not now, she thought. She just didn't have the strength to deal with this at this moment.

"Adam? What are you doing here?"

"What did you mean when you said I see nothing?"

"Adam, please, I'm tired."

"I need to know what is happening between us Eve. First, Lainey says something about seeing more than you want me to, and then you. Tell me what's going on."

Eve frowned. Why would Lainey say that to him? She was just too drained to think about that now. Tomorrow, when she could think straight, when she called Lainey, she would ask her about it. Eve sighed. "I said I'm tired. I can't do this tonight." Eve tried walking past Adam to her door, but he blocked her way.

"I'm not leaving. Whatever's going on between us is keeping me up at night. I can't eat, I can't concentrate. You're consuming my thoughts. We're going to talk about this. Before you go out of town."

Eve glanced over and saw her nosey neighbor peeking through her door. Annoyed and exhausted, she pushed past Adam and unlocked her door. "Come in then."

Whatever he was going to say was forgotten when he saw Eve standing there facing him, her powder blue button down shirt slightly wrinkled and un-tucked covering most of the short black skirt. She looked irritated, tired and amazingly sexy.

Before she could move away, he took her in his arms and crushed his mouth to hers in an almost desperate attempt to relieve the need for her that had been building up inside him.

Eve clung to him. Adam awakened this primal need in her, one that only he knew how to satisfy. Everything, except what was happening to her at this moment, was forgotten as Adam pushed her against the door. His hands were rough, but skilled, touching her to arouse her beyond imagination.

Not able to control himself, Adam pulled Eve's shirt apart, popping the buttons off, sending them to the floor. He just needed to feel her to soothe this burning desire throbbing inside him. With his powerful thighs, he pushed her legs apart, using one hand to pull her skirt up and the other to unbuckle his own jeans. Finally, they were both exposed and he picked Eve up, wrapping her legs around his waist. He entered her, savagely, pounding inside her. He couldn't get enough. The chain on the door clanked as his thrusts became faster.

"God, I missed you, Eve." Adam's voice was rough with desire as he buried his face in her neck. "I love being inside you."

Through her burning desire, Eve remembered the scene at her restaurant with Adam and the other woman and the way he placed his hand at the small of her back, the way they laughed with each other. Of course she had done some checking of her own to find out who she was.

"Do you say that to Camille when you're fucking her, too?"

As quickly as it had begun, Adam froze.

"What?"

"You heard me. Do you say the same thing to her?"

"Eve..."

"Put me down, Adam." She pushed his shoulders, but he didn't budge.

"Let me..."

"Put – me – down."

The look in Eve's eyes had Adam obeying. Confused, still aroused, Adam buttoned his jeans back up and looked at Eve. She was straightening her skirt and furious.

"How do you know her name?"

It wasn't what he had planned to say. He didn't want to be talking about Camille, he wanted to talk about them, but nothing was going the way he had planned it.

Eve's laugh was humorless. "How did I know? You take her to my restaurant, my club, you son of a bitch, and you wonder how I know? Why, Adam? You knew I'd find out, why did you do it? Did you want to make me jealous?"

"Did it work?"

Eve struck him before she could stop herself. It was the first time she had ever hit anyone and she found she didn't enjoy it at all. "I'm sorry," she whispered. Running her hands through her hair, she slumped back against the door. When she had slapped Adam, she saw the look of shock on his face, and now, she couldn't look at him at all.

"I can't do this," she said.

She looked so vulnerable and fatigued that all he wanted to do was hold her.

"You once asked me if I ever hurt." He heard her say softly. Eve looked up at Adam, and for the first time since he met her, he saw tears brimming in her eyes. "I do."

His heart dropped. He had never meant to hurt her this way. "Eve." Adam stepped to her but she held him at arm's length.

"No. I'm not the one for you, Adam. I'll never be able to give you want you need. What you deserve. And, what you deserve is to be happy. If she's the one who can do that for you, then I have no right to keep you from her."

"You make me happy, Eve. Please don't do this." He was scared. More scared than he'd ever been in his life. He couldn't lose her. "I did it to make you jealous. I admit that. God, baby, I never slept with her."

He reached out and touched her cheek with his fingertips, relieved when she didn't push him away. "You have to believe me. She wanted to, but I couldn't. I never slept with her."

"It doesn't matter anymore, Adam." Eve sighed heavily. "I believe you, but it doesn't change anything. I can't do this to you anymore. Go. Please, Adam, just go. Don't look back, don't call, and don't come to the gallery anymore." The lump in her throat was painful and her head was pounding.

"I'm not leaving you. I need you, Eve, and I know you care about me more than you want to admit."

"I do. My God, I do. But there are things you don't know, things I can't even begin to explain to you, Adam. You would never understand."

"Try me, baby. Talk to me, please."

"I can't," she whispered. "Please go. You have to go." Eve pushed him back and opened the door. The tears stung, but she willed herself not to let him see her weep. "Please. It's what's best. Forget me, Adam." *Forgive me,* she added silently.

"You're asking the impossible. Please, don't push me away. I love you, Eve. Let me be there for you."

"No, don't say anymore. Please. Don't make this harder than it already is. Just go." Eve pushed him towards the door. "I'm sorry. I'm so sorry. For everything." On impulse, Eve pressed her lips to his in a brief kiss, regretting it instantly. At that second, she wanted nothing more than to close the door and take Adam to her bed. She just needed him to hold her, to tell her everything would be alright. But, she couldn't. Not until this mess with Tony was over. When that happened – and it would be soon, she vowed – she could only hope that Adam hadn't moved on, and could forgive her for hurting him this way.

"Goodbye, Adam," she said gently, and closed the door before he could do or say anything else. Eve leaned against the wall and closed her eyes. She never imagined she could hurt this much.

"I'm not giving up on you, Eve." Adam was trying to comprehend what was going on, but he was hurting too damned much to figure it out. "I hope you can hear me. This isn't over."

He waited for a moment to see if she would change her mind and open the door. When she didn't, he took a deep breath and walked away. He would have her back, he swore to himself. He was in too deep to let her get away.

"I hope it isn't over," Eve whispered.

Eve stayed huddled on the couch all night, afraid not only of the ghosts that awaited her upstairs but also of the loneliness that filled every part of her.

Lainey lay quietly in bed, awake, worrying about Eve and the journey she will be making tomorrow. She wished, with all her heart that she could make that trip with Eve, to help her fight whatever demons she had to face.

Jack stirred next to her, rolling onto his side and crossing an arm over Lainey's chest. He felt warm and safe. This part of her life was uncomplicated, she thought when Jack snuggled closer, the total opposite of her relationship with Eve. There were no hidden enemies in Jack's life, no ghosts haunting him every day, no dangers awaiting him at every corner. The life she had thought of as boring and uneventful, was now becoming a blessing. As much as she wished she had the words, the courage, or even the knowledge of how to make these things disappear for Eve, she didn't. And, it made her feel unnecessary and incredibly useless in Eve's life. Here, in this bed, in this house, Lainey felt needed, by her sons, by Jack. Perhaps it was selfish, but it was something that made her feel good inside. But still she couldn't forget how alive and desirable Eve made her feel. Eve was the embodiment of excitement and passion, life, love, and even that undeniably fascinating element of danger. Lainey needed Eve in her life as much as she needed her family, and the realization of that rocked her.

She was surprised when Jack lazily stroked her breast, and she could feel him getting hard as he pressed against her body. He had become gentle and loving again, like the Jack she had fallen in love with twelve years ago, and her body reacted the way it had back then. Everything, apart from what Jack was doing to her, escaped her troubled mind, and she turned into his arms. He kissed her softly and rolled on top of her.

"I love you," he whispered in her ear as he slowly slipped inside her.

"I love you, too." Lainey arched into him, wrapping her arms around his neck. This is what they have been missing, she thought. The compassion, the attention to each other's feelings - the love. She gave herself to Jack then, freely and wholly as never before.

Eve sat quietly in the back of the limo. She had taken the time to change her clothes before leaving for the airport, but hadn't made the call she had promised to make this morning. She didn't know if she had the strength to let Lainey go the way she did Adam the night before. Lainey would never understand. She would never leave Eve, even if Eve told her that her life depended on it.

She was also not looking forward to telling Lainey about her time with Adam, knowing it would upset her. She hadn't planned on being with Adam at all, but now found herself wishing she hadn't stopped him from making love to her, hadn't told him to leave. She had sat on her couch all night, longing for Adam's arms to be around her, and the feelings made her experience guilt, even more confusion and contempt for herself. She knew that all she needed was rest, and a little time to think about how she was going to explain any of this to Lainey, but she was so exhausted, she couldn't think of anything to say that would help her at the moment.

She let her cell phone ring three times before she decided to answer it. After the third ring, she broke down and picked it up, not bothering to look at the caller ID. She knew exactly who it was.

"Good morning, Lainey."

"Are you okay? I got worried when you didn't call me." Lainey relaxed considerably when she finally heard Eve's voice, but there was something different about it. Something wasn't right.

"I'm fine. A little tired. I'm sorry I didn't call, I was trying to get a little rest."

"Oh. I'm disturbing you."

"No, you're not," Eve interjected. "I'm glad you called. It's great hearing your voice." It was the truth. Just hearing Lainey brought Eve a little bit of peace.

"You had a bad night?" Lainey noticed her hand was shaking slightly, and tightened her grip on the phone. How was she going to tell Eve that she had made love to Jack the night before? She hadn't planned it, of course, but she couldn't stop it from happening. And, when Jack was holding her in his arms, she realized she didn't want him to stop. For the first time in a long time, Lainey had felt the way she had when she and Jack were first married. But now, the next day, all she felt was guilt, which was ridiculous. She was married to Jack. She loved him. But she also loved Eve, and the last thing Lainey wanted to do was hurt her. How did she fix the mess she was in now?

"I didn't sleep very well," Eve admitted. "Lainey, there's something you should know."

"I made love to Jack last night," Lainey blurted out. "And I feel like I should apologize to you. I didn't..."

"Stop," Eve interrupted. "It's okay." The nagging pain in her head worsened. "You don't owe me an apology. He's your husband and I should expect that you would be with him. I should even be happy for you."

Eve made sure her voice didn't betray the hurt she felt inside although she knew she had no right to be jealous or angry. Perhaps if she kept telling herself that she would come to believe it.

Lainey frowned. She should have been happy that Eve was making this easy on her, but she wasn't. It was absurd to Lainey that she would be offended by Eve's lack of a reaction. "You're not upset?"

"Of course I am. I'd be lying to you if I said I didn't care. But, what can I say about it? I know you love your husband, Lainey. The original plan was to get your relationship with him back on track. You should be happy that it's happening."

Eve paused, and rubbed her temple to relieve some of the pain. "In fact," she went on, "oddly enough, I was just going to tell you that Adam was waiting for me when I got home last night."

There was a silence on the phone, long enough for Eve to think she had lost her connection.

"Did you fuck him?" Lainey immediately regretted the words the second they left her mouth. Damn it, why couldn't she keep her emotions in check.

"For you it's making love. For me it's fucking?" Eve sighed, too tired to be infuriated. "Forget it," she said before Lainey could apologize. "Yes, I fucked him. Or, started to at least."

"I don't understand." God, could she feel any more guilt?

"I made the unfortunate mistake of thinking about the woman I had seen him with at the restaurant at a very inopportune time. Then, of course, there's all of the other shit that's going on in my life. I just couldn't let it happen. I told him it was over."

Eve laid her head back on the seat. If she wanted to win this life and death game she was playing with Tony, she needed to focus on something other than her messed up love life.

"Oh, Eve. Are you sure that's what you want?" Jealous or not, Lainey still believed that Eve and Adam belonged together. She still saw that Eve felt more for Adam than she would ever divulge.

"No. I want him." She closed her eyes and thought of Adam. "God, I want him so much. And, I'm truly sorry if saying that hurts you, Lainey. You know how I feel about you."

No, I don't, Lainey thought silently, I wish you'd tell me straight out and not in some slip of the tongue.

"If you want him," she said aloud, "why did you let him go? And, please don't tell me it was because you're not good enough for him."

"It's what's best. For everyone. Let's just leave it at that, okay? Maybe one day, I'll be able to give him more of me, but for now, this is how it has to be." Eve paused, remembering what Adam had said to her last night. "He told me what you said to him."

"I didn't mean to get involved," Lainey said quickly. She had never thought about the possibility that Adam would tell Eve. "I hate seeing you hurt, and I thought if I could just say something to help you and him..." Her voice trailed off, and she sat there listening to Eve breathe.

The silence was deafening, and she wished that Eve would yell at her, scold her, anything to break this silence.

In her peripheral vision, Eve saw that the driver had made the final turn onto the airstrip, and she would be at her plane in minutes. "I have to go," she said. There would be no endearments to end this conversation, not when she felt as wretched as she did. "I'll call you when I get to Paris."

"Eve, wait. Please. Are we okay?" Lainey couldn't stop herself from asking and hated the weakness. If she could just hear Eve tell her everything would be alright, she would feel better. When Eve didn't answer right away, Lainey's heart sank.

"Yes, we're okay," Eve answered finally. "Don't worry about anything. Don't feel bad for making love to your husband. Don't feel any guilt. You're doing nothing wrong. I - I'll call you."

Eve hung up the phone quietly before Lainey could respond, and Lainey sat there listening to the silence for a long moment before replacing the receiver. "Be careful," she whispered in her empty bedroom. "I love you."

~ Twenty-One ~

A shiver ran through Eve as she stepped out of the limo in front Madame Bussiere's cafe. All of the horrible feelings and images came back to her with a vengeance, and it took her by surprise. She thought she had been prepared for this. She was stronger now. Nothing could hurt her. She was here to find answers, and that's exactly what she was going to do, no matter what she had to do to achieve that.

"Is everything alright, ma'am?" her driver asked her. "This is where you wanted me to take you, no?"

"Yes," she answered quietly. "Yes. Stay with the car, please. I don't know how long I'll be."

"Yes, ma'am."

Eve nodded and gave him a small smile. With a deep breath, she squared her shoulders and walked back into her nightmares. It wasn't fear that chilled her to the bone. She knew she was safe, knew there were people watching over her. It was the memories, the smells, Madame Bussiere herself that made her feeling nauseous and even more enraged than she wanted to be. And yet she knew that she must be careful. Anger could cause her to make mistakes. Eve stood at the entrance of the café and scanned the filthy, smoky room. Not much had changed, she noticed. Though the customers' faces had changed, they were the same sort of people she had served all those years ago. Eve could even recognize a few of the regulars that came in for the watered down wine and awful food. She supposed their taste buds really didn't matter as long as they could get some gambling in, and any other illegal activities Bussiere could provide for them.

And then she saw her. Madam Bussiere was standing by the bar, one massive arm supporting her weight as she leaned. She was wearing what looked to be the same black dress Eve had seen her wear countless times. The years had weathered her round, unattractive face making her looks even more evil to Eve. Eve's hands clenched involuntarily by her side, and she willed herself to stay calm. This woman would pay for what she had done to her. But, first, she would give Eve the information she needed.

"Madame Bussiere." Eve's voice was smooth, cold and businesslike. "What? No hug for your young protégé?"

Madame Bussiere's eyes widened in recognition. "Eve? Mon dieu! Is it really you?"

Eve read the greed in the older woman's eyes as she took note of Eve's Versace suit, her Jimmy Chu pumps and the gray Louis Vuitton pocketbook. "Shall we go somewhere a little more...private?" Eve suggested.

"You have money now, no?" the older woman said, her eyes narrow, covetous. "You want something from me, petite fille, you'll have to make it worth my while."

The woman's accent grated on Eve's nerves as much as the request, but she smiled coldly at her. "I'll make it worth your while, Madame, by not telling the authorities what you're doing in this dump, what you've been doing for years. Don't fuck with me. I will destroy you and everything you think you have here." Eve's icy whisper, and the fire in her eyes, had the woman taking a step back. "Now, let's go somewhere where we can talk."

"Oui, bien sûr," Madame Bussiere agreed. She gave the bartender a look, then turned and marched off towards her office.

Eve leaned onto the bar and crooked her finger at the bartender. When he was close, Eve wrapped a hand around his tie and pulled. "You're being watched," she told him in perfect French. "My men are all over this place." She watched, satisfied as the bartender's nervous eyes darted around the bar and dining area. "You won't know who they are, or where they're coming from, but if you go for that phone, they'll come after you. You don't want that, now do you? Of course not. And, you'll keep anyone from disturbing Madame and myself, right?"

The man nodded his head and Eve smiled. "Very good," she said. "Au revoir pour le moment."

Patting him on the cheek, she walked off to join Madame Bussiere, leaving the man staring after her. He didn't know who the American was, but she had a dangerous look about her. He wasn't about to find out just how dangerous.

Eve walked into Madame Bussiere's small, dingy, paper strewn office and closed the door behind her. She knew what people saw when they looked at her. The tailored slacks, the fitted button shirt, the designer heels, down to the manicured fingernails. All of it said money and prestige. Even her carefully applied, yet minimal make-up, gave on-lookers the impression that this was a woman born into privilege. No one would have guessed that she once had to do despicable things just to stay alive. And, that was how Eve was determined to keep it.

Taking the seat in front of Bussiere's desk Eve crossed her legs. "It seems like someone has been talking about things that happened here years ago, Bussiere," she said scornfully. "You wouldn't have any idea who that is, now would you?"

"I don't know what you're talking about. I have talked to no one."

"You're lying. I hate liars." Eve sat back and threaded her fingers together as she watched the older woman fidgeting. Her thick hands clasped together tightly with anxiety. "You have a couple of choices here. You can tell me what you know. Or, you can keep telling me you don't know anything and see what the consequences are."

"There's nothing you can do to me. I know nothing." The woman shrugged. "Now you must leave."

"Sit down." The words carried with them such an underlying violence, that Madame dropped heavily back into her chair. "I don't like you, Bussiere," Eve continued. "I hate what you did to me, the things you made me do. I could take care of you right now, like that," she said snapping her fingers, "and feel no remorse for it at all. However, maybe I'll spare you if you tell me what I want to know. Maybe," Eve repeated with a vicious smile.

She saw the doubt in Madame's eyes, but it didn't hide the uneasiness that was there as well.

"Don't underestimate me, old woman," she hissed. "I'm not the same little girl you smacked around back then. This time, I get to do the smacking."

"I haven't been talking. I swear," Madame told Eve, her dark eyes shifting nervously.

"You're lying again," Eve told her. "If you haven't been talking, then one of the men you sold me to have. So, if you want to help yourself, give me names and addresses, whatever information you have that I can use. If you can't be of use to me…"

"He made me do it," Madame Bussiere spat out. It was clear to Eve that the woman realized that she had no way out. She had no choice, really, but to make a deal with Eve, to give her information in exchange for protection. Whatever else Madame Bussiere was, she was no fool, not the sort to take the fall for having obeyed Tony's orders.

"Who made you do what?" Eve asked carefully.

"Your father. Tony made me do what - what I did to you back then. Je jure! I didn't want to, but he threatened me. He told me that if I didn't make you do those things, the authorities would be after me, and I could very well end up dead."

Eve couldn't believe what she was hearing. Her own father? It shouldn't have surprised her. After all, he had been using her, abusing her for most of her life. But, the news stunned her nonetheless. "How did he know I was here?" Eve hadn't realized she asked the question aloud, until Madame answered.

"I told him," she said nervously. A trickle of sweat dripped down her temple.

"You swore to me that you wouldn't tell him. I should have known. You bitch!" Eve started to rise.

"Wait! Écoutez moi." Madame Bussiere raised her hands as though to protect herself. "I was greedy. Word was out that you had run away and there was a reward for any information on you. It was a lot of money, Eve…"

"Don't you dare speak my name," Eve said scathingly. "I gave you everything I had, made you money, worked my fingers to the bone for you – goddamnit, I gave my body to strangers for you. All because I thought I was safe from my father. Now you tell me he knew all along. You conspired with him with selling my body as well?" She was so furious, she could imagine her hands wrapped around the other woman's neck, squeezing the life out of her, the same way the life was squeezed out of Eve all those years ago.

"That was his idea," Madame Bussiere said quickly. "Not mine. Your father had debts he couldn't pay. When he found out you were here, he used you as payment. I never saw any money from...those times."

"You lying bitch. Some of those men weren't the type to have loaned my father money. How many did you sell me to?"

"Je suis désolé, I had to make a living." She shrank back in her chair as Eve's look turned venomous. "You were already doing it for you father. I never thought a couple more here and there would matter. After all, I made sure they didn't hurt you."

"You watched?" Eve grabbed on to the arms of the chair, digging her nails into the fabric to keep herself from killing the woman in front of her. "I will destroy you for what you did to me. For watching and doing nothing when those men brutalized me."

"That last night wasn't my fault." Madame's face was as white as a sheet with fear. "I was told to disappear, and that if I didn't you and I would be killed."

"Perfect. So you left me alone to be raped and beaten - for my sake," Eve said, her voice dripping with sarcasm.

"I didn't know they were going to do that. I swear. S'il vous plait! You must understand..."

"Understand?" Eve repeated with exasperation. "Fuck you! Don't say another word." Eve held up a hand, cutting the other woman off. "All you're doing is pissing me off even more. What you are going to do now, is get up and walk over to your safe. I want every document, every name, every piece of information you have on those men my father 'paid off'. And that list had better include the men you sold me to as well." Eve leaned forward and gave Madame Bussiere a piercing stare. "If anything is missing, I'm coming after you. After what I've learned today, your death will be excruciatingly painful for you, and extremely pleasurable for me."

Obviously the older woman was terrified. There was on old fashioned iron safe in the corner. Eve watched as she turned the combination and opened it. Bringing a pile of envelopes and files back to the desk, Madame Bussiere dumped them in front of her.

"This is everything. All I have. Je vous promets."

"Your promises mean nothing to me." Eve picked up a stack of papers. They included names and addresses of the patrons that frequented Bussiere's bar, some with notes underneath them.

Evening with Eve. Paid. Disgusted, Eve picked up the black leather Tavecchi briefcase that she had brought with her. She put the papers into the case and looked through more of the papers from the safe, until she came to a brown envelope. "What is this?"

Madame said nothing, but her eyes widened with fear.

"I asked you a question."

"Ph-photos," Madame Bussiere stammered.

"Photos of what?" Eve looked on as the older woman lowered her eyes. "Oh my God. You took photos of..." She couldn't bring herself to finish the sentence. The thought alone was nauseating. "Why?"

"For no reason," Madame Bussiere muttered. But Eve saw the narrow look in her eyes and suddenly she understood.

"You're a cruel and repulsive woman," Eve said with loathing. "Did it turn you on to watch men abuse me? Tell me, Bussiere, did it arouse you to watch a child being raped? No. Don't tell me. I don't want to know what your vile obsessions are. Who else has these photos?"

"No one," she said and Eve saw her as she was, not the demon from her past but a frightened old woman.

"Don't fucking lie to me."

"Je ne me trouve pas. It's all there. The film, the prints, everything. They were for me. I gave them to no one, showed them to no one."

"You better hope I don't find out if you're lying to me." Eve took the rest of the papers and contents that came from the safe and threw them into the briefcase, slamming it shut. She needed to get out of there. Her head was pounding. "If you pick up that phone to call Tony after I walk out that door, it will be the last thing you do," she told the old woman who was cowering in her chair, her face sunk in deep lines. "Do you understand me?"

There was no need for Eve to wait for an answer.

"Go in and clean up the mess," Eve told the man in dark sunglasses as she walked outside. Her mood was foul, and all she wanted to do was go home. No, she thought, that wasn't the only thing. She wanted to hear Lainey's voice telling her everything would be okay.

"Do you want her dead?" he asked.

Eve hesitated as her driver held the door open for her. "No," she answered, finally. "But I want to make sure she suffers for what she did to me. Destroy everything in sight. Scare her — a lot — but keep her alive." As the limo drove off, she saw him slip discreetly into the café and knew that within the hour her order would be carried out to her complete satisfaction.

Eve sat in the dimly lit living room of her home in Paris. The heavy, velvet drapes were drawn over the long windows facing the Avenue Foch, and there was a silence that surrounded her as she sat in the middle of the room with papers all around her. She had spent her evening reliving the horrors of her past, and her head was throbbing. What she needed was something familiar, someone to reassure her of who she was now. But Eve was confused about whom exactly that was for her. When she closed her eyes, she could feel Adam's arms around her, holding her and keeping her safe. Then her mind would change gears, and Lainey would be there telling her everything would be all right, that she would always be there when Eve needed her. Who was it that she needed? It was a question that plagued her as she sat there alone in the city that had stolen her innocence, and her ability to give herself fully to either of the people who loved her.

The names of each of the men who used her body however they pleased stared back at her. She had all of the information she needed to devastate their lives. Everything she needed to exact her revenge was right here at her fingertips. Everything, except the desire to do just that.

Suddenly Eve realized that she was tired of fighting, tired of living her life with the shadow of Tony and her past following her every move, hiding in every corner. She wanted the burden she has lived with her entire life to be lifted at last. It was time to live a happy and normal life, whatever that may be. But before that could happen, she had to finish this game with her father once and for all.

Picking up the envelope she had been avoiding, she took a deep breath and opened it. Much as she hated to, she must be sure that Madame Bussiere had told her the truth about the film being in there with the photos. She took a hold of one of the glossy photos. Before she could stop herself, she slipped one of the pages out. Her breathing turned rapid and bile rose up into her throat when she saw the image. Quickly, she replaced the photo and closed her eyes, but the vision was still there. "Stupid," she whispered. Without thinking, she picked up the phone next to her and dialed.

Jack moved in a steady rhythm on top of Lainey as she wrapped her arms around him and held on tight. Sounds of their lovemaking filled the room. It felt good, Lainey realized as Jack buried his face in her hair. He had surprised her with flowers and candlelight, even sending the boys to their grandparents so they could be alone. He had seduced her with kisses and loving words, and she had fallen willingly into his arms. Their minds and hearts were so entirely interwoven that, when the phone rang next to them, it startled them both.

"Who the hell is calling at this time of night?" Jack muttered. "Let the machine get it, Lainey."

Lainey thought of Eve. "I have to get it," she told him. "Something might have happened to one of the boys."

"Lainey?" The moment she heard Eve's voice, Lainey knew that something was terribly wrong. She sounded so scared and alone.

"Eve?" she said, pulling the sheet around her. "Is everything okay?"

"Ask her why she's calling at this time of night," Jack demanded. "Don't shush me! Why should I be quiet? She's the one calling in the middle of the night. She's the one interrupting us while we're making love."

Eve's heart shattered. "I'm sorry," she whispered, hanging up the phone quickly before she made an even bigger fool of herself.

"Goddamnit, Jack!" Lainey exclaimed, pushing him away as he tried to put his arms around her. "Why did you do that? You have no idea what's going on, what she's going through."

Hurriedly she dialed Eve's number, praying she would pick up.

"What she's going through? What about us, Lainey? Does she think she's the only one in your life?"

Lainey held up a hand, shaking her head. She heard Eve's voice mail come on, and almost screamed in frustration. "Eve? Please call back. Please." Jack rolled away from her and got out of bed. Lainey said nothing to stop him when he put on his robe. She was worried about Eve. What if something had happened?

"Perhaps the truth is that she's the only important person in your life," he muttered as he slammed out of the room.

Lainey considered going after him and apologizing. She had believed they were on the right track, that they were getting back to the way they were before the kids were born. But she couldn't ignore the reality that Eve needed her right now even more than Jack. Maybe she was taking for granted the fact that Jack would always be there, but she had to believe he would be. All she could think about now was that she had made a promise to be there for Eve who had been alone almost all of her life. Jack would understand that, she reassured herself as she picked up the phone and dialed again. Again Eve didn't answer. Glancing at the door to make sure it was closed.

"Eve? Honey," Lainey said. "Please call me. I'm sorry. God, I'm so sorry." A tear rolled down Lainey's cheek. "Please, baby, call me back." She hung up the phone, staring at it, willing it to ring.

"Please, baby, call me back." It was the third time Eve had listened to the message this morning, and each time she had wanted to call just as she had the night before, but found she couldn't. She was too hurt, and too ashamed. She didn't want to hear Lainey apologizing for doing something that should be natural and guilt free for her. But she had made Lainey feel that way, and the reality of that mortified her. How could she ruin Lainey's life, her marriage, by being so selfish? She knew what it was like to have nothing, to lose everything. How could she put Lainey through that?

But, the thought of a life without Lainey hurt like hell. When she was gone, Eve knew she would have lost the only true friend she ever had, the one person who knew everything about her, and yet still loved her.

If you really cared for her, Eve, you'd let her go, she told herself. You're only hurting her. Eve sighed and put her cell phone away as the limo pulled up to the curb in front of an apartment building in the exclusive Trocadero district. Time to put your game face on, Eve. She took a deep breath, and pushed everything else to the back of her mind. This was her last stop before returning back home and it was the going to be the most difficult.

After a quick stop at the concierge desk, Eve knocked solidly on the door of the apartment. She was shown to the parlor by the uniformed maid, who then went to get the man who had used her body as his personal punching bag. She didn't sit. She wasn't going to give him any kind of advantage. Instead, she took in her surroundings. Wealthy, important man, bad taste in decorating, she thought. The room was dark and cold. Antiques decorated the room in a cluttered manner. There was no order, no sense of style, just chaos. It didn't surprise her one bit, knowing what he was inside. Studying the painting on the wall, she could see clearly that it was not an original. "Cheap bastard," she said quietly with disgust, though she knew of a few treasures the bastard kept hidden.

"Can I help you?"

His voice was like nails on a blackboard to her. Slowly, she turned to him and silently watched as recognition hit him. Alarm and confusion crossed his face in rapid succession and he was immediately defensive.

"What's the matter, Laurence?" Eve said. "You don't look happy to see me. Or, maybe you are. Isn't it amazing what ten years can do to a child's body? Because that's what you remember, isn't it?" She had dressed deliberately in a short Gucci skirt and tight fitting shirt that dipped low to show off her cleavage.

"What do you want?" He couldn't keep his eyes from traveling the length of her body, lingering on her cleavage and bare legs.

"To kill you," she answered with fierce quietness. It wasn't what she had planned to say, until she saw the look in his eyes.

He took a step towards her, then froze when his daughter came in the room.

"Papa, shall I bring you tea?"

"No. Thank you, fille. Papa needs to speak with this – this lady, alone." He pushed his daughter to the door. "Go play. Stay out of trouble."

"Cute kid," Eve commented when he closed the door again. "She looks like she loves you."

"Leave her out of this." He took a step towards her again. "Tell me what you're really doing here," he demanded. "I don't like jokes."

"I've come to kill you," Eve repeated. "But, first, I want to find out how your daughter is going to react knowing what kind of monster you really are."

"That will never happen."

"Are you sure, Laurence? Are you certain that there is no evidence of what you did to me?"

"What are you talking about?" he demanded and she recognized that look in his eyes, knew what he was capable of, remembered what had already been done.

"You'll never hurt me again," she hissed through her teeth as her hand snaked out and grabbed him, squeezing tightly where she held him.

His crotch throbbed painfully, and trying to pull away only made it worse. "Let go," he whispered, and started to sweat.

"Why? Does it hurt? Would it hurt more if I did this?" Eve twisted her wrist, and smiled when Laurence cried out in pain, his knees buckling. "What would your men think of you now, seeing a woman bring you to your knees?"

"I'll kill you for this," he spat out the words.

"No you won't. For your daughter's sake, you're going to do as I say. I have people outside just waiting to come in here to kill you, so make your choice. Do what I tell you to do or I make your life hell."

"What do you want?" It was clear that the pain had become unbearable. "I'll do anything."

"Anything? Then walk with me over to the desk. That's right. Now, I've learned that you have four original paintings by Van Gogh. I want them."

"Like hell..." He stopped when she took a gun out of her pocket. Letting go of her grip, she aimed it steadily at him. "Fine, okay."

"I'm not done. You also have two original Monet's. I don't know how or where you got them, but I want them, too."

"Do you have any idea what those are worth?" he demanded.

"Oh yes. I do." She unfolded the legal document that would transfer ownership of each of the paintings to her, then pushed it towards him. "Sign it."

"Put the gun away."

"Sign it. The faster you sign, the faster I get out of here, you son of a bitch!"

He grabbed the pen and scribbled his name on the line.

"There. I've signed it, now get out!"

"Good," she said. "These almost make up for what you did. But, not quite."

"What else do you want?"

"Your dick on a platter," she said simply, and he looked at her sharply. "Don't worry; I won't put the order out just yet. You're still of some use to me."

Laurence sat in the chair and held his throbbing crotch in his hand. "What do you mean?"

"Those men you had with you..."

"They're not on my payroll," he protested. "They were just men your father owed. I had nothing to do with that."

"That's not what Tony says," she lied. "He said you masterminded the whole thing, he said you were the sick son of a bitch that liked to fuck little girls, and watch them get fucked."

"Merde! Ce bâtard menteur! I'll kill him."

Eve smiled with satisfaction. "You sound upset, Laurence."

"You come to my home, stealing from me by forcing me to sign away the most valuable things I own, all because your cunt of a father lied to you. Of course I'm upset."

"I didn't steal anything, Laurence," Eve said. "You gave it to me. Now you're telling my dear old dad lied to me? The anguish."

"I don't find your sense of humor amusing," he told her. "Millions of dollars is what you've taken from me. This time, your father is going to pay me back."

"No. My father will deal with me. What I want is for you to take care of these people he has in his employ." Taking a folded envelope out of her pocket, Eve laid it on the table and walked to the door.

"What makes you think I'll do this for you?"

"Because if you don't, I will destroy you," she promised him. "There's a little surprise in that envelope for you, Laurence. A little souvenir. A few photographs to remind you of the animal you really are. Enjoy."

~ Twenty-Two ~

Lainey stood at the kitchen door, watching Jack drink his coffee and read the paper. It was a morning routine that she had witnessed every day for twelve years, and over the years it was a habit that had gone from endearing to monotonous. Nothing ever changed, and for her, the monotony was how her life had ceased to move forward.

Going back to work had been an attempt to help her find the woman she had forgotten so she could be that woman again for Jack. She had expected to be happier as a result of taking the job in Eve's gallery, had expected to become a better mother to her sons because of it. And for awhile that had happened. When she had met Eve, her whole life had changed.

But now, Lainey had more questions about herself than before. Was she still in love with the man she was watching now, or had she fallen in love with a woman she had not even known a month ago? Were her feelings for Eve true, or had they been aroused by the novelty and excitement of having something different in her life? They were true, Lainey told herself now. But how much was she willing to sacrifice because of them?

"Jack?"

"There's fresh coffee," he said without looking at her.

Lainey sighed and pulled out a chair to sit across from him. "Are we going to talk about this?" she asked.

When he had left her that night Eve had called, he hadn't returned, opting instead to sleep in the guest room. When he had returned to their bed the past couple of nights, he slept with his back to her.

"No. I'd rather not hear how more important Eve is to you than me over breakfast."

"She's not more important to me, Jack. You won't even let me explain."

Jack folded his paper and laid it on the table. "Explain what, Lainey? That our marriage, our love making, wasn't enough to keep you from answering her phone call?"

"That's not true! I'm sorry that you feel that way, but you don't know what she's going through. This is a very difficult time for Eve."

"Yes, let's hear about Eve's 'difficult time'. What's wrong with the poor, beautiful, rich girl? Too much money weighing her down? Is her boyfriend not good-looking enough? Has she run out of things to buy for you?"

"Stop it! You know nothing about her, and you have no right to judge her! Eve has given me opportunities no one else would have. She has treated you and our sons with nothing but kindness and respect." Lainey hesitated. Once upon a time, she had told Jack everything, but she couldn't do that now. Now, she had to decide how far her explanation should go.

"There are things that have happened to her, things that are happening now that no one should have to go through, Jack," she said, choosing her words carefully. "Especially alone. And, she's completely alone."

"She's not completely alone, she has – what's his name? Adam? That's why I don't understand why you have to be so involved with this."

"She's my friend, Jack. I can't just turn my back on her. Besides, she and Adam are - well, they're not together right now."

"That's too bad; I think he really liked her," he said thoughtfully. And then he shrugged. "Maybe she should talk to one of her other boyfriend's. Women like that usually have more than one lover. Or perhaps she could buy another one."

"Jack! That's enough. If you want to be mad at me for the other night, or for any of this shit we're going through, then fine, I deserve it. But, leave Eve out of it. This is not her fault. She's not the reason we're having problems."

"Who is the reason, Lainey?"

Lainey looked him in the eye. "We are. Both of us. We are going to have to talk about what's happened between us, and what we're going to do to fix it."

"I thought we were fixing it the other night and the night before that."

"You think this is only about sex? Jesus, Jack, it's about this!" She picked up the paper and threw it across the room. "It's about every day being the same. It's about us not talking anymore. We don't have a relationship or companionship anymore. You wake up each morning, read your paper and drink your coffee for exactly twenty minutes, and then you go to work. When you come home, you sit down and watch TV, you eat, play with the boys and then you go to bed and fall asleep. We hardly make love. Did you know that more than two months went by without you touching me at all? When I made the first move, you were annoyed with me. You barely say two words to me throughout the course of an entire day. You've stopped asking me how my day was. I thought it was because every day was the same with me and you were just as uninterested as I was. But, then I got this wonderful and exciting job, and you still never ask me how my day was. When did this happen, Jack? When did things become so familiar that we don't even notice each other anymore?"

"I didn't realize that being familiar with your spouse was a bad thing," Jack said quietly. "I also didn't realize that I was the one to blame for all of this." He looked at his watch and stood up. "I have to go. It's been more than twenty minutes."

"Jack."

She swore under her breath when he didn't stop, and laid her head down on her folded arms. Nothing was going right. Eve wasn't returning her calls, Jack was pissed off at her. Lainey felt like her life was spiraling out of control and there was nothing she could do to stop it. With a sigh, she pushed away from the table.

She had to get up and do something, because dwelling on things was not helping her. Even though it was her day off, Lainey picked up the phone and dialed the gallery to check in on Mikey.

"Sumptor Gallery, this is Mikey."

"Hi, Mikey, it's Lainey. How are things going over there?"

"Mrs. Stanton! Things are great. A little busy. You won't believe the new paintings Ms. Sumptor brought in!"

Her smile faded. "Eve is there?"

"Yes, ma'am. I'm sorry, I assumed you knew."

"I-I guess I got the days mixed up. I thought she was due back tomorrow." Ordinarily Eve would have let her know. Why hadn't she called? She let out a laugh, hoping it didn't sound as strained to Mikey as it did to her.

"I understand, I was surprised to see her this morning, too. Would you like to speak with her?"

Just the request had her pulse jumping. "Yes, please."

"Okay, hold on a minute and I'll let her know you're on the phone."

Lainey's heart pounded in her chest. For the past couple of days she has been trying to get Eve to talk to her and now she didn't know what she was going to say. Her anxiety was about to boil over when she heard the line click.

"Mrs. Stanton?"

Lainey held in her sigh when she heard Mikey's voice.

"Yes, Mikey?"

"Ms. Sumptor is busy with a client at the moment and can't come to the phone. Do you want me to give her a message?"

Lainey struggled with the tears that threatened to fall. She knew how good Eve was at the avoiding game. "No, no message. Thanks." She hung up the phone quickly before her voice betrayed the pain she felt inside. "Damn it, Eve, I'm not going to let you do this."

Determined to speak to Eve, Lainey left for the gallery. Eve couldn't avoid her if they were face to face. She was going to listen to her whether she liked it or not.

"People are dropping like flies here, Eve. This morning, two FBI agents were found murdered. With their bodies, were confessions and evidence that they worked for your father. Five other men in Paris were found murdered in their homes. They were all tied to your father. He owed them all gambling debts in excess of three million dollars."

Eve registered the words and said nothing.

"It has been reported that you were in Paris recently," Billy continued. "Is this true?"

"Yes," she answered without hesitation.

"Damn it, Eve! Why didn't you tell me you were going there?"

"I don't report to anyone."

"Eve, you are being investigated for a murder and a disappearance. You go to Paris and suddenly five people are dead."

"Do you think I killed them, Billy?"

"No, of course not, but that's not the point, Eve. How is it going to look for you when the detectives that are investigating you find out you were there?"

"Was I the first one you thought of when you heard of these deaths?"

"No. I thought of Tony, but..."

"Exactly," Eve interjected. "I may be on the list, but it sounds to me like Tony is cleaning house. Have you seen his financial statements lately? He's running out of money, Billy. Which means he can't pay for their silence anymore - or his debts. They know too much, what better way to keep them quiet?"

"We have to have proof of that."

"That's not my burden, Agent Donovan. If Tony is behind this, it's the FBI's job to find the proof. After all, two of your agents were killed. Word of advice, though. Tony never does his own killing. He'll want to keep his hands clean, so there will be someone else doing the dirty work for him."

"I've already taken that into consideration, but I need names and a reason to investigate them."

"You'll get what you need."

"Eve, you can't get any more involved with this. Take a vacation. Get as far away from Tony and this mess as you can."

"I'm not running, Billy. I ran before and where did it get me? I've been running for thirteen years. It's time to face my father, and put an end to this game he's playing with my life."

"Eve!"

"Stop. Nothing you say can change my mind about this. I called you in to help me. Can you do that?"

She heard him sigh and knew that he must be frustrated. When would he and all the others learn that she could take care of herself?

"Fine, yes, I can do that," he told her in a resigned voice. "You'll be happy to know that I've cleaned out your file. No trace of the falsified records exists now. To ensure it doesn't happen again, we've set up a trap of sorts. If anyone tries to access your file, we'll know about it, and act accordingly."

Eve closed her eyes with relief. Not many things had worried her in life but that file had been one of the things that had.

"What have you found on Detective Carter?"

"Not much, at least nothing incriminating. A couple of reprimands for excessive force during arrests, but that's all. It tells me he has a hot temper, but it doesn't mean he's a murderer. I'll dig deeper, but that means going through channels. It's going to take me a while."

"Do what you have to do," Eve said and hung up the phone. "And, I'll do what I have to do."

She pressed the power button on her monitor. With a click of the mouse, Detective Carter's most private information flashed on the screen.

"Someone has been a bad, bad boy, Maurice," she mused as she scrolled down the page. "I'm going to enjoy bringing you down."

Eve studied every bit of data on Carter's records until she knew them by heart. Getting the information illegally would make it hard for her to go public with it, but going public wasn't her concern. She would use everything she had learned to give Carter just enough rope to hang himself.

When she heard the knock on her office door, Eve knew it would be Lainey. When Mikey had told her that Lainey was on the phone, she had known that a meeting would be inevitable. But, God, she wasn't sure she could face her right now. She had listened to the messages Lainey had left over and over again, just to hear her voice, but she had never called her back. It was weak, she knew, but that's how Lainey made her feel. Weak. And strong. Loved. Vulnerable. Excited. She felt so much when Lainey was around that it confused her. Never knowing how she was going to feel at any given moment, scared her. Eve closed her eyes for a moment and took a deep breath. It wouldn't do to let Lainey see just how much her being there affected Eve.

"Come in," Eve called out and switched off her monitor, hiding Detective Carter's records from view.

The silence was deafening, even to Eve, and the room seemed to be closing around her, but she couldn't speak until she was sure her voice wouldn't betray her.

"Mikey showed me the new paintings." Lainey was the first to speak, no longer able to endure the silence. "They're beautiful." And extremely expensive, she thought silently.

"Mmm hmm."

Lainey shook her head at Eve's bent head. "Where did you get them?"

"They were a gift," Eve said simply.

"A gift? Those are multi-million dollar paintings, Eve. Who would just give them to you?"

"They were payment for services rendered long ago." Eve answered, still not looking at Lainey although she didn't know what she was even writing anymore.

Lainey frowned. She didn't like the sound of Eve's explanation. "What services? Who gave them to you?" She waited for Eve's answer, but Eve just sat there, silently working, never looking up from the papers in front of her. "How long are you going to ignore me?" she demanded finally.

"I'm not ignoring you, Lainey, I'm working. I realize this is your day off."

"Don't!" Lainey sighed. She didn't want to be fighting with Eve, so, she decided to try a different approach. "I've been calling you," she said. "I guess you must know that."

"I received your messages," Eve admitted.

"And, you couldn't call me back?" Lainey asked, exasperated. "I've been worried about you."

"Nothing to worry about," Eve assured her. "I'm fine. I didn't call because I didn't want to interrupt anything."

Lainey stood up and grabbed the pen out of Eve's hand. "If you want to make me feel like shit – make me feel guilty for making love to my husband - then you are damn well going to look at me while you do it!"

Eve stood herself. "I don't want to make you feel guilty!" she cried. "I didn't call you because I don't want to hear you apologize. I don't want to hear the pain and confusion you're going through because of me!"

Lainey was taken aback by Eve's outburst. Never once had she thought about how hard this was on Eve as well. "Eve..."

"No," Eve interrupted and sank back down in her chair. "It's true, so don't try and deny it. I knew you were unhappy with the way your marriage was going. I knew this would happen – this guilt and regret you have and yet I still seduced you." Her voice was filled with self-loathing.

"I don't regret anything, Eve," Lainey told her gently. "And, you didn't seduce me. I knew what I was getting into, and I wanted it. I wanted you. I can't help feeling guilty, I'm married for crying out loud, but I don't regret anything that's happened between us."

Eve looked into Lainey's eyes. "I've put you in the position of having to choose between your husband and me, and that's not fair to you."

"I put myself in that position, Eve. I'm not sorry I did."

Eve remained silent for a moment. "Tell me, Lainey," she said. "When you were making love to your husband – No! Look at me. Look me in the eye and tell me the truth. When you were making love to Jack the other night were you happy? Did you think of me even once?" And then, when Lainey did not answer, "You don't have to say a word. I know the answers."

"Damn it, Eve!" Lainey exclaimed. "It's not as black and white as that. Nothing is that easy. Yes, I'm happy that Jack is paying more attention to me, but that doesn't mean I don't want or need you anymore.

I'm so incredibly confused. I never expected I could be in love with two different people..."

Eve's jaw dropped. "What?" The single word was barely a whisper.

Lainey saw the pure shock in Eve's face. She hadn't meant to say it, but now that it was out, she couldn't deny that it was true. "I've tried to talk myself out of it, to tell myself that what I was feeling wasn't being in love," she said slowly. "I've tried to believe that it was just the excitement that you bring to my life. But it all comes back to one thing. I'm in love with my husband, Eve. But I'm also in love with you."

Eve sat in stunned silence. Every thought in her brain, every clever saying, fled her.

"Say something, Eve," Lainey begged her. "Please, say something, anything, just speak to me."

"Come home with me."

"What?"

"Come home with me," Eve repeated. "Right now. There's something I want to do. Not that," she said with a little smile when Lainey blushed. "Something else. Will you come home with me? Now."

Lainey stood in Eve's bedroom, alone. The drive from the gallery to Eve's apartment had been made in complete silence. Now Lainey was here, not knowing why, and Eve had left her by herself to go through the hidden door into her studio.

She climbed the steps to the bed and ran her hand lovingly across the comforter. She knew what it was like to be in this bed, to make love with Eve in this bed, and yet, her pulse still raced at the thought of Eve lying there. Sitting down, she put her head in her hands. What in the hell was she going to do about the mess she was in? How could she have let herself fall in love with two people, and how long could this double life go on before she just couldn't handle the guilt anymore? No matter who she was with, she felt guilty for betraying one of them. She knew she owed her loyalty to Jack. She had made a vow to him on their wedding day, and that's what she should be holding to. But, when she was here, sitting on Eve's bed, smelling that unmistakably unique scent that was purely Eve's, she couldn't bear to think that she would never be in this bed again.

Eve watched Lainey from the doorway, torn by conflicting emotions. She felt need, desire – and something deeper than she could admit to. And witnessing the weariness in Lainey made her feel shame, as well.

"I'm sorry," she said. "I didn't mean to make you wait so long."

Lainey's eyes widened as she saw that Eve was setting up an easel and canvas at the foot of the bed. "What are you doing?"

Eve didn't answer right away. Ever since she had laid eyes on Lainey, she had wanted to capture that classic beauty, that touch of virtue coupled with the sexuality that was the core of Lainey.

This was the time to do it, Eve thought, before she lost the chance along with everything else she cared about.

"Eve?" Lainey joined her at the foot of the bed, and watched Eve. She's so beautiful, Lainey thought as she observed how expertly Eve worked with the equipment, remembering just how much an expert Eve was with her hands.

Eve placed a fingertip on Lainey's lips. "Let me paint you," she whispered. "Please?" Keeping her eyes on Lainey's, she reached down to unbutton her shirt. "You're shaking. Do you want me to stop?"

"No," Lainey answered softly. She didn't ever want Eve to stop.

And, Eve didn't. She continued to unbutton Lainey's shirt before slipping it slowly off her shoulders. She had told herself that she would be professional about this, and not let her emotions get in the way. But, with Lainey standing here in front of her, she wasn't sure if that was going to be possible. Closing her eyes, she reached around Lainey to unfasten her bra, and let it follow the shirt to the floor. Eve didn't open her eyes until Lainey was standing naked before her. Then she stepped back and took in the amazing sight. "You're so beautiful." Eve smiled when Lainey blushed. "Will you lay down for me?"

"Lay down?" Lainey couldn't believe how unbelievably nervous she was. It was ridiculous, really. Eve has seen her body before. Hell, Eve has done unimaginable things to her body before, but there was something extraordinarily intimate about what was happening now.

"Here against the pillow," Eve said. "Good. Now, bend your right leg for me, leave the left one straight."

Although she found herself violently aroused, Eve tried to let the artist in her take over. When Lainey did as she was told, Eve placed her hand gently on Lainey's bent knee and pushed it into the position she craved. Her hand lingered on Lainey's soft skin for a breathless moment. Then clearing her throat, she walked away. Once she was safely behind her canvas, she sat on the stool and looked over at Lainey.

"Place one hand over your head," she told her. "Yes, like that. The other one, place on your hip. Lower. Mmm, perfect." Absolutely perfect. Eve picked up her palette, and began mixing her paints. "Are you okay?" she asked.

"Yes. A little cold."

"You're just nervous. It gives a nice effect, though," she teased.

"Well, in that case." Lainey tweaked her nipples. "All for artistic value."

When Eve laughed, Lainey placed one hand over her heart. The sound of it was magical. Deep, throaty...sexy, and all too rare. Her eyes lit up with amusement, making the wonderful shade of gray brighter. There was a small dimple in Eve's right cheek that Lainey hadn't noticed before.

"That's the first genuine laugh I've heard from you since I've been with you today," she said, and then, as Eve's smile faded, "Talk to me."

"You moved," was Eve's only response.

Lainey sighed and returned to the position Eve had placed her in. "I'm sorry about the other night," she said.

"Don't be. I shouldn't have called you. I didn't take the time change into consideration, and, to be honest, I didn't think about Jack. I'm the one who should apologize."

"Why did you call, Eve?" Lainey asked as Eve began to paint.

"Bring your chin down a little. That's right. To answer your question, I was upset. I made the mistake of looking at a photo that I never wanted to see."

Lainey frowned. "A photo of what?"

"Me," Eve replied as her brush captured all of those beautiful curves.

"I don't understand."

"She watched," Eve told Lainey. "Madame Bussiere was more of a pervert than I ever expected. It was all a show to her. Not only did she watch, she took photos."

"Oh my God."

"I found this out when I went to find out who was talking about my past. When I called you, I had just looked at one of the photos." Her laugh was humorless. "As though I needed a photo to remind me of the things that happened to me."

"I'm so sorry." Lainey hadn't thought she could feel any worse than she already did for not being there that night for Eve. But she was wrong. Now she felt as though she had let Eve down during her most vulnerable moment. "Oh, Eve," she said. "Is that how someone knows? Is she using these photos against you?"

Eve shook her head. "No. She's a pervert who admitted to taking the photos for her own pleasure. I have the negatives, and she knows that if she lies to me she'll be sorry."

"Then who is doing this to you?"

"My father."

"What! But how does he know?"

"He knows because he's the one who told Madame Bussiere to use me that way." Eve sighed. She was sorry now that she had told Lainey about the photos. She didn't want to be thinking about this now. All she wanted now was to lose herself in painting her. "It's a long story, and one I don't want to get into now, but he's the one that's behind everything."

Lainey was having a hard time comprehending what Eve was telling her. She just couldn't understand how a father could do such horrific things to his daughter. But, she didn't want to make Eve talk about it if she didn't want to, so Lainey changed the subject.

"Tell me about the paintings you brought back," she asked. Eve looked up at her, and the sadness in her eyes brought tears to Lainey's eyes. She wanted to go to Eve, to hold her in her arms.

"Don't move." Eve stopped Lainey's movements with the soft words. "You still want to know everything, don't you?" she asked with a hint of reluctance in telling her everything. "I told you they were payment for services rendered, and that's the truth. I visited one of the men – a very prominent and important man who had - used me. After a little persuasion, he signed over the paintings that were in his possession."

"Persuasion? Did you threaten him, Eve?"

Eve held Lainey's eyes for a moment, then turned back to the painting. "The photos came in handy," she said simply. "It's amazing what someone will do to keep their reputation – and family – safe." Eve studied the strokes of paint on the canvas. It was taking shape, she thought. The painting was going to be a priceless addition to Eve's collection when she finished. "Relax, honey. You're tensing up."

"How can you be so calm?"

"It's all a façade," Eve confessed. "There's something else you need to know, something that you're probably going to hear about anyway. Two FBI agents and five other men in Paris have been killed."

Lainey's felt her heart skip. "Why would I hear about that?"

"Because I'm going to be a suspect."

"What? Why?" Lainey was too alarmed to sit still anymore.

"Lainey, please don't move."

"You're telling me that you're going to be a suspect in multiple murders, and you expect me to just lie here while you paint me? What's going on, Eve?" she asked as she pulled a blanket over her naked body.

Eve sighed and laid her brush and palette down. She walked over and sat down next to Lainey. "Everyone who was murdered was tied to my father. To me."

"But you didn't have anything to do with it," Lainey demanded. "Did you?"

"The five men in Paris raped me," Eve told her. "The two FBI agents worked for my father. I didn't kill them. But, after I got what I wanted from that 'prominent' man in Paris, I gave him a list of people I knew were tied to my father, and told him to take care of them."

"Jesus."

Lainey made a move to get up, but Eve stopped her. "I didn't tell him to kill them, Lainey, but I don't live in a fantasy world. I knew it would be a possibility."

"I don't want to hear anymore!" Lainey told her, then swore violently. "Eve, wait."

Lainey rose, oblivious to the fact that she was still naked, and took Eve in her arms. "I'm sorry. No, don't pull away from me. Things like this have never happened in my life, so I don't know how to react. It's like a bad dream, or a movie – like it's not even real."

She guided Eve back to the bed and sat with her. How in the hell was she supposed to respond to everything Eve was telling her? How was she going to make it right?

"I don't know what I would do if I were in your position," she went on. "Maybe I would do the same thing. God, I hate it that you have to go through this, and that there's nothing I can do to help you."

"It's not your fight," Eve said quietly. Lainey may have been unaware of her nudity, but Eve wasn't. "I shouldn't have even involved you, or told you any of this, Lainey. You shouldn't be here."

"But I am here, and there's no turning back from anything that either of us has said or done." Lainey told her. "I don't know how to help you. Hell, I don't even know how to help myself. But I'm here."

Not for long, Eve thought silently. It was difficult trying not to be selfish where Lainey was concerned, especially when Lainey was sitting on Eve's bed completely naked. She should be letting Lainey go, getting her out of harm's reach, and that's exactly what she was going to do.

"I want to finish this painting," she said abruptly.

"Soon," Lainey said, and pulled Eve to her. She had detected the distance in Eve's eyes, could feel her slipping away, and it scared her.

"Lainey, I didn't bring you here for this."

"I know." Lainey was amazed by how steady her fingers were as she unbuttoned Eve's shirt. "You want me relaxed. So, relax me. Then you can paint me as much as you want." She fell back slowly on the bed, bringing Eve down on top of her. "Make love to me," Lainey whispered in Eve's ear.

No matter how much Eve told herself this shouldn't happen, she couldn't stop it. One last time, she told herself. Just one. Then she would set Lainey free. Eve hoped that was true. It had to be. For Lainey's sake. But now, Eve would savor these last moments with Lainey, a luxury she would never have with Adam. Closing her mind to everything else except the woman beneath her, she poured every bit of her heart and soul into being with her now.

Eve lay alone in her bed, studying the finished painting of Lainey. Her beautiful subject had left moments before, on her way back to her husband, her family, and Eve hadn't moved from her position on the bed since. Now, all she had to keep her company was the painting and her memories. Each brought her a great amount of pain. Reaching over, Eve turned off the light and was instantly surrounded by a darkness and emptiness that eerily mirrored what she felt inside.

Lainey took a deep breath before opening the front door of her home, the home she shared with Jack and their sons. Every night it became increasingly difficult for her to pretend that everything was normal with her mixed emotions pressuring her to make the decisions she didn't want to make. She could still feel Eve's hands on her, hear Eve's breathing and soft moans in her ear, and feel their bodies entwined. Driving home, those feelings made her conscious of the warmth she felt inside. But, here and now, coming home to her husband, that warmth turned into immeasurable guilt.

Lainey laid her keys on the hall table and found herself hoping that Jack and the kids would be asleep by now so that she wouldn't have to tell them more lies. Instead she found all three of them wrestling on the floor of the living room. She stood in the doorway for a moment, just watching them. A single tear slid down her cheek, and she quickly wiped it away. She had no right to feel sorry for herself. All of this guilt was the result of choices she had made.

"I can't do this anymore." Lainey didn't realize she had said the words out loud until she saw Jack look up her questioningly. Before either of them could say anything, Darren was out of his father's arms and leaping up into hers.

"Hi, Mommy! We waited up for you." Darren planted a loud kiss on Lainey's cheek. "Were you at Eve's?"

The pain in her heart worsened, but she smiled at her youngest son. "Eve sends her love," she told him, "and she told me to tell both of you that she hopes to see you soon." Lainey looked over at Kevin and smiled warmly at him. "Don't I get a hug from you, too?"

Kevin bounded up from the floor and ran to her. "How much longer will you have to work late?" he asked as he hugged her.

Tears threatened again. "I thought you liked taking care of yourself," she told him, brushing his cheek with her lips.

"I do." He shrugged, a little embarrassed. "It's just that I miss you."

"Oh, honey. I miss you, too. Both of you. I'll try not to work so much, okay?"

"Okay, Mom. Maybe Eve can come here. That way you work and we can see Eve, too," Kevin suggested.

"Maybe." It was the most noncommittal answer Lainey could give him, and still give him hope.

Jack stepped up to the three of them. "Why don't the two of you go up and get ready for bed." He ruffled Kevin's hair, while keeping his eyes on Lainey. "Let your mom get settled in. Then, we'll both be up to tuck you in."

"Yes, sir," the boys said in unison. Giving their mom one last hug and kiss, they hurdled up the stairs.

"Did you mean what you said?" Jack asked her. "Are you going to try not to work so much?"

"Yes, I meant it." She tried to pull her hand away, but he held on.

"Are you going to divorce me, Lainey?"

"What?" His question took her completely by surprise. "No! Why would you ask that?"

"When you came in, you said you couldn't do this anymore. If you're not divorcing me, then what did that mean?"

"I – I just meant that I don't like being away from the boys so much."

"I told you not to go back to work," Jack began.

"Stop it. Please. I don't want to go through this every time we're together. I want to work. I enjoy it, and I hate it when you make me feel guilty about it."

"You're the one who..." Jack stopped. He could see that Lainey was tired and irritable, and the last thing he wanted to do is fight with her. Her words had scared him enough to want to try harder in their marriage. "I'm sorry," he said. "I shouldn't have said that."

His apology surprised her almost as much as his question about divorce. She was prepared for a fight, as it happened almost every day. But, she didn't quite know how to handle his apology.

"We should go tuck the boys in," she said.

Jack pulled her to him when she began to move away. "What about me?"

"What about you, Jack?" she asked warily.

"Do you dislike being away from me as much as the boys?"

She looked into his eyes, saw the concern, the fear, the love, and melted because in those eyes, she could also see the young man she had once fallen so deeply in love with. Lainey lifted her hand to Jack's face. "Let's put the boys to bed," she told him. "Then, we can put each other to bed."

She stood on her tiptoes and kissed Jack lightly on the lips before silently leading him up the stairs.

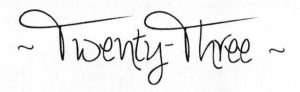

~ Twenty-Three ~

She pushed open the door of the police station and breezed her way through the bullpen full of officers with suspects, victims or family members looking for help. She had an agenda and she was not stopping for anyone. In the back of her mind she could mourn for those who were there reporting their lost children, or reproach those who were there because of their own lack of common sense. But, these people and their problems were not her concern today. Today, she was armed and dangerous, with information and determination.

"Can I help you, ma'am?" Sweat stained the officer's collar and armpits, and he had a gun holstered at his side.

"I'm looking for Detective Harris," she said keeping her voice light and friendly. "Could you tell me where I can find him?"

"He's down the hall, first office on the right, Miss. I can show you if you want."

"That's okay. I'll find it. Thank you."

A plastic nameplate adorned the glass door, dingy, white blinds the only thing allowing any kind of privacy. Out of courtesy, Eve knocked lightly before entering the office. Detective Harris was just finishing a phone conversation which, judging by what she heard, Eve assumed was about her.

"Eve," he said amicably after hanging up the phone. "I have to say that I'm surprised to see you here."

"Are you? Where's your partner?" She asked the question even though she knew the answer. Eve had made sure that Detective Carter would not be here for this particular meeting. But, Detective Harris didn't need to know that.

"He took some personal time today." He paused for a moment, his fingertips tapping together at his lips. "What can I do for you, Ms. Sumptor?"

"Why do you do that?" she asked curiously.

"I'm sorry?"

"You call me Ms. Sumptor whenever you're scrutinizing me, waiting for me to make some mistake. Or perhaps waiting for me to confess all my sins. Then, you turn completely around. Your face changes and you look at me as though I could do no wrong, and all you want to do is protect me. That's when you call me Eve. So, which is it, Detective? Am I guilty or innocent?"

"You tell me."

Eve smiled. "Would you believe me?" Her smile faded then. "I'm no angel, Detective, but I'm not a murderer either. That's not my style."

"My partner thinks you had something to do with the recent murders in Paris."

Eve's lips curved, again. "Predictable. And, what do you think, Detective?" she asked.

"He has good reason to believe that," he told her. "You were in Paris. These men were associated with your father."

"I was here, in beautiful New York City, when those men were murdered," Eve countered. "They were not 'associated' with my father. My father owed them money. Money he can't pay back. Your partner would know that if he stopped this obsession he has with trying to find me guilty of something, and investigated a little more closely. And, you didn't answer my question. Do you think I murdered these men, or had anything to do with their deaths - Detective?"

"No, and I've bought you some time."

Eve glanced at the phone. "So I heard. How much time do I have?"

"Not long. The press is biting at our heels wanting a suspect. I've done my best to keep your name out of this, Eve, but I don't know how much longer I can do that."

"You've done your best, and so has your partner – probably against his will because the Commissioner told you to. I'm a big contributor to the Police Fund," she said with a shrug. "He's also aware that you have no real evidence, and that I could sue the city for wrongful accusation and, of course, mental anguish." She tilted her head, and turned up the heat in her stare. "Not to mention, you could lose your job."

Satisfied by the faint film of sweat on his brow, Eve sat back in her chair and crossed her legs, the small slit of her pale pink skirt revealing her smooth thigh. "How is the investigation on my father going?"

Harris looked away. "Not going as well as I expected. Every lead we get ends up at a dead end."

"Of course it does," Eve said quietly. Harris wouldn't have been as surprised by her lack of concern if he had known what she did. Things were about to change. "Maybe if you would stop focusing your energy on trying to bring me down, things would be easier for you," she added.

"We're not focusing on you, Ms. Sumptor. But we do have to cover all angles. There's been no harassment. Your business affairs are not suffering."

"Do you think I care about business, Detective?" she interrupted heatedly. "The family of a young woman that worked for me actually thinks I killed her. Two other women in my employ are missing. One is safe, the other - I don't know. Another woman employed by me has been hospitalized, having been severely beaten. My garage attendant at the gallery has been hospitalized and I don't know if he'll ever walk again. The people I care about the most are being threatened, and the only way I can keep them out of harm's way is to get them away from me. All of this is because of my father's hatred for me." Eve sighed, feeling the weight of the guilt on her shoulders. "Money means absolutely nothing to me," she continued. "I have more than I'll ever need. But your focus on me is accomplishing nothing except letting people get killed or hurt. The longer this goes on, the more those around me will be in danger."

"I admit that my partner is a little obsessed with pinning this on you," he told her. "But more circumstantial evidence is piling up on your side than your father's. I can't simply ignore that." He picked up a pen and tapped it on his desk. "I don't think you killed Miss Sawyer, Eve. But, what am I supposed to do when my partner keeps digging up this evidence?"

"Have you ever wondered why you keep going in circles? When it comes to Tony, he always comes out smelling like a rose, the perfect citizen, even though he's a known murderer. Have you ever wondered how he could get out of prison so soon after being convicted of murder? And, yet, when it comes to me, 'circumstantial' evidence practically throws itself in your lap." She leaned forward once again and laid the folder she had brought with her in front of the detective. "No. Don't open it yet, wait until I'm gone. Things are not always as they appear to be, Detective. Your partner has it in for me. Why? And, is he turning you towards me to keep your attention off someone else? Sometimes, the answers could be right under your nose."

She knew she was taking a gamble by giving Harris the information she had, but she had to trust him. She had no other choice. "I can help you, Charlie. Stop working against me, and maybe we can save another innocent person from getting in the line of fire. This started thirteen years ago when my mother was murdered. One way or another, it ends now."

And with that, Eve took her departure, leaving Harris wary and confused. Turning his attention to the file, he opened it. He frowned, and started reading the information that accompanied a photo. "Son of a bitch!" he whispered with disbelief and picked up a folded piece of paper which had fallen onto his desk when he opened the file, a piece of paper which was to make all the difference.

The elevator doors opened, and Eve stepped into the gallery, her routine cup of coffee in hand. Her visit to Detective Harris had proven to be beneficial since she had subsequently been informed that he had made the phone call she had predicted he would make not ten minutes after she walked out of his office.

The wheels were now set in motion, and it was up to her to keep them on track. One of her next steps would be one of the hardest things she would have to do yet. When she had fallen asleep, eventually, the night before, her dreams had been filled with Adam and Lainey, with

Lainey dominating the first half, angry with Eve, overcome with hatred, and unwilling to forgive, leaving Eve feeling vulnerable and miserable. Then Adam had crept in, and Eve's heart had been filled with regret. She wanted him, needed him, and dreamt of making love with him. She could feel him moving inside her, loving her. Then, as abruptly as he had appeared, he disappeared, and she was left alone, cold and trembling with no one to turn to.

Lainey did not look up from what she was doing as Eve came into the gallery. After last night with her husband, she knew that facing Eve today would be difficult. She would have to deal with that later.

After telling Mikey that she would be spending most of the day in her office and expected to be left undisturbed except for a single visitor, she started down the hall, only to be greeted by the young couple Lainey was helping.

"Good morning, Ms. Sumptor." The young, enthusiastic couple with Lainey greeted Eve as she walked by. They were regulars from when Eve first opened the gallery here in New York. He was a hot shot on Wall Street, she, beautiful and blonde, somewhat of a princess, liked spending his money on the art. It was a perfect arrangement for Eve.

"Mr. And Mrs. Cates, it's always nice to see you. I trust you are being well taken care of."

"Yes, of course. You always did have great judgment in the people you have around you."

Eve simply smiled. "If you'll excuse me, I have tons of work to do. I have no doubt you'll choose something spectacular for your new apartment. Mrs. Stanton will take good care of you."

Lainey tried to keep her composure, but all she wanted to do was sit down and cry. Why had Eve called her Mrs. Stanton? What did she know? With Eve, that answer could be everything. Lainey relied on her professionalism to make it through this sale, but her mind was on Eve. She determined that in her first free moment, she would make her way up to her office and find out what was going on.

Eve closed her office door softly behind her. She had seen the pain and shock in Lainey's eyes when she had called her Mrs. Stanton, and it hurt. Still, Eve kept telling herself that she was doing the right thing, that

Lainey would get through this and be happier in the long run, even if Eve was giving up her own happiness to make that happen. Sitting down at her desk, she rested her pounding head in her hands, reviewing what she intended to tell Lainey. She was going to be harsh, but Eve felt she had no other choice. Picking up the photo they had taken at Disney, she ran a fingertip over Lainey's image and found that the pain was even worse when she focused on the two little boys she was so fond of. The memory of their trip to Florida was one she would cherish for the rest of her life – however long that would be.

She had been so happy since Lainey had come into her life and now, because of her father, she would once again be alone. Her stomach churned sickly as she thought of what she had to do. Eve snapped out of her daydreams and back into reality when she heard the knock. Carefully, as though it would hurt to let go, Eve set the photo back down on her desk and called out, "Come in."

"I must say that I was surprised when I was told that you wanted to meet with me," Dee said by way of greeting. "I was having a rather nice vacation."

"I'll make sure you go back to Hawaii for a real vacation when all of this is over," Eve told her. "I'm ready to make a statement."

Surprise flickered in Dee's eyes. "My camera man's outside," she said.

"No cameras."

"I don't understand. You just said you wanted to make a statement. I'm a T.V. reporter. Remember?"

"I said I'm ready to make a statement, but I can't do it on camera."

"That wasn't the deal, Eve," Dee protested. "You told me you'd go on air."

"And, I will," Eve promised her. "But, I can't do that now. All I can do is give you information that I need you to make public. Dee, it's important that you do this my way."

"Eve, my boss is breathing down my neck for a story on you. We've been pressured by you and the police to keep names out of it, but I need something."

"I'm about to give you something. And, I'm not going to lie to you. If you do this story, there'll be a contract out for your head. So, you need to make sure that you and your boss are ready for that."

"Are you saying I could get killed because of what you're about to tell me?"

"Yes."

Eve waited. She knew something about brinksmanship, enough to be fairly certain that, when push came to shove, this woman would put her career before her own safety. Eve knew ambition when she saw it and she knew how to manipulate with it.

Dee sat down and took a notebook and pen out of her tote bag. "We'll do it your way," she said, "but only because I'm going to take you at your word that you will give me an exclusive. On camera."

"Before I say anything," Eve told her, "you have to agree that you'll do exactly what I tell you."

"I'll do what I can."

"That's not good enough, Dee. In order for any of this to work as I've planned..." Eve's voice faded. There was too much on her mind, and she was becoming sloppy.

"In order for what to work, Eve?" Dee's eyes narrowed.

"I have no time to waste, Ms. Cummings," Eve told her, her voice and eyes expressionless. "This is the statement I want you to report."

Lainey watched as Dee Cummings left the gallery. She knew Dee had been in Eve's office for more than an hour, and she couldn't help but be curious as well as annoyed that her confrontation with Eve had to be delayed. But now that Lainey had the chance, she felt her blood run cold with fear. All morning, she has had a sick feeling in her stomach, as if she knew something was awfully wrong. She just couldn't pinpoint what it was. Then, Eve had called her Mrs. Stanton and that sick feeling intensified. Leaving Mikey to take care of things she made her way up to Eve's office.

Eve fought the sick feeling in her stomach as she waited for Lainey to come to her as she knew she would now that Dee had left. Second thoughts plagued her. Could she really go through with this? But, when she heard the light knock at the door, she knew there was no other choice. Eve closed her eyes and took a deep, steadying breath. "Yes?"

God. Lainey closed her own eyes and prayed for her quaking hands to work. Her breath shuddered when she sucked it in, and opened the door. "Hi." Lainey's voice wasn't as confident as she would have liked it to be, but she refused to clear her throat. "Are you busy?"

"I'm always busy." Silently thanking God that her voice was light and careless, Eve gestured to the chair. She waited for Lainey to sit, but didn't look up from the papers in front of her. "Did you make the sell to the Cates?"

"Yes."

"What did they end up buying?"

Exasperated, Lainey sighed heavily. "I don't know."

Eve looked up and cocked a brow. "You don't know?"

"Damn it, Eve, I can't think about what I sold when I'm trying to figure out what's going on between us." Lainey paused for a moment to think. "A-a sculpture from a local artist and a Pissarro. Would you like the tickets, too?"

"No, that won't be necessary," Eve said. "What can I do for you?"

Lainey stared at the top of Eve's head for a moment. "Is this how it's going to be?"

"What do you mean?"

"What was that Mrs. Stanton bit about?"

Eve looked up at Lainey again, praying her eyes didn't betray the pain she felt inside. "That's your name, isn't it?"

"It never was with you. Especially after everything that we've been through."

"I was being professional, Lainey. I said hello to Mr. and Mrs. Cates, and to you. You shouldn't take it so personally. Besides, your marriage is getting better, isn't it? You should be happy to be called Mrs. Stanton?"

"What do you know about the state of my marriage, Eve?" Lainey demanded. "We haven't talked about the most recent installment." It was, she found, impossible to keep the sarcasm out of her voice. At least Eve could tell her what was going on. She owed her that.

So she was angry. Eve couldn't blame her. And perhaps anger was better than grief. "What I know is, I'm no longer going to stand in your way," she said evenly. "Things with Jack are going well. I can see it in your eyes."

"Just because things are going better with Jack, doesn't mean I don't still need you, Eve," Lainey said. At least she could be honest even if Eve was determined to play games with their relationship.

"You made love with Jack last night." It wasn't a question. Neither was it an accusation. "That's nothing to be ashamed of, Lainey," Eve continued. Eve rose and, standing in front of Lainey, leaned against her desk, folding her arms across her breast. She shrugged. "Look, what we did was fun. But, we knew it couldn't last."

"Fun? 'What we did was fun'? You make it sound like it was nothing more than an experimental fling."

"Isn't that what it was?"

Lainey recoiled, as though she had been physically punched in the stomach. At that moment, Eve hated herself more than she ever thought possible.

"It was more than that," Lainey said accusingly.

Uncrossing her arms, Eve gripped the edge of her desk for support, hoping Lainey didn't notice. "Look," she said. "I was intrigued by you the moment I saw you. That was the artist in me. The lines of your face, the curve of your lips, I always knew you'd make a beautiful portrait. You opened your mouth and your voice and intelligence only intrigued me more. I admit that I was attracted to you, and I was curious to know what it would be like to kiss that mouth."

Eve couldn't keep her eyes from moving to Lainey's mouth when she said that. How could she bear never kissing her again, never making love to her again, or never having her cherished friendship again.

"That kind of feeling was new to me," she went on. "It became something I wanted to explore more. I could tell you were attracted to me, too. So, I thought, 'why not take advantage of the situation'. I've never had this kind of experience before, so I took the chance."

"Stop it! Why are you doing this?"

"Doing what? I'm telling you the truth." Eve's grip tightened and she leaned forward slightly, closing the gap between them a fraction. "You're making this too personal. Telling me you're 'in love' with me, lying to your husband to stay with me. It was just an experiment, Lainey, something different to try. You weren't supposed to let your feelings get involved."

Lainey leapt to her feet. "Are you telling me that your feelings aren't involved?"

"If you knew me as well as you think you do, you'd know that I have no feelings," Eve responded flatly. She wanted to move, to go back to her chair and sit down before her legs gave out beneath her, but she couldn't move. "It was different, being with you. Nice. And fun," she added with another careless shrug. "A lot of fun."

Before she knew what happened, Eve felt a hot sting on her cheek and her head whipped to the side as Lainey slapped her, hard. Slowly, Eve turned her head back to Lainey and locked eyes."I'll give you that one," she said quietly, licking the trickle of blood from the corner of her mouth.

The slap shocked Lainey as much as it did Eve. What Eve had told her had cut her straight through to the heart.

"Look me in the eye and tell me that you don't care about me," she said. "That you don't love me."

Lainey's voice shook with anger and hurt as she watched Eve's lips curl. Suddenly it was as though she were a stranger, someone Lainey had never really seen before.

"I don't love you. It was sex, it was fun, it was experimental. And you can't tell me that it didn't feel good, that I didn't do things to you that made you feel alive again. You should be thanking me. Can you tell me that sex with your husband isn't better than it was before we were together?"

"Thank you?" Tears fell in a rush down Lainey's cheeks. "How can you do this to me? Why did you make me fall in love with you? Why did you treat me as though I were more than a friend to you?"

"I didn't make you fall in love with me, Lainey." Eve had to force the words. "I may have taken advantage of the situation, but you didn't fight it. You wanted it as much as I did. You were just as curious as I was."

"You bitch!" Lainey whispered vehemently. "You goddamn bitch." She was having trouble breathing and her heart was beating too fast. "I hate you." She had to get out of Eve's office, to breathe in fresh air before she collapsed.

"I'm sorry you feel that way." Eve's voice was cavalier, her composure relaxed, but inside she was dying. Every part of her soul was falling apart as she saw hate and disbelief in Lainey's eyes. Suddenly she remembered seeing that same hurt in Adam's the night she told him goodbye. And at this moment, Eve didn't care if her father made good on his promise to see her dead, because, at this moment, she was dead.

"I can't even look at you anymore," Lainey said, grabbing the framed photograph off the desk. "All of this was just bullshit, wasn't it? Did you use my sons to make me trust you more? They love you, Eve. What am I supposed to tell them now? How do I tell them that you're not the woman I thought you were, that we all thought you were?"

Her anger and hurt grew with every second she stood there in front of Eve. She threw the photo on the floor, shattering the glass that held the photo in place. "I have to get out of here," she said. "I can't bear to be in the same room with you anymore."

Eve wanted to reach out to Lainey, to take her in her arms and hold her until Lainey knew just how much Eve really did care. When Lainey left, she would take Eve's heart with her.

"I trusted you, Eve. I loved you," Lainey told her, not looking back because it hurt too much for her to bear. "I was there for you. I gave you everything, all of me. You were the one person I thought could never hurt me. How could I have been so wrong about you?"

It was with an effort that Lainey resisted slamming the door after her and running out of the gallery. As calmly as she could, she walked down the stairs, bypassing the customers, and ignoring Mikey who called her name.

Lainey couldn't get away from the gallery fast enough. Her hands were shaking uncontrollably as she tried to open her car door, and start the engine. She couldn't breathe and her eyes blurred from the tears.

Inside her office, Eve was trying to catch her own breath, but every intake hurt like hell. She felt like she was dying a very slow and painful death as she kept hearing Lainey's voice in her head. *'I hate you.'* The words, repeated and over, shattering what was left of her soul. The rapes, the beatings, everything that she had endured in life before this moment, seemed like nothing compared to the way she was feeling now.

Through the shards of glass from the broken frame, she saw Lainey's face looking up at her. All of the strength she was trying to hang on to, poured out of her in a rush, and her hand flew to her mouth just as a sob escaped. Her legs finally gave out, and Eve, the woman who everyone saw as strong and unaffected, unemotional, fell to her knees, uncontrollable sobs racking her entire body. She didn't notice, or maybe didn't care about cutting her hands as she brushed the glass away and took the photo, holding it to her aching heart. "I'm sorry, Lainey," she whispered. "I'm so very sorry."

Hours after he saw Lainey leaving the gallery in a hurry, Mikey flipped the switch to the last light shining in the gallery. He hadn't seen Eve leave, but when he knocked on the door of her office and there was no answer he assumed that she had left. Locking the gallery door behind him, he headed home.

The pounding in her head wouldn't stop. Eve hadn't moved from the spot where she had collapsed after Lainey had left. She wanted to go home, and bury herself under the covers of her bed, but she couldn't gather the strength to get up. For a long time she was aware of nothing except the throb in her head and the excruciating pain in her heart. And then she thought of Tony. This was all his fault. He had better kill her, because when she had the chance, she was going to kill him for what he's put her through. And she would make certain that his death was as unbearable as the pain she was experiencing now. Her life had been one incredibly difficult journey. And then, for the first time, she had found something to believe in. She had finally found a way to open her heart and care for, not just one person, but two. And that had brought her so much happiness, so much joy. And now it was all gone. Everything was gone, she thought sadly as another hot tear slid down her tear stained face. Somehow she would find the strength to make her father pay, but now, all she wanted to do was sleep. At this moment, she didn't care if she ever woke up again.

After leaving Eve and the gallery hours before, Lainey finally pulled into her driveway and switched off the ignition. She sat there for a few moments, absently wiping away the never-ending tears. The drive she had taken did nothing to calm her. Everything seemed to remind her of Eve. Even the music on the radio made Lainey remember being with Eve so vividly that she had to turn it off. She had gone over and over every word Eve had said to her, but she couldn't understand what had changed, what had happened to make Eve treat her that way. There were no answers. Only questions, questions that she could no longer bear to ask.

Lainey rested her head on the steering wheel for a moment. She knew that her eyes were red and swollen from crying, and she had to get a hold of herself before facing her family. She had been so excited about taking a job, had fought with Jack about it, had fought with Jack about Eve, and for what? And now there was no one to turn to. She needed to just be held and told that everything would be fine, but the arms she wanted to be in were closed to her forever.

Taking a deep breath, she opened her car door and slowly stepped out. She wasn't sure if she could put up a happy façade, but she could try, at least, to appear as though nothing had happened. Lainey braced a hand on the car when a wave of dread and sadness swept over her. Once she walked into that house and told Jack she no longer had a job, it would all be true. This horrible, horrible nightmare would become reality.

Lainey squared her shoulders. Given the way Eve had treated her, she should feel lucky that it was all over, she told herself. Eve's true colors were finally in the open. Lainey just wished she could be sure that the woman whose lip had curled when she looked at her was the true Eve.

Rufus met Lainey at the door, but instead of jumping on her, he sat and observed her sadly, whining when she bent to pat him.

"What's the matter, boy?" Lainey asked.

He whined again and licked Lainey's cheek, scarcely thumping his tail as he usually did when she scratched behind his ears.

"Am I that obvious?" she asked him with a sad smile. "She's gone, boy. I loved her so much, and now she's gone," she whispered. Lainey felt the tears coming again. She wanted nothing more than to go upstairs, lay down in her bed, and sleep away all of this hurt.

"Mommy?"

Quickly, Lainey wiped her face with her hand. "Darren, honey," she said. "You startled me."

"Are you sad, Mommy?" Darren's bottom lip poked out in a small pout.

"No, honey. I'm not sad." Lainey forced herself to smile and took Darren in her arms. "How can I be sad when I have a son like you?" She kissed his whole face until he started giggling. It was so good to hear his laugh. She needed to hear it. "Now, I know you're not home by yourself. Where is everyone?"

Darren giggled again. "Daddy and Kevin are in the kitchen, Mommy. We're making macaroni and cheese for dinner!"

"Macaroni and cheese? From a box?" Darren nodded, and Lainey shook her head. "I'm sure we can find something better to make for you to eat. Come on. Let's go show them how to make a real meal." She lifted Darren in to her arms, holding him there for a minute. "I love you," she whispered.

"I love you, too, Mommy." Darren kissed her on the cheek.

When Jack turned from the stove and saw Lainey standing at the door with Darren in her arms, he frowned slightly. "You're home early."

"Yes." She set Darren down on a stool, and turned to Kevin. "Hi, honey," she said, kissing him on the top of the head.

"Hey, Mom! Dad's making us some macaroni!"

"So I heard." She walked past Jack, afraid to look him in the eye. Picking up the pot of boiling water, she dumped it in the sink. "Hot dogs and macaroni and cheese? Is this what you've been feeding our sons while I've had to work?" She couldn't keep the bite out of her voice.

"I'm doing the best I can, Lainey," Jack responded quietly. "Why are you home so early?"

"Now you don't want me here?" She walked to the refrigerator and took out items she thought would make a healthy meal.

"I didn't say that. Boys, why don't you go upstairs and wash up for dinner."

Both boys left the room without a word. It was clear that they sensed that something was very wrong.

"I don't know what I did to deserve this attitude..."

"Macaroni and cheese, Jack? We have all of this food in the refrigerator and all you can come up with is something unhealthy for the boys to eat?"

"If it's so damned unhealthy, Lainey, why do we have it? I can't believe you're getting this upset over something so trivial."

"Our sons' health is trivial?" No matter what she did, she couldn't stop the anger from taking over. He didn't deserve this, she thought to herself. In a huff, she turned off the stove and pushed the food away from her. "Order pizza. Order whatever the fuck you want. I'm going upstairs."

"Lainey!" He watched, confused and angry as she stormed out of the room. What the hell was all of that about, he wondered, and looked at all of the food she had brought out. Surely there was something he could cook to make her happy.

Lainey hurried into her bedroom and shut the door, leaning on it for support. The sobs were catching up to her again. She took three deep breaths, trying to calm herself, but the goddamn pain just wouldn't go away. Walking to the bed, she caught a glimpse of the Buddha that Eve had bought for her, sitting on the nightstand. Sorrow filled her heart as she picked it up. "Why did you do this to me?" she asked quietly. "How could you hurt me like this?" The urge to throw the sixty-thousand dollar little statue was so strong that she tightened her grip. God, how was she going to make it through this?

He found her sitting in the chair, staring out the window. Jack thought that he had never seen her look so sad.

"You'll be happy to know that I won't be going back to work," Lainey said quietly. She saw his reflection in the window, and knew that she had startled him, not by what she said but how she said it. But it was impossible for her to keep the bitterness out of her voice.

"I don't understand." The set of her shoulders told him that she didn't want to be touched.

"What's not to understand?" she said. "You got your way. You should be happy."

"I never told you to quit."

"Bull shit, Jack." She wanted to yell, but didn't have the strength to do so. And she didn't want the boys to hear. "You told me multiple times to quit. Not that it matters. .I'm not going back, so you got your way. Happy?"

"No. If it's making you this miserable, why did you quit? And, please don't blame me. If I asked multiple times, you've refused just as many. Why now? And, how does Eve feel about this?"

Just hearing Eve's name made Lainey's pulse jump, and her heart ache. "I don't want to talk about it."

Jack saw her close herself off and knew that he wouldn't be getting any information from her now.

"Well, maybe you'll be happy to know that I cooked something healthy for the boys to eat," he said. "There's some chicken and rice downstairs if you get hungry."

It only made Lainey more miserable to hear that he had gone through the trouble after she was such a bitch to him. But she remained silent until she heard him sigh, and walk into the bathroom, shutting the door with a distinct click. Only then did Lainey let the tears flow once again.

"I'm going to watch some TV," Jack said when, having showered, he found her still huddled in the chair. Although he was beginning to worry about her, he had decided that she needed a little more time to deal with whatever it was that was bothering her. Switching on the eleven o'clock news, he sat back in bed with a book. It was another one of his routines that Lainey found annoying. *"You're either watching TV or reading. You can't do both."* She would say.

But tonight she didn't notice or simply didn't care. Clearly she had other things on her mind.

"In our top story tonight, Eve Sumptor, owner of Sumptor, Inc. whose employee, Jackie Sawyer, was found murdered in her home earlier this month, has made her first statement to the press. She talked to our own Dee Cummings about who she thinks is responsible for the young woman's death. Dee?"

The mere mention of Eve's name snapped Lainey out of her trance.

Thinking that hearing about Eve might somehow upset Lainey even more, Jack switched off the television.

"What are you doing?" she cried. "Turn it back on!"

Dee Cummings' face filled the screen. "In a recent interview with Ms. Sumptor," she began, "she stated how terribly sorry she was for the loss of such an excellent employee and wonderful young woman. Ms. Sumptor has extended her condolences to Miss Sawyer's family, and has offered to help them in any way she can. Recently, Miss Sawyer's family has been told conflicting stories about Ms. Sumptor's involvement in their daughter's death, resulting in a lawsuit against her. In light of new evidence, this lawsuit has since been rescinded. I asked Ms. Sumptor about the allegations made against her, and she has told me – and I quote 'I had nothing to do with the murder of Jackie Sawyer, and will do everything in my power to bring down those who are responsible'."

"Dee," Bill, the anchorman of Channel 9 News cut in. "What about the allegations that Ms. Sumptor is a suspect in other related deaths in Paris?"

Dee smiled to her audience. "Ms. Sumptor admitted to having been in Paris recently, but records will show that she was indeed here in the States when those murders occurred. In her statement, Ms. Sumptor acknowledged that her father, Tony Sumptor – recently released from prison – is now quote 'out for revenge, and will stop at nothing to bring me down. Including framing me for hideous crimes I did not commit.' Some members of our listening audience may remember that evidence from Ms. Sumptor brought her father to justice for the murder of her mother."

"Is she accusing her father of murdering Ms. Sawyer?" Dee's fellow anchor asked.

"Well, Bill, she wouldn't go into details with me," Dee replied. "But she did tell me that she had evidence that there were quote 'players in this game' who include city officials and even government officials that she knows of. She went as far as saying, 'This game will be over soon, and all of those involved will be brought to justice one way or another'."

"Is that how she thinks of this, Dee? As a game?"

"Ms. Sumptor knows this is anything but a game," Dee told him. "After speaking face to face with Ms. Sumptor, I can say that she is extremely distressed by what has happened. She says that, to her father, this is a game, and for the sake of everyone, one she does not intend to lose."

"Thank you, Dee." The voices on the television faded as Jack turned down the volume.

"Why didn't you tell me about any of this?" Jack demanded.

"Don't start." Lainey's voice was quiet, but held a warning that Jack heard loud and clear.

"Were you in any danger being with her?"

"No. She would never let me get hurt." Unless it was by her, Lainey thought sadly.

"Well, maybe it's a good thing that you won't be around her anymore," he told her. "You shouldn't have to worry about your safety each time you go into work and I shouldn't have to worry about the mother of my children. Eve was selfish enough to involve you in that mess, and I'm just glad you're out of it now."

"Goddamnit, Jack, she was not selfish! She did everything..." She cut off her rant, afraid to say too much, and too tired to fight. "I'm not talking to you about this anymore. Don't bring it up, don't speak Eve's name."

"Where are you going?"

"To be by myself." She answered simply, and walked out. She couldn't be with him, not now, not when she had to think about everything she had just heard.

~ Twenty-Four ~

"Son of a bitch!" The sound of a crash was followed by a string of curse words that would make a sailor blush.

"How long has he been like that?" He had seen the news last night as well, and had known that Tony would not be happy with Eve when he heard about the interview she had given Dee Cummings. He just wished he knew where Eve was.

"All morning," his companion answered. "Ever since he saw the paper this morning, he's been scaring the hell out of everyone here. She's in trouble, man. I hope she knows what she's doing."

"She knows." He was sure of it. Eve Sumptor never did anything without having a plan. He took a breath. "I'm going in."

"You sure you want to do that?"

"Someone has to." He lowered his voice. "I can't get a hold of her but he hasn't gotten to her yet if he's still this upset. See if you can find out where she is."

Then squaring his shoulders, he cautiously opened the door, only to close it again when a crystal tumbler flew towards him.

"Hold your fire, sir!" he called out. "I'm coming in."

"I want her dead! Do you hear me?" Tony's chest heaved with frustration. He sat down at his desk and looked at the paper for the umpteenth time this morning. His face was plastered on the front page, and the story wasn't flattering.

"She's missing, sir."

The news only infuriated him more. "What do you mean she's missing?" he roared. "What the hell am I paying you morons for?" Swiping his arm across his desk, Tony sent papers flying. "Get out of here! I'll take care of her myself! Get out!"

Tony waited for him to leave before opening the top drawer of his desk. Carefully, he picked up the .22 caliber gun that lay in there, together with a photo of Eve. "You think you've won, Little Eve?" he said in a low voice. "Think again. I'm coming after you, and this time, the game is going to end."

Lainey sat quietly, alone at the kitchen table. Her coffee was cold, and she was still in her pajamas, but she just didn't care. She had spent the night in the guest room, but sleep had evaded her. She kept remembering the scene at the gallery, the way Eve looked at her as though everything they had done was a joke or an experimental fling. She could still see the cruel smile. All night she had wondered why Eve had had to be so cruel. The story on the news was unexpected, but perhaps that had something to do with Eve's attitude. She just couldn't believe that Eve had meant any of it. But, she did, Lainey, she thought to herself, sternly. She doesn't want you anymore, and you need to just get over it and move on. You have your sons, your husband, forget about Eve.

When the phone rang and she heard Mikey's voice, Lainey became instantly alert. "What's wrong?" she demanded.

"I need your help, Mrs. Stanton. The gallery is full of people, and I'm here alone. I don't know what to do."

Lainey took a steadying breath. "Mikey, I'm sorry. You're going to have to call...Eve. I don't work at the gallery anymore."

"But I can't find Ms. Sumptor," he told her. "I've called everywhere, and no one has seen her. I don't know Adam's number. I was hoping you would know where she was, or at least could come in and help me for a while until Ms. Sumptor showed up. I'm sorry; I didn't realize that you had..."

"It's okay," Lainey interrupted. She was worried. It wasn't like Eve not to show up at the gallery. She had to have known that the News last night would have stirred things up. Oh my God, she thought, the News.

What if she had angered her father enough for him to have taken some sort of revenge?

"Mrs. Stanton? Are you still there?"

"I'm sorry, Mikey. I-I don't know where Eve is."

"What am I going to do? There are so many people here right now. I think a lot of them have come because of the News, because they're curious."

"I'll be right there," Lainey told him. "Just stay calm and I'll be there to help you as soon as I can."

Lainey hung up the phone, only to pick it up once more. Her hands shook when she tried dialing Eve's phone, and when no one answered, she became terrified that something had happened to her.

Hours passed before Lainey finally had the chance to escape to her office. After everything that has happened, she still felt as though it was hers. Maybe she was just being stupid, but she just couldn't believe that all of this was over. Lainey had given the task of trying to contact Eve to Mikey. Every thirty minutes, he was to call Eve's cell and apartment until he got an answer. She had finally let him off the hook as evening approached so he could clean up and go home.

Now Lainey sat back in her leather desk chair and closed her eyes. "Where are you, Eve?" she said aloud. She would know if anything was wrong. Wouldn't she? The light knock at her door had Lainey's pulse jumping.

It was Adam. "Where is she, Lainey?" he said, not bothering to even say hello. He looked exhausted in jeans and a slightly wrinkled Harvard t-shirt. "I have to see her."

"I don't know, Adam," Lainey told him. "I'm sorry."

He fell into the chair in front of Lainey's desk and held her eyes. "I saw the newscast last night. You knew about all of this didn't you?"

Lainey sighed. "Yes. I did."

"Why didn't she tell me about it? We've been together for two years. Why didn't she trust me enough to tell me?"

"She was trying to protect you, Adam."

"From what?"

"From everything. From her, from her past – her present. She didn't want you getting hurt."

He sat up very straight in his chair. "Doesn't she understand that what she's doing to me is hurting me more than anything else ever could?"

"Adam, you don't understand. There are things about Eve that you don't know. She has gone through things – is going through things - that no one should ever have to endure."

Adam pushed himself to his feet in frustration. "Why do I keep hearing that when no one wants to tell me what the hell it means? You know don't you?"

"Yes."

"Then tell me. Please, Lainey. I need Eve. Help me."

I need her, too, Lainey thought sadly. "It's not my story to tell, Adam. Eve has to tell you when she's ready."

"She won't talk to me. Damn it, Lainey, she won't even see me."

Lainey watched Adam pace her office, dragging his hands through his hair. Obviously he was just as miserable as she was. "I'll help you," she said rising. "I'll tell you when she gets back. Then you can talk to her about all this. Adam, there's more there than she wants you to see. There's more there for her to give than even she knows. Be there for her."

"I want to. I've wanted to for a long time, Lainey, but she always pushes me away."

Lainey struggled to keep her uneasiness hidden from Adam. How could she tell him that no one knew where Eve was? "Then don't let her," she said quietly. "Push back, Adam. Eve needs to know you're not going to run. Now I'm sorry, but I have to get this work done. I have two sons and a husband to get home to."

"You'll call me when she gets back? Thank you, Lainey."

He really was made for Eve, she thought miserably as he turned to leave the office. It only meant that her relationship with Eve was indeed over. "Adam," she called out before he closed the door. "Don't judge her. Later you'll understand."

Somehow Lainey knew that he would, if Eve would only give him a chance.

As Lainey began packing up to go home after the long day the phone on her desk rang. But, it wasn't Eve, as Lainey hoped. Detective Carter was on the line, demanding to speak with Eve. He was a police officer, but deep down, Lainey felt she couldn't trust him. How much could she tell him?

"I'm sorry, she's not available," she said cautiously.

"This is police business, Mrs. Stanton. I need to speak with her now. Could you just tell her that I'm on the phone?"

"I'm sorry, Detective. Eve's not here."

"Do you know where she is? Is she at home?"

"No, I'm sorry, I don't know. No one has heard from Eve since yesterday afternoon." The pit of Lainey's stomach churned with sickness. Nothing happened to her, Lainey, she assured herself.

"Who was the last person to see Ms. Sumptor?"

His tone put Lainey on edge. Had Eve talked to anyone after Lainey had left? Mikey had mentioned that he hadn't seen Eve leave the building. "I'm not sure," Lainey said. "I guess that would be me."

"You? You were the last person to see Ms. Sumptor before she disappeared, Mrs. Stanton? Is that what you're telling me?"

Was he accusing her? She couldn't comprehend how he could even think she could do something to Eve. "Yes, I suppose I am." She would be honest with him. She had nothing to hide. "We had a disagreement," she confessed.

"You had a fight? And, now Ms. Sumptor is missing?"

"Are you accusing me...?"

"What did you quarrel about?"

"I told you, I don't know where Eve is. How dare you accuse me?"

"Have I accused you of anything, Mrs. Stanton? Just where did you go after this 'fight' you had with Ms. Sumptor?"

"Home." God, was this how Eve felt everyday knowing that people accused her of crimes she didn't commit?

"Is there anyone who can confirm that?"

"Yes, my husband. I went straight home after leaving Eve here at the gallery." It wasn't quite the truth, but driving around aimlessly didn't technically qualify as going somewhere else. She just took a very long way home.

"What was your disagreement with Ms. Sumptor about?"

Lainey's fists clenched. She had never liked this detective, though she couldn't have said why before. Now, she despised the way he had treated Eve and how he was treating her now. "That's none of your business."

"We'll see about that." Was there a hint of a threat in his voice? First he demanded to know where Eve was without giving her any reason and then he somehow managed to twist things around to imply that she was responsible for Eve's disappearance.

"You're right, we will. I've done nothing wrong, Detective. Next time you want to question me, you can do it through my lawyer." Lainey hung up with a snap. "Son of a bitch," she whispered. She was not going to let the police intimidate her. But, he did frighten her, no matter that she had put up a brave front. With trembling hands, she picked up the phone and dialed.

Eve woke up in her living room where she had passed out hours before. Her neck ached from her position on the couch, and the smell of alcohol and cigarettes filled her nostrils, making her sick. But, instead of getting up to clean the mess, Eve sat up and picked up the pack of cigarettes. She didn't have to look to know that pills, bottles of liquor and cigarette butts littered the expensive coffee table. She didn't care. Lighting a cigarette, she inhaled deeply, letting the sting of the tobacco fill her lungs.

Last night's binge did nothing to clear her conscience of what she had done to Lainey or Adam. It only served to make her feel worse.

Lightheaded and nauseous from the hang-over, she went to the wall opposite of her, removed a small but charming landscape by Bazille from the wall and opened the safe behind it.

Her hands shook as she removed her three prized possessions from the safe and took them back to the couch with her. Setting the letter and journal aside, Eve held the locket close to her heart before opening it.

"I can't do this anymore, Mama," she said, looking at the picture of the lovely, familiar face. "I've lost everything. Everything I've ever loved has been taken away from me, and I just can't take anymore."

Laying the locket on the table, she picked up the leather bound journal. It had always brought her peace or strength when she read it. That's what she needed right now. The strength her mother had promised her. As she flipped through the book, her fingers brushed against a bump in the back that she had never noticed before. Balancing the cigarette on the ashtray in front of her, she picked at the edges until she found an opening, and then gingerly took out a folded piece of paper.

My dearest Eve, her mother had written. *My hope is that this letter will find you when you need it most. Don't let him win, my Eve. He beat me, in more ways than one. Please, don't let him beat you. Do what I could never do. I love you, my sweet Eve, and I am there with you, always.*

Love,

Mom

The tears she failed to shed for her mother years ago, finally came. "I love you, too, Mama," she whispered. "I don't want to let you down."

When the phone rang, she ignored it. This moment was too precious to share. But then she heard Lainey's voice and a flood of joy and sorrow washed over her.

"I – I know you don't want to speak to me," Lainey said, "but I didn't know what else to do. God, I can't even believe this is happening. If you get this message, please call me. Call anyone. It doesn't even have to be me. There are people who are - damn it, I'm sick with worry about you, Eve."

Eve felt hope when she heard Lainey's words. Maybe when this was all over, Lainey would forgive her for everything she had put her through.

"I think I'm a suspect in your disappearance," Lainey went on. "If I weren't so worried about you, I think I'd be laughing at Detective Carter right now. Please, Eve, call. I don't understand anything that's happening or why you treated me so horribly..."

Eve heard Lainey's small sigh and felt a pang of guilt go through her.

"At least call Mikey and let him know you're okay and when you'll be back at the gallery. I can help him for now, but not for long."

She heard the chill creep back into Lainey's voice, and couldn't blame her for it. She deserved it. It was her fault Lainey was in this mess. And it was her responsibility to get Lainey out.

"You think you're a clever boy, don't you, Carter?" She smiled slowly, coldly. "You have no idea what you've gotten yourself into."

Eve's strength was back. She felt it inside her. Her determination to bring Tony and those who worked for him down was more intense than ever now. As was her determination to get back everything he had taken away from her. She looked around her in disgust. This is what you let him do to you, Eve, she scolded herself. Now, you need to set things right.

She walked out of her bathroom, still naked from her shower. The hot water and stinging spray had helped clear her head, and she knew what she needed to do now. Picking up Adam's shirt from the foot of her bed, she held it close for a moment, remembering how Adam felt, how he looked. She missed him more than she ever dreamt was possible.

Lainey had reassured Eve that Adam would understand, that he would not judge Eve for her past and she hoped that that was true. She also hoped that, in time, Lainey would forgive her for the despicable things Eve had said to her. Although she was certain now that she needed

Adam, she realized she needed Lainey as well. When her cell phone rang, Eve slipped into the shirt before answering.

"Hello?"

"Where in the hell have you been?" he demanded.

"Excuse me?" No one spoke to her that way.

"I'm sorry," he said quickly. "It's just that Tony is on a rampage, Eve, and everyone has been trying to get a hold of you, with no luck. We've been to your apartment, but there was no answer. I thought something had happened to you."

Eve barely recalled her night. It was blurred by booze, pills and tears. The whole world could have been at her door, and Eve would never have noticed. "I – I needed time to myself," she said, frowning. It wouldn't do to get caught unprepared again, she thought.

"I see. That must be why you didn't let Adam in."

Hearing Adam's name was pain for Eve. "Adam?"

God! He had been here. But there was no time to think about that now. "Why is Tony on a rampage now?" she said, keeping her voice expressionless.

"It's about the statement you gave to Dee Cummings. He saw the newscast, Eve. I think you've finally succeeded in pushing him over the edge."

Eve barely managed to keep from swearing aloud. How could she have forgotten about Dee's report? It had been her plan, and she knew the trouble it would cause once it was aired. Damn it! That's why Lainey was worried. And, Adam must have watched as well. How was she going to explain everything to him?

"Good," she said, aloud. "He'll make mistakes now."

"If he doesn't kill you first, Eve."

"That's not going to happen. I have a job for you. Tomorrow morning, there will be someone waiting for you at the warehouse. Eight o'clock. Go there and get instructions from them, and do exactly as you're told. This could get very dangerous for everyone involved."

"I understand. I'll be there, and I'll be ready."

"I hope you are," she said quietly. "I'll be in touch." Tomorrow was going to be a big day, she thought to herself. If everything went the way she planned, one or more people would be brought to justice.

~ Twenty-Five ~

Lainey was tired and irritable after a long day at the gallery. The night before had been spent fighting with Jack, a fight that had rolled over to this morning. She hadn't slept well, opting to stay in the guest room again. With everything that was going on, she couldn't find it in her to be with Jack. He didn't understand her. He couldn't sympathize with how miserable she was, and she couldn't tell him how worried she was about Eve.

Lainey had sat up most of the night, willing the phone to ring, praying that Eve would get her message and call her, reassuring her that everything would be alright. At the gallery, she willed the elevator doors to open and have Eve appear. They never did. Lainey couldn't even find it in herself to be mad at Eve anymore. The more she thought about it, the more it made sense to her that Eve hadn't meant anything she had said to her. As she had told Adam, Eve had wanted to protect him, so she sent him away. Why hadn't Lainey realized that about herself?

She unlocked the door of Eve's office. Lainey had avoided coming in here all day, but once the gallery doors were closed for the night, she couldn't stay away. Closing the door behind her, she stood there for a moment, just trying to breathe. Eve's scent was all around her, and Lainey remembered every moment they had spent together.

As she pushed away from the door, the first thing that caught her eye was the dark stain on the floor in front of Eve's desk. When Lainey realized the stain was blood, she felt faint. All sorts of horrible images went through her mind and she had to brace herself on Eve's desk before she collapsed.

"Oh my God." Lainey sank to her knees, praying Eve was alright. Gingerly, she touched a hand to the stain, jerking it back when she felt the sharp slice of glass. Lainey turned her palm over, mesmerized by the blood that trickled down it. So Eve had cut herself on the glass she had broken. There was the frame. But not the photo. Eve had taken the picture with her.

"You didn't want to say those things to me," Lainey told the empty room. "You didn't want to hurt me, but you felt that was the only way you could keep me safe."

"I always said you see too much."

Eve's voice was quiet, but Lainey jumped nonetheless. Slowly she rose to face the woman who had invaded her thoughts. "Eve." Lainey wanted to run to her, throw her arms around her, but she found she couldn't move. Her voice caught in her throat.

It was Eve who made the first step towards Lainey. "I'm sorry," she said. "I know that doesn't make up for the horrible things I said, but I am so sorry. I thought that I was doing the right thing. I had no right to put you in the middle of all of this that's going on in my life. I had no right to make you choose between me and your husband."

"You had no right to push me away like that," Lainey told her. "You had no right to tell me that what happened between us meant nothing."

"No. I didn't. And I'll never be able to apologize enough for that." She closed the gap between them and cupped Lainey's face in one hand. "It meant everything," she whispered.

Lainey turned away. "Why?" she asked. "Why did you push me away? After all that we've been through, didn't you know that I'd stand with you?"

"Yes, I did know that. That's why I did it. Damn it, Lainey, don't you understand that you're in danger when you're around me? I couldn't live with myself if anything happened to you."

"Do you not realize that what you said hurt me more than anyone else ever could? Adam feels the same way."

"You saw Adam?" Eve's voice trembled.

"Yes, and he's just as miserable as I am."

Eve turned away and pushed her hands through her hair. "I didn't think I could feel any worse than I did but I was wrong. I suppose I deserve it."

The tears startled Lainey. "You're crying." Her voice was incredulous.

"Yes, I seem to be doing that a lot lately."

Lainey didn't know whether to feel guilty for making Eve cry, or delighted that Eve finally found the tears that had avoided her all of her life.

"Oh, Eve!" Lainey took Eve's hands in hers and saw Eve flinched. "Your hands." More carefully, Lainey took Eve's hands and turned them palm up. Small cuts covered them. "This must have hurt a lot."

"Nothing that alcohol, pills and nicotine couldn't cure," Eve admitted with a shrug. "Besides they didn't hurt nearly as much as I did inside."

The admission, both of them, rocked Lainey. There were too many emotions inside her that she didn't know which one to address first.

"I seem to do that to you a lot," Eve said quietly. Lainey looked at her questioningly. "Confuse you," she elaborated. "Make you feel conflicting feelings. Probably things you never wanted to feel in the first place."

"And you say I see too much. Why, Eve? Why did you go back to that time in your life and do those things again?"

Lainey tried not to sound judgmental or disappointed, but her voice betrayed her.

"I was lost, Lainey," Eve told her carefully. "When you walked out of this office that day, you took part of me with you. And when Adam walked out of my apartment after I told him it was over, he took a part of me with him. I had nothing left. That's how I felt. I could have killed myself, died the way my mother had, without any regrets. That's what I thought."

Lainey couldn't stop her hands from trembling. "What changed your mind?"

Eve remembered the letter. "Different things," she said. "I remembered how Tony had beaten my mother, and I knew that I couldn't let him win this time." She lifted Lainey's chin until they were looking in each other's eyes. "And, I thought of you. You gave me your love, your friendship, and I hurt you. I needed to make that right. I needed you to know how deeply sorry I am."

"I do know," Lainey said softly. The selfish part of her didn't want to ask the question that crossed her mind, but she did. "What about Adam?"

Eve saw the sadness in Lainey's eyes, and was sorry for it. "I thought of Adam, too. I need him, Lainey. When all of this is over, I hope that he will be with me. I want him to stay the night with me."

"I see."

"Do you? Do you really, Lainey?"

"Yes. I've been thinking about all of this as well, Eve. I couldn't think of anything else. I realized that I scared you when I told you I was in love with you."

"Lainey, wait. You're wrong. You didn't scare me, you gave me joy. Joy I had never experienced before. But, honey, you're not in love with me."

"But Eve."

"You're not in love with me," Eve repeated. "You love the excitement of the new experiences you and I had. Lainey, honey, don't look at me that way. I'm not trying to upset you. I know you love me. But, you're in love with your husband. Once this is over, I'm going to fulfill my promise to you and help you fix things with Jack."

"I don't know if that's even possible anymore."

"Yes, it is. He loves you. How could anyone not love you?" Eve's eyes burned into Lainey's. "We can both have what we want."

"And, if what I want is you?" Lainey's pulse raced. Eve had practically admitted to loving her. But, hadn't she done the same with Adam?

"I'll always be here, Lainey. I'm not going anywhere. But, you know that you're in love with Jack, that you need him. Don't you?"

Lainey lowered her eyes and nodded.

"Oh, Lainey, that is nothing to be ashamed of. I understand. Honey, I think I could live without ever making love to you again. At least I hope so. But, I can't live without you in my life. You're the best - the only friend I have and I need you."

Tears welled and spilled over as Lainey took Eve in her arms. "I need you, too," she whispered in Eve's ear, holding her tightly.

"How touching."

Eve's grip tightened around Lainey instinctively when she heard Tony's mocking voice. "No."

The word was barely past Eve's lips before Tony grabbed Lainey's hair, yanking her back to him. He held the .22 in his right hand, and pressed it to Lainey's temple. Eve fought the wave of sickness that washed over her.

"Leave her alone." God, she had never been so scared in her life.

"What's the matter, Eve? Afraid I'm going to kill your lover?" He smiled and pressed the gun harder against Lainey's head. "How do you suppose people will react when they find out that you and Mrs. Stanton are sleeping together? Especially Mr. Stanton?"

"Leave her out of this, Tony. This is between me and you." Eve's eyes met Lainey's briefly, but long enough to see that Lainey was terrified. "Let her go."

"Well, now, Eve, you're being selfish. If this woman is good enough for you to sample..."

"No!" Her temper was rising and she fought to stay in control. She had to outthink him. Damn it, Eve, think! You can't let him hurt Lainey! And yet she knew what he was capable of. He wanted to make her suffer. "She's not that experienced, Daddy," she said, shrugging. Eve began unbuttoning her shirt.

"Eve, don't!"

Tony clamped a hand over Lainey's mouth. "Shh, shh, shh. No interrupting. This is our family reunion after all. Go on, little Eve."

Eve imagined taking the gun from Tony and pulling the trigger as she held it against his forehead all the while continuing to unbutton her shirt slowly. "She's only been with two people, Daddy," she said, smiling, trying not to see the shock and disbelief in Lainey's eyes. "I haven't begun to teach her everything I know." She pulled the shirt from her waistband. "You know I'm experienced. Don't you, Daddy? You made sure of that. Let her go." Eve began stroking her breasts.

Lainey felt Tony's grip loosen but she didn't dare to try to break away. She wanted to help Eve but there was a gun at her head and she thought about her sons. She was too stunned, too scared to do anything but pray.

"Come on, Daddy. It's me you want." Eve spread her arms, her shirt open. "Here I am. Let Lainey go, and we'll - play."

"Do you think I'm stupid?" he asked her. Eve could see the desire burning in his dark eyes and it turned her stomach. She knew all too well how little it would take to make him lose control. "If I let her go, she'll run straight to the cops."

"She won't go to the police," she murmured. If she could just get him to let Lainey go and get close to him she would feel more in control. "Right, Lainey?"

Lainey's eyes met Eve's, and she shook her head in answer.

"She watches then," he said, pushing Lainey towards the couch. "If she goes near the phone, I'll kill her while you watch. When I'm done with you," Tony smiled, "I get her, too."

"That's not a good deal, Daddy. I need to know that Lainey will remain safe, and unharmed. Once I know that, I'm all yours."

"I'm the one who makes the rules here! I'm in charge!"

"I know. You're in charge." Eve feathered a finger over her cleavage. "So, tell me what you want."

He pointed the gun at Lainey. "Sit down. Don't say a word. Do you understand me? All right, little Eve, take off your clothes. Show me what you can do. If you satisfy me, I'll let her go."

"Oh, I'll satisfy you, Daddy." And, I'll show you what I can do, you sick son of a bitch, she added silently. "You know how much practice I've had, don't you? It'll be much better if you undress me, Daddy."

Eve positioned herself strategically between Tony and his line of view of Lainey. She didn't want Lainey to see the things she would have to do, didn't want to see her face as she was forced to watch.

Tentatively, Tony reached out with the gun and touched Eve's skin with the cold metal.

She could do it now, Eve thought. She could reach out and take him by surprise, but something told her he was cautious enough still to be ready for that. She had to throw him off his game.

"Tell me something." Eve's voice was low and inviting, and she raised a hand to seductively brush a finger down the barrel of the gun. "All I want to know is why. Why did you turn me into a whore?"

Tony looked into her eyes now, and smiled. "Are you going to tell me you didn't enjoy it? You liked having those men want you. I know you did." He cupped a hand around her breast. "Besides, you owed me. Because of you, I was in prison. I needed some way to pay off my debts."

Eve fought the wave of nausea that passed over her when she felt his hands on her. "You were in prison because you killed my mother. How did you manage to get out so soon?" She saw him smile, and answered for him. "You always did line your back pocket with officials."

"I didn't kill your mother little Eve. The bitch killed herself."

Eve's body tensed and she had to struggle not to attack him.

"She liked having the men want her, too," he told Eve in a low voice. "She tried telling me that she didn't, but I knew. Just like I knew you enjoyed it. I'm sure both your lover over there, and, of course, Adam are grateful for your 'experiences'."

He was close enough to her now so that if the gun went off, she would be in the line of fire. She knew that. But Lainey would be safe. No matter what she had to do, Tony was not going to hurt Lainey. If that meant dying and taking Tony down with her, then she was ready. With a burst of fury, for her mother, for Lainey, for Adam and for herself, Eve made her move. In one swift movement, Eve grabbed the gun, struggling to take it away from him.

"You bitch!" he hissed furiously.

"And, you are a sick bastard!" she retorted, matching him strength for strength. She felt as if the world's existence depended on her winning. To her, it did.

Lainey sat on the couch, stiff with terror. She had watched the exchanged between Eve and Tony in a state shock, trying to comprehend what was really going on. Now, as the two struggled, she knew that she should do something but her body wouldn't move. When the first shot rang out, she couldn't even scream.

The struggle halted in stunned silence for a split second after the first shot. And then two more shots sounded.

"Go to hell," she whispered as Tony slumped to the floor, a look of disbelief in his eyes, blood spurting from his mouth.

Eve watched him die there in front of her. There was no remorse, no sense of sadness anywhere inside her as he took that last breath. There was no sense of guilt. Only a great rush of relief she felt.

"Eve?" Once Tony had fallen, Lainey found the strength to move again. Relief flooded through her body as she ran up to Eve, seeing her still standing.

She turned to Lainey who was as white as a sheet. "I'm so sorry. Oh, baby, I'm so sorry."

"I'm okay." She laughed nervously. "I'm scared shitless, but I'm not hurt. God, I was so afraid I'd lost you." Lainey threw her arms around Eve and squeezed her tight.

The pain was so immense, that Eve had to fight the wave of nausea that washed over her. Woozy, she pushed Lainey away, but held on at the same time. "Lainey, I..."

She covered the wound with one hand, using the other to keep her balance.

"It was self-defense, honey," Lainey told her. "You had to do it."

Another explosion of pain hit Eve. "I need to sit down," she said, letting her hand slip.

Lainey saw the gaping wound, saw blood pouring from Eve. "Jesus." Finding strength she never knew she had, Lainey took Eve's weight on herself, and guided her to the couch. "Sit down. God, baby." Grabbing one of the designer pillows from the couch, she pressed it against the wound. "Hold this here, honey, as firmly as you can."

"Don't leave me."

"Eve, baby, stay awake for me," Lainey cried as she dialed 9-1-1. "Don't close your eyes, Eve. Look at me. They'll be here soon, honey. Stay with me."

"Lainey..."

"No, don't talk. Rest."

Eve's eyes closed again. The pain was gone, replaced by a chilling numbness. She knew how scared Lainey was, she was scared herself, but her strength was rapidly deteriorating. She had to make sure Lainey knew how she felt.

"Eve, open your eyes! Please, baby, you have to stay awake!"

"Lain..." She couldn't stay awake any longer. She was so incredibly tired, and just needed to close her eyes. Weak and exhausted, Eve slipped into unconsciousness.

"Eve! Damn it! Don't you die!" Lainey bent to kiss Eve's lips. "I know," she whispered in Eve's ear. "I know how you feel. I know you love me. Please, don't leave me."

Lainey paced the waiting room of the hospital, waiting for someone, anyone to come out and tell her what was going on. Eve hadn't regained consciousness during the ride to the hospital, and Lainey was terrified that she never would. She couldn't still her hands that were still covered with Eve's blood. Her heart raced as she could see how the blood gushed from Eve over and over in her mind.

"Lainey?"

Lainey spun around at the sound of her name and saw Adam standing at the door, his hair disheveled, the rims of his eyes red. His face was lined with worry. She had called him from the ambulance and told him about Eve. By the time the ambulance had arrived, camera crews surrounded the gallery, cops and investigators filed in and out, and the coroner stood by waiting to take Tony's body away. She hadn't wanted Adam to hear about the shooting on the news, but it was one of the hardest calls she had ever had to make. Now Lainey's heart broke for him.

"There's no news yet," she told him. "No one will tell me anything."

Adam pulled her into his arms, and held on tight. "She's going to be okay," he whispered.

"Lainey?"

Lainey broke away from Adam and faced her husband.

"Come here," he said softly. Jack could see how much she was hurting, and it was painful for him. He held her in his arms, and watched Adam pace away. Lainey had told him that Eve and Adam were no longer together, but one look at the man and Jack knew that Adam was in love with Eve. He could see the pain and fear in every move Adam made. "Is he okay?" Jack asked.

"He's scared. So am I, Jack."

"I know, honey." He brushed Lainey's cheek with his hand, unable to hide the fact that he was trembling.

When she had called him about the shooting, he had been alarmed and relieved at the same time. She was calling him, which meant she was okay, but he had been so close to losing her. He'd never been so frightened – or thankful – in his life.

"She saved my life, Jack." Lainey's voice shook. She couldn't help feeling guilty for what Eve is going through now. If she died, Lainey didn't know how she could live with herself.

Jack heard the guilt in Lainey's voice. "It's not your fault," he told her. "She cares for you; she did what she had to do."

Silently Jack thanked Eve for the sacrifice she made. He was sorry about the outcome, but his wife and mother of his children was safe, in his arms. The feeling of relief was overwhelming.

"Lainey Stanton?"

Lainey's pulse jumped painfully as a doctor in green hospital scrubs walked into the waiting room. "Yes?"

"I'm Dr. Roman." He glanced at Jack. "Are you Adam?"

"No. I am." Adam hurried to Lainey's side and fixed his eyes on the doctor.

Dr. Roman nodded. "Eve mentioned both of you briefly when she woke up. Does she have any family? Someone you can call to be here?"

Lainey's heart plummeted. "No," she answered quietly. "Just us. We're her family." The only family she has left, Lainey thought silently.

The doctor looked from one of them to the other. Hospital policy was to speak only with immediate family when cases like this came in, but he decided, seeing the anxiety in their faces, that hospital policy was not going to apply here.

"Eve is going to be fine."

"Oh, thank God." Lainey held on to Jack for support as relief washed over her. She placed a hand on Adam's arm and squeezed.

Dr. Roman smiled. "She's a very lucky woman. The bullet missed every major organ and made a clean exit. No internal bleeding, no surgery."

"Can we see her?" Adam was having a hard time holding back tears of happiness. All he wanted to do was see Eve. He wanted to make sure for himself that she was okay.

"Not before we do."

They all turned and saw Detective Harris and Detective Carter entering the waiting room, holding their badges up for the doctor to inspect.

"We need a statement from Ms. Sumptor," Carter said peremptorily.

Lainey heard the contempt in his voice. This was no friend of Eve's. She was certain of it.

"Not tonight you don't," Dr. Roman told them.

"This is police business, doctor. You have a murderer..."

"Murderer? That's bullshit!" Lainey confronted Detective Carter angrily. "I was there, Eve did not murder anyone! It was self-defense!"

Detective Harris stepped between Lainey and his partner. "My partner misspoke, Mrs. Stanton. We're not accusing Eve of murder. We just need to get her statement. We'll need yours as well."

"I'll tell you everything, but right now I need to make sure Eve is alright." Lainey's eyes pleaded with him.

The detective turned back to the doctor. "How long before Eve is strong enough to talk to us?"

"She needs to rest tonight. I suggest you come back in the morning."

"Tomorrow isn't good enough," Detective Carter began.

Harris held up his hand, cutting off his partner's tirade. "We'll come back tomorrow. She's not going to be much help to us tonight anyway. We can get your statement tomorrow as well, Mrs. Stanton. When you're done here, go home and get some rest. You've been through quite an ordeal."

An 'ordeal' doesn't even begin to explain it, Lainey thought as she watched them leave. She was emotionally exhausted by the time she was able to see Eve.

She was in pain, but she was alive. She had won. "Don't get ahead of yourself," she said quietly in the empty room. Tony was down, but there were more players in this game. She shifted her position on the hospital bed, and winced as the pain shot through her stomach. The first thing she needed to do, she thought, was get out of here. Hospitals made her anxious. All she wanted was to go home, call Lainey and Adam to make sure they were okay, and then sleep for hours. Eve laid her head back, and closed her eyes.

"Eve?" Lainey whispered from the doorway.

Eve opened her eyes. "Hey," she said. Her smile was slow, and her voice was weak.

Lainey tried to hold back the tears, but seeing Eve lying there, so pale, so fragile it was too much for her.

"Don't cry, honey. I'm okay. Come here." Eve lifted her hand for Lainey to take. Although it hurt her to move, she didn't flinch for Lainey's sake.

"You scared me," Lainey told her quietly.

"I know. I'm sorry. I would have preferred not getting shot myself. Are you okay?" Eve shifted again, and couldn't keep from flinching this time.

Another tear fell down Lainey's cheek. She hated seeing Eve in pain, and wished there was something she could do to take it away.

"Hug me," Eve whispered. "That would help a lot."

Lainey made a noise between a laugh and a sob and bent down to hug Eve. "You read me so well," she whispered in Eve's ear.

"I'm sorry, Lainey."

"You have nothing to be sorry for, Eve." Lainey lifted her head until their eyes locked. "You saved my life."

"It was the least I could do for putting you in that situation in the first place," Eve said with a grin. It wasn't a subject that should be taken lightly, but Eve couldn't dwell on 'what might have been'. If she did, she wouldn't be able to finish what she had to do.

"I hated what you had to do. I couldn't stand watching you..." She broke off shuddering. "I could have killed him for touching you, for what he'd done to you."

"Shh. It's over now." Eve lifted a hand to Lainey's cheek and pulled her close. Without thinking, she kissed Lainey gently on the lips.

Though Lainey loved the feeling of Eve's lips on hers, she glanced nervously at the door.

Eve saw Lainey's uneasiness. "I'm sorry."

"No, please don't be. I love the way your lips feel," Lainey confessed and then sighed. "Eve, Jack is here."

Eve dropped her hand from Lainey's cheek. "I see. Is everything all right?"

Lainey hated the tension that filled the room. "Yes. He's just happy that I'm okay. Not that he's happy that you were hurt," she said quickly.

Eve smiled. "I understand."

"You were right, Eve." Lainey pulled a chair close to Eve's bed and sat down. "I am in love with my husband. Tonight, when all that was happening, when I knew I might die, I thought of Jack and our sons. I wanted to be with them. I wanted to tell them how much I loved them. I was afraid I'd never have the chance to do that again." Lainey tucked Eve's hair behind her ear. "That's not to say that I don't love or need you, Eve."

"I know, honey." Eve kissed the inside of Lainey's palm. "I understand everything you're saying to me. When that gun went off, you were the first thing I thought of. I knew I had to make sure you would be safe, for your husband, your sons, for me. So I kept fighting." It was such a relief to speak from her heart. She had kept her emotions hidden for so very long, reserving her spontaneity for sex. And now she could say exactly what she felt. "Once it was over, and I knew Tony was no longer a threat to you, I found myself thinking of Adam. Lainey, the last time I saw him, I told him goodbye and I regretted that more than anything. I was afraid he'd never know how much I really need him."

"But a little of the jealousy is still there, isn't it?" Lainey asked her. "I'm still a little envious of Adam. Are you of Jack?"

Eve smiled. "Yes." She rubbed the back of Lainey's hand with her thumb, and her smile faded. "You know this is what's right. It's what we need."

"I know, but I don't want to lose you, Eve."

"I'm not going anywhere. I think we both know that we'll always have something special between us. Nothing will ever change that."

Lainey nodded and took a deep breath. "I don't know if I'll be able to live with never making love to you again," she said in a low voice.

"I was hoping you would say that," Eve told her. "I'll always be here if you need me."

"What will you say to Adam now?" Lainey asked. "Are you ready to tell him everything?"

Eve sighed. "I'll never be ready to tell him everything. I wasn't ready to tell you. But, it's time. If I want any kind of future with Adam, he needs to know the truth about me. I can't hide from him anymore."

"He's here."

"I know. I can feel him." It still amazed her that she could feel so deeply for two different people. "Just as I can feel you when you are near."

The quiet words spoke volumes to Lainey. "You're not upset with me for calling him, are you? I just couldn't let him find out from the News."

"Of course not. I'm glad he heard it from you. How is he?"

"He's scared, and ready to see that you're okay for himself. Do you want me to get him?"

Eve lifted Lainey's hand briefly to her lips. "Yes. Will you get Dr. Roman for me as well?"

Concern lit Lainey's eyes. "Are you in pain? Do you need something?"

Eve smiled. "I'm fine. Really. Now go!" Eve closed her eyes again and tried not to focus on the pain. Her heart pounded in her chest when she thought of seeing Adam. Would he understand? Would he be able to handle Eve's past? She drew in a breath and winced at the pain it gave her.

"I hate seeing you hurting," Adam said quietly.

Slowly, she opened her eyes and saw the strain and the fatigue. She was the one who had done that to him, and the realization of that hurt.

"I'm okay," she told him, her voice low and soft.

He kept his hands at his side, afraid to touch her, though he wanted to so much. "You've been shot, Eve. It's okay to let people know that you're human and can feel pain."

If you only knew how I felt when I lost you, she thought. He was so close to her, yet she felt an enormous distance between them. "I'm in a lot of pain," she confessed. "I'm in pain because I had to hurt you. I'm in pain because of things in my past that haunt me every day. I'm in pain every time I watch you walk out of my apartment after we've made love."

He was shocked to see tears in her eyes. In the two years they had been together, he had never seen any kind of emotion from Eve except passion.

Eve caught his hand and brought it to her lips. She pulled him closer to her until his face was inches from hers. "I've missed you," she whispered.

The sentiment of the words rang in his ears and, although he thought it impossible, he fell in love with her even more. "I've missed you," he replied, gently kissing her lips, savoring the electricity that passed between them. "You should have told me what you were going through, Eve. I would have been there for you. Let me be there for you now."

"I want to. But there's so much I need to tell you."

"Later," he said, and pressed his lips against hers. She felt that familiar need for him burning inside her. Eve wrapped her arms around his neck, ignoring the pain from her wound, and lost herself in his kiss.

"Ahem." Dr. Roman grinned as they drew apart.

Lainey and Jack were close behind him, Jack's arm around Lainey's shoulders.

"Excuse me for interrupting but Lainey told me you wanted to see me."

"Yes, doctor," Eve said, her hand in Adam's. "I'd like to go home."

It was Lainey who began to protest, but Dr. Roman cut in. "I don't recommend that, Eve. You've lost some blood. I think you should stay here overnight for observation."

"Is there a possibility that I might die, doctor?" She felt Adam's grip tighten, and knew in her heart that he was scared of the answer. A glance at Lainey revealed the same fear.

"No. I don't feel that is a possibility, however..."

"Will I slip into a coma, or hemorrhage?"

"No." He knew what she was doing, and couldn't blame her. Being a doctor, he knew how horrible being in a hospital could be, especially if you were the patient. But, he couldn't, with a clear conscience, let her walk out of here without knowing the potential dangers. "There's a possibility of infection, of an allergic reaction to the medicines that we've given you. I feel it's necessary that you have someone with you at all times for the next twenty-four hours."

"I will have someone with me," she said quietly and looked up at Adam, the question in her eyes.

Adam felt a jolt inside him. She was asking him to stay with her. After all this time of him asking her to let him stay, now she was asking him. "I'll be with her," he said.

"Very well," Dr. Roman said. "You'll have to sign a release form stating that you are leaving against my advice."

He saw Eve's satisfied smile and shook his head. The woman certainly knew how to get her way.

"Come with me," he told Adam. "You're going to need instructions on which meds to give Eve and when."

"Yes, of course." Adam bent and kissed Eve gently. "I'll be right back."

"You should take your wife home, Jack," Eve said as soon as they had left. "She's had a very rough night."

"You're right," Jack replied. He looked exhausted and undone in his khakis and t-shirt that he must have thrown on in a hurry after receiving the call from Lainey.

"Don't thank me, Jack," Eve told him, reading his mind. Her hair was pulled back into a pony tail and she looked incredibly young. "You know as well as I do that your wife wouldn't have been in that position if it weren't for me."

"Eve..."

"It's true, Lainey."

"Maybe so, Eve," Jack said. "But, you more than made up for that by sacrificing yourself for her. I'll never forget that."

Eve turned her head on the pillow. Jack should hate her for bringing Lainey into this mess, but instead he was grateful to her. It was something she didn't know how to respond to.

"Let me help Eve get ready to go home," Lainey said, seeing Eve's discomfort. "And then we'll go."

"Of course." Jack planted a kiss on Lainey's cheek. "You should know that the press is everywhere. You may want to ask if there's a back way out of here."

Eve grinned. Having the press here could only help her with what she had left to do.

"You need rest," Eve told Lainey. "Go home, kiss those two wonderful boys of yours, make love to your husband, and God willing, have a dreamless night of sleep. I'm going to be in good hands."

Lainey took Eve's outstretched hands and gently pulled her until she was standing. Eve's breath became ragged as she fought the darkness that threatened to pull her under. The pain was almost unbearable.

"Eve, you shouldn't be moving. Please stay here for the night."

"I can't. Just give me a minute," she said, resting her forehead on Lainey's, willing the pain to subside. "You know, you once told me that I was good at turning my emotions on and off. You were wrong. I'll always need you. I'll always love you." The admission rocked both women to the core. Eve saw tears in Lainey's eyes, felt her own threatening to fall. "I probably shouldn't have said that to you, it's not fair."

"I've been waiting for that for a very long time. It was amazing to hear," Lainey said with a watery laugh. "It makes me feel better saying this. I think you're ready to let Adam in. You're ready to admit to yourself that you're in love with him."

"Well, I'm not as confident about that as you seem to be." Eve felt the muscles in her stomach tighten and her heart beating faster at just the thought. "But then I didn't know I was ready to tell you."

"Just be completely honest with him, Eve," Lainey told her. "Trust him. I think it's going to be hard for him to hear, but in the end, he will be there for you. Here, slip on this robe."

Eve frowned. "Why haven't the detectives been here to see me?"

Lainey looked up at Eve. "They were here. Dr. Roman sent them away. You're supposed to be resting."

"I'm sure Detective Carter was happy about that," Eve murmured.

Lainey's brow creased in curiosity. "Why do you say that? Is there something about him that you're not telling me? Because he accused you of murder tonight."

"There's a surprise," Eve replied her voice edged with sarcasm.

"Why aren't you surprised?"

Before Eve could answer her, Adam walked in, rolling a wheelchair in front of him.

"I'm not getting in that," Eve told him defiantly.

"Doctor's orders, baby," Adam said with a shrug.

"And hospital rules," Dr. Roman added from behind Adam. "I'm giving you what you want, Eve. You can give me this."

"Fine," she said sulkily. "But only as far as the front door."

"Eve, what about all of the press? Is there a back way out of here, doctor?" Lainey asked.

"No. I want to go out the front," Eve said. "I want to make a statement."

"That's really going to piss off Detective Carter," Lainey told her.

Eve turned to Lainey and smiled radiantly. Exactly, she thought silently.

"Stop here," Eve told Adam when they were near the exit. "I don't want a photo of me in a wheelchair making the papers tomorrow."

"Fine, no wheelchair," Adam said. "I hope you don't object to a photo of me carrying you to the car."

"You wouldn't dare..."

Before she could finish protesting, Adam was lifting Eve into his arms. "It's one way or the other, baby. Your decision."

"Well, if I only have these choices," Eve began and playfully nipped Adam's ear with her teeth. "Then I choose you."

Eve's quietly spoken words were not lost on Lainey. She heard them and took them for what they were meant to be. Smiling, she linked her arm through Jack's.

Dozens of flashbulbs from photographer's cameras went off when Adam stepped out of the exit with Eve in his arms. Reporters shouted questions from every angle, each of them wanting Eve's account of what happened.

Eve searched the crowd until she spotted Dee, and motioned for her to join her.

"They wouldn't let me up to see you," Dee told her, breathless from pushing her way through the crowd. "It doesn't always pay to be a part of the press. How are you?"

"I'm well, considering," Eve replied. "If I had known you were down here, I would have had them send you up. I'm ready to make that statement."

"Are you sure you're up for it?" Dee glanced at Adam and saw that he was holding Eve as though she was his entire world. It would certainly make for great TV. Dee waved her cameraman over and held up her mike so that Eve could speak into it easily while all around her, members of the press pushed and shoved their way closer to Eve.

"Can you tell us what happened tonight, Ms. Sumptor?" Dee asked in a loud voice.

When Eve began to speak, the crowd of reporters hushed to take notes or record the story. "As I'm sure you know already, my father paid me a visit at my gallery," she said in a clear, carrying voice. "Lainey, my assistant and dear friend was there, and he threatened her. Words were exchanged and a struggle ensued. During the struggle, the gun went off three times, wounding me and killing him."

"Can you tell us what he said to you?" Dee asked, raising her voice again over the questions the others were shouting.

"All I can tell you is that he confessed to killing my mother," Eve told her. "He also revealed to me who his accomplice was in the murder of Jackie Sawyer, and the disappearances of Meredith Lansky and Katherine Bushnell."

The questions flew at Eve from every angle, and grew louder with fevered anticipation.

"Can you give us a name?" Dee asked, clearly excited.

Eve shook her head. She had set the bait. Now she would wait and see if the fish would bite. "That's all for now," she said. "I'm exhausted, and I'm sure Adam's arms are getting tired from holding me." Eve smiled into the lens of the camera. "I'm going home now to rest. Tomorrow, I'll give my statement to the police."

~ Twenty-Six ~

Adam pushed open Eve's apartment door, Eve asleep in his arms. She looked so frail that he wanted to weep. Taking her straight up to her bedroom, he laid her gently down on the bed.

Eve stirred awake when she felt Adam kiss her softly on the lips. "You're not leaving, are you?" she asked him.

"Of course not," he said quietly. "I told you I would stay with you. I was just going to go in the sitting room so you could rest."

"Lie with me."

"Eve." His body reacted to her words and he chastised himself for having these feelings about her when she was in such pain.

"Please? I want you here." She saw how his body reacted, too. It felt amazing being with him again.

He sat gingerly on the bed next to her. "You really should be resting."

Eve frowned. She had been petrified about how the night would turn out, and now it seemed as though he didn't want to be there. "You're right. I'll probably sleep through the night, so you're not obligated to stay."

He heard the bite in her tone and turned to her. "Don't do that. You know I want to be here. This is all so much for me to take in, Eve. I don't know how to react. I never knew that any of this was going on in your life. You've always told me that there are things that I didn't know, but I never expected anything like this. All of a sudden, you're hurt and in the middle of something big. I still don't even know exactly what's going on. And then, to top it all off, I feel guilty."

"Guilty? Why?"

"Because I want you," he answered quietly. "I want you so much."

Eve's eyes fluttered closed. Looking at him again, she touched his face. "Why should you feel guilty about that?"

"Because you are hurting, Eve. You've been shot and all I can think about is making love to you."

"Adam, do you have any idea how much I want that, too?" She wanted to just forget about everything else that he had said, but she knew she couldn't. He needed answers, explanations about what was going on.

"Unfortunately, I don't think I'll be able to make love to you tonight," she said. "But, I can try and explain the most important things to you. I want you to know why I've had such a hard time letting you in, Adam. You asked me once who had hurt me."

And, saying a little prayer, Eve settled in to tell Adam everything.

"How could you?" Adam was pacing in Eve's bedroom, unable to sit. He had listened, intently, to everything Eve had to say, growing angrier with each moment that passed.

Eve's heart dropped. Every fear that she had about telling Adam was becoming a reality for her. "I had to," she said. "I didn't know what else to do." Her eyes pleaded with him to understand.

"No, Eve, I mean how could you keep this from me?" He walked back to her and knelt by the bed. He brushed a tear from Eve's cheek. Did she have any idea how beautiful she was, he thought. "I would have killed your father for you," he said in a low voice.

Eve's laugh was soft and sad. Relief filled her, overwhelmed her. He wasn't leaving. Af.ter everything she had told him, he wasn't leaving her. "I believe you would have," she told him.

"My God, baby, I would have been there for you. If you would have let me, I would have fought every ghost that ever haunted you. Because I'm in love with you."

He kissed her gently on the lips, then kissed another tear that trickled down her cheek.

"I've been in love with you since the moment I met you, Eve. Maybe even before that. You're the one I've been waiting for. What you've told me only makes me love you more. You are an extremely strong, courageous, beautiful woman. I'm honored that you have chosen me to be in your life."

His eyes drifted to her lips and he remembered how she had told him that he was the first, and only man to have kissed them.

"I will be here for you," he told her. "Not to fight for you, but to fight with you. You proven you are strong enough to fight for yourself. But, I will be here beside you now. Forever."

Adam bent his head and kissed Eve passionately, a kiss that rocked her to the core. Their love making, their kisses have always been extraordinary, but this was something more. These emotions were something she's never felt before. "I love you," she whispered, her lips a breath away from his.

Never had words sounded so beautiful to his ears. Never had he thought he could feel this kind of joy. "Say it again," he pleaded.

Eve chuckled and touched his face with her fingertips. "I'm so in love with you," she whispered again and brought his lips back to hers.

The phone rang, startling both of them.

"Let the machine get it, baby." Adams voice was rough and full of desire.

Eve's breath was ragged and need for him was driving her insane. The way he touched her body left her wanting more than she could have right now.

"I have to answer it," she said apologetically. "It could be Lainey, and I don't want her to worry about me. Besides, I think I need a little break to calm down," she told him with a sly wink.

Adam handed the phone to Eve.

"Your friends out in the hall are disturbing me," a familiar voice announced.

Eve frowned, bewildered. "Mrs. Jenkins?"

"It is very rude to have visitors this late at night. I should say, that woman friend of yours will not be happy either. They plan to visit her after their visit with you. From what they say, it's going to be a surprise. I think this is something you should take care of, Ms. Sumptor."

Eve sat there listening to the silence for a moment. You really are my watch dog, she thought silently. "Thank you," she said aloud into the silence. "Bye." Deliberately shielding the worry in her eyes, she handed the phone back to Adam.

"Mrs. Jenkins? Your next door neighbor?" he asked, amused. "What did she want?"

Eve wanted to tell him the truth. But she had just found this thing called love, had just let him in. She was not about to lose him. "She wanted to know if I was all right," Eve lied. "Adam, I want to show you something."

"What? Now? Baby, you're still in pain."

"Please. I want to do this now. I want you to know everything." And, you will know everything, she promised silently, after this is all over.

Adam hesitated, and then sighed. "You really want this?"

As worried as she was about his safety and Lainey's, it was difficult for Eve to flash a smile. But she did. Adam had a bad feeling about this. He had no idea why, but something just didn't feel right. But, it was what Eve wanted.

"Wrap your arms around my neck," he said.

"Hmm, I'd love to," Eve purred. "But I want to walk. I'm all right, Adam."

He followed her every move as she led him into the sitting room to press the remote and open the secret door.

Adam's brow creased. "Has this always been here?"

"Just another one of my secrets," Eve said dryly. "I'm sorry I didn't tell you about it before."

"I'm just glad that you're telling me about it now." Adam replied, bending to kiss her on the cheek. And then he saw what was inside the studio, the paintings, the photographs and he brushed past her.

"Amazing!" he exclaimed.

Eve stood outside the door and watched him move from painting to painting. "I love you," she whispered, and closed the door.

Once she was back downstairs, she used the remote to close the panel. At least now Adam would be safe, she thought silently, and then picked up the phone. "It's time."

Eve sat in a chair next to her bed, and waited. Her robe fell open over one leg exposing her silky thigh. Her perfect breasts were framed by the V of the robe that was tied loosely at the waist.

She knew what she looked like, knew that the image could bring a man to his knees. It worked for her before. She just prayed it would work this one last time. She could hear them outside the door, Carter's voice a low grumble. When he opened the door stealthily and walked the length of the sitting room, she was waiting, smiling.

"What took you so long?" she asked when he came into the room, gun drawn. "Enjoying the view, Detective?" Eve sneered.

"You were expecting me!" If she knew he was coming, she would be ready for him with a gun of her own. He looked around frantically, as though waiting for someone else to appear.

"Look," she said, reading his mind, holding her hands out in front of her. "No gun. No one is here but you and me." She glanced at the other man in the dark suit. "And your friend there. I'm wounded. Really, Detective, what can I possibly do to you?"

She could see him begin to relax. "So, Tony really told you it was me?" he said. "He always was a sniveling piece of shit who was too scared to do his own dirty work."

Eve smiled and nodded. "Yes that he was. Incidentally, why did you kill Jackie? She was innocent of any of this."

Carter shrugged. "Tony was told that she was talking. He thought she was a threat after hearing she had been seen with you. It was too bad really. She was - nice." Carter smiled cynically. "So innocent."

Eve felt fury rise deep inside her.

"It's going to be a better experience having you, I think," Carter told her with an ugly smile.

"Don't count on it," she told him. "I'm not exactly at my best."

"You'll still fulfill a lot of my fantasies," he replied and took a step towards her.

The man with him, who had remained quiet, placed a hand on his weapon, and poised himself.

"What about Katherine and Meredith?" Eve asked.

"I don't know about Katherine," he said pausing. "Meredith, on the other hand, will never be able to testify against me or anyone else."

"You killed her," Eve said quietly. Deep down she had known this, but the confirmation troubled her.

"Yeah," Carter said proudly, puffing out his chest. "It was easy. She was messy but I made sure that if she was ever found, your name would be linked to her death. It pays to be a cop."

"So I've noticed," Eve said calmly.

It was becoming extremely difficult to remain composed, but she kept Adam and Lainey in her mind. Adam was upstairs, out of harm's way. She had to keep telling herself that. Carter made no indication that he knew Adam was here, and Eve held on to that.

"You've been busy with all of the killing and trying to frame me," she said. "The false juvenile records were a good touch."

"That was good wasn't it? It was my idea. You'll have to tell me how you fixed that one." He glanced down at her wound. "You always seem to come out of things with only scratches. You've been pretty lucky." He stepped closer. "Too bad your luck has run out."

"Are you sure about that?" Eve countered. "I think it's your luck that has run out."

Carter laughed. "You've lost too much blood. You're not thinking clearly. If you haven't noticed, I'm not alone." He turned to see his companion pointing his gun directly at him. "What the fuck are you doing?" Carter said, laughing nervously, raising his own gun tentatively. "Hey, if this is about who's going to take over for Tony, we can discuss it later. I'm sure we can work something out."

The man smiled and took a badge out of his pocket. "That's okay. I already have a job. Maurice Carter, you are under arrest for the murder of Jackie Sawyer and Meredith Lansky. I would run down the list of other violations, but I'm sure Ms. Sumptor is tired."

Carter looked at Eve in shock, and then back at the man standing in front of him. "Is this some kind of fucking joke?"

"Not a joke. I'm Agent Monroe of the FBI, and I have been watching you for some time now. It's time for you to drop your weapon."

"Fuck you!" Carter spat out. "Drop yours, asshole! I'm a fucking ace shooter!"

"Don't make this any harder than it has to be, Maurice." Detective Harris appeared in Eve's doorway.

"What the fuck are you doing here?" Carter was breathing heavily, sweat running down his face.

"It's over Maurice. Put down the gun," Harris said, hand on holster, his face full of anger and sadness.

"This has nothing to do with you, Harris. Get out of here now!"

"You're surrounded, Maurice." Agent Donovan stepped into the room, his gun already aimed. "There's nowhere you can go. Put down your weapon, and let's end this now before anyone else gets hurt."

Carter began to shake. Pivoting, he pointed the gun at Eve.

"Maurice!" Harris called out. "Don't! If you shoot her, you're dead." Drawing his weapon, he pointed it at his partner's back.

Carter's chest was heaving as he stared at Eve with hatred in his eyes. "You fucking bitch!" he growled. "I should have killed you a long time ago."

"Yes, you should have," Eve agreed with a mocking smile. "But, now, I win."

"We'll see about that you fucking bitch."

The first shot made Eve's ears ring. A searing pain shot through her and her eyes dimmed. Three more shots rang out, one after the other. Closing her eyes, her head fell back on the chair, and she prayed for the pain to go away.

~ Epilogue ~

Eve sat on the swing of her back porch, letting the breeze caress her face. The gardens surrounding the painted, white, wooden deck were colorful and so beautiful that she could sit out here forever and forget that the whole world existed. She would never forget though, no matter how much she tried to. The world had tried to come crashing down on top of her. Somehow, someway, she had made it out alive. But barely, she thought now as the porch swing's creak kept her thoughts company.

She could still remember that night over a year ago when she woke up to find Maurice lying dead on her white carpet. She remembered how red the blood had been in contrast to the white. She remembered the smell of gun powder and death, the same smell she had encountered only hours before with her father. Chaos had ensued after the shooting, but somehow she had managed to make it back to Adam.

When she opened the door, she found him on his knees, crying. She had never seen someone so furious and relieved at the same time. It had taken her what seemed like months of apologizing before he was able to get over what happened, although, she knew deep inside, none of them would truly get over it.

They had, however, found a way to move on with their lives. Eve toyed with the ring on her left hand, and smiled when Adam walked out of the sliding glass door to join her, a seven month old fidgeting in his arms. Eve looked up at them both and beamed.

"I think our little Bella Marie wants her mommy," he told Eve with a grin. "Daddy's not doing something right." He held the bundle of joy out to Eve, and sat next to them on the swing.

"Aww, hey baby girl." Eve smiled down at the little chubby face and saw part of her and part of Adam staring back at her.

Bella certainly fit her name, Eve thought proudly. With her daddy's black hair and a mixture of Eve and Adam's eyes, she was beautiful. Eve would give her life to protect her from any harm.

"Are you okay, baby?" Adam asked her.

She looked at him, love beaming in her eyes. "Yes," she said. "I'm happy."

"Me too," he whispered, and leaned over to kiss Bella's forehead. "You have the magic touch," he added as Bella quieted in Eve's arms.

"So do you, baby," Eve told him, grinning. "You're a wonderful father. It's just that Mommy has the food."

"Hello?" Lainey poked her head out of the sliding glass door and smiled at the vision of the three of them sitting together. A perfect little family, she thought, moving to one side as her own two sons came bounding through.

"Hi, Eve! Is she talking yet?" Darren looked at Bella curiously, clearly prepared to hear her say something.

"She can't talk yet, dufus. She's not old enough," Kevin told him with authority.

"Boys, that's enough arguing. Let Eve breathe a little." Jack came through the door carrying a plate covered with slices of steak and chicken. "Up for a little grilling, Adam?"

"You bet." Adam leaned in to give Eve one more kiss, laughing at the boys' disgusted sounds. "Let me know if you need anything," he told her.

"I will. Go. Have fun." Eve patted his behind when he got up and he shot her a look of desire before walking away.

"Can we play with Bella, Eve? We'll be careful, we promise!" Darren looked at Eve pleadingly.

"Hmm." Eve tapped her lips with a fingertip, pretending to think about it. "Of course you can, silly. Why don't you take her over there on her blanket?"

"Be careful," Lainey reiterated as Kevin reached out to take Bella.

Darren paused and turned back to Eve. "I got my wish, Eve," he told her shyly referring to the time in Florida when he threw a penny in Eve's fountain.

Eve smiled brightly as he walked away, talking to Bella.

Once they were safely situated on the blanket, Lainey sat down next to Eve. "How are you?" she asked cheerfully.

"Wonderful. How are you?"

Lainey returned the smile. "Wonderful." Her pulse jumped when Eve lightly touched her hand. Both women glanced over at their husbands and their children. "You look radiant," she whispered.

"So do you," Eve replied. "I love you." She winked at Lainey, whose face flushed with happiness.

"I love you, too," Lainey replied.

Eve sat back. There was the smell of food on the grill, the sounds of Adam and Jack talking, the gentle breeze, the sound of the children's laughter, and Lainey beside her. She had never been happier.

He watched her through the binoculars, focusing in on her pleased face. "Take it in while you can, Eve. You won't have it for long." He moved the binoculars until they were focused on Adam, and then on Bella. "There is so much for you to lose now. Let's see how happy you are when it's all gone." He lowered the binoculars and looked around. When he was satisfied no one had seen him, he walked away.

~ Acknowledgements ~

Something About Eve is the first novel I have finished. When you don't write for a living, it gets difficult to find the time it takes to put your mind and imagination to a book. You also have to rely on those around you to pick up your slack when you just *have* to write.

Being a first time writer, there are really no other people than those around you to thank. Your family, your friends. Those are the ones who listen to your obsessive talking about this book you want to write. Those are the ones who have to answer the questions like; "How does this sound?", "Do you think she would do this here?", etc. And, those are the ones that you insist on reading your book and give you feedback, as long as it's completely honest. Fortunately, those are also the ones that really do give you complete honesty.

So, thank you to my family and friends who have endured this process with me, bought the book to support me, and bragged to others for me. Your love means the world to me, and I give it right back to you.

~ About the Author ~

Jourdyn Kelly was born in California in February of 1975. She now resides in Texas and writes as well as design web pages. Jourdyn has always enjoyed the arts in one form or another. She has been writing songs and stories since the age of fourteen and has recently just finished her second novel, *Destined to Kill*. She believes that her love of writing comes from the fact that she loves to read. She was captivated by books that led you into different and exotic places and through impossible scenarios, letting you become someone else for a time. As she read, she was inspired to write herself and bring the characters in her mind to paper. She hopes that her writing will inspire others or just give them a way to escape from everyday life even for a moment.

Jourdyn graduated from high school in a small town in Arkansas and promptly moved to Florida and attended college where she majored in Commercial Art and minored in Video Production. Since 1997, Jourdyn has spent her time working in a different area of the arts. As web designer, etc. for singer/actress Deborah Gibson, Jourdyn has had the opportunity to be involved in wonderful experiences, travel around the country and meet exciting people. Jourdyn believes this has helped with creating unique and lovable characters.

Currently living in the Houston area, Jourdyn hopes to continue to bring her characters out for everyone to meet. Her goal is to bring *Something About Eve* to the big screen and finish three more novels she is presently working on.

Made in the USA
Lexington, KY
08 August 2013